Call Me Lonesome

OTHER FIVE STAR TITLES BY BRETT COGBURN

Two-Dollar Pistol (2015)
Smoke Wagon: A Morgan Clyde Western, Book 1 (2017)

A MORGAN CLYDE WESTERN, BOOK 2

Call Me Lonesome

Brett Cogburn

FIVE STAR
A part of Gale, a Cengage Company

Farmington Hills, Mich • San Francisco • New York • Waterville, Maine
Meriden, Conn • Mason, Ohio • Chicago

This novel is a work of fiction. Names, characters, places, and incidents are either the product of the author's imagination, or, if real, used fictitiously.

The publisher bears no responsibility for the quality of information provided through author or third-party Web sites and does not have any control over, nor assume any responsibility for, information contained in these sites. Providing these sites should not be construed as an endorsement or approval by the publisher of these organizations or of the positions they may take on various issues.

LIBRARY OF CONGRESS CATALOGING-IN-PUBLICATION DATA

Names: Cogburn, Brett, author.
Title: Call me lonesome / Brett Cogburn.
Description: First Edition. | Waterville, Maine : Five Star Publishing, 2018. | Series: A Morgan Clyde western ; book 2
Identifiers: LCCN 2017047228 | ISBN 9781432831912 (hardback)
Subjects: | BISAC: FICTION / Action & Adventure. | FICTION / Westerns. | GSAFD: Adventure fiction. | Western stories.
Classification: LCC PS3603.O3255 C35 2018 | DDC 813/.6—dc23
LC record available at https://lccn.loc.gov/2017047228

First Edition. First Printing: March 2018
Find us on Facebook–https://www.facebook.com/FiveStarCengage
Visit our website–http://www.gale.cengage.com/fivestar/
Contact Five Star™ Publishing at FiveStar@cengage.com

Printed in the United States of America
1 2 3 4 5 6 7 22 21 20 19 18

Call Me Lonesome

Chapter One

Somewhere on the Salt Fork of the Arkansas River, Indian Territory, 1872

Another bullet hit the saddletree with an angry thwack of splintering wood, followed quickly by the bellow of a big bore rifle somewhere in the distance. The man down on his belly behind the dead horse pressed himself tighter to the earth. The midday heat reflected off the prairie like hot iron held to an anvil, and sweat salt stung his eyes. He spat the dirt from his lips and brushed at the splattered bits of bone and horse brains that dotted his face before he craned his neck around enough to glare up at the sun hanging there blurred and shimmering, as though it, too, were his enemy.

After that gunshot had faded away there was no sound but the incessant buzz of a blowfly. The fly's fat blue body flitted lazily about, drawn to the smell of guts and putrid death. The first shot had taken the horse in the flank and busted its paunch. A great loop of intestines and half-fermented belly juice had spilled out onto the ground while the horse thrashed and struggled in pain, and before the second bullet struck it in the head and put it out of its misery.

Despite the smell and the heat, and despite his cramped muscles and the fear, the man behind the dead horse remained still. He fought off the temptation to peer over his saddle enough to see if he could spot his attacker, for he knew to do so was to die. From the direction of the shots, the rifleman was positioned somewhere on the hilltop several hundred yards on the far side of the dead horse, which now sheltered him, and a man that could hit a horse in the head from so far away was a man that could hit about anything he wanted.

It was an old game that the man behind the dead horse knew well, and the primary rule of that game was that the first one to make a wrong move died. The second rule was that there was no second-place winner.

He pushed tighter against the horse carcass and looked up at his rifle stock, which he could see protruding out over the animal's flank. He wondered how quickly he could draw the gun out from under his stirrup leather, and how much of himself he would have to expose by doing so and for how long.

A cackle of laughter sounded from out there on that far-off hilltop, wicked and raspy, and more than half-crazed.

"Clyde," the same voice called out, and it drug out the name so slow that it was like an echo.

The man behind the horse didn't answer.

"Hey there, Clyde," the voice repeated.

The man behind the dead horse did not want to hear that voice, but he was not shocked at the sound of it. He had known all along who was out there, without so much as laying eyes on him. And that was the bitterest thing of all—lying there knowing he had been ambushed by the man he himself had sworn to kill. But that was another rule of the ancient, bloodthirsty game of men hunting men. The hunter often turned into the hunted.

Chapter Two

Ironhead Station, MK&T Railroad, Indian Territory

Red Molly O'Flanagan fanned the sweat-damp curls of red hair plastered to her forehead with one hand, and her bosom heaved as she sucked in a breath of heavy, humid air while she sat on the bench in front of the ruined shell of what had once been the depot house. Carpenters hired by the railroad had already torn most of the building down. Only the single wall behind her remained standing, charred from fire and leaning precariously, and with the planking shattered and blown off in places.

The man beside her on the bench wore a sweat-stained, gray wool Johnny Reb cap, and held a pipe clenched between his jaw teeth on one side of his mouth. He coughed when he drew on the pipe, and had to put it aside while he hacked up smoke and phlegm and spat it off the depot platform into the street.

"You ought not be smoking with that lung of yours still mending," Red Molly said, her accent laced with more than a touch of the Irish brogue.

The man in the Rebel cap touched a hand to his chest, but said nothing to that. Instead, he continued to watch the work crews the length of the street dismantling tents and the plank false fronts of what had been most of the railroad camp's structures. They worked like a steady stream of ants, tearing things apart, carrying those things to the train cars parked on the tracks at the head of the street, then returning to repeat the process.

"They'll have the whole camp torn down and loaded up by dark," Molly said, more to herself than anything.

"Not all of it," he replied. His slow, Alabama drawl and country twang was almost as heavy as her Irish brogue. "Some of those people that moved over from North Fork are staying, and I hear Bill Tuck's gonna keep his saloon here. I don't know what they're thinking with the railroad pulling out."

"They're thinking they're going to build a regular town," she said. "Simple as that."

Both of them continued to watch the tent camp torn down, each lost in their own thoughts. The idling locomotive parked close by them was drifting a cloud of smoke and cinders over everything.

A troop of black cavalry soldiers rode up the street, and the white officer leading them reined his horse over close to the depot platform. He didn't stop, but he tipped his hat brim to Red Molly and the man in the Rebel cap.

"It's all yours," the officer said to the man in the cap. "Good luck."

The cavalrymen crossed the tracks, heading north, and were soon out of sight. A few of the men at the train stopped their work to watch the soldiers pass, and more than a few of them mumbled harsh words about the army.

"Not everybody loved those sodger boys' heavy-handed ways," the man in the cap said.

"I'm glad they came, but at the same time, I can't say I'm sorry to see them go," she answered.

The man in the cap nodded his head in agreement. "First time I've seen martial law since the war, but like you say, it was needed, no matter what some of them cutting their eyes at those sodgers think."

She looked behind her at the pitiful remains of the depot house. Bits of shattered window glass and splinters of wood littered the boardwalk, the depot platform, and the ground around it. "If they had only come sooner . . ."

He gave the destroyed depot house a glance and sniffed the air. "I swear I can still smell that burnt nitroglycerin like it was yesterday. Should have known not to put anything past that Missouri border scum. Dangling a railroad payroll in front of them was like hanging raw meat in front of a wolf's nose."

"The Katy people were going to paint the depot maroon like their locomotives." She referred to the Missouri, Kansas, and Texas Railroad, the MK&T, like all the locals did, as the Katy. "Would have been a pretty building beside the tracks. First thing you would've seen when you came to Ironhead."

"Ironhead don't look like much now, does it?" he asked. What had been the main street was now only a strip of hoof-torn earth running in an arrow-straight line through rows of brown squares where the grass had been beaten away for tent floors. Where once the wagon yard had been, there was nothing but trash littering the grass. And the depot house wasn't the only black scar on that strip of has-been street. Bits of charred tent framing and an ash pile marked where Irish Dave's Bucket of Blood saloon had stood.

They listened to the screech of a nail as someone down the street tried to pry it loose from the bite of the wood it was driven into, and watched a man beating a mule towards the railroad tracks dragging a sled load of salvaged pine lumber with a cast-iron stove piled on top of the stack.

"Who's gonna run Bill Tuck's saloon for him?" he asked.

Red Molly didn't answer him. She pulled a white lace handkerchief from her wrist purse and coughed into it several times.

"You sound like you're getting sick," he said when she was through.

"It's nothing. This spring weather has given me the croup.

Hot one day, cool and wet the next." She glanced down at the handkerchief, and then folded it quickly and put it away.

He tapped his pipe bowl against the heel of one boot he had propped up on his knee, and watched the ashes fall out of it onto the boardwalk. "You didn't answer my question about Tuck's saloon."

"No, I didn't."

"That's what I thought."

"What did you think?"

"You're gonna run the Bullhorn Palace, ain't you?" He scraped at the inside of the pipe bowl with the blade of a small pocketknife he pulled from his vest pocket and glanced at her out of the corner of his eye.

"Tuck asked me," she said.

"Wouldn't have thought you would work for the likes of him. Not after everything he's done."

"I said he asked me. Never said I accepted."

"I can tell."

"Just what can you tell, Dixie Rayburn?" Her green eyes widened and bore down on him, and her large breasts heaved again as if she was drawing a breath and about to say more.

The man she called Dixie looked at her with a bland expression. She was truly a pretty woman with thick, dark red hair and a figure that made most men look twice at her, and a smile, when given, that could light up a room. But all the same, he noticed the faded, faint yellow bruises on her face mostly covered by the rice powder she wore, the smear of some kind of red lipstick on one corner of her mouth, and the sweat-soaked dress where it pressed between those two great breasts. He also noticed for the first time the wrinkles at the corners of her eyes and the way her skin hung looser on her jaw. And then there was the chronic cough that she seemed to have developed as of late, and the way her hands shook from time to time.

Maybe it was that he hadn't looked close enough at her before, but he couldn't help but think how she looked like she had aged five years in the short time he had known her. And the thought crossed his mind that he didn't know how old she really was. Maybe a hard-lived thirty, or maybe ten years older. The kind of woman she was, and the kind of life she lived, made it hard to tell. Women in her profession didn't stay young long, no matter their years.

She caught him staring at her, so he focused his attention across the street where the big canvas tent that had been the company store had once stood, and at the two men leaning against the rear wheel of the wagon parked there. Both men wore broad-brimmed hats and pistols on their hips, and both men were trying to act casual, as if they had nothing better to do than while away a hot afternoon leaning against a wagon and telling stories. The sunlight flashed for an instant on one of the badges they had pinned on their chests.

Dixie waited to speak until she saw where he was looking and who he was looking at. "Are they still asking you questions about Johnny Tubbs?"

"Not in a few days." Her voice lost some of its edge and went a shade quieter, as if the two men across the street at the wagon might hear them. "But they're still asking questions of everyone else left in camp."

"Don't know why they're so all fired up to find out who shot that miserable little peckerwood. Nobody's missing him and nobody's complaining. It ain't like there ain't plenty of bad men in the Nations for those federal boys to go hunting. They ought to leave you alone. Picking on a poor . . ." His voice trailed off.

"Picking on a poor whore. That's what you mean, isn't it?" She was looking right at him again with those green eyes flashing.

"I was about to say 'poor defenseless woman.' "

"Don't try and sugarcoat it now."

"Those marshals think you killed Tubbs. And so do a lot of other people."

"And why would I kill him?"

"You know why, and almost everybody else has a pretty good idea what he did to you. Ain't no shame in it, but some would say you had a pretty good motive. I'm not saying you did it, but if you killed him, well, can't say as I blame you. Might have done it myself if I had caught him."

"People ought to shut their mouths and stick to their own business."

"I think . . ."

"What do you think, mister lawman? What do you think, now that they're calling you *Chief* and you've got all the answers?"

Dixie looked down at the MK&T Railroad Police badge pinned to the lapel of his vest with the little pendant hanging on chains beneath it that said *Chief,* as if surprised to see it there. "I ain't made up my mind whether I'm taking the job or not."

"You pinned on his badge."

They both knew who she was talking about when she said *his badge.*

"He's gone. Told me I had his blessing if that's what I wanted to do."

She gave a bitter scoff. "What a load of blarney. You're fussing at me for considering running Bill Tuck's saloon, and yet you're willing to work for Willis Duvall and his railroad? I'd say that's the pot calling the kettle black."

"I said I haven't made up my mind."

"And that's what I told you about Tuck."

"Fair enough," he said.

"Fair enough," she replied equally as curtly.

They said nothing to each other for a long spell after that, as if the hot, humid day pressed down on them to the point that even speaking took too much energy. The two U.S. deputy marshals across the street soon gave up their watch and went elsewhere to find some shade or a cool drink of water.

Bill Tuck came up the street a half hour later walking beside a loaded wagon. Several women waved at him from a six-seater surrey with bright red wheels and a canvas sun top as they passed him headed east in the opposite direction of the tracks.

"I guess Sugar Alice and her girls don't like paying railroad fair," Dixie said. "Or else those railroad boys wouldn't swap tickets for a little dose of Sugar Alice's wares. Either way, Alice looks like she's going overland to the next camp."

Red Molly glanced at the buggy load of prostitutes wheeling out of the camp, but her real attention was on Bill Tuck, although she tried to act like she wasn't watching him.

"Why, good day, Molly," Tuck said like he was some gentleman on a Sunday stroll after church, rather than a pimp and a saloon owner who everyone in Ironhead Station believed was behind half the bad stuff that had gone on in the construction camp during the past winter and spring.

Neither Molly nor Dixie answered him, and remained leaned back against the wall of the depot house to keep under the limited shade it offered. Dixie adjusted his cap and studied the saloonkeeper.

Tuck, as always, was dressed fashionably in a silk vest with a floral pattern, and bright blue garters worn around the upper sleeves of his white shirt. A gold watch chain hung across the front of that fancy vest, and the white handle of a little pistol stuck out of the opposite slit pocket. He was hatless, and his head was shaved as slick and clean as baby skin. Despite the muggy day, his shirt looked fresh and ironed, and only a few dewdrops of sweat could be seen on his bald head.

He stopped in the glare of the sun and squinted into the shadows at Dixie and Molly. When he squinted, the sharpened, waxed ends of his mustache lifted and twitched like cat whiskers. "You thought on my offer?"

"Some," Molly answered.

Tuck looked at the wagon where the marshals had stood earlier, and Dixie knew that Tuck somehow had known what the marshals were up to that day. Knowing the whereabouts of lawmen was probably a requirement for a man of his questionable leanings.

"Well, don't think too long on it," Tuck said. "We're about loaded up."

"I'm still thinking on it," Molly answered, and her voice was flat and emotionless.

Tuck laughed. "Who are you fooling, Molly? You're either staying here and working for me, or you're going down the tracks to Canadian and working for me there."

"I've got choices."

"What choices?"

"Maybe I'll go on to Canadian and go into business for myself."

He laughed again. "Talk tough all you want, but you and I both know better."

"I'll give you an answer when I'm good and ready."

Tuck looked again to the wagon where the marshals had stood. "Might be if you answer right, I could help you with some of your problems."

She didn't reply to him, and Tuck moved on, walking rapidly to catch up with his wagon and shouting orders to his hired help on how he wanted his stuff loaded on the train.

Dixie noted the roulette wheel perched atop Tuck's wagonload. "Looks like he's taking most of the saloon with him. Don't know what he's leaving you to run here."

"He knows the real business will be down the tracks at Canadian, but he's leaving enough behind to keep the doors open long enough to see if those North Fork people get this town off the ground."

"Town? This?" Dixie said.

And he was remembering and seeing earlier days when he asked it. He was seeing how Ironhead had been in its ugly, boisterous prime, with hundreds of booted men living in the camp they were now tearing down, and the majority of them bellied up to the bar on a Saturday night and swilling down cheap rotgut until they thought they were half man and half alligator and ready to take on any man who said any different. And what it took to keep those hardworking, hard-drinking devils in line, and even more so, what it took to keep a lid on a camp that drew the other, worse kind of human, like flies on a fresh cow patty. They were the kind that followed such places looking for easy pickings and easy prey—dope peddlers, cardsharps, pimps, prostitutes, pickpockets, and holdup men. And worse.

"You know how these end of the tracks boom camps work," he added with equal disdain and skepticism. "They live hard and die fast, and then the next one springs up and nobody remembers the one before it."

"All I know is what they're saying. I heard yesterday that they're going to build a hotel soon. The Katy is going to fix the depot, and the supply warehouse across the tracks is still here. That means railroad business, and with the wagon roads that come through here . . . Well, maybe they're right, and this place can make a go of it."

"A hotel? Nothing but big talk and big ideas."

"Everything starts with nothing more than talk and ideas," she said. "Maybe I want to be in on the beginning of something."

"When did they start calling the next camp Canadian?" he asked. "I didn't know it had a name, yet."

"You're the new police chief, and you don't know what

they're calling what's fixing to be your new home?"

"I haven't talked to the superintendent in a while." He touched his chest gingerly, as if to remind her of his wound. "This bullet hole has had me under the weather, in case you didn't notice, plus I needed time to think on things."

"Call him by his name. You sound like every other kiss-ass on the Katy line calling him the superintendent."

"Duvall is . . . well, he is what he is," he said.

"He's got it coming."

"Got what coming?"

"Nothing. Just what we all got coming, I guess."

He noticed the funny way she said that, but didn't let on like he had. And he thought about Bill Tuck and his fancy vest and that smart-aleck smirk always on his face, like a cat that had just swallowed the canary and with the tail feathers still poking out its mouth. Hard to believe he had come through it all virtually unscathed. If anybody had it coming, it was him, but that wasn't the way things had to work. What was fair didn't always have anything to do with the way things were. Dixie had learned some of those lessons as a boy, and more of them in the late war and since. Things happened the way they happened, and a man often couldn't do a thing to stop them.

His gaze drifted back to the black square and ash pile where Irish Dave's saloon had been, burnt and gone like the depot house in those days of the past when the Katy railroad was trying to get the trestle bridge built over the South Canadian River, and Ironhead Station truly was the wildest hell-on-wheels construction camp west of anywhere. And he looked beyond the camp to the little knoll with the giant oak trees that had become the camp's Boot Hill. Fourteen grave markers lay under the spreading arms of those trees. Fourteen men gone, and all kinds of other suffering that couldn't be marked with tombstones or wooden crosses—that's what it had taken to build the Katy's railroad trestle and get the tracks moving on to Texas.

"Irish Dave was one of a kind," Molly said absentmindedly as she, too, looked at the ash pile where the Bucket of Blood Saloon had burned down.

"You might say Fat Sally was every bit as eccentric." He laughed and then gave a mock shiver. "Meanest, foulest, toughest woman I ever had the misfortune to run across."

"Well, they're both gone now."

"Gone like Ironhead Station, and maybe we're the better for it."

"Maybe. What do you think he would say about all of this?"

Dixie knew who she meant—that *he* again. *Him.*

He twisted around on the bench and looked at the charred, splintered plank wall behind them. A yellow-stained sheet of paper was tacked there. It read:

Welcome to Ironhead Station.

1. *No firing off guns in camp.*
2. *No running horses, mules, or other saddle stock or wagon stock through camp.*
3. *Saloons or other establishments selling liquor or ardent spirits will not open before noon and will close no later than 2 o'clock in the morning.*
4. *All games of chance will be run honestly, and such games and the establishments housing them shall be inspected at will by the railroad police or other authorities.*
5. *Anyone found to be loitering, wandering, or loafing about the saloons with no visible means of employment will be deemed a vagrant.*
6. *All persons will go fully clothed while in camp.*

7. *Those not employed by the MK&T will not follow the construction crews to construction sites, or otherwise distract or hinder those employees from their work.*
8. *Trash or dead animals must be buried or hauled out of camp by the responsible party.*
9. *No destruction of MK&T property.*
10. *All other applicable rules and laws of the MK&T Railroad, the Indian Territory, and the United States of America will be enforced.*

The handwritten poster was signed at the bottom by the chief of the MK&T railroad police, Dixie's predecessor. A pair of bullet holes cut the middle of the paper like the eyeholes in some kind of a mask. And he noticed that somebody had scribbled out the name of Ironhead Station and written something else in place of it.

"What's that?" he asked, pointing to the crude edit.

"That's what those North Fork folks are calling it now. Eufaula," she answered.

"Eufaula?"

"Some kind of Creek Indian word."

"What's it mean?"

"I don't know. I think Agent Pickins and his Indians out at the Ashbury Mission came up with it."

"Leave it to old Useless Pickins to change a perfectly good name."

"His name is Euless."

"That's what I said, Useless. Everybody calls him that." Dixie gave something between a grunt and a chuckle. "Now there's an accurate name if I ever heard one. Never had any use for that whiny preacher."

"Well, it's his place now, him and the rest of them that are staying on," she said.

"Hate to think what we did cleaning this place up was only

so that his kind can reap the rewards."

"Thought you said this place wouldn't ever amount to anything?"

"I'm just saying . . ."

"There you go again. What are you saying?"

"This is Indian land. White folks have to marry into the tribe or get them a work permit from the Federals to live in the Nations legal-like. Nothing but the railroad right-of-way belongs to the Katy, from what I hear, and all that talk about a three-million-acre land grant has been thrown out the window unless Superintendent Duvall and the money men can sway Congress and the courts to change their minds."

"Folks are staying, no matter what. There is good farmland here along the river. Plenty of timber for building or for selling. You ought to think on staying yourself. Throw away that badge."

"Lay down the sword and take up the plow?"

"Something like that."

"What do you know about farming?" he asked.

"People can learn. We don't always have to stay the same thing."

"Well, I followed a plow near half my life, and I never ended up anywhere but at the end of the next furrow, and hungrier than I started." Dixie stood to his feet stiffly after such a long sit, and making slow work of it and favoring one side of his body.

"Does it hurt much?" she asked.

"A little, time to time, but I'm healing proper. Another week or two and I ought to be right as rain," he answered. "Lucky the Traveler didn't shoot more to center, or I wouldn't be here now complaining."

The mention of the Arkansas Traveler made her face go still, and he knew what she worrying about and wished he hadn't said what he said. It was the same thing he had been worrying over for more than two weeks.

The deadliest hired killer to ever kiss a rifle stock, and a man that had put more men under the sod than half the undertakers west of the Mississippi, that's what they said about the Traveler. And Dixie had reason to know the truth of some of that, for the assassin had put a bullet in him at better than six hundred yards away and put him within a frog hair of the bone orchard. And he was still out there somewhere, hunting, and with a certain killing yet undone—not Dixie, but the man the Traveler really wanted dead. *Him.*

The engineer had climbed up in the locomotive cab and let off a long blast of his steam whistle. Dixie moved his holstered pistol around to a more comfortable position on his hip and made as if to go.

"Train's about ready to leave," he said.

"Yeah. Are you going with it?"

He looked down at the badge on his chest. "I guess that's what he would do. He always said it was an honest living, even if I'm not sure about the honest part."

"Where do you think he is right now?"

Dixie stepped to the corner of the depot platform and looked to the west, as if he could see right through the train blocking his view, and as if he could see for days and days ahead into that distance. He looked back at her, and then he looked one last time at that poster of camp ordinances tacked to the wall behind her. He paid particular attention to the signature at the bottom of that poster.

Morgan Clyde, MK&T Chief of Railroad Police. Him.

"I reckon he's getting by. Morgan's a hard man," Dixie said.

"You say that so calmly. And with him out there all alone, and in who knows what kind of trouble."

"Morgan is used to being alone. I think he's like that most times, even when he's got company."

"You should have gone with him."

"I know . . . but he said that it was his to do, and nobody else's."

"He always says that."

"The Traveler challenged him to come out and face him, alone and on his terms, or get ambushed here in camp with no fair chance at all. Wouldn't have it any other way."

"Men and their damned fool pride. He could have gotten a posse together and ran that Traveler out of the hills. Or he could have got the army to help him."

"No posse is going to want to hunt the Traveler. Not with him lying out there somewhere in the distance with a rifle likely pointed their way."

He noticed a tear running down Molly's cheek, and when she saw him looking at it, she swiped it away and gave him an angry scowl.

"You ever told him how crazy you are about him?" Dixie asked.

"I haven't, and don't you go making stuff like that up," she snapped back at him. "Me and Morgan go way back, that's all. I'm proud to call him a friend, same as you are."

"Right." He rubbed at the whisker stubble on one cheek in an attempt to hide his grin.

"Have you told Ruby Ann you're leaving?" she threw back at him.

He rubbed that whiskered cheek more vigorously and his grin changed to a grimace. He shifted his feet restlessly, and everything about his pose said he wasn't going to answer that question.

"Oh, come now, Dixie Rayburn. You've got all kinds of wisdom when it comes to other people's business," she said. "You know she's sweet on you."

"Ruby Ann . . . she's . . . she's all messed up right now. I've been nice to her during her convalescence, that's all. She'll think different when she's had time." He stepped off the depot platform and started for the nearest passenger car on the long line of the train. "You'll tell her I'm gone, won't you? Explain things?"

"You knew you were going, didn't you? You already had your belongings on the train."

"Reckon so. Man's gotta make a living."

He was halfway there when he heard her speak again. Maybe she meant him to hear it, or maybe she was only talking to herself.

"I wonder where he is right now?"

Dixie was still thinking about those words when the train rolled and rattled across the high trestle over the South Canadian River a mile and a half south of Ironhead. He looked out the window of the passenger car to the west again, at all that wild country the government had set aside as the Indian Territory, or what some called the Nations. The whole damned territory was meant to replace the land that the government had taken from the Indians elsewhere, but like all things the government messed up; it had become as much a haven for bad men and outlaws of every color and creed as a reservation, and the kind of place where law and order was as scarce as hen's teeth. A lot could befall a man in that kind of country, and he, like Red Molly, wondered what had happened to Morgan Clyde.

Chapter Three

Morgan Clyde lay on his belly behind the dead horse, unmoving, and exactly the same way he had lain for the past two hours. Only one other shot had been fired his way in all that time since the one that had struck his saddle. But that last shot had blown another hole in his dead horse's belly. The flies and the smell of guts had gotten worse as a result.

The hill where the gunshots had come from ran for a mile or better on the northern horizon. Morgan knew it was only a matter of time before Old Death out there got tired of playing with him and changed positions on that hill, and only a matter of time until he was situated where he could shoot around the dead horse.

Old Death, Morgan didn't say it, but that's how he had thought of him for a long time, like an old nightmare that he had somehow gotten on a first name basis with. When people talked of him, they mostly called him the Arkansas Traveler, but Old Death fit better. Everything about that man out there reeked of death, worse than the smell of horse guts, and as wicked as the crack of his rifle.

Morgan twisted his stiff neck around enough to look at the sun. He had maybe an hour or a little more before sundown. Old Death, the Traveler, wasn't going to let it get dark. He would finish it when he became bored with tormenting Morgan, and while it was still light enough to see his gunsights. Morgan was going to have to make a move, and do it soon.

Again, he glanced up at his scabbarded rifle stock sticking out over the dead horse's hip. He might pull that rifle free without getting shot, but there was no way he was going to be able to reveal himself from behind the horse long enough to find his attacker in his sights before he took a bullet in the skull. The facts were the facts, as bad as they were, and there was no getting around them.

"Clyde!" that cackling, hillbilly voice called out to him again.

Morgan's throat was so dry that it took him two tries to answer back. "Is that you out there, Traveler?"

"You know it is." Again, came that half-mad cackle of laughter. "Gotta say I'm plumb disappointed in you, Clyde. Ridin' out in the open like that was a fool thing to do. You're takin' all the challenge out of killin' you."

Morgan tried to pinpoint exactly where on that far-off hilltop the Traveler's voice was coming from. Was it farther to his right than the first time the killer had called out to him?

To make a wrong move was to die, but so was doing nothing. Morgan reached for the rifle stock and yanked the gun to him. His movement drew no shot from the Traveler, and he wondered if he had picked a perfect moment while the Traveler was moving positions and out of sight of him. Morgan fought off the strong temptation to run, but there was nowhere to flee. To his south, at least a mile away, was the Salt Fork of the Arkansas River. To his north was the long hill where the Traveler hid. Everything in between was wide-open prairie. Maybe there might be a chance to hoof it out of the rifle range of a normal marksman, given some distraction to grant him a running start, but the Traveler was no normal marksman.

The closest cover was the very hilltop where the Traveler had taken his stand. It was more of a long, prairie ridge than it was a hill, rising up fifty or so feet from the level ground he lay upon, and free of anything but grass and a few scattered clumps of woody brush. Morgan looked past his horse's rump at the ridge and guessed it to be at least four hundred yards from him.

In his youth, he had been a decent foot racer, but he wasn't a fleet-footed boy anymore and it was going to take him at least a couple of minutes to cover that much ground loaded down with his guns and hobbled by old wounds yet to heal. All the while, the Traveler would be shooting at him.

Morgan rolled back on his belly and propped himself up on his elbows. He fitted the curled Schuetzen buttplate of his heavy-barreled R.R. Moore target rifle to his shoulder and scanned the portion of the ridge he could see past his horse's tail through the twenty-power Malcolm telescopic sight. A slight turn of the focus ring on the riflescope, and the hillside came into clearer view behind the hair-fine crosshairs. If the Traveler was moving that way, he wanted to see him first and he wanted to shoot first.

He lay like that for a quarter of an hour, scoping the hillside until his eye needed rest. He raised his head from behind the riflescope and twisted it around to look behind him. The sun had moved a little lower down on the western horizon. He wished he could turn around behind the horse so that he could scan the ridge beyond his horse's head, but there was no way to do so without exposing himself.

There was only one thing he could think to do, and it was the worst of long shots at best. He moved his legs as much as he could, trying to stretch the kinks and the stiffness out of them after lying there so long. And he thought about what he knew about the Traveler.

Very few men claimed to have laid eyes on the assassin, but Morgan had seen him twice. The first time was only a glimpse of him in the distance many years before, but the second time was much more. It was the memory of the second occasion back in Ironhead Station that he called upon, and the image of the Whitworth rifle that the Traveler carried that wouldn't leave his mind.

The Whitworth was a British-made muzzle-loading rifle that some Confederate snipers used during the war. Morgan knew little about such guns, but one thing he remembered about those rifles from campfire talk was that the tight tolerances of the hexagonal bore that made them so accurate was also said to make them damned slow to reload. If he was to have a snowball's chance in hell of making that ridge without getting shot, he needed to egg the Traveler into firing at him while he was still behind the dead horse. A good soldier with a muzzle-loader and minié balls could fire a shot a minute, or maybe a little better if he was an unusually calm, skilled sort. But the Traveler might have a hard time ramrodding a tight-fitting bullet down the fouled bore of that Whitworth. And time was what Morgan needed.

His canteen and his other rifle, a Henry repeater, were pinned under his horse. But even if he could have gotten to them, there was only so much he could carry, especially when he needed to move fast. He rolled onto his back and heeled off one boot and then the other. Gently, he raked them within reach of his hands with his legs. Then he yanked two saddle strings off his saddle skirt and tied them into one longer piece, secured the tops of his boots together, and hung the string between them behind his neck.

Back on his belly and with the target rifle in his hands, he reached out with it and tried to drag his hat to him with the end of the barrel. The hat was a good two feet past the tail end of his horse, but if the Traveler saw the movement, it didn't bait him into shooting.

The hat was barely out of his reach, but Morgan gave up on it, unwilling to stick his head and most of his upper torso out past the horse. Instead, he grabbed the saddlebag on the up side of the horse and flopped it over to him. He unbuckled the straps that held it closed and let the items inside it spill out on his chest.

There was nothing much there that he needed or that wouldn't weigh him down, but he did take the waterproof tin of matches and a little brass picture frame that folded in the middle and clasped closed. He slipped both items inside his shirt, then he checked his Remington-Beals pistol to make sure it was still on his hip with the hammer thong secure.

He put a hand under the saddlebag and began to flop it up and down. The Traveler had shown that he wasn't above popping off a few shots to show off or to torment Morgan, and from that hilltop the moving saddlebags might appear like a man's head or some other body part.

Morgan didn't have long to wait, for a bullet ripped through the saddlebag and thumped into the ground on the other side of him with a solid whump. In the same instant, Morgan was up on his feet and running for the hill.

He held the Moore rifle in his left hand, leaning far forward as if through sheer will alone he could force his knees to pump faster. He was a tall man and his strides were long. His socked feet flew over the ground, and he gritted his teeth and fought against the pain every time his tender foot soles stepped on something sharp. His stiff right shoulder hampered him some, but worse than that was the other old wound in his left leg. By the time he had covered forty yards, his run was more a swift, limping hobble.

And still no shot from the Traveler came his way. The foot of the ridge was a little closer.

Twenty more yards and he was laboring for all he was worth. The twenty-pound target rifle was weighing him down, and his bad leg was weakening more with every stride. Still, he ran on, for there was nothing to do but keep going, no matter how slow he felt himself to be moving.

When he was two hundred yards from the ridge he began to zigzag and alter his pace. Seconds ticked off in his head, measured and counted by his frantic mind with each stride he took.

He was within a hundred yards of the foot of the ridge and a small clump of shinnery oak brush that he had been aiming for, when the Traveler finally managed a reload and found him in his rifle sights.

Chapter Four

The Traveler's rifle roared again from somewhere up on the hilltop to Morgan's left, but Morgan had no clue where the bullet went or how close it had come to him. His lungs felt like they were on fire, and he wheezed with every sobbing breath. All he could think was to focus on that clump of bushes and make his legs keep moving. He felt like he had been running for hours, and the thought he couldn't shake was that he was never going to make it.

He fell headlong into brush and landed on his face. He lay motionless there, and the time it took him to catch his breath and to slow his beating heart was time enough for the Traveler to reload once more. Another bullet whipped through the grass beside Morgan and knocked a limb off a clump of brush. He scrambled on his belly, crawling uphill following a shallow runoff gully barely deep enough to hide him. He fought the urge to move too fast and was careful to navigate around any clumps of taller grass or any other vegetation that might bend or sway and draw the Traveler's attention. He belly-crawled ninety feet or so before the drainage petered out and became too shallow to give him cover. He stopped there behind a clump of buffalo grass. The sun was directly in his face, and made it hard for him to look for his adversary. And that same sun was also likely to reflect off his scope lenses if he aimed the rifle in that direction.

His heart rate and his breathing approached normal after a

time, and he could think more clearly. The lack of water, the run, and the constant vigil he was keeping was wearing on him. But he also realized that he felt more alive than ever, despite his worries and his pains, and not only because he had survived the run. An old rush that he hadn't felt in a long time pumped through his veins. Fear and aggression and adrenaline mixed together in some powerful concoction. It was the feeling of knowing a man out there was stalking you, and you stalking him in turn—a cat and mouse game where either man could wind up the mouse.

Old dreams and old memories pushed closer to the surface, and he knew that he was becoming more the man he had left behind so long ago. And he knew that to survive he was going to have to relive old sins and hold them dearly. He was going to have to find the Traveler in his crosshairs and kill him.

He looked down at the Moore rifle laid across his forearms, and at the fat octagonal barrel so heavy that it only left room for a thin slab of forearm at the end of the darkly oiled walnut stock. The browned steel of it, and the long tube of the Malcolm scope running almost the length of the barrel, smelled of oil and sulphur. He had fired that gun on only one occasion in all the days since the war was over, and never at a man in that time. He couldn't even say why he had kept the rifle, or why he had packed it along with him hidden in its leather traveling case for almost nine years.

It was a benchrest rifle too heavy and cumbersome to carry for hunting. Originally it had been built to shoot accurate groups at paper targets for men with enough money and leisure time to entertain themselves with such hobbies. A fine piece of craftsmanship, but to his mind it was something darker and more alive than a Saturday afternoon gun-club plinker and a rich man's toy. It was a mark of Cain and a thing made for killing. Yet, he had been unable to part with it, and there he was about to wield it again.

The Traveler couldn't be far away, but such a man was an expert at concealment and the art of a sniper. He would likely be where Morgan least expected him, and he would be waiting for him to make a mistake. One wrong move, one moment of foolish impatience, and the deadly game would end. The distance between them was now close enough that neither man was likely to miss if he got a good, clean look at his opponent. One shot and one kill, the measure of a long-range man hunter.

Morgan looked down at his rifle again, at the clumsy, blunt beauty of it, and then he twisted his head to see down the ridge towards his horse. He could barely discern it through the grass. One shot, one kill—one was all he was going to get, for the Moore rifle was a muzzleloader carrying but one .54 caliber patched bullet in its bore, and his ramrod, spare bullets and powder, percussion caps, and the rest of his things were down there in his shot bag pinned beneath that horse. One shot in the rifle, and then nothing but the ten rounds of rimfire cartridges for his pistol—five in the pistol itself and five more in the spare cylinder he carried in a pouch on his gun belt. And he had his sheath knife, but it was almost as poor of a weapon as the Remington Army was for the kind of fight the Traveler specialized in.

Morgan scanned the hillside over and over again, starting close to him and then working his way out as far as he could see with his naked eyes. His guess was that the Traveler would be somewhere near to the top where he had the high ground and the most commanding field of fire. His horse was likely tied on the other side of the ridge, and he might want to keep it handy or within sight.

The high ground mattered a lot. But no advantage came without some risk of its own, and the Traveler might skyline himself up there.

The sun was so low that the orb of it was gone from sight, and all that remained were smears of glowing orange and yellow and red, slowly fading and sinking like trails of oily firewater off the edge of the world. Morgan grunted and considered what that meant. Shooting light was about gone.

He felt it now safe to use his Malcolm telescopic sight, and he shouldered the gun and pressed the stock under his cheekbone like the kiss of an old girlfriend. He used the magnification of the scope to more closely search several spots where he thought the Traveler might be hiding. But the hired killer wasn't to be found. Either he was that damned good, or he had pulled up stakes and moved on. Morgan wasn't about to count on the latter.

He waited until the sun was down before he decided on his next move. Had it been a dark night, he would have had more options, but a ripe full moon was already visible, and within another hour it was going to be bigger and bright enough to possibly shoot by with a telescopic sight. To go back down to his own horse to retrieve the shot bag for his rifle was going to mean being out on that open prairie lit up by that moon. And the Traveler had other options if he wanted to stake out the dead horse. He could move close and wait for Morgan to come. Less likely, for close work at night was better suited for a shotgun or a pistol, but Morgan didn't rule out anything.

He needed things off his horse, but when he finally moved it was in the opposite direction, towards the top of the ridge and in the gray gap between daytime and full dark. It took him less than half an hour to get over the top of the ridge and hunkered down in a new place. He listened and he searched for sign of the Traveler, and then moved on when he felt that he could.

He found the Traveler's horse a quarter of a mile away, more by luck than anything. The backside of the ridge was rougher terrain and dropped off more steeply, and he found the little zebra dun gelding tied in a cedar gully, still saddled. He ran a hand over the horse's right shoulder, feeling the brand there and knowing it was a lightning bolt only by the tips of his fingers traced over the scar. He slipped into his boots and tightened the saddle cinch and got up on the horse as quietly as he could, cringing at every creak of the leather.

When he left the gully, he left at a dead run, headed north. He thought he heard cursing from the top of the ridge behind him as he was leaving.

When he was a mile away he pulled the horse up and looked back the way he had come. The ridge was only a shadow in the distance. He took the Traveler's canteen from where it hung on the saddle horn. The water in it was lukewarm and stale, but right then it felt like sweet nectar wetting his dry mouth and trickling down his parched throat.

When he had drunk enough, he turned the horse and made a wide circle back to the south towards the river. An hour later he made a cold camp along a timbered dry creek bed leading down to that river. He kept the horse saddled and propped himself up against the trunk of a hackberry tree with the Moore rifle cradled in the crook of his elbow, and watched the prairie to the north and west of him. The Traveler was going to need water of his own soon, and he was likely to head for the river.

Morgan would be waiting for him.

Chapter Five

Red Molly sat alone in her rocking chair inside her little tent behind the Bullhorn Palace. The single kerosene lamp she had burning on the empty nail keg that served as her bedside table barely lit the room and cast feeble shadows on the canvas walls. She had her dress sleeves rolled up, and she scratched at one forearm absentmindedly, the loose dowel joints in the chair creaking as she rocked it back and forth in a steady rhythm, lost in thought as she had been for the last hour.

She stopped the rocker as the sound of footsteps outside drew her out of her daze. She grabbed her wrist purse off the back of the rocker and pulled a tiny Manhattan revolver with pearl grips out of it.

The footsteps were right outside the tent flaps. She didn't cock the little pistol, but held it in her lap half concealed by her dress.

"Are you in there, Molly?" Bill Tuck's voice called to her.

"I'm here."

He stepped through the tent flaps without waiting to be asked inside, and he noticed the pistol in her lap right off. "I thought you would have had sense enough to throw that thing in the river."

"This?" She revealed the pistol to him more, but didn't lift it. "What's wrong with a woman having some protection?"

"I hear Tubbs bought the farm with seven little .22 bullets in his chest. Doc Chillingsworth cut a couple of them out after they drug Tubbs off that shitter they found him on," Tuck said. "I'd bet you twenty dollars that pop gun you're holding is a .22."

"What's that supposed to mean? I'm not the only one in camp with a pocket gun." She gestured at the nickel-plated Smith & Wesson pistol in his vest pocket.

"This isn't a .22, and I'm not the one those marshals suspect," he said.

"Condescending bastard," she said under her breath.

"You call me what you will if it makes you feel better, but don't play me for the fool. I know what Tubbs did to you," he said. "But maybe you don't remember me finding you on your bed looking like something the dogs had drug in, curled up all pitiful and crying like a baby."

"Shut up."

"Close your ears if you want to, but it doesn't change what I saw. Him practically carrying you back to your tent after the other one had his fun with you. And he took a long time leaving, like maybe he cut off a piece of you himself."

"I said shut up!" Her hand clutched her pistol so hard that she felt the tip of the hammer bite into her palm. She started rocking again, trying to focus on the sound of the chair instead of what he was saying to her.

"You're not near so tough as you let on, are you, Molly dear? They tore you up bad. Broke you down."

She sniffled and wiped at her nose, and glared at him. Her voice was quieter when she spoke again, but no less angry. "I thought you had left for Canadian."

"My crew can handle getting the new saloon put up. And how could I leave when I haven't made my delivery?"

He pulled a tiny, square glass bottle from one of his vest pockets and set it on the cheap dresser beside him. He looked at himself in the mirror while he did it, then saw her reflection watching him over his shoulder and smiled. His teeth were white and perfect. "This ought to steady you some. Give you a better outlook on the world."

"I didn't ask you for that," she said.

He continued to look at himself in the mirror. "No, but I thought it was about time you would be running low. Wouldn't want you to be getting all itchy and shaky when those marshals come back around again."

"What if I don't have the money to pay you?" She hated that she couldn't keep her eyes off the bottle, and that he had noticed the tremble in her hand that held the little pistol and the way he smirked at the sight of it. She hated the power he held over her with that little bottle, and despised herself, most of all, for listening to his filth. His words settled on her like sour fog, and she could feel the slime of them on her skin.

He quit the mirror and turned to face her. "Call it a present, or call it an advance on your wages."

"Oh, the gall of you."

He clucked his tongue and shook his head at her. "Poor thing, all this mean talk."

"How long do you think you can keep spitting on me?" She stopped the rocker and leaned forward as if to rise, or as if she intended on striking him. "You come in here and ask me to work for you after what you did to Morgan and what you did to this camp?"

"You'll take it, Molly, like you always have," he said without emotion. "You won't like it, but you'll take it. You're a survivor if you are anything. I knew it the first time I met you when you were still with that tinhorn gambler husband of yours."

"You mean my ex-husband that you murdered?"

"You know I did you a favor. All he ever did was bust you up and steal from you. And it was him that gave you the habit." Tuck jerked a thumb at the little bottle on the dresser.

"You didn't kill him for me. Tell it how it really was. You did it because he owed you money and wouldn't pay. You never do anything that doesn't fit into your schemes."

Tuck shrugged his bullish shoulders. He wasn't a tall man, but heavy muscled and with the joints and bone of a much bigger man. His shadow loomed wide and large on the tent wall. "He was a rat, and you and I are long past that."

She leaned back in the chair, and her voice went quieter. "If I was any woman at all, any stronger, I would have killed you for what you did to him, no matter how mean and lowdown he was to me."

"Like you killed Tubbs? Did that make you feel powerful? Do you like that, sweet Molly? Killing?" Tubbs laughed after he said it.

"I'm not like you." She fought back the tears building in the corner of her eyes, unwilling to let him see her cry.

"No, Molly, you're only a dope fiend whore with a bad choice in men and worse luck. But you do know how to run our kind of business, and you know how to keep your mouth shut when it matters. Funny, how I trust you."

"You ought not trust me."

"I trust that you know what I do to those that bite the hand that feeds them. You might hate me, Molly, but you need me. That's what bothers you most."

"I know it was you that set Deacon Fisher and those Kingman brothers on Morgan. I know it and he knows it," she spat back at Tuck. "How do you like that? Knowing there will come a time when Morgan settles the score with you?"

"I suspect dear Morgan's got enough troubles of his own right now. If the Traveler doesn't get him, what's left of the Kingman boys will. And then there are those Pinkertons that were fussing around after him. I suspect they've got plans for him that he won't like." Tuck clucked his tongue and shook his head at her as if he were dealing with a child. "No, it's likely I don't have much to worry about when it comes to Morgan Clyde, however much that will break your rotten little heart. Never did see what you saw in that law dog of yours. Guess you like your men tall and dead, but hell, I've seen stranger tastes."

The pistol in her lap shook in her hand, and lifted slightly from her dress without her realizing she had moved it. "You dirty, selfish bastard."

Again he laughed without an ounce of humor in it. "Careful, Molly, with that talk. Don't make me hurt you."

Make him hurt her. That's how all of his kind said that, as if the blame belonged to their victims. And the sad thing was that they could make you believe them.

He pitched a folded piece of paper at her. "There's the combination to the safe. You go to work running the Bullhorn tomorrow. There's enough money for you to get started if you run things right, and I'm leaving you enough liquor to tide you over until we see how things shake out. If it looks like you can show a profit I'll send you more help from down the tracks. If not, I'll send for you, and you get that big sweet ass of yours down to Canadian."

Her chin trembled as badly as her hands. So badly, that she couldn't reply. It wouldn't have mattered, anyway. He knew she was going to take his offer, and him knowing that without her saying it, and him so confident that she needed him, was almost worse than anything.

He started for the tent flaps, but paused halfway to them. "You got Tubbs, but you forget about that other one. Forget about him, you hear me?"

"I'm not forgetting anything."

"You can't touch him, no matter how badly you want to. Maybe if you were smarter you could, but you're not."

"What do you care?"

"I care because I've got other plans for him. Say you got away with it and they didn't hang you, then I would cut your pretty throat."

"Why don't you do it now?"

He laughed at her again, that cold, spiteful chuckle that cut into the raw soul of her. "And you get rid of that pistol tonight. I don't need any trouble from those marshals. Bad for business. Remember, we don't let the personal get in the way of business. You always understood that, and I'm hoping you still do once you've had your fix."

"Leave," she said. "Now."

He slipped the .32 Smith from his vest pocket, and the Manhattan in her lap cocked under her thumb as if by its own volition. For a moment, both of them faced each other with guns in their hands, and nothing but the final aiming and a pull of their triggers for one or both of them to die.

"You silly bitch. I'm not going to shoot you." He turned the Smith around and pitched it to her butt first. "Take it, and get rid of that .22 like I said. If those marshals come back around you tell them you never owned such a gun."

She had to scramble to keep his pistol from hitting her in the chest, and he was already going out the tent door by the time she had caught it.

In a moment, when she could no longer hear his footsteps outside, she started rocking again, alternating her attention between the bottle of opium tincture on the dresser and the two pistols in her lap. She resisted the urge to scratch at her itching arms, the feel of them like a thousand tiny needles were pricking her from the inside. And it wasn't long before she began to look at Tuck's pistol more, watching how the lamplight shone on the shiny nickel plating. Almost everyone in Ironhead knew that pistol on sight, with its fancy ivory grips always sticking out of his vest pocket. Wasn't a day in the last year he hadn't worn it like most men wore a watch.

She swiped at another tear on her cheek and inhaled with a repressed sob and a gasp. Slowly, a thin hint of a smile spread across her face. Not a happy expression and not a sad one, but rather something else. As if she had only recently come to some new conclusion with the working of it fitting together so tightly and perfectly, like the gears in a clock, that it gave her pleasure. A cunning thing she was driven to, and once the idea came, there was no turning back.

She put Tuck's pistol in a dresser drawer, and poured herself two fingers of whiskey from the bottle stashed in the same drawer. She pulled the cork stopper from the opium bottle with her teeth and trickled a few drops into the whiskey. And then a few more. It was going to be a long night, and she needed steadying.

When she had downed the whiskey, she put her Manhattan pistol in her purse and went outside. Soon, the sound of her quick footfalls faded.

It was a long walk to the river and it was well after midnight when she returned. She poured herself another shot of whiskey laced with the opium, drank it, and then undressed while she stared at the dresser drawer where she had put Tuck's pistol

The same cold smile was on her mouth when she blew out the lamp and lay down on her bed. She had gotten Tubbs, and she was going to get the rest of them.

Chapter Six

The sun had barely risen enough to see by when Morgan stripped from his white shirt and took it down to a sandbar on the river and rubbed it in the mud. He took handfuls of the same mud and smeared it over his pants legs. Back at his camp, he hung the shirt on a tree limb to dry and examined his aches and pains.

He dropped his pants and unwrapped the bandage on his left thigh enough to check the wound there. The scab was still intact, and the fresh puckered scar there about the size of his thumb hadn't busted open during his exertions. In fact, the wound looked like it was healing well in the weeks since he had ridden out of Ironhead Station. Other than some stiffness and an occasional twinge or two when he moved it wrong, the leg was pretty much mended to the point it didn't hinder him. As far as such wounds went, he had gotten off lucky. The pistol ball that had torn through the muscle could have just as easily struck a major artery or busted bone.

But it was the other pistol wound in the chord of muscle and tendon above his right collarbone that grieved him most. While he couldn't see it well enough to examine it, the right side of his chest and ribcage was covered in dried serum where the wound had drained. He felt the lump beneath the crusty bandages and beneath his skin where the doctor had sewed the wound closed and knotted a tendon back together. That same doctor had told him to make sure he moved it and flexed it frequently to keep it limber and the scar tissue from forming and permanently limiting his range of motion. He had done so, but it still caused him pain when he moved it wrong.

And then his gaze drifted down to the puckered scar on his right ribcage that ran all the way down to his hipbone—a far older scar, and an ugly one, as if a hot iron had been drug down his side and gouged away flesh that could never regrow. And there were more scars and bumps and bruises, all little ones, some new and some old, but each with a story to tell. He tallied up his history of wounds against the money he made as a lawman, and knew then why he had never succeeded at his earlier profession as a businessman. There was damned little profit in packing a badge and a gun; not enough to outweigh the risk.

But he wore no badge then, and was considering never pinning one on again. Not that it mattered, for it wasn't a matter of law and order between him and that one out there hunting him. It was something more primal, an old, unfinished thing that remained between the two of them that could only be solved by a killing. The Traveler would have it no other way, and as uncivilized as it sounded, Morgan, too, welcomed a reckoning.

Once the shirt had time to air-dry a little, he donned the garment again. For the most part, he had managed to brown the shirt enough to camouflage most of its whiteness, and while his wool pants were gray, the mud smeared on them might help him blend in with the countryside a little more. It bothered him to ruin good clothes, for he was a man that liked to dress well, but such a sacrifice was a small price to pay to stay alive.

He belted on his pistol, took up his rifle, and headed for a tall cottonwood tree growing about twenty yards away from the riverbank. A fork high up in that tree provided Morgan a clear view of the prairie, all the way out to where his dead horse lay. The carcass was at least five hundred yards away—too far to make out any detail with the naked eye, but close enough that he could see if the Traveler tried to retrieve the canteen off the dead horse or cross that open prairie on his way to the river. The odds were against it, but there was a slight chance he might end it there and then.

But being literally up a tree wasn't to his liking. A man caught up in the air like that was nothing but meat for the pot if he was spotted or snuck up upon. The old training and the old lessons hard won came back to Morgan. Always allow for means of retreat; be careful about firing more than one shot from the same stand; always expect counter fire. The quick ones learned that early, and the slow ones often didn't get a chance for a second lesson.

Three buzzards were already circling over the dead horse, and more of them fluttered and fussed with each other down on the carcass. He studied the scene many times through his riflescope, and thought he could see a mound of fresh earth where something had dug under the down side of the horse. Maybe it was coyotes or some other predator or scavenger, or maybe the Traveler had already been there.

Morgan stayed in the treetop until late into the morning. The Traveler never appeared. In time, Morgan climbed down and went to the dun horse and took off the saddlebags from behind the saddle. He slipped the horse's bridle and let it graze at the end of a lariat while he went through the Traveler's belongings.

Morgan didn't know quite what he expected to find, but it was readily apparent that the Traveler was a frugal man. One of the bags contained a homemade kettle fashioned from a tin can with a piece of wire for a bail, and inside the kettle wrapped in a rag was a knife, fork, and spoon set that fastened together for packing and were stamped *WORMAN & ELY* on the handles. Salt and pepper shakers were also wrapped in the rag, and a little cast-iron skillet and a tin mug completed the rest of the

Traveler's mess kit. A box of Lucifer matches, some fishing line and a hook wrapped around a short piece of stick, a whetstone, a mason jar full of bacon grease, a little sack of cornmeal, another sack half full of coffee, and a tin of soda crackers was wrapped inside an India rubber rain poncho.

Morgan dumped the other bag on the ground. There was a small glass jar of sperm oil, a spare shirt, a pair of Indian moccasins with holes in the soles, and a gray wool Confederate Army coat. And wrapped inside the coat were three little black books, all leather bound with a flap and tuck loop that held them shut. Morgan thumbed open one of the books and read the first page. *POCKET DIARY, 1861, A BLANK SPACE FOR EVERY DAY IN THE YEAR WITH CALENDER, PUBLISHED FOR TRADE, DENTON AND WOOD, MASSACHUSETTS.*

And handwritten at that top of that first page in clumsy handwriting were the words, *"Erastus Tuck, Pvt., Co. A, 3rd Arkansas Inf."*

Somehow, putting a name to the ghost that had haunted him for almost nine years was unsettling for Morgan, and it took effort to comprehend what he read.

The Union soldiers fighting in the east during the war had known that man out there as Old Death, and the Confederate boys called him the Arkansas Traveler. As the war drug along its bloody years, his reputation grew. When a boy in blue fell to a hidden marksman's bullet, there were always questions about whether it had been the Traveler's kill. To the fatalistic sorts, when your time came it came, and the Traveler was another symbol of hopeless fate and the fickle, chaotic whims of war. There was nothing you could do when Old Death wrote out a ticket with your name on it, no more than a man could stop an artillery shell randomly dropping in his trench. He was something you couldn't fight or face, the boogeyman, the taker of souls. And when he came calling, you were as good as gone, and you would never see him or hear the bullet that got you.

And when the war was over, the Traveler didn't quit shooting men. The difference then was that he got paid a premium for his unusual skill set, like some men hired out to build things with a hammer or the sweat of their brow. Only, the Traveler didn't build things. He tore men down with the pull of a trigger. And there were many that had need of such a man—the kind that wanted their enemies or their competitors done away with and no questions asked.

Morgan had known bad men and morally weak men, but the Traveler was something else altogether. His former encounter with the Traveler back in Ironhead and their brief conversation haunted him as much as anything he had ever heard and brought him no closer to understanding what made a man like that tick. Maybe he was mad dog crazy and once he had a taste for killing he couldn't let it go. Or maybe a man like that was simply born and not made. For such a thing as evil existed.

Morgan reread those handwritten words inside the diary again, and repeated them in his head. *Erastus Tuck. All of that, and he was simply a man with a name like Erastus. Flawed and twisted and evil, but a man just the same.*

And another realization came to Morgan after that naming had time to soak in. *The Traveler's last name was Tuck.*

From the moment the Traveler had arrived in Ironhead Station the winter before, Morgan had wondered who had hired the assassin. The Traveler didn't come cheap, if the rumor mill was correct, yet for all that talk of him over coffee and campfires, Morgan had never met a single storyteller who knew what the Traveler exactly looked like or how his clients contacted him. For such a mysterious man that thrived in the shadows, the fact that he shared a last name with Bill Tuck was no coincidence, especially not considering the kind of man Bill Tuck was and how he hated Morgan.

If the two were family, as it seemed, then the saloonkeeper would have access to him. Morgan couldn't prove it, but he firmly believed that Bill Tuck had a large hand in the attempted robbery of the Katy payroll the previous winter that had resulted in an all-out gunfight pitting the railroad police, and a small force of Pinkerton detectives and soldiers, against a gang of Missouri bushwhacker trash. And he knew for sure that Tuck had no qualms about paying for a killing. He had hired another bushwhacker gunman from the old Clements gang, Deacon Fischer, to gun Morgan down, and the Deacon had as much as admitted it before he and three other outlaws put two pistol balls in Morgan's body—the same unhealed wounds that grieved Morgan at that moment.

Morgan put the books down and took up the jar of sperm oil and the Traveler's spare shirt. He sat and unloaded his pistol, and cleaned the weapon with a rag torn from the shirt and dabs of whale oil. He worked intently, but often glanced at the three black books lying there on the ground as if he were drawn to them but disliked giving in to the urge.

Satisfied that the pistol was well oiled and free of rust, he reloaded it. He glanced at the diaries again, and he inhaled deeply before he picked up the one he had opened previously. He turned it to the first page and the first journal entry. Again, there was that same crude penmanship, with all of its inkblots, scribbled-out words, and poor grammar and misspellings.

May 6, 1861—Me and Solomon got to Hot Springs today. Come a fair piece over the mountains to join up to fight. We was supposed to take turns ridin the mule but Solomon refused to give up his turn very often and I walked most of the way. He thinks he is really somethin since he whipped Bessie's brother at the schoolhouse dance last week and she promised she would marry him when he got back from the war. He may be my big brother but he is always full of himself and as proud as a strut-

tin tom turkey. Says one man like him is more than a match for any whole company of Abe Lincoln's abolitionist Yankees and the war will be done and us back home by winter. I am not sure about that. I hear there is a lot of them Yankees and I reckon there is some fighters among them same as us. No matter. Solomon is probably right not to be scared though. We will whip them one way or the other and then we will come back home and all the girls will say what heroes we are and how handsome we look in our uniforms. Bessie's sister Sarah might look different on me wearing a smart uniform.

Hot Springs is the biggest town I ever seed. Ma wont believe me when I tell her about how the people from the capital down at Little Rock and even lots from way back east in their fancy clothes and their fancy carriages come there to spend their money and soak in the mineral springs. They got a whole street of hotels and bathhouses with them people standin around on the porches like they got no work to do. I wore my good shoes over my neck on the way here so as not to wear them out walkin. Those people laughed at my bare feet when they saw that. Never seed people so foolish or uppity. There is more colored folks here than I ever seed all at once. We never had no slaves to do our work and I do not know why Solomon is so all fired up talkin about filthy abolitionists. It was ten cents to have a hot soak in one of those bathhouses but I saved my money. I aint never been sick and dont need no healin and I reckon I can fight Yankees dirty same as I can clean. Solomon thought that was funny when I told him but he took him one of those baths and then had to borrow the money from me later to buy him some roasted ear corn from a man sellin them on the street.

May 7, 1861—Stood in line half the morning with the other men from the county wantin to join up. The officer making up the muster list of volunteers took Solomon but he did not take me. Said I was too little and sickly to pack a rifle in his infantry company and my feet was too flat for walking. Solomon is dead set on being a soldier and he told me to go back home cause I was too young for war fightin anyways. He gave me Pa's spare rifle to take back with me cause the army was going to give him a better one.

The next several pages and date spaces were empty of writing, and Morgan flipped through them until he found the next entry:

May 25, 1861—Walked all the way down to a town called Portland. Reckon it was nigh 200 miles or better but I have always been a good walker. Swampy and feverish country and no good kind of woods or mountains down here. It does not look like Arkansas proper. Not like home. Bad thickets of piney woods and too many mosquitos. Colonel Rust and a man named Captain Tebbs is making up a company of volunteers. They was not going to take me on either but I set up a target way down the street and knocked it over with Pa's rifle gun. That was enough for them and they signed me on for what they called the durashun of the war or something like that. Said we will not quit until the war is over. I ruined my shoes walkin here but they gave me new ones and a gray sack uniform coat with brass buttons and trousers the same color that the town ladies was sewin at the courthouse. I feel like one of those fancy folks back at Hot Springs wearin my uniform. The Enfield rifle they give me is as long as a plow furrow but it looks like a good one and I am anxious to try it out. I had no way to send Pa's gun back to him so I sold it to have money to buy me a mess kit and some other things for my pack. They say we will be going to Virginia soon by train. I look forward to ridin a train.

Morgan thumbed past more entries that consisted of the

daily living in a Confederate infantry company. In places Erastus Tuck, the man that would become the Arkansas Traveler, seemed to have been so driven to write down his experiences that he wrote in the margins or so tiny it was almost impossible to read. Morgan stopped once again over another page that caught his eye.

> *July 15, 1861—They formed our companies up into a regular regiment since we got to Virginia. They got us Arkansas men camped with a bunch of those Virginians and two other regiments from Georgia. They all talk tough and call us a bunch of hill hoppers and razorbacks but they aint been in a battle no more than we have. Just lots of patrollin and drillin and sittin around camp tellin stories and watchin down the mountain for the Federals to come. Done wore out my shoes I was so proud of and I do not think I will get any more for a long while. Good mountains hereabouts but wet weather and many of the men taken sick. I took the croup myself and lay in bed in the hospital tent for the past week. This is the first day I felt like writin and I have to be careful not to let the doctor see me sittin up. Cannot hardly breathe and I am wheezy as a windbroke horse and runnin a fever so hot I think you could rub me against a pine knot and start a fire with me. They say the Federals are goin to try us soon. Every man in camp is rearin to fight and nervous at the same time. They dont say that but I can see it. Hope I am well enough to stand on my feet when the time comes. I would hate to lay here while other men fight for me.*

Again, there were many blank pages and then sporadic entries that told how Erastus Tuck had lain sick for weeks. Then more marching, camp living, work details, and rumors of battles to come. Morgan scanned those pages more than read them, until he picked another entry to read closely.

> *October 2, 1861—Camped at some place called Cheat Moun-*

tain above the Greenbrier River. Same old soldier livin. A few of the companies on road patrol have had little skirmishes with the Federals but not us. Men bored and in low spirits. Some good food and a letter or two from back home would help but I get neither. All the men in my company are teasin me about the fight that is sure to come once the Federals get their nerve up. Those Federals are dug in not far away. The men say I will piss my pants and cry like a baby the first time I hear cannon shot. They call me a kid anyways but I dont let it bother me. Got to admit I am nervous though I dont tell them that. Hope I can be brave when it matters. The Tucks might be poor but we never raised no cowards. Granddaddy lost a leg at New Orleans with Andy Jackson and the Tennessee militia and Pa lost his eye with Old Rough and Ready Taylor at Palo Alto. Pa says a Mexican soldier poked his eye out with a bayonet but Solomon always says that Uncle Phineas claimed that Pa was drunk and a Texas Ranger knocked it out in a fight over a woman in a tavern before they ever got into Mexico. Pa is always mean when in his cups and bad to fight even though he aint no bigger than me.

And then another entry, longer than any before it. The dates for several days on two pages were scratched out to make room for so much writing, as if Erastus Tuck had much on his mind. Morgan read on.

October 4, 1861—Battle came faster than we expected. Federals overrun our camp yesterday. Our pickets fell back and they were on us without warnin and then most everyone broke and ran. Some was so scared that they could not figure out how to shoot their rifles. Captain Tebbs was hollerin at everyone to turn around and shoot their damned guns and he whipped some of them with the flat of his sword and finally put some backbone in them. We fought for about five hours and whipped those Yan-

kees back to where they come from but we lost two men from our company and three more wounded. The high up officers is claimin a victory today but I would call it a draw. The rumor is that our side lost 15 men altogether and about 40 wounded and we are still in the same camp we started in without moving so much as an inch forward. The Federals went right back where they was before we fought. That is no kind of victory I know of.

October 5, 1861—This is not what I expected. We do not fight smart. The officers want us to stand firm in front of the enemy and trade shots like fools. And we do what they say and we charge the Federals positions screamin like crazy men cause if you quit screamin the fear will set in and you cannot go nowheres. We shoot and reload and shoot again while the other side does the same. They tell us to go one place and we go no matter how the cannonballs are flying and no matter that you cannot see what your shootin at for all the smoke and shrapnel and men falling around you. I seed grown men curled up on their sides whimperin like suckling babies and others callin out for their wives or mothers. And I seed brave men too but it dont matter whether you are brave or coward. Its all the same with this kind of fightin.

A cannon shell does awful things to a man. Saw what was left of a Federal boy blown way up in a tree. He was run through and pinned on the stob of a limb and just hangin there with his eyes open and a terrible surprised look on his face. The crows was at him before the litter crews could find him the next mornin. Crows always peck for the eyes first.

October 6, 1861—I do not like cannons and I do not care for this kind of fightin. It dont make sense. No Cherokee Injun would fight this way. Pa did not teach us this way. I think if we took good cover with our rifle guns we could have our way with those Federals and not get all cut up standin in lines out in the open beggin to be shot or digging trenches and puttin up dirt walls to fight behind. We dig like moles and then the fool Federals try to dig us out. Next day they dig them a fort and we come along and let them shoot some of us while we try to dig them out. Its like we all are willin to die over some mounds of dirt and some muddy ditches. I spent more time with a shovel this fall than I have totin my rifle. Many of the men here are hunters and woodsmen and they know the ground and how to handle a rifle. But the officers do not use them right. At this rate I will not live long. None of us will. I think I am as brave as the next man. I did not run yesterday but this is not what I expected.

Morgan nodded his head while he read those words. The war hadn't been like anyone expected, and he suspected no war ever was. He folded the diary closed and stuffed it back in the saddlebags, and when he did he saw that his hands were shaking. He opened one of the other diaries, but only long enough to see that it was for the year 1862. He put it away without further examination, but the third one gave him as much pause as the first sight of the Traveler's real name had.

It was in the roughest condition of the three, torn and stained with the bound edge broken and with a piece of twine keeping it from falling apart. He untied the string and opened it gently and held it in the palm of his hand and looked upon the first page. It was as if he was hesitant to close it or go further. He swallowed once while he studied those simple numbers printed there, *1863,* as if that year had meaning to him.

But he did not read any of the entries and finally put it away in the saddlebags along with the others and the rest of the items. He was about to buckle the bags closed when he saw something else on the ground that he had not noticed earlier. It was a small buckskin bag about the size of a tobacco pouch decorated with beadwork and porcupine quills. Morgan had seen such worn around the necks of Indians as medicine bags.

He loosened the drawstring at the top and dipped two fingers inside it. When he pulled them out he was holding a wad of white feathers pinched between them. The feathers were soft and small and felt as if they might be goose down. Only feathers to some, but he knew they were the Traveler's mark and as much a part of the legend of him as anything. The Traveler left one of those feathers on the body of every man he killed. Left them like a signature, or like some men left a business card.

Morgan bridled the dun and rode out onto the prairie. He circled to the east of the dead animal, and climbed the ridge where he had been ambushed from the previous day. He rode down the spine of it, stopping often.

When he was sure that the Traveler was gone, he rode down to the dead horse as warily and as cautious as a lobo wolf approaching what he thought might be trap bait on the downwind side. The buzzards lifted and flew away, and he saw that it wasn't them or the coyotes that had dug underneath the dead horse. The Traveler had come down to it during the night and Morgan's saddlebags and his Henry rifle were gone, as well as everything else other than his saddle. Looking closer, he found that his hat was gone, too.

And the other thing that he saw was a crude arrow scratched into a spot of bare ground not ten feet from the horse. The arrow pointed southwest towards the river and upstream, as if daring him to follow its direction. He thought on the words the Traveler had said during their encounter back in Ironhead. The Traveler had the drop on him then and could have killed him at point-blank range. But that wasn't how he wanted it, for it wasn't his style.

"You take up your rifle and come out of camp before too long. I'll be waiting for you, and don't you make me wait," the

Traveler had said while he covered Morgan with a pistol. "Gonna be like old times, me and you. The ol' Devil is gonna tune up his fiddle and we're gonna dance the way we was made to. Dance 'til one of us can't dance no more."

Morgan unsaddled the dun and put his own saddle on its back. Then he remounted and laid the Moore rifle across his saddle swells and clucked to the little gelding and nudged it towards the river with his heels, following the direction of that arrow. He did not know the country ahead where the arrow pointed, but he knew what was coming somewhere out there. The Traveler had already started the music, and it was time to dance with the devil.

Chapter Seven

Morgan found his Henry rifle a mile upriver from where the Traveler had ambushed him. The gun had been hit against something and the stock splintered and broken free of the receiver. The Traveler had also ramrodded the bore full of dirt and gravel, knocked off the front and rear sights, and left the rifle stabbed into the sandy riverbank for Morgan to find. Morgan's black frock coat and his wool vest of the same color hung on the rifle.

He tied the vest and coat behind his saddle, pitched the ruined gun into the river, and rode on. Four miles more upriver and he came into sight of a building.

The trading post—that's what it was according to the little sign tacked to the roof eave—lay on the south bank of the Salt Fork. It was nothing more than a sod-brick shack with a timber frame and plank room that looked like it had been added more recently sloping off the rear of it. A single freight wagon was parked alongside it, loaded down with bundles of dried buffalo hides. More hides were stacked beside the wagon. A team of big Missouri mules and a couple of saddle horses stood in a pole corral that joined the opposite side of the soddy. Inside the corral were the only trees within two hundred yards of the setup, a few straggly, half-dead ones that the livestock had already chewed the bark from.

Morgan watched the building and the area around it from a clump of cedars on the other side of the river through his riflescope for the better part of an hour.

Only one man appeared outside the post. Morgan watched him scraping green buffalo hides that he had staked out on the ground in front of the shack, and he watched him hobble the mules and the horses out one at a time to graze a little in turns on the nearby grass. There was no sign of the Traveler, but Morgan was unwilling to cross the river in broad daylight with such a man possibly lying in wait inside that shack and looking out through the shutters of the single window facing the river.

So, Morgan waited in the cedar break until it was well after nightfall. Storm clouds blew in from the southwest, hiding the moon for the most part. He rode across the sandbar and splashed through the shallows of the wide, low-banked river. Once on the far side, he dismounted and led the dun horse behind him. The Moore rifle was hanging barrel down from his saddle horn by a string he'd rigged to its grip, and he held his Remington revolver in his right hand, watching the shadow of the trading post as he neared it.

He feared that one of the horses or mules in the corral would give him away with a nicker or a bray, but they seemed uninterested when he unsaddled the dun and turned it in with them. Crossing behind the shack, he circled around the end of the wagon on the far side and took a seat on the ground against a back wheel where he could see the front door, but out of direct view of it.

And he waited.

A little after sunup he heard somebody stirring from within, and then, a little later, he smelled smoke coming out of the stovepipe in the dirt roof. Shortly thereafter, a scrawny, shirtless man in nothing but his long johns, pants, and with his suspenders hanging down beside his leg came out the plank door carrying a coffee pot. He had dumped the coffee grounds and turned back to the door before he looked Morgan's way. That startled him so badly that he flinched and almost dropped the coffee pot.

What he saw sitting against the wagon wheel was a tall, middle-aged man with a shock of coal black hair and a thick but well-trimmed mustache and a jutting chin. He was hatless and his clothes were filthy, but the blue steel of the Remington pistol in his hand shone with oil and the sound of the cocking hammer was as brittle and crisp as river ice cracking during a spring thaw. The man held it not necessarily aimed at him, but laid along his leg and pointed close enough in the general direction to get the point across. There were dark half-circles under his pale blue eyes, as if he hadn't slept in a long time.

Morgan jerked his head at the shack. "Anybody else in there?"

The man with the coffee pot said nothing, but shook his head fervently to indicate that he was alone.

Morgan stood, letting the Remington hang alongside his leg, with his thumb hooked on the hammer. He looked at the buffalo hides, then back at the man. "Is this your place?"

"It is."

"Long way out here to work alone."

"Had a partner, but he couldn't take it and left me." The trader scratched at a week's worth of gray whisker stubble below his chinless mouth. He was so thin and rawboned that his shoulder bones poked out of his long johns like knife blades. He gave a shrug of those narrow, bony shoulders, as if that told the whole story.

"What about a man that might have come through here yesterday or the night before?" Morgan asked. "A little man on foot. Blond hair he wears in braids like an Indian, and talks like he's straight out of the woods."

"He was here. Bought a horse off me. I didn't have a saddle to spare him, but he had him some breakfast and rode off bareback yesterday about lunchtime. I thought he might be another one come to hunt buffalo with that big rifle he was carrying, but it didn't take me long to see it wasn't buffalo he was hunting."

"Which way did he head?"

"West. Upriver towards the salt plain."

"So, if we go inside, I'm not going to find any surprises I don't like?"

"Not unless you're expecting something more than dirt floors, pack rats, and centipedes. This ain't no hotel, not by a long shot."

Morgan took up his Moore rifle from where it leaned against the wagon wheel and motioned with the pistol for the trader to walk inside the shack ahead of him. "Any surprises, and I'm going to make sure you like them a lot less than me. I'm going to bust a cap at you first. Understand me?"

"I hear you. Done told you, ain't nobody here but me."

Morgan followed close on the trader's heels. The plank door was hung on leather hinges and the wind slammed it closed behind them. Morgan stepped quickly to his left with his back to the corner of the room, trying to let his eyes adjust to the gloom.

As the trader had promised, there was no one else in the shack. The entire place didn't measure twenty-four by twenty-four, with the peeled cedar pole rafters so low they barely cleared the top of Morgan's head. Cobwebs and miscellaneous gear hung from those rafters, and a single countertop made of stacked boxes with a plank laid across them ran down the left-hand side of the room. Two chairs sat on either side of a potbellied stove on the other. A doorway in the center of the back wall led into the framed addition, and the blanket hanging down in front of that door led Morgan to believe it was the man's sleeping quarters.

The trader saw him looking at the blanket. "You look if you

want, but there's nobody back there, either."

"No, you're going to look." Morgan motioned him towards the blanket.

The trader went to the blanket and held it aside, pointing into the back room with the coffee pot in his other hand. "Just like I told you. Nobody here but me."

Morgan peered into what he could see of the room without putting himself directly in front of the door, and slowly moved until he could see it all. The ceiling in the back room was even lower than the one he stood in, and there was nothing there but two cots, a few boxes, and sacks of supplies.

Morgan went back to the counter, and his host let go of the blanket and followed him. Morgan laid his rifle on the countertop and pointed at a couple of bottles of whiskey sitting on top of a wooden keg of Laflin & Rand black powder against the wall behind the counter.

"Is that for personal use or for sale?"

"Both, and I'm thinking that you and me could use a drink. You're more than a little on edge, and that sure enough puts me on edge." The trader went behind the counter and put down his coffee pot. He pulled his suspenders over his shoulders and took up a bottle and two tin cups and poured drinks.

Morgan paused with his cup half lifted to his mouth. "You do much business here?"

"Not yet, but I aim to," the man said. "Hiders got most of them big shaggies up north killed out up above the Arkansas. Me and my partner thought we might come down here first and get the best of it. We could have fresh pickings and maybe sell a little powder and lead and other supplies while we hunted. Buy some hides on the cheap from those that don't want to leave fresh hunting grounds and haul to market up on the railroad in Kansas. Thought maybe we could pick up some extra business from the trail crews coming up the Chisholm Trail, but like damned fools we set up too far west for that. The buffalo are too thick out here and tend to stampede trail herds, and the Indians don't like cowboys any better than they do buffalo hunters."

"Lots of buffalo out here, I take it?" Morgan still didn't drink the whiskey.

"Most I ever saw. Late spring and summer they leave the breaks for open country. Those salt flats west of here draw them like you won't believe."

"How many hunting crews have you seen in these parts?"

"There ain't but maybe two or three crews out hunting now, cause the word ain't spread much about the southern herd and nobody but a big crew is going to chance it with the Indians as bad as they are. But when that Fort Dodge bunch finally gives up hunting up north, this country and the Texas Panhandle will be crawling with shooters and skinners. And I'll be right here waiting for them. You mark my words."

"How much does one of those hides bring?"

"Two to four dollars, depending on the hide. Twenty-five cents a tongue packed in brine."

Morgan drank the whiskey and nodded. "Hoped I might see one of those big herds before they're all gone."

The trader behind the counter pointed at the Moore rifle. "That man with the yellow hair had him a big bore scoped rifle sort of like yours. Like I said, first I took him for someone looking to hire on as a shooter with one of the crews, but he wasn't interested in that kind of hunting. And I don't think you are, either."

"What makes you think that?"

"Besides the fact that you're asking about him?"

"Besides that."

"Well, he said you'd come along maybe yesterday evening, or this morning."

"What else did he say?"

"Said he'd be out there waiting for you. Said he was having fun with you up to now, but that you had stolen his horse and now he was a little mad. Said he thought you weren't ever going to get in the game, and he thought you were better than what you've showed so far. But now that you were here, he could wait another day or two. Said he wanted to savor it."

"Is that all he said?"

"That's about it. He didn't talk much, other than that, and to dicker for a horse. And I was careful not to ask him too many questions."

"What kind of horse is he riding now?"

"Scrawny little Kiowa pony I took in trade last month. Black."

"Barefooted or shod?"

"Barefoot mare. He bought him a blanket to throw on its back, and an old cavalry bridle and bit that I found washed up on the sandbar."

"You can drink your whiskey," Morgan said and holstered his Remington. "And quit acting like I'm going to kill you. I've got no problem with you."

The trader swallowed his whiskey down so fast and hard that his eyes watered. "That's good to know."

"What's west of here?"

"Salt plain if you go to the head of the river. Gypsum butte country for a big swathe northwest after that and towards the Cimarron. Nothing on the other side of that but lonesome and empty. Bear a little to the south and you might hit Camp Supply where the Beaver River and Wolf Creek meet."

"That all?"

"And plenty of Indians. Kioway, Comanch, Southern Cheyenne, and maybe a few Pawnee and an occasional Osage or Kaw hunting party from the east."

"Apt to cause a man trouble?"

"Who can say about how an Indian thinks? But the Pawnee ain't been bad for many a year, and the Osage and the Kaw will leave you alone. Cheyenne, well, maybe or maybe not, depending on their mood. Steer clear of any Kioway. They're treacherous on a regular basis."

"What about the Comanche you mentioned?"

"If you've got to ask, then you don't know nothing about Comanch. Comanch like to fight more than about anything. They'll kill ten horses apiece to run down a white man, especially one with a fancy rifle like yours to steal, and more so for anyone they think is killing their buffalo. Best watch your topknot if yore intent on going west."

"I aim to." Morgan ran a hand through his thick black hair. "I'm kind of partial to my own scalp."

"He left your hat for you, and some other things." The trader pointed to the corner beyond the stove at the back of the room.

Morgan went over and saw his broad-brimmed, black felt hat on the floor there. He donned the hat, and beneath it was his shot bag for the Moore rifle. He took it up and slipped one arm through the strap and then put it over his head. It was nothing more than a leather bag with the steel ramrod for the rifle run through a loop on one side of it.

He knew what the Traveler had meant by leaving his hat and his shooting things behind for him. It was a taunt, the same as leaving his coat and vest had been, and an invite to finish what they had started—not back in Ironhead only, but a thing from many years before.

He returned to the counter and pointed to two stacks of folded clothes in a row of wooden crates that was nailed to the wall behind the counter to serve as shelves. The trader took down both stacks and laid them on the counter. Morgan chose a brown cotton shirt with a button-down shield on the front of it that looked like it would fit him.

"Got any .46 shorts?" Morgan asked while he stripped out of his muddy shirt and pulled the new one over his head.

"No rimfire stuff other than some .44s, and the only other brass cartridges I got is four or five boxes of .50-70s. Got plenty of bar lead and black powder. Percussion caps, too."

Morgan tucked the shirt in and adjusted the Remington's holster until it sat on his left hip where it ought to be. He looked at the Colt 1860 Army cap-and-ball revolver hanging by its belt from a peg on the wall at the far end of the counter. "That Colt of yours there shoots a little harder than my conversion Remington if you load it right, but I never did carry one of those roll-your-own pieces but that I worried the damned thing was going to misfire or chain fire on me."

The look on the trader's face showed that he still wasn't certain he wasn't going to die, and even Morgan's attempt at casual conversation unnerved him. That said a lot about how alone he was and the kind of men that passed through his establishment. "I guess I ain't caught up with modern times. Folks always said I was set in my ways."

"You shouldn't leave that pistol hanging there when you go outside. Not if it's Indian country like you say it is." Morgan took up the bottle and poured himself another drink. Not paying particular attention to the man behind the counter or anything else, only sipping at the whiskey and thinking.

"I'll try to keep that in my mind. Is it all right if I put on my boots?" the trader asked and gestured to a pair of tall-topped, flat-soled boots with mule-ear tugs next to the front door. "I got tender feet, and I never could get all the gravel in this floor packed down."

"Suit yourself."

The trader came out from behind the counter at the end closest to the front door, but as he was bending over to pick up the boots he happened to glance out the window. "You expecting company?"

Morgan set the whiskey down and went to stand at the window. The boards in the shutter had shrunk as they dried out over time, and gaps a half-inch wide between them gave him plenty of room to see the stretch of open ground between the trading post and the river. Two white men in city clothes and on good horses were crossing the sandbar. Both of them had rifles laid across the front of their saddles.

"And just when I thought I might get out of the rest of this day without any more trouble," the trader said.

"Why do you say that? Do you know those men?"

"Never laid eyes on them, but it's plain they're hunting someone. Same as you and that little blond-haired killer."

Morgan didn't argue with him, for even a blind man could have seen what he said was true. The two horsemen stopped on the near bank of the river and surveyed the trading post for a long time. After a while, one of them, the one in the bowler hat and the beard, circled his horse and rode wide of the shack until he disappeared from sight around the back of the corral. The other man cracked the receiver on his Winchester enough to see that he had a round in the chamber.

"Anyone home?" he said loudly.

Morgan was already back at the counter nursing his whiskey by the time the trader turned to look at him.

"Do you want me to answer him?" he asked.

"Suit yourself. It's your place."

"You think they're outlaws? A friend of mine had a month's take of hides robbed from him up on the Republican River last year."

"You think those two look like hide thieves?"

The trader shook his head. "No, I don't."

"Me, neither."

"Are they looking for you?"

Morgan turned up the whiskey cup, finished it, then sat it down on the plank with a hard rap. He wiped at his lips with the back of his hand, then turned his head slowly to look at the trader. “Don’t know why they would be, but if they are, I guess they found me.”

Chapter Eight

The trader looked down at his bare feet, wiggled his toes once, and hastily tugged into his boots without so much as putting on a pair of socks first. He went to the door and cracked it open, and then looked back at Morgan.

"Go ahead," Morgan said.

The trader rubbed the thin patch of hair on one side of his balding head fretful-like, then yanked a slouch hat off a peg beside the door and jammed it in place. He gave Morgan one more look before he pushed the door wide open.

"I got no part of whatever this is," he said.

"Things like this don't care if you want to be a part of it or not. You're here, and they're here. Go see what they want."

"Might be they're looking for somebody else. Maybe that blond-haired fellow."

"I don't make a habit out of expecting the best." Morgan dragged the whiskey bottle and his cup to the far end of the counter and put one hip against it and faced the door. He wore his pistol holster on his left side at a cross-draw, the butt of it facing forward. He took hold of that holster with his left hand, and his thumb reached forward and pushed the keeper thong off the hammer.

The trader went out the door, but stayed in front of it and stopped two steps outside. Morgan could see the rider with the brass-framed '66 Winchester carbine sitting his horse not twenty yards away over the trader's shoulder.

"Light and sit," the trader said to the man on the horse. "I ain't got much, but I'm hospitable."

"Who else you got in there?" the man on the horse asked.

"Just me and my hunting partner."

"How come he doesn't come out?"

The man on the horse had an accent straight out of Chicago, if Morgan wasn't mistaken. And he was wearing a dress coat with a checkered wool vest under it, despite the heat and the way he was sweating. The butt of a revolver carried in a shoulder holster barely showed under one armpit through the front of the unbuttoned coat.

"This here's a troublesome country," the trader said. "You never know who's friendly and who's not. We were watching you and wondering which kind you were."

"You had any company lately?" The rider pointed the Winchester at the corral. "Maybe a man on foot and looking to buy a horse?"

"Yellow-haired man, so tall?" The trader held out his hand beside him, about five feet off the ground.

"Yellow-haired?"

"Long blond hair braided like an Indian's. Traded me that striped-legged dun horse in the corral yonder."

The second rider, the one in the brown bowler hat, came into view with his Spencer carbine's butt resting on his thigh. His accent was a little different from his partner, but definitely New England Yankee. "Other than that blond-haired man, nobody else came by here yesterday or today?"

"Nobody. There's a few hider camps around, but we've had no company of late," the trader answered.

The two riders exchanged a look and held a brief, whispered conversation. They pointed at the dun horse a few times, and then back in the direction of the river.

"You got a sign there that says you're a trading post," the

man in the bowler hat said when they were finished with their private conversation. "You wouldn't happen to be a cook, too, would you?"

"Not normally. Ain't got much in the way of fixings, and I'm not exactly fancy with a skillet. Barely can eat my own cooking, much less serve the public."

"We're hungry enough not to be picky, and we would like to meet this partner of yours."

The trader headed back inside, and called over his shoulder at them, "Well then, you boys get down off those horses and I'll see if I can stir up some breakfast. I ain't had any myself and I'm nigh famished."

The two riders dismounted and disappeared out of sight of the doorway while they led their horses over and tied them to the corral fence. The man in the bowler hat was the first one through the door, and he stepped to one side of it and put his back against the inside wall. The other one came in behind him and stepped to the other side. Both of them held their rifles pointing down at the floor, trying to appear harmless, but ready for trouble, just the same. And both of them studied Morgan carefully and with a twitchy edge to them.

"Good morning," Morgan said.

"Same to you," the man in the sweaty coat said. "You his partner?"

Morgan glanced at the trader, who was feeding dried buffalo chips into the stove, and making busy rattling his pots and pans. And then Morgan looked back at the two strangers.

"That's me. The partner, as you say," Morgan said.

The man in the bowler hat went to the far end of the counter and laid his Spencer carbine on it. He laid it so that the barrel was pointed Morgan's way, end to end with Morgan's own rifle. Neither of the long guns on the plank countertop was far out of the reach of their hands. The other man stayed where he was near the door.

"You wouldn't happen to know anything about a bay horse we found dead a few miles downriver, would you?" the one at the counter asked.

"Bay horse?" Morgan said.

"Are you hard of hearing?"

Morgan set his whiskey cup down and gave an innocent, bland look. "I don't know anything about a dead horse."

"You never heard any shooting, maybe yesterday, or the day before? Not much left of that horse, but what there was showed a bullet hole in its head and the saddle was lying on the ground next to it."

"No," Morgan replied, and then he looked at the trader. "Did you hear any gunshots?"

"Not a one," the trader answered him while he kept his attention on the slabs he was cutting off of a side of bacon with a butcher knife. "Could have been wild Indians, or maybe that yellow-haired fellow had something to do with that dead horse you found."

Again, the two men shared a look between them, much the same as they had when they were still outside, as if they knew things they weren't saying.

It was an old game that the two were playing. You simply kept putting your questions out a little at a time, first the little ones and then the big ones, like fishing and teasing with the bait and seeing what would get you a nibble from your fish. They weren't especially good at it, and Morgan knew the tactic well, for he had often used it himself.

"We're looking for the man that was riding that bay horse, not Indians or this yellow-haired man you keep talking about," the one beside the door said.

"Well, I was just thinking that the yellow-haired man might . . ."

"This yellow-haired man, did he have a name?" the man in the bowler hat asked.

"Never said it, and I didn't ask. Kind of struck me as a private sort of fellow," the trader answered, and then continued like he had never been interrupted. "Maybe he killed that horse and the man that was riding it."

"We didn't find a body."

"Coyotes or the wolves could have drug it off."

"Not likely."

"Oh, you ought to see the size of some of those old lobos. Anything that can pull down a yearling buffalo calf could drag off a man's body."

The man in the bowler hat frowned, and more irritation crept into his voice. "We've told you straight up, we're looking for the man that was riding that bay horse. Simple as that. Tall fellow with black hair."

"Lots of tall fellows with black hair," Morgan said.

"Yeah." The man in the bowler hat had odd eyes, and he blinked them so seldom that it almost made Morgan's own eyes water to watch them. He looked down at Morgan's left hand on his pistol holster, and then back up at Morgan's face.

In fact, both of the men were watching him closely, and nobody said anything for a bit. The only sound was the bacon sizzling in the cast-iron skillet on top of the stove.

The man at the door ran a finger inside the celluloid collar of his shirt and flung away the sweat he gathered. "Miserable, hot country."

"It ain't hot, yet. Not really. Wait 'til real summer gets here," the trader said.

"It's hot enough already."

"Not so bad when you get used to it, but some don't," Morgan said. "Some can't stand the heat."

The man at the counter pointed at Morgan's rifle. "Unusual weapon."

"Buffalo gun," Morgan said.

The man reached out to touch the rifle.

"I didn't say you could touch my gun," Morgan said.

The man withdrew his hand, slowly, and then gave a slight shrug of his shoulders, as if in apology. "A man that knew what he was doing could shoot something a long ways off with that kind of gun."

The trader cracked an eggshell on the edge of his other skillet. "When a hunter takes him a stand on a herd of shaggies, he'd best be downwind and far enough off not to spook them if he wants to make any money at this game. You want to tip over as many of them as you can close together so that you don't run your skinners ragged chasing all over creation."

"Where does a man learn to shoot long range like that?" the one at the counter asked, and the look he gave Morgan implied that there was more to the question. "The war?"

"Maybe for some," Morgan said, and then looked at the trader's back. "Where did you learn to shoot?"

"Ah, I don't know. Popping squirrels and deer and such back when I was a boy in Mississippi. I was a quartermaster during the war and never saw any fighting."

"But you said some might have learned like that," the man in the coat leaning against the wall beside the door said.

"Like what?" the trader asked while he slopped half-raw fried eggs on four plates.

"Maybe a man that had served with one of those sharpshooter outfits." The man by the door looked to his partner. "What was that regiment they're always talking about? You know the ones that march in the parades and show off their green jackets and medals?"

"Berdan's Regiment," the man at the counter said, and he

was focused on Morgan again. "First U.S. Sharpshooters."

"Yeah, that's the one," the man by the door said.

"There's all kinds of shooters amongst the hide camps. Young ones, old ones, Americans, Mexicans, Irishmen, Germans, Britishers . . . you know, just like anywhere else," the trader said. He forked the cooked bacon onto the plates and stepped between Morgan and the other man at the counter and set their breakfast down on the plank. "I reckon there might be some of them that served in the war. There is almost anywhere you go. One side or the other, many a man served the cause."

"Old man, why don't you get back over at that stove and make us a pot of coffee?" the man at the counter said.

The trader did as he was told, and began rattling the coffee pot as much as he had the skillets, whether because he was nervous or because he was a man that spent too much time alone and liked the sound of such things. It was hard to tell.

"What about you, tall man?" the one at the counter asked. "What do you think? Were you ever a sharpshooter?"

"I think you ask a lot of questions," Morgan replied.

The one at the counter looked to his partner by the door and they both had them a little chuckle. When they were finished the one at the counter pulled back the lapel of his coat and revealed a silver-colored shield-shaped badge with the words "Pinkerton National Detective Agency" engraved on it. The one by the door shifted his rifle to his other hand and pulled a folding wallet out of his vest pocket. He opened that little leather case and revealed a Pinkerton badge of the same kind inside it.

"We're hunting a man of the kind we're talking about," the Pinkerton detective at the counter said. "Former commodities broker and a New York policeman. Made him a name as a Union sharpshooter during the war, and then as a peace officer out here. Goes by the name of Clyde. Morgan Clyde."

Morgan saw how both of the strangers were watching him to

see how he reacted, but he didn't bite for them. "Heard of him when I was passing through Baxter Springs two years ago on my way out to the Fort Hays country. Not a man I'd want to be hunting, from what I hear, but it strikes me unusual that you are, considering you say he's a lawman. What did he do?"

"That's our business," the man at the counter said.

"All right, it's your business." Morgan shrugged.

"I didn't catch your name," the man at the counter said.

"Smith. John Smith."

"You hear that?" the Pinkerton at the counter said to his partner. "Smith."

"Now that's a common name," the other Pinkerton answered him.

"I'm an ordinary man," Morgan replied.

"You say you rode down here from Fort Hays?" the Pinkerton at the counter asked.

"Thereabouts. Hunted the Platte River country for a while, and then back down to Hays before I came here." Morgan looked at the trader by the stove. "When was that? Last spring?"

"Yep." The trader answered Morgan without turning away from his coffee making. "Took us most of the summer to build this here post. Would have gone faster if you weren't in such an all-fired hurry to go out hunting hides."

Maybe their act was working, or maybe the Pinkertons were simply willing to take a little longer and dig a little deeper. Or they had already made up their minds and were looking for more of an edge. Either way, the Pinkerton in the sweaty coat left the door and went to the counter. He leaned his Winchester against it, butt down on the floor, and took up a plate of food. He forked the eggs down without stopping and then took up a piece of limp bacon dripping grease.

"You're right, old man. You're not much of a cook," he said.

The other Pinkerton on the far side of him forked at the food with disgust and didn't take a bite. "Wasn't expecting Delmonico's, but damn."

When the Pinkerton closest to Morgan was finished with his breakfast he pointed at the whiskey bottle beside Morgan. "How about you share that?"

Morgan slid the bottle towards him, and without stepping closer or changing position. The Pinkerton leaned over the counter and retrieved two more tin cups. He sat them before him on the plank and made as if he was going to pour drinks for him and his partner. But he didn't pour. Instead, he held the bottle by the neck, unmoving.

"Your pants look like you might have waded the river," he said without turning his head to look at Morgan and staring only at the wall in front of him. "Man that lost his horse might have done that."

"It doesn't have to be this way," Morgan said. "You could ride on."

The Pinkerton shook his head. "Not going to happen. Mr. Pinkerton himself wants you."

"Ah, well then, I guess there's that."

"Yes, there's that." The Pinkerton continued staring at the wall.

"The old man and I had an agreement to let this lie."

"The old man is paralyzed. Stroke or something. His sons are running things now."

"I take it this is about New York?"

"We don't give the orders. We only do what we're told."

"That was a long time ago. Why now?"

"You killed a good agent, and hurt two more real bad. William Pinkerton wanted more effort put into finding you then, but the old man wouldn't let him."

"It was self-defense."

"Maybe the way you tell it, but that's not how the boss tells it." The detective still wouldn't look at Morgan, and continued staring at the wall. "They were only going to rough you up a bit. Scare you, you know. Make sure you had the message to leave the boy and his mother alone."

"That boy was my son. And I don't scare worth a damn," Morgan said.

"They're telling back in Ironhead how you shoved one of ours off a train. William took special offense to that. Thinks you need taught a little respect."

"He was an unpleasant traveling partner and a little clumsy on his feet. Man like that can have a bad fall."

"And what about the other one? The one you beat with a stove poker? What about him?"

"Disorderly and resisting arrest."

The Pinkerton turned his head slowly to Morgan. "Suppose you unbuckle that pistol belt and lay it up on the bar? Real slow so that you don't make me and my partner here nervous. Let's do this the easy way."

"I got a better idea. You ride out of here and none of us gets hurt. Nobody bleeds. Nobody dies."

"He talks too much to be tough as they say," the Pinkerton in the bowler hat at the far end of the countertop said. "Never seen a talker that wasn't mostly bluff and bluster."

"Try me," Morgan said.

"You think you're that good?" the Pinkerton in the bowler asked.

"Been good enough so far."

"Maybe you're right." The Pinkerton in the coat next to Morgan exhaled heavily, almost a sigh, and tried on a half-smile for size, as if resigned to something. And then he looked at his partner at the far end of the bar and shrugged before he looked back at the wall. "Maybe this can wait for some other time."

"Some other time." Morgan nodded.

"Let's have us a drink. One for the road, eh?" The Pinkerton next to him adjusted his grip on the whiskey bottle while he shoved a cup under it.

Morgan knew what the Pinkerton was going to do before he did it. The man waited too long planning his move, and he was holding the bottle all wrong to pour a drink. When he twisted and swung the bottle at Morgan's head, Morgan was already pushing away from the counter.

Chapter Nine

Morgan threw up his left hand and took the bottle on his forearm, and at the same time the Pinkerton in the bowler hat went for his Spencer on the plank countertop. He didn't pick the carbine up, but cocked it lying where it was and touched off the trigger. But Morgan dove towards the blanket door leading into the sleeping quarters, and the .52 caliber bullet smacked into the wall where he had been an instant before.

Morgan's stiff shoulder gave him trouble getting his Remington drawn from his holster. He was already falling through the blanket when he got the gun clear. The Pinkerton with the whiskey bottle held it high for another blow, and standing like that he blocked Morgan's view of anything else.

Morgan cocked the Remington and leveled the eight-inch barrel at the Pinkerton's middle as he landed flat on his shoulders halfway into the back room. The instant he hit the floor he fired and the Pinkerton dropped the bottle and lunged out of view of the doorway, bent over and clutching his belly with both hands.

Morgan could see the other Pinkerton behind him, the one in the bowler hat, picking up that Spencer and swinging it his way, so he dug his heels into the floor and scooted backwards, all the while thumbing the hammer on the Remington. His first shot went wild and slammed into the window shutter, but the next one must have either struck home or hit close enough to throw off the Pinkerton's aim, for his next shot from the Spencer went through the blanket above Morgan and knocked the feathers out of the tick mattress on one of the cots beyond him.

Morgan rolled to the side and out of sight of the doorway, and he barely had time to push his back against the plank wall that divided the two rooms before he heard that Spencer lever rack another round into its chamber and the clack of the hammer thumbed back. A third rifle shot boomed in the tight confines of the shack, and another bullet whipped through the wall barely an inch to one side of Morgan's head.

Morgan flinched at the sting of splinters and grit hitting his cheek, but twisted around and got on his knees. He could see the Pinkerton in the bowler hat through either of the two bullet holes in the wall, and he put his pistol barrel to one of them and fired two more shots back through it.

His Remington empty, he dropped back to the floor and flipped down the loading lever on the pistol and slid the cylinder pin forward and took out the empty cylinder. He took the spare loaded cylinder from the pouch on his gun belt and put it in the pistol frame and snapped everything closed. The reload took him only a matter of seconds.

He could hear one of the Pinkertons cursing and groaning, but no more shots came through the wall. His left elbow was throbbing where the bottle had struck him, and the fingers on that hand tingled with numbness.

A tiny ray of sunlight passed through the bullet hole in the blanket and shone on the back wall. Morgan glanced at that dot of light and the dust motes floating in the sunbeam, and waited and listened. Besides the man doing the cursing and groaning, Morgan could hear someone else breathing heavily, and with a frothy gurgle to it like a lung-shot man will do.

There was only one way out of the back room, and that was through the blanket door. He thought he had hit both of the Pinkertons, but that was no guarantee that they were down.

Morgan had seen many a man take bullets and still stay in the fight, and he didn't relish going through that door when the time came. Both of those Pinkertons could be out there waiting for him to show himself.

"Damn you! Damn you to hell!" one of the Pinkertons called out, and his voice filled with pain and somewhere between anger and weeping. It was the one in the suit coat that had hit Morgan with the bottle. "Come out and fight, you son of a bitch!"

There was no sound from the other Pinkerton. Even the raspy, gurgling had gone silent. Morgan peered through one of the bullet holes in the wall, and saw the Pinkerton at the end of the counter sitting slumped on the floor with his back to the wall. He looked out of the fight.

Morgan stood and kept well to the side of the blanket door, and when he was near it he took the edge of it in his free hand and gave it a hard jerk. The blanket ripped free of the nails securing it to the top of the doorjamb and fell to the floor, and almost simultaneously a bullet whipped through the opening. Morgan saw the Pinkerton in the suit coat kneeling behind the cast-iron stove in a cloud of black powder smoke. He had a Colt Police Model resting on the stovetop. Nothing but the gun and his head was visible above the stove, and Morgan shot him just above his right eyebrow. The Pinkerton flopped back against the wall, and then to the floor, dead before he hit it.

Morgan waited a long count of ten before he lunged out into the doorway and swung his pistol towards the far end of the counter. The other Pinkerton was still there. He had slid down the wall and landed in a seated position with his Spencer carbine held across his thighs and his bowler hat lying in his lap. A blood trail was smeared down the wall where his back had slid against it, and his chin was resting against his chest. The front of his vest was heavy with blood.

The Pinkerton's head jerked like he had the hiccups, and

bloody froth bubbled out his lips and down his chin. He didn't raise his head until Morgan was standing over him with the Remington pointed at his face.

"Finish it." The Pinkerton choked out the words and glared at Morgan through shiny, wet eyes.

Morgan reached down and yanked the Spencer away. "You're already finished."

The trader was curled up in a ball on his side with his hands over his head in the other corner of the room beside the front door. It was only then that he took a look around and saw that it was over. He rose on shaking legs and looked at the dead man behind the stove, and then at the Pinkerton gargling and choking out his last breaths at the foot of the counter.

"Aren't you going to do something for him?" the trader asked.

Morgan leaned the Spencer against the stove and went behind it. He squatted down and began checking the dead Pinkerton's coat and vest pockets. "Nothing I can do for him."

"You don't know that." The trader gestured to the man at the counter, asking without saying it if he could go to him.

"Go ahead," Morgan said as he stood once more.

The trader knelt beside the Pinkerton at the counter, but he was too late. Before he could do anything, the Pinkerton's chest expanded in one final gasp and then his head sagged farther down against his chest and he breathed no more.

The trader looked up at Morgan. "He's dead."

Morgan walked past the trader to the dead Pinkerton at his feet. He checked the man's vest pockets as he had with the other one.

"What are you looking for?" the trader asked.

"A warrant."

Morgan laid three dollars on the counter. "That ought to square me for the shirt and the whiskey."

He took up his own rifle and the Winchester and went out of

the shack and walked to the corral. He rummaged through the saddlebags and bedrolls on the Pinkertons' horses, but found nothing he wanted other than a box of .44 rimfire cartridges for the Winchester. He caught the dun gelding from the corral and was saddling it when the trader walked outside.

The trader was still so scared that he was shaky. "Good Lord, you got 'em both. Never seen anything like it."

"They gave me no choice."

"They were lawmen."

"Pinkertons, and that's not the same."

"They work for the government sometimes."

"Neither one of those men in there had a warrant for me, and you heard what they said. It was a personal matter, nothing more."

"Are you really a lawman yourself?"

"Was."

"You going to help me bury them?" the trader asked.

"No. There's two good horses there and some gear to pay you for the burying," Morgan said. "Or haul them across the river and leave them to the buzzards if it's too much trouble for you. Makes no difference to me."

He put the box of .44 cartridges in his saddlebags, shoved the brass-framed Winchester into his saddle scabbard, and swung up on the horse with the Moore rifle in one hand.

"That ain't right," the trader said. "Not burying them, you know. It ain't Christian. A man ought to respect the dead."

"I don't have time for burying, and whatever they had to say to the Good Lord, I guess they've already said it by now. Nothing either one of us could say will change things for them, one way or the other."

"What do I say if more Pinkertons come?"

"Tell them whatever you want, but they had best leave me alone. I won't be pushed."

"How come they're after you? What was all that about New York?"

Morgan tugged his hat down tighter on his head and looked down at the trader. "History, my friend."

"History?"

"Bad history. Story of my life." Morgan gave a tip of his hat brim and nudged the dun gelding towards the river.

Chapter Ten

It was pitch black when Dixie Rayburn made his last round of the night through the new construction camp of Canadian. A train was parked alongside the camp, offloading supplies, and he passed along its side. The steam and smoke from the locomotive writhed and coiled about his legs like serpent ghosts under the dim lanterns hung on the telegraph poles along the tracks.

He left the train and passed through the cluster of tents that made up the camp proper. Unlike Ironhead had been, the new camp was laid out with no rhyme or reason, like the men were in a hurry and gave no thought to where the tents should be staked. Somewhere toward the back of that cluster of haphazard layout a piano sounded, and he waded through the grass and amongst the tents with his ears guiding him towards the music.

The tin-panny sound was coming from Tuck's new saloon erected on a hump of ground in the middle of a grove of trees at the foot of a timbered little mountain that marked the north edge of the camp. Dixie stopped several yards away and studied the place. Tuck had forgone the carpenter work required to construct the usual false front on his establishment, and without it, the saloon looked like nothing more than the big tent that it actually was, stained with mildew and mud until it wasn't true white anymore.

Lamplight spilled through the open tent flaps and men came and went through the entrance, most of them as drunk as they were loud. And, in that very same pool of lamplight, Dixie could see that a post had been set in front of the saloon with a wide plank nailed crossways to it at the top. A man with a bucket of paint was putting the last brushstrokes to the rough pine plank while Dixie watched, regardless of the fact that it was almost midnight and the painter had to work by lantern light.

Dixie read the words the painter had almost finished in big red letters. *CROW'S NEST.* And then in smaller letters beneath: *FINE SPIRITS & GAMES OF CHANCE. WILLIAM TUCK, PROPRIETOR.*

Dixie leaned over and spat a thick stream of tobacco juice on the ground, and then he straightened and looked upon Tuck's saloon sign once more. He had spent his first day wandering through the camp learning it, and passing the saloon twice in his rounds. But he had yet to step foot inside it.

"The Crow's Nest," he muttered to himself and gave a disgusted grunt. "More like a rat's nest."

Two of Tuck's bouncers were standing to either side of the entrance. Both were big men, but one of them was especially so. In fact, he was the biggest man Dixie had ever seen, a veritable mountain of muscle and bone, with arms as big around as most men's legs and heavy, sloping shoulders. He wore no hat, and his long black hair hung in thin, scraggly strings from a high, square forehead. His eye sockets were like dark caverns as he gave Dixie a cursory glance with his booted feet braced wide and his fat thumbs hooked behind his belt buckle. Dixie took one last look at the behemoth of a man, and noted the Colt's Dragoon revolver holstered on that very same belt, and the big walnut-handled knife worn in a sheath suspended over his belly from a strap worn across his chest.

The giant bouncer said nothing nor gave so much as a bored nod to Dixie, but Dixie thought he saw the other one glance at his badge and smirk as he was passing by him.

"Little squirt, ain't he?" that second bouncer said to the big one. "Expected him to be at least full grown."

Dixie kept walking as if he hadn't heard, but a tight-lipped frown formed on his face. True, he wasn't near the size of the two bouncers, but he was not a short man. The bouncers' contempt and cockiness continued to rankle him as he moved inside the tent. Obviously, the two meatheads had wanted a look at the new chief of the railroad police, and what they saw didn't impress them.

The tent was divided by a row of support posts under its ridgepole and running the length of the room. On the left side of those posts was a bar made of long planks resting on beer kegs that stretched half the length of the room, and on the right side were tables for the customers. On the same side in the front corner next to the door was the piano, and in the back corner were two faro layouts and a roulette wheel.

It was a busy night, and Tuck's two bartenders and his handful of women were busy keeping drinks served and the customers happy in the crowded room. The place smelled of tobacco smoke, stale beer, and piss. And the clicking spin of the roulette wheel, the clink of beer bottles and glasses, and the drone of loud voices marked the kind of place it was, even if Dixie had been blind. And rising above all of that was the sound of the piano.

Dixie glanced at the piano player propped on his stool before the instrument while two drunken railroad workers lurched over him. The duo of music lovers sang at the top of their lungs while they stood with arms over each other's shoulders and slopping beer on their boots. Neither of the two were what could be called "talented" singers, and their rendition of whatever they were trying to sing was decidedly off-key. Although the piano player didn't seem to mind and continued to bang away at his keys with an enthusiasm almost equal to their own.

Dixie pressed through the crowd until he found a place at the near end of the bar. Bill Tuck met him there, standing on the opposite side of the bar with both palms flat on its top and leaning over it with his weight braced against his arms. A gold-plated toothpick was tucked in one corner of his mouth.

"Good evening, Chief," Tuck said. "We were beginning to think you weren't coming."

Dixie leaned closer, unsure exactly what Tuck had said because of the noise.

"I said good evening, Chief," Tuck repeated. "That's you, isn't it, the new chief? I hear Duvall gave you the job when Clyde quit him."

Dixie glanced at the badge on his vest as if it had only then appeared, and then back up at Tuck. "That's right."

"Well, you'll have an easy job of it in this camp. No trouble." Tuck straightened and waved an arm around the room. "Nothing here but men blowing off a little steam after a hard day's work. Good, honest fun."

Dixie's attention was drawn to a man at a nearby table. That man had one of Tuck's soiled doves sitting in his lap. She wore nothing but her stockings and some sort of white chemise, and one of her breasts was hanging out of the untied neck of her undergarment. The man she was sitting on was playing with it and showing it off to the other men at the table with him. The whole group was as inebriated as they were boisterous, and the man and the harlot were so drunk that they threatened to fall out of the chair at any moment.

"Tell her to take it out back," Dixie said.

"Ah, now, Chief. What does the showing of a little flesh hurt?" Tuck shifted his gold toothpick to the other side of his mouth and smiled. The toothpick shone brightly against the white of his teeth. "Like I said, it's only good, clean fun."

"Tell her to put her tit up or take her business to her crib.

Stuff like that only causes trouble."

"And here I was thinking you might be a man of reason. In case you haven't noticed, this is a saloon and not a church." Tuck brought that wolf smile back as soon as he finished.

"You tell her, or I will."

Tuck called another of his ladies over to him and leaned close to her and whispered something in her ear. She headed across the room towards the other whore sitting on the man's lap. While Dixie watched to see what happened, Tuck motioned to one of the bartenders.

The two whores had a brief conversation that Dixie couldn't make out, but when it was over, the whore on the man's lap shoved her breast back in her top and gave Dixie a sour look before the man she was sitting on buried his beard in her neck and distracted her.

The sound of a glass mug thumping on the bar top got Dixie's attention, and he stared at the beer that had been placed before him and at the retreating bartender who had brought it to him. Dixie reached in his vest pocket to pay for the beer, but Tuck held up a hand to stop him.

"No need to pay," Tuck said. "Not our fine new chief."

Dixie pointed at the beer before him. "And what does this beer buy you, Tuck? What favor are you expecting from me as its price?"

The smile on Tuck's face disappeared and his eyes went cold. He took in a slow breath before he answered. "Does everything have to have a price?"

"With you it does."

"I was merely offering one on the house as a token of my esteem." Tuck's words were like honey oozing over the razor blades hidden in them.

"Save that for somebody else, Tuck. I've known you too long."

Tuck took the golden toothpick from his teeth, stared at it a moment, then put it in his vest pocket before speaking again. "There's no reason why we can't work together. Our former chief never understood that. Hardheaded man, that Clyde."

"I work for the Katy. Nobody else."

"So that's how it is?"

"That's how it is."

"And how much does the MK&T pay you? Not much, I imagine."

"Enough."

The two men stared at each other across the bar top for a moment, before Tuck shrugged. "So be it, but maybe you will find out I'm not the man you believe me to be and rethink your position. Working relationships take time, and we haven't even got to know each other properly."

"I know enough already."

"Careful, now. An insult is something you can't take back. No different than pulling a gun or a knife on a man, and cuts the same."

"No insults here, Tuck. Only wanted you to know how I stand. Get it out in the open so that there aren't any misunderstandings."

"I'm a businessman, nothing more, regardless of what your friend Clyde may have told you."

"You tried to have him killed. Everybody knows it, even if Deacon Fischer has his head sewn back on and can't tell the truth of it."

Tuck to a deep breath, as if to gather patience. "The trouble between me and Clyde is personal."

" 'Cause he killed your brother-in-law up at Baxter Springs. Everybody knows that, too."

"Grant you, I have no love for Clyde, but I had nothing to do with that trouble between him and the Deacon."

"Be that as it may, I heard a funny thing while I was on my

way here from Ironhead."

"And what's that?"

"Somebody found your old faro dealer . . . what was his name? Charlie Six Fingers, that's him. Found poor old Charlie with his head shot off not a mile up the track from here. Varmints had mostly eaten him, but there was enough left to tell it was him."

"Charlie quit me almost a month ago. Last I heard he was headed to Texas."

"Rumor is that he took a little coin from your faro bank for traveling expenses before he left."

"I don't like what you're implying."

"I wasn't implying anything. Merely stating facts and relaying rumors to you so that you could see how your lily-white reputation might be stained." Dixie finished the beer and set the empty mug on the bar top.

"I don't think I'm going to like you, Chief." Tuck's voice was flat and emotionless, and had dropped almost to a whisper.

"Why, that really pains me, Tuck. It surely does."

"You make enemies where you don't have to."

Dixie put some change on the bar top and took up the beer. "There's the price of your beer."

Tuck left for a while, leaving Dixie to nurse his beer and watch the room. There were plenty of men drinking, but Tuck's roulette wheel and his faro layouts were doing slow business. Dixie tried to remember when the next payday would come, and knew that Tuck's business would pick up when the railroad workers had fresh money to spend.

Tuck came back at the same time Dixie was taking the last swallow of his beer. He gestured at Dixie's empty mug. "Care for another?"

Dixie shook his head. "Noticed you didn't put up a false front on the tent," he said when he had finished wiping the beer foam from his upper lip.

"Wasn't worth the trouble. This camp won't be here more than a week," Tuck said. "Maybe less."

"That so?"

"Duvall sent his powder monkeys and one grading crew and a party of tie cutters to work ahead while we were still back in Ironhead last winter waiting on that damned bridge to get built. The track crew is laying better than a mile a day now and sometimes two, and they're saying we'll be at McAlester's Store before the month is out."

"Haven't been here long, but it looks like Superintendent Duvall has more workers than he had back in Ironhead."

Tuck nodded. "Lots more men. He has been rehiring everybody he let go when the bridge held him up, and anybody else that wants to sweat and break their back for a dollar and a half a day. Says he intends to get his railroad through to Texas by Christmas."

"I see you're the only saloon in camp."

"The only one." Tuck smiled again. "Guess the competition doesn't want any part of the Katy's camps since what happened in Ironhead. You know, with Irish Dave getting burned out and the camp getting shot up by those bushwhackers, and the army roughing everybody up and all."

"Well, tell your girls to keep some clothes on in public and tone things down. Nothing makes trouble between these hardworking devils more than women, unless it's whiskey and gambling. Nobody would put up with me running either of those out of camp, but we can try not to stir the pot too much where we can help it."

"I'll tell my girls to tone it down a little if it will make you happy. I'll trust you'll tell Sugar Alice and her girls the same thing?"

"Already have."

Tuck slapped the bar top with one palm. "There, now. See, that wasn't so hard. Nothing that reasonable men can't work out."

Dixie took his pocket watch out and glanced at the time. "I want you closed up by midnight from here on out. Same as in Ironhead."

Tuck's face went still with anger, trying to hide it but doing a poor job of it. "We didn't close until two in Ironhead."

"Well, it's midnight here. Duvall is going to want his men to have plenty of rest and not staying in here all night getting too tanked up to work the next day," Dixie said as he put his watch away. "You're open late tonight, but we'll let it go this once."

Tuck pointed at the badge on Dixie's chest. "You haven't been chief but a little bit, and you're already turning pushy."

"Keep it within the law, Tuck, and I'll treat you fairly, same as everybody else, whether I like you or not."

"Who have you got helping you, Chief, since the army is gone and the Pinkertons decided they had better things to do than work for Duvall's railroad?"

Dixie didn't answer him, only stood there and stared back at him.

Tuck grimaced. "Alone, huh?"

"I'll hire a policeman or two as soon as I can find suitable sorts."

Tuck nodded at the pistol on Dixie's hip. "You any good with that?"

Dixie turned and started for the door without answering.

Tuck called after him. "I was only asking out of concern for you, Chief. A man not careful can get himself hurt in a hurry in a camp like this. Hate to see a good man like you come to trouble."

Dixie didn't stop walking.

"You better go find your boss. He's looking for you," Tuck

called from across the room as Dixie went out the tent flaps. Dixie thought he heard Tuck laughing.

Dixie paused outside the tent, cast a dirty look at the two bouncers staring at him, then spit on the ground. "How do you work for that son of a bitch in there?"

The giant bouncer said nothing, only staring at him out of those deep-set eyes, but the other one laughed and reached out and slapped Dixie on the back. "Yeah, Tuck's a son of a bitch, all right, but he pays a sight better than anyone in this camp."

Dixie walked on. He was twenty feet away from the bouncers before he spoke again. And when he did it was under his breath. "Kiss my Rebel ass."

"What's that, little man?" the same bouncer called to him.

"I said good night. Sweet dreams," Dixie called over his shoulder as he disappeared into the night.

Chapter Eleven

Dixie had yet to arrange for permanent lodging, and the only place he had been able to find a bed was in one of the company tents set up to house the railroad workers. It was twenty men to a tent, and the space between the cots was narrow. He awoke long before daylight to the sound of snoring men, and dressed without lighting a lamp. His cot was in the middle of the room, and it was a chore to pass out of the tent in the dark without barking his shins.

He went straight to the cook tent in the middle of the camp. It was early, yet, and nobody was in the tent other than the cooks preparing breakfast. He went to the coffee pots already warming on a stovetop and was pouring himself a mug of coffee when he heard someone approach him from behind. When he turned around he saw a short, wiry built black man wearing a white apron tied over a pair of overalls, and carrying a plate of food.

"Mornin', Dixie," the black man said.

"Morning, Saul."

"Guess I ought to call you Chief now."

"Call me what you want to. You and I have been friends for a good while, and I've been bragging on your cooking longer than that."

Saul handed the plate to Dixie. "Three eggs sunny-side-up, two strips of bacon, and a hot buttered biscuit, just like you always want."

"How'd you know I was coming?"

"I watch things."

Dixie took the plate and went over to one of the long tables, motioning Saul to have a seat on the bench beside him.

Saul shook his head. "No, sir. I gots too much work to do to sit down. Won't be long before all those hungry men will be in here wantin' they bellies full before they goes to work."

Dixie chopped up the fried eggs with the edge of his fork and slurped at the coffee mug in his other hand. "You seem really happy this morning."

"I is. Gonna be a good day for sure."

"How's that?"

Saul grinned and gave a shy look to the floor. "My woman is comin' today."

"Your woman?"

"Yes, sireee. She comin' all the way from Fort Scott up in Kansas. Catchin' the train and gonna be here sometime tomorrow mornin'."

"You've been holdin' out on me, Saul. I didn't know you had a wife."

Again, Saul grinned. "She ain't my wife. Least, not yet, but we goin' to get married soon as she gets here."

"How'd you find yourself a woman? All you do is rattle pots and pans."

"Knowed each other since we was striplin' chillen. We was on the same plantation back before the war. Found her again in Kansas not two years ago and knowed I couldn't let her go again."

Dixie finished his last piece of bacon and sucked the grease from his fingers one by one while he gave Saul a measuring look. "Is she pretty?"

"Prettiest woman on God's good earth, and I ain't only braggin'. Wait 'til you see her and tell me it ain't the gospel truth,"

Saul said. "Pretty and as smart as they come. Educated, not like me."

"Can't wait to meet her," Dixie said. "I'm proud for you."

"Can't say why a woman like her chose me, but she did."

"A woman like that, and you're bringing her here?"

"She gonna find work here, maybe washin' or cookin', or such, and then when we save a little money we gonna take up some farm ground and see if we can make a go of it."

"You ain't Indian. This is Indian land."

"We ain't Indian, but her brother is," Saul said.

Dixie gave him a confused look. "Say that again."

"Her brother and some of her cousins were Seminole slaves, and when those Injuns freed them they made them a member of the tribe. Did that for all they colored folks," Saul said. "We gonna partner with her brother, and maybe she can take up school teachin' the Injun chillen."

Dixie wiped the egg yoke from his plate with his last chunk of biscuit. "You say you watch things?"

Saul nodded. "A man watchin', 'specially a black man that nobody pays no mind, he sees lots o' things. Hears a lot o' things."

"What about that big new bouncer working at Tuck's saloon?" Dixie asked. "Ain't seen him before."

"You must mean the Hilltopper."

"Hilltopper?"

"That's what they calls him."

"Know anything about him?"

"Nothin' but what I hear the railroad men sayin'."

"And what are they saying?"

"They sayin' that the Hilltopper come down here from Taney County. Used to ride with the Union home guard up there, chasin' Missouri bushwhackers and Reb insurrectionists and such for Governor Gamble and General Fremont."

"That all you heard?"

"No. They say he was real good puttin' down those insurrectionists and Southern sympathizers. So good that he hung all the folks in some settlement up there, old men and young, innocent and the guilty, and the Union army there outlawed him for his heavy-handed ways. And they say after that Bill Tuck used to match him against the river men for prize money sometimes around Memphis. You know, like some men fight pit dogs and roosters, only sometimes they fight men against each other, too. The Hilltopper, he ain't never been beat fightin' for Tuck."

"Well, he's a big man. I'll give him that," Dixie said. "Must be damned near seven foot tall."

"Yes, sir, he big. Real big."

Dixie swirled his coffee mug to get the grounds in the bottom of it floating, and then swallowed the last of it. "Think I'll send a telegraph up the line and find out what I can about this Hilltopper."

"You steer clear of him. He a killuh."

"I will, Saul. I'm sure if I was going to pick a fight I could find somebody smaller than him." Dixie got up from the bench with his plate. "Best I got back to my rounds."

"Mistuh Duvall is lookin' for you," Saul said.

"I'll go see him today."

"You better. The superintendent was hoppin' mad at you for gettin' here so late, and he ain't one to be kept waitin'. Mistuh Clyde always kept him waitin', and Superintendent Duvall was always cussin' and threatenin' to fire him. Best you stay on his happy side."

"Saul, you told me once that the gamblers in Ironhead gave odds on how long Morgan would last as chief."

"I did."

"Are they giving odds on me?"

"Not many of those gamblers here 'cept for Tuck's men. Least, not yet. That old army done put the fear in those kind. Be a while, I reckon before they come tricklin' back."

"You didn't answer me. What odds are they giving?"

"No odds, Chief. Nobody I hear is talkin' about you much at all."

Dixie arched one eyebrow. "I don't rank that high, huh?"

"You ain't gots the reputation Mistuh Clyde had. That's all."

"Anybody in camp that I should know about besides that Hilltopper?"

"Not that I recollect. Quiet here, so far. Nothin' like Ironhead was, and that's good. That place was like regular fireworks, and I don't sleep good when the pistols goes to poppin'."

"What about the Kingman brothers? Have they been around?"

"You mean the two of them that Mistuh Clyde didn't kill?"

"Yep. Texas George, and what's the other one?"

"Bennie."

"Yeah, that one."

"Ain't seen either of 'em. My guess is they's hidin' in the brush on the scout, what with the army and those marshals and what all lookin' for them to hang."

"Good."

"Or is you thinkin' what some say? That those Kingmans went off lookin' for Mistuh Clyde tryin' to get they evens?"

"You let me know if they show up here."

"I will. Superintendent Duvall would cuss somethin' fierce if Texas George was to steal any more horses from his railroad. And when the superintendent gets all hot and bothered like that he's liable to fire anyone. Might forget what a good cook I am should I have his coffee too cold or his eggs too runny some mornin' when he's mad like that."

"Duvall won't fire you. You're too good of a cook to lose."

"The superintendent ain't his usual self lately. On edge most of the time. Eyes all red and his face puffy like he ain't sleepin' proper or sippin' the devil's tonic too much." And then a wicked twinkle came into Saul's eyes. "Could be that New York woman is keepin' him up too late."

"Is Helvina still with the superintendent? I thought she might have had her fill with us and gone back east."

"Yep. That woman got her claws buried deep in him."

"I guess I'd best go see him now. Get it out of the way." Dixie rose and took his plate to the washtub. "It's liable to be too early for her."

"That it is, and I don't blame you for wantin' to catch Mistuh Duvall alone."

"It's no wonder Morgan got rid of her." Dixie gave a mock shiver of fear and grinned at the cook.

"Chief?" Saul asked before Dixie could leave the mess tent.

"What?"

"Is it true what they say? That the Deacon is still alive?"

"Was the last I heard. They moved him out to the mission church at North Fork, but from what I hear, he's still a long way from living through it for sure."

"Did Mistuh Clyde really about cut the Deacon's head off?"

"Ear to ear." Dixie made a knife motion across his throat with the edge of his hand. "But he didn't cut deep enough or we wouldn't be talking about the Deacon anymore."

Saul clucked his tongue and wiped his palms on his apron. "Texas George was scary, and so is that Hilltopper. But neither one of them hold a candle to the Deacon. Maybe it ain't Christian, but I'd feel better if that man was in the ground."

"See you later, Saul."

"You take care out there, Chief. You know what they did to Mistuh Clyde, and you ain't half as tough as he was."

Dixie grinned. "Saul, someday me and you are going to start

us a restaurant. Make us a slew of money the way you cook."

"I know I can cook, but what you goin' to do to earn your keep? You can't cook, and the Good Lord knows you's too lazy to wash dishes or sweep floors."

"I'll talk to the customers. Take their money when they're through."

Saul laughed. "That's just like you white men. Get me to do all the work, then take all the money."

It was Dixie's turn to laugh, and he was still laughing when he went out of the tent and headed for the tracks where Superintendent Duvall's private Pullman was parked on a siding. When he came into sight of it, he saw lamplight glowing through the windows and knew that the superintendent was already up and about.

He grabbed hold of the ornate, cast-iron handrail at one end of the private car, and went up the steps until he stood before the door. He knocked twice before a gruff voice from within told him to enter.

It was his first time in the superintendent's private car, and while he expected it to be fancy, he was still impressed and uncomfortable within its confines. He closed the door behind him and stood with his back to it and his feet barely off the edge of a Persian rug, as if he were afraid to step on such a thing, lest it bite him. The lower walls of the modified passenger car were wainscoted with raised mahogany panels and everything above that covered in pale blue, diamond-checked wallpaper. The long row of windows along each side of the car were framed by burnt red curtains with gold tassels dangling from their edges, giving the room the feeling of a French parlor.

A short, bulldog of a man, with mutton-chop whiskers, sat behind a desk at the far end of the room. Normally a fastidious man, Superintendent Duvall's suit coat was hanging off the back of his chair, as was a paisley silk vest, and he was dressed only in a wrinkled white shirt with the sleeves rolled up to his elbows. His black hair streaked with gray, usually parted with perfect precision down the middle of his skull, was in disarray, and his eyes were bloodshot.

He closed the ledger book he was reading and an impatient frown crinkled his mouth when he looked up at Dixie. He motioned to one of the chairs in front of his desk. "Have a seat."

Dixie glanced at the door on the far end of the car behind the superintendent, obviously leading to his bedroom. Helvina was most likely still sleeping back there, for she rarely got up before noon, and that suited Dixie fine. He could more than do without the presence of Helvina Vanderwagen. Woman like that was always tormenting a man, either from the wanting of her, or the wanting to kill her.

Superintendent Duvall cleared his throat and repeated himself. "I said, have a seat."

Dixie went around the fancy rug and sat down in one of the high-backed chairs facing the desk. He took off his cap and set it on one knee.

"Took you long enough to get here," Duvall said. Then he poured himself a half-glass of bourbon from the decanter on the desk before him. "Damn throat is so dry I can't hardly talk. Care for a toddy to get the day off on the right foot?"

Dixie shook his head. "Don't think I will. Too early for me. Fact is, I didn't expect you to be up, yet."

Duvall tossed down half the glass before he answered. "I've got a railroad to run, in case you haven't noticed. But then again, if you had cared anything about that you would have been here sooner."

"Needed time to heal up."

Duvall grunted. "I take it you're now fit for work?"

"I started making my rounds yesterday."

"And what did you see?"

"Quiet camp, mostly. The majority of the riffraff haven't followed you here since the army sent them packing."

Duvall grunted again. "At least not yet."

"Not yet."

Duvall took another slug of whiskey, and finished his glass. "So, you think things are running smoothly?"

"I said the camp was quiet."

"Quiet, yes, but I'm three months behind schedule," Duvall growled.

"You didn't hire me to build your tracks," Dixie said. "You hired me to police your construction camps."

"I didn't hire you at all. Morgan Clyde did."

"You offered me his position when he quit you."

"And I expect results for my money." Duvall slapped both palms on the desk and leaned forward. "I expect you to show me why Clyde recommended you for the job. Results, Mr. Rayburn. That's how I judge my employees. That's how the world judges us all. You're either a man that can, or a man that can't. Which one are you?"

"What is it that you've got your tail in a wringer about, besides me not getting here quick enough to suit you?"

"My crane operator didn't show up for work yesterday," Duvall said. "And I imagine that I'll soon find out that he isn't going to work today, either."

"I'll look into it."

"You do that. You find him fast and get his sorry ass to work," Duvall said. "And I also want you to do something else."

"What's that?"

"I want you to find out who is peddling the dope in my camp, and I want you to put an end to it," Duvall said. "I need my men on the line every damned day. Every single one of them."

"There are no opium dens in camp. Not like I hear those

Chinese camps had when the Central Pacific was working east from California."

"Somebody is peddling the stuff in my camp, and it's getting worse."

"Couldn't stop the laudanum fiends if we wanted to," Dixie replied. "You know how that is. And half that snake oil and remedy tonic has some kind of poppy in it. You know that, too."

Duvall's chair creaked when he pushed back from his desk and laced his fingers together over his belly. His bloodshot eyes bore into Dixie like raw, wet gun barrels. "That's not what I'm talking about. I'm talking about somebody with the straight stuff. Lots of it. Stuff you drink. Stuff you eat or smoke. Stuff you needle. And God knows what all else. I don't give a rat's ass how most idiots want to screw up their miserable little lives, but I won't have it slowing my railroad down. I won't have it wrecking my operation. You hear me?"

"Any ideas on who it is?"

Duvall rocked forward in his chair again. "If I knew I wouldn't be telling you to look into the matter. I wouldn't be paying you twice too much to wear that badge."

"I'll see to it."

"You'd better." Duvall flipped open his ledger book. He looked down at it for a moment, then back up at Dixie as if surprised that his policeman was still there. "Thought you were going to do something about it?"

Dixie stood, but hesitated.

"Something else on your mind?" Duvall asked. "Spit it out if you've got something to say. My time is precious."

"You don't look well, Mr. Duvall. Maybe you ought to get some sleep."

"I don't pay you to give me medical advice."

"I was only . . ."

Duvall cut him off. "You know what it's like to have worries,

Mr. Rayburn? Real worries?"

"Everybody has worries."

"If most people had my kind of worries they would shoot themselves in the head and get it over with. Damned board members and politicians, bankers and cutthroat competitors breathing down my neck like panting whores, and half of them would like nothing better than to see me fail." Duvall tossed another slug of whiskey down his gullet, and some of it ran off his chin. "That fool bridge over the South Canadian and those damned bushwhackers that hit us have my margins razor thin. Every tinhorn speculator and big idea man has been like a fox in the henhouse the past few years, and lots of deals went bad. You could pave the road from here to California with the bad bonds floating around. And now those dumb bastards in Washington are threatening to mess with the silver market, and all the moneymen are scared. Those damned fool politicians will break the whole nation, you watch and see."

"I understand . . ."

"No, you don't. How could you? I've got a five percent stake in the MK&T. Three of it I bought, and they're paying me two more, depending on my completion of this line. Do you know how much money five percent represents?" Duvall poured himself another glass of whiskey, then frowned at it and shoved it aside. "I'll tell you what it is, that's a hell of a lot of money. I've got everything I own sunk in this project, and that's a speck compared to what some of the other ownership has invested. This railroad is already over budget and behind schedule, and if I can't turn it around, they'll run me out and find somebody else that can."

"You've made it this far."

Duvall seemed to not even have heard Dixie, and talked as if to himself. "And now my sources tell me that damned Jay Cooke and his Philadelphia bank and his Northern Pacific are about to go belly up, and I'd come closer to fornicating with a unicorn than I would getting anybody with more than two dollars in their pocket to invest in a railroad and help me see it through."

Dixie went to the door, donned his cap, and turned back for one more look at the superintendent while he put his hand to the doorknob. "Like you say, boss, you got worries."

Duvall waved a dismissive hand. "You go find my crane operator and see to it that he goes to work today. Maybe you can manage that much."

"Kiss my ass," Dixie said under his breath as he stepped out onto the rear deck and had the door almost closed behind him.

"What's that?" Duvall called after him. "What did you say?"

"I said I'll get right on it."

"That's the right attitude," Duvall said as Dixie closed the door. "I like a man that knows his place."

Chapter Twelve

The little Texas gelding that Morgan had taken from the Traveler, not bigger than fourteen hands tall and maybe 900 pounds, was a stepper. The horse clipped along at a ground-eating walk, bobbing his head to the quickness of his stride, and with his ears perked forward as if he enjoyed seeing new country. Morgan, too, would have enjoyed the traveling, for it was a fair country with a lot of horizon and a fresh feel, as if you could go on forever and never see it all. But there were two dead men at the trading post behind him, and the Traveler waiting ahead for him.

The river turned northward and passed between a cluster of hills covered with oak trees and scattered glades of lush grass. He kept the horse close to the river, taking advantage of the more broken ground and vegetation to provide him cover. The river itself became no more than scattered potholes of water and long stretches of nothing but dry sand bed. He rode often in that channel, liking the way it muffled the sound of his horse's hoof falls and that being below the riverbanks hid his movement.

In the middle of the afternoon he came to a point where the pass between the hills ended and the country before him opened up. He left the river and rode up the side of a hill until he found an open glade of grass that provided him a view of the terrain ahead and below him. Two miles to his north the river made a bend to the west once more, and between it and his position was a plain as flat as a tabletop, and on the west bank of the river in the middle of that plain was a stretch where the ground was as pure white as if it had snowed.

He watched that salt flat for an hour, not liking the thought of crossing it, but also wanting to look closer at it, for never had he seen such a place. He could see scattered small bunches of buffalo on the flat or moving and grazing not far from it. And a summer band of antelope was headed toward the river to water.

Nothing else moved on the flat, and he rode down from the hill and worked his way across it toward the bend of the river. The ground beneath his horse's hooves was so white that it was almost blinding under the afternoon sun. And when he dismounted once and took up a scoop of that ground he found it was coarse-grained salt that had leached up from the depths below. Intermixed in the salt were scattered, larger crystals, some milky clear and some pinkish. He pitched aside one of the crystals and scraped the soul of his boot against the sand to listen to the scuff of it, then climbed up on the zebra dun's back once more.

He crossed the salt flat and took a noon break under the shade of a large elm tree on the south bank of the river with the zebra dun picketed on the end of a rope to graze. Morgan wasn't hungry, and soon tired of watching the horse pick grass. He reached inside the shooting bag hanging beside his hip and laid hand to the folding picture frame that he had stuffed inside his shirt the day he had run for the hill with the Traveler shooting at him. He took the picture frame and one of the Traveler's diaries and went back to sit under the shade tree.

He opened the picture frame first, thumbing free the latch and folding the two brass frames away from each other on the hinge that joined them. On one side was a photograph of a young woman, light of hair and beautiful. On the other side was a similar photograph, but not of the woman but a boy. The boy was seated on a studio chair, in his boy's suit coat and string tie, with his legs too short to reach the floor, and with an impish gleam to his eyes as he stared at the camera. He was maybe nine or ten years old.

"Eight," Morgan said to himself. "Ben was eight that year."

He continued to stare at the photograph of the boy. "Grown man now. Probably wouldn't recognize you if I saw you, nor you me, either."

Morgan gave one last glance at the photo of the woman. "It didn't have to be that way, Helvina. Didn't have to be that way at all. He is my son, same as yours."

He folded the frames shut with a snap and put it back in the shooting bag. He stared at the nothing around him for a half hour and kept watch for signs of movement on the salt flat. Eventually, he picked up the Traveler's diary. It was the one he'd last been reading, dated 1862.

He opened it at a random point about halfway into it. He scanned several pages, stopping to read in more depth several times before moving on again. He didn't know why he continued to pour over the diary. He told himself he simply wanted to learn more about his enemy, but he found his hand tingling and his chest felt funny reading such words and accounts of skirmishes and battles. He had not been at those same places, but the story was familiar to him.

June 7, 1862—Reckon it is about hog scalding time back home. Miss home more than ever and I can almost smell them cracklins and good cornbread sopped in lard but I will not cry about that. Does no good to cry. Lots of rumors in camp. We are to march into Maryland or maybe Pennsylvania and give the Federals some on their home ground. I do not know where those places are except for they are up north somewhere. They made Rust a general and Captain Manning a major and Captain Tebbs got promoted to Lt. Colonel. The rest of us is still privates and rifle totin razorbacks who sleep in the mud and live on food a dog would not eat and get no thanks for it. Meat for the grinder.

July 6, 1862—Got a letter today that said Solomon was killed in the fightin at Beaver Dam Creek back in June. Marched thirty miles today thinkin about him. Do not know how he was killed but reckon it surprised him as much as me. Knowin him I would guess the head knockin fool was out front tryin to show what a fighter he was. He always wanted to match Pa's medals from the Mexican War and never thought he could be touched. But anybody can die. Most do in this war.

July 18, 1862—The Second Arkansas Battalion was shot up so bad they mustered them into our regiment and did away with theirs. Wasnt but about a hundred or so of them left and the ones joinin us are mostly sick or wounded and in low spirits and not much fight left to them. Rumor is they left their battle flags in the trenches at Mechanicsville for the Yankees to have. Talked to several that had served with Solomon but none of them knew how he got it in the end. It doesnt matter no how. Dyin is all the same. You are here and then you are gone. Some ways is worse than others but you are still gone in the end.

September 16, 1862—We marched to some place called Sharpsburg. Maryland I think. We dug in along Antietam Creek and southeast of the Potomac River. Captain Tebbs sent three of us across a rock bridge to scout for the enemy. We come in sight of some water wells at a crossroads in the middle of this apple orchard. The Federals was hot and thirsty and had no water but they was scared to fetch them some cause they didn't know where our main force was. Before long they could not take it anymore and sent runners out loaded down with canteens. We hid in the loft of a good hay barn and watched them til an offi-

cer come out with them. One of the men with me says how he would like to shoot that Yankee son of a bitch cause he had just got word of how his cousin was stabbed and killed in a trench outside Richmond with Yankee bayonets and with him tryin to surrender and beggin for them to take him prisoner. I never had shot that far but I gave it a try anyways. Must have been better than three hundred yards but I hit that officer in the head with my Enfield. Never knew a head shot man would flop like that. I cannot say what I felt watchin him. Most times I feel empty. The men with me bragged on my shot and told everybody about it when we ran back across the bridge and joined up with our company.

September 18, 1862—The battle our officers was wantin came yesterday. Worst fightin I seed yet. They put us on top a little rollin hill and we dug in along a wagon road where it was rutted deep enough to form a natural trench and give us some cover. Heard bad fightin all morning to the north of us. All the cannons and muskets in the world must have been goin off at onest. Late mornin the Federals came at us hard. Must have been thousands of them and two or three times our number. But we held fast. There was so many of them that a man couldnt miss. Their dead stacked up like chord wood but they still kept comin. Shot my Enfield so hot that it blistered my hand to touch the barrel. Had to take up the rifle gun off Charlie McElroy's body to keep fightin. He was dead and half buried in the dirt but had his gun gripped so tightly in his hands that I had to fight him for it. Charlie was a good sort and I hated to do him that way but he would understand.

The whole Union army must have decided to dig us out of that road cause then the Irishers come at us marchin in ranks out of the woods at the foot of the hill with their green flags floppin in the wind and one of them pope types riding back and forth in front of them on his horse shoutin holy words to egg them on. But God didnt like them Irishers no more than he liked us and we shot them down like meat same as we had the rest. Little before noon some of the Federals flanked us and got the high ground where they could shoot down into our line. Went to killin us like hogs in a fattenin pen. There was nothing to do but run or leave our meat to rot in that trench. What was left of us fell back as best we could. The Federals would have gotten us all but our artillery laid heavy canister shot on their advance. None of us wanted any more of the fight but the officers was callin for those fit enough to form up and make a counter attack. We was mixed companies and regiments but we formed up just the same. Boys from North Carolina and Arkansas and Virginia all with our ears ringin so bad from cannon shot and rifles crackin to do anything smarter than what they said. Wasnt but a couple of hundred of us but we hit them hard again and ran them out of that sunken road bed. But they was as crazy with blood as we were and we couldnt drive them no farther away. Must have been thousands died along that wagon road and nothin changed for it. All that dyin and some on both sides is goin to say how they won.

I shot me another officer yesterday afternoon. They say it was a major this time. Was not a real long shot but the men in my company made much of it. There wasn't much to cheer about today. I took a bayonet in the leg durin the counter attack on that wagon road. Not bad but I will limp for a while. Most of Co. L is all but gone and the rest of the regiment is in little better shape. Co. A started with 127 men but there are only 74 of us now. I can still hear Solomon sayin how it wouldnt take a month or two to end this war. None of us knew what this would be like. The thing I come to know is that a soldier is nothing but meat. Sounds awful and cowardly but that is the way it is.

Sept 19, 1862—Colonel Tebbs called me to his tent today and give me a new rifle gun. He called it a Whitworth and it is made all the way over across the ocean in England. Said the Confederate army was formin up sharpshooters from every regiment and I was gonna be one. That Whitworth shoots the heaviest .45 bullet I ever seed. Long as your thumb and they aint round but have got six flat sides. And its got a telescopic sight on it that you can see a far piece with like things are up right close. Kind of like a spyglass mounted on your gun with crosshairs to put on what you aim at. Shot it this evenin and that scope tube hit me in the eye and cut me to the bone when the gun kicked back. Goin to take me practice to get used to it but I think when I do I could hit a man most anywhere I can see him. Colonel Tebbs said I needed to keep a lookout for Federal officers and get them first. Said I would not be on the line with the rest of the men much anymore and would usually be scouting on my own or with other sharpshooters. That suits me right down to the ground. A man ought to pick his own way of dyin.

Morgan closed the diary, and went to the dun. He took the canteen off his saddle, slung the canteen strap over one shoulder, and took one last look to make sure the zebra dun's picket rope was staked securely before he pushed through the brush and found his way down the high bank of the river with the diary in one hand and the Moore rifle in the other.

He found a narrow channel of water running between the bank and a sandbar and unscrewed the cap on the canteen and submerged it. Once filled, he screwed the cap back on and left the canteen in the water to cool the blanket insulation on it while he took a seat on the sloping, sandy riverbank. He propped the rifle against one shoulder and opened the diary once more.

November 16, 1862—What was left of the men in Co. L are

put over into Co. A with us. And the whole regiment is swapped over to join with General Hoods Texas Brigade. Those Texans have worked them up a big reputation as scrappers but they are as ragged as we are and just as shot up. The officers want us sharpshooters to work in pairs where we can and most of those chosen like it that way. Makes them feel safer to work in teams or groups away from the lines and scouting the enemy and raisin Cain where they can. They got me paired with a man named George from San Antonio. He speaks Spanish as good as he speaks English and is always talking about pretty Mexican girls and them cattle they got down there with horns big enough to run a horse through. George is a good enough shot but he dont have the callin for this kind of work. I complained to my lieutenant that I like to work alone but he says George will be all right once he has the nerves shot out of him. What a thing to say. What I say is that George hasnt learned that we are all dead anyways. Only difference is that some has fallen and some is still standin and waitin their turn. No sense in bein scared.

December 12, 1862—Got ordered into Fredricksburg yesterday and loaned out to General Barksdale with other sharpshooters from up and down the lines. Federals were tryin to lay pontoon bridges across the river and we took stands in the town and tried to slow them while General Longstreet and Stonewall got their defense in order. Me and George found us a place in the basement of a shoe shop. It had little windows even with the street and we could see the river fine from there. George shot one of those Yankee engineers through the guts and he was screamin and cryin at the edge of the water and the other sharpshooters in the city shot at him but none of them could hit him good. Must have been ten bullets hit him but they only kept hurtin him more. The sight of it made George sick and then the Federals started lobbin cannonballs in among the city to try and run us out. The noise of it and the buildins busted to pieces was somethin awful and George lost his nerve and ran back to our lines. Hope he made it but I wont hunt with him anymore.

That artillery brought whole buildins down but I was all right in that basement. When the Federals started buildin their bridge again I waited until I spotted me an officer. Couldnt tell for sure what his rank was but I could see him givin orders through my scope. I meant to hit him in the chest but he was a far piece away and I ended up hittin him in the knee my second shot. He fell and was callin out and carryin on like the one George shot and it wasnt long before his friends started comin out to try and carry him away. I got one more of them and the sharpshooters hid nearby got some more. Good trick that. Have to remember it. Shoot you some bait and then wait for more fish to come. Funny thing was I didnt feel nothin watchin that man suffer. Shames me to write that but it is the truth. I ought to quit writin such things down in case somebody were to read them after I am gone but I cant. Writin this to myself is somehow soothin maybe. Seein what I write lets me know what I am becomin. And if anybody ever reads this it means I am gone anyways and it wont matter what they think of me.

December 14, 1862—Worked alone the last two days. Federal skirmishers crossed the river on boats and run us sharpshooters out of Fredricksburg near their landin. Some surrendered but the rest of us worked from hidin place to hidin place takin our toll on them. Hid under a piece of sheet iron beside the train tracks and waited til daylight come while the Federals crossed the river in force. Was so foggy yesterday it was like the Devil's breath. Used that fog to work my way downriver along the tracks past where the Federals had another pontoon bridge. Took a stand inside a warehouse and pulled loose a board so I could shoot out the wall. Our horse artillery was givin it to the Federals pretty hot and I figured out that nobody was goin to think anything of men fallin around them in all that noise and confusion. Shot two Yankee lieutenants before the Federals started shellin my hidin place and I had to move. I am findin I am good at this kind of fightin. More like huntin than fightin and I know how to hunt. Swear I wont fight like before ever again. I will be the hunter and the chooser of the slain. If I die it will be because I failed and not because some officer told me where to go or where to make a stand. I ask no quarter of my enemy and I will give none. God help their souls and mine.

December 15, 1862—Some bobtailed lieutenant tried to take me to task for not reportin back to my company when I should have. I didnt pay him any mind. The officers above him like how I hunt. Brought Colonel Tebbs the officer's bars I took off one of those Yankee colonels. Crawled half a mile in the dark to get them before the Federals could drag him off the battlefield. Colonel Tebbs didnt say nothin but I know he was pleased. Our brigade is givin ground and formin up farther north. I am the only one to have brought in my share of meat.

December 25, 1862—Been out huntin for a week. Found little other than two Yankees hidin in a farmhouse. Waited for a whole afternoon for them to come out. When they did I let them get in the middle of a stubble field before I shot. Got the first one fairly close but the second one took to running and was five hundred yards by the time I reloaded. Guess they were deserters from the way they was hidin and how they waited until almost dark to leave that house. No need really to shoot them but it was good practice. Still learnin' my Whitworth gun and how my bullets do at farther ranges. Slipped to them the next mornin to see where my shots had hit them and found one of them was carryin a down pillow in his rucksack. My bullet had gone through that pillow before it busted his backbone and there were little white feathers everywhere. Raked me up a handful of those feathers and drug those dead Yankees to the edge of the road. Stuffed a feather in each of their noses and left them like that. Dont know why I did that unless it was to leave some kind of mark like a dog pissin on a post. But I am doin lots of things lately and I have quit thinkin much on them. Only good thing about this war is that a man can be what he is. The hunter gets to pick his own rules and the meat live by them.

Morgan closed the diary. He, too, had hunted men in the war, but he had never enjoyed it like young Erastus Tuck in the diary was slowly learning. He had seen many soldiers go crazy during the war and understood how the violence could numb a man to all the killing and the horror, but that didn't explain the Traveler. Maybe he was already a little twisted before he went to war, born with a black streak of evil or insanity running up his middle that the violence set free like a mean dog set loose from its chain.

Morgan looked up at the sun and realized how long he had been reading. He took up his canteen and rifle and started up the riverbank back to his horse. He was skirting around a clump of sagebrush at the top of the bank when he saw the zebra dun facing to the south and with its ears perked up like it was watching something.

A bullet smacking the ground beside him and the crack of a rifle were all in one instant, and Morgan toppled backwards down the bank. He half rolled and half slid back to the water's edge, and he was on one knee and looking up at the riverbank when he heard the sound of running horses.

He took a better hold on the Moore rifle and sprinted down the sand, heading upriver towards a clump of trees tangled with vines and underbrush that extended on a narrow point out into the river channel. He had only gone a few yards when he heard the creak of saddle leather and the riverbank crumbling under a horse's weight. He threw a wild look over his shoulder as he ran, and caught the silhouetted form of a man on horseback at the top of the bank. No sooner than he saw that, than a bullet smacked into the canteen swinging in his left hand and knocked it from his grasp. Another gun roared and a spray of buckshot pelted the sand in front of him. He twisted at the waist, never stopping, and extended the heavy rifle one-handed behind him like a pistol towards the rider. His rifle bellowed and the horse staggered. The man on its back let off a second round from his rifle into the sky and yanked hard on the bit as if that would keep the animal upright. But the horse bent its neck and gaped its mouth and fell sideways off the high riverbank, taking its rider with it.

Morgan skidded to a stop, shifted his rifle to his left hand, and snaked the long-barreled Remington from his holster while he watched man and horse roll over twice and come to a stop in a cloud of dust at the edge of the water. The rider had somehow kept from being crushed by the weight of the dying horse, and he struggled to get to his feet. Morgan's pistol was leveling on him when another load of buckshot fired from above him whipped so closely past his head that the wadding behind it fluttered to the ground a few feet away from him. Morgan looked up at the riverbank above him, with the sun hitting in the face and all but blinding him. He caught a flash of movement and the black silhouette of another rider, and he threw a hurried pistol shot into the sagebrush and tall grass there and sprinted for the timber. Two more shots were fired his way while he ran, but neither one hit him, nor could he tell how close they had come.

He hit the thicket in a headlong dive, and another bullet clipped the limbs and brush near to him. The trunk of a fat cottonwood tree and a pile of driftwood, sand, and leaves made a breastwork between him and the men coming after him. He hunkered down flat on his back behind that cover and reached inside his shooting bag and took out a cylinder made of walnut wood about the length of a finger and twice the diameter. He grounded the butt of the rifle, pulled the plug on one end of the cylinder with his teeth, and poured a premeasured charge of black powder down the barrel of the gun. The quick-load cylinder had separate chambers hollowed out at each end, and the other contained a bullet and cloth patch. He unstoppered that end and poured them out in the palm of his hand and set patch and then bullet over the muzzle. He could hear the two men shouting to each other, and another shot cracked through the thicket over his head while he whipped the ramrod free from its loop on the shot bag and started the bullet down the bore.

Even with the quick-load he used with its premade charge, the Moore rifle was slow to load. The mating of the rifle bore to the patched bullet was tight for accuracy's sake, and he usually, when given time, used the aid of a bell-mouth false muzzle shaped like a funnel that fit into the end of the barrel and made bullet starting easier and protected the lip of the bore from damage by the ramrod. There was no time for such, and he strained to get the bullet started and then drove down the bore and seated home against the powder. The metal ramrod bowed and flexed like a buggy whip, and his knuckles turned white with the strain.

The man behind the dead horse had found his rifle after his fall, and apparently, it was a repeater, for he was shooting as fast as he could work the action. His searching fire was scattered through the thicket and knocked chunks of wood and leaves around Morgan as he drew the ramrod free and fit a percussion cap on the nipple under the side hammer. Once loaded, he hugged the rifle close to his chest and waited for the hail of bullets to slow or stop.

It seemed like an eternity before the firing ceased, and Morgan rolled on to his stomach and crept up the hump of flood debris until he could peer down the river. His effort was immediately rewarded by another bullet kicking sand in his face and sending him back down behind cover.

"I think I got him in the head!" a high-pitched voice shouted.

While Morgan tried to rub the grit out of his eyes, he could hear a horse pushing through the vegetation on top of the riverbank to the side and above him. That would be the one still on his horse, and the one with the shotgun.

"Careful now, he might be playing possum!" the same squeaky voice called from the dead horse downriver to the one riding on the riverbank.

Morgan shouldered the rifle and searched the top of the riverbank beside him with its scope, but could make out nothing. He lowered the rifle and waited, listening to the sound of the horse in the brush and trying to approximate its general location by listening.

"You see him, yet?" the voice from downriver called again. "I tell you I got him."

Morgan slid his Remington once more from its holster and listened for the rider in the brush to move. When he heard the distinct crack of a limb and saw a sway of the grass some fifty yards away he fired three pistol shots in that direction as fast as he could thumb the hammer and pull the trigger. He heard a startled yelp of pain or surprise, and he rose quickly behind the drift pile and looked downriver and saw the man whose horse he had shot down on one knee behind it. He fired his revolver empty at that man, then lurched to his feet.

He ran wildly upriver with one arm held across his face to protect him from the tearing limbs and vines, and the other toting the heavy rifle. Twice he fell, only to get back up again. He broke out of the thicket, and before him was a long stretch of open river channel with grassy banks and nothing to provide him cover. He considered, for the briefest of instants, wading the river to put it between him and his attackers, but the channel was too wide and the going would be too slow wading and fighting against the suck of muddy sand. They would plug him in the back before he made it halfway across.

An eroded rut in the riverbank made by buffalo showed itself on his side of the river, and he immediately started up it, hoping to get out of the riverbed before whoever was up there on the horse could make it that far. What he needed and his only chance of survival was to somehow gain some distance between himself and his attackers, and take a stand.

The narrow trail up the riverbank was steep and the buffalo hooves had churned it to powder, and he made slow headway despite his panting and straining. He was shaking and his lungs were heaving by the time he landed on his knees on level ground. A head in a broad-brimmed hat showed itself above the grass and sagebrush not fifty yards down the riverbank, carried along at a trot by the body and the horse somewhere beneath it and out of sight. Morgan shouldered his rifle and tried to find that head in his crosshairs, but the sun gave him problems again. Dust and tiny flecks of mud had settled on his outer scope lens, and with the sun hitting the dirty glass all he could make out was a blurry, bobbing dot amidst splotches and bubbles of light. His exhausted body and shaking arms swung his crosshairs all over the dot that was the rider's head. He took a deep breath, exhaled, and his finger caressed the trigger.

The .54-caliber rifle boomed and the dot disappeared. Morgan set the gun down and clawed at his holstered pistol while he watched the rider and the horse appear out of the grass and brush. The rider seemed unhurt, but the gunshot at such close range had frightened the horse to the point it was lunging and rearing.

Morgan dropped back in the grass and exchanged the empty

cylinder in his Remington for the loaded one from his belt. By the time he was finished, the rider had gotten the horse under some control and was spurring it away at a dead run and firing a pistol behind him at Morgan to guard his retreat. That rider was already a hundred yards away, but Morgan took a two-hand hold on the Remington and fired a shot at him anyway. He missed, but did succeed in motivating the rider to greater speed.

As soon as he fired the pistol he took up the rifle again and headed upriver, following the edge of the riverbank at a jog and glancing over his shoulder at his back trail often. Ahead of him, a low, flat-topped butte jutted out into the river channel. The sides of the butte sloped gently to its top, and fell off in an almost sheer bluff into the river on the other side. He made the top and fell to a prone position facing back the way he had come. It was a hundred and fifty yards or so to the thicket he had fled from, and all around his hill there was nothing but miles and miles of open country, except for the eyebrow-thin line of vegetation along the river. Nobody was going to come at him without him seeing them.

The rider he had chased away showed himself in the edge of the thicket on the riverbank, and Morgan took another long shot at him with the pistol. He couldn't tell how close his aim had been, but the rider did duck back into cover. Morgan used the time to reload his Moore rifle.

When finished reloading the rifle, he glanced at the sun again, gauging the time left until sundown. Maybe two hours. He held the high ground, a good field of fire, and they weren't going to root him out before darkness fell unless there were more than two of them. He hoped there were only two of them.

He hadn't gotten a good look at either of the men he had fought, other than to tell they were white men, but he had recognized that squeaky voice belonging to the man whose horse he had shot. That was Texas George, and he assumed the other rider might be his brother, Bennie. George had tried to ambush him once in the dark while he was still back in Ironhead, and got shot in the hand for his troubles. And he had faced off against all of the brothers and Deacon Fischer later, and killed Grat Kingman, once the third of the brothers, during the bloodletting. He wasn't shocked that the two surviving Kingmans would want his life and come so far to take it, but he was surprised that the army or the federal marshals hadn't caught them and hanged them before now. Much effort had been put into the hunt for them after they participated in the attempted robbery of the Katy payroll and tried to blow up the railroad trestle on the South Canadian.

But Texas George had always been a good judge of fast horseflesh, and if he wasn't the sharpest tool in the shed, he was at least crafty when it came to looking after his own neck.

His brother, Bennie, Morgan didn't know much about, other than he was bigger and talked a whole lot less. All of the Kingman brothers supposedly had ridden with some Texas cavalry company. The story was that George commanded the company as an officer. Morgan couldn't imagine the mean little runt commanding anything, or anybody willing to listen to him, but he had to admit that he had taken orders from men not a whole lot better during the war. A man didn't get to pick his officers.

The only truth that mattered was that there were two of the Kingmans out there, and they would stick after him until they saw him dead. Both were men with "scalps on their belts," as the saying went for men who had killed, and they had put him on foot.

And then there was the Traveler.

Morgan gave a weary grunt. It was high time his luck changed, and he hoped it would happen soon, before anybody else showed up to kill him.

Chapter Thirteen

"Son of a bitch shot my horse," Texas George said in a voice gone squeakier than its usual high pitch due to his excitement. He was always a nervous, spastic sort, and he had already paced back and forth enough beside his dead mount to have worn a rut in the sandy riverbed. He kicked a spray of sand with one boot and then kicked the dead horse.

"Wasn't your horse's fault," the man looking down at him from the top of the riverbank said. "Don't know why you're kicking him."

"I'm kicking him because I want to." Texas George looked up at his brother, Bennie, sitting on his horse. "I suppose you let him get away."

"He didn't go far. He's up the river a ways on the other side of that thicket. Bellied down on a hilltop." Bennie's calm voice didn't change, regardless of his brother's scornful tone.

Bennie was a big man, made bigger by the size of his hat and the long, thick beard spreading wild and ungroomed from his face to his chest. His whiskers grew so high up his cheeks that only his eyes and the tip of his broad, flat nose were visible between the beard and his hat brim. He shoved the double-barreled shotgun he carried down in the saddle boot hanging beside one leg, and wrapped his bridle reins once around his saddle horn to free his hands. He took a plug of chewing tobacco from his vest pocket, cut a piece of it off with his knife, and stuffed it in his mouth. Texas George paced some more and cursed while Bennie worked the quid methodically around inside his cheek and watched his brother's antics.

"How the hell did he get away from you when I flushed him out of that thicket like a rabbit on the jump? Should have been easy," Texas George said and kicked the dead horse again.

"He was waiting on the other side and liked to have put a hole in me." Bennie took his hat off and spun the brim until he found the bullet notch in the edge of it. He held it up for George to see. "See that? Lucky it didn't bust my melon, instead."

Texas George looked down at the bullet hole in his dead horse's neck. "What the hell kind of rifle is he carrying? Dropped my horse like it was poleaxed."

"Big 'un, I reckon."

Texas George was little more than half the size of Bennie, a half-pint man as thin as he was short, and the Starr single-action .44 he wore on his right hip in a cut-down army holster was the most conspicuous thing about him. He put a hand to the walnut pistol butt to keep it from flopping while he paced some more.

"Bastard is lucky is what he is," George said.

Bennie gave no reply, other than to spit a stream of tobacco juice off the riverbank. He twisted in the saddle and looked upriver. "We're going to have a hard time getting him up on that hill."

George looked around at the terrain. "Lucky bastard. Only hill on this whole damned flat, and the son of a bitch finds it. But we'll get him. I didn't ride across the whole damned territory not to."

"Won't be easy."

"Easy? Who said anything about easy?" George kicked the horse again and broke into another string of profanity.

"You kick that horse one more time and it won't be Clyde you have to worry about," Bennie said.

"What the hell do you care? It ain't your horse."

"You're mean with animals, George. Always have been. And I'm in no mood for it."

Texas George thought about kicking the horse again simply to spite Bennie, but saw how his brother was looking at him and didn't. Bennie was a slow thinker and a deliberate mover, but he was a hard man to stop once he decided on violence.

"Don't you threaten me, Bennie," George said to save face.

Bennie took up his reins and kicked his horse downriver.

"Where the hell are you going?" George called out. "Clyde is the other way."

Bennie circled his horse back to where he could see George again over the lip of the riverbank. "What are you squawking about?"

"That Clyde maimed me. Made a cripple of me. He killed Grat and shot a hole in you," George held up his left hand and showed the nub of the pointer finger gone at the knuckle, as if the sight of it would remind Bennie of everything. "Texas George don't let nobody do that and get away with it, and the Kingman brothers don't, either. And here you are riding off while that Clyde sits up there on the hill laughing at us."

"That all?" Bennie asked.

"Is that all? Ain't that enough?"

Bennie turned the horse around again and started off the same way he had before.

"Where are you going?" George called after him. "I say where are you going?"

"I'm going to fetch you that dun horse. 'Less you want to chase Clyde down on foot," Bennie said.

George took a pause to gather his thoughts, but quickly recovered. "Yeah, bring me that horse. And then we'll go get Clyde."

Bennie returned shortly, leading the zebra dun. "Gonna be

hard with him up there on that hill with that big gun."

"You're good with a rifle. You take my Henry and pick him off first time he shows himself," George said.

"I ain't that good," Bennie said. "Maybe if I could get within a hundred yards or so I might hit him."

"Then we'll Injun up on him."

"Easy for you to say when I imagine it's me you want to do the Injun work," Bennie replied in his laconic way. "They say Clyde was some kind of sharpshooter for the Yankee army during the war, and I got a quick look at the rifle he was carrying. He ain't going to let me get within a hundred yards, nor you, neither."

"He can't stay up on that hill forever. He's got to drink and he's got to eat. We'll wait him out. Let the sun fry his brain until he's got to come down." Texas George bent over his dead horse and began loosening his saddle cinch. He made hard work of pulling the saddle free with the animal's weight mashing one side of it into the sand. "You could come help me, you know."

Bennie remained on his horse atop the riverbank, and his attention was aimed in the direction of the hill where Morgan had gone to ground instead of his brother.

"If that Clyde would give me a fair fight I would have already finished this," George said as he decided it was too much work to dig his saddle loose.

"Fair fight? You laid for him back in Ironhead and didn't get nothing for your trouble but your finger shot off."

"He got lucky." George trudged up the riverbank.

"You keep saying that. He ain't lucky. That man is good. He bested us back there with the Deacon to help us. Shot us to doll rags," Bennie said.

"The Deacon messed that up," George said when he got up on level ground. "We put lead in him then, and we'll give him another dose before the day is out. You mark my words."

George frowned at Morgan's saddle, thinking how he was going to have to unlace the stirrup leathers and shorten them considerably to fit him. He wasn't finished building up his energy to tackle that when Bennie let go of the dun's reins. George had to make a grab at them to keep the dun from walking off and leaving him. Bennie was already riding away, paying him no mind, and giving him no time to readjust the stirrups. But Bennie was always inconsiderate like that.

"I get the sense you ain't as fired up to kill Clyde as you once was, and that worries me," George said as he gave the saddle a shake by the saddle horn to check that it was secure enough to mount. "Family used to mean the world to you. Never seen you quit on something when we was done wrong. Eye for an eye, tooth for a tooth, and all of that. Blood is thicker than river water."

Bennie kept riding away, casting looks over his shoulder but ignoring George.

"Are you listening to me?" George tried to place his boot in the stirrup, but the dun horse stepped away from him. "Hold still, you stupid horse."

Clyde had left a new Winchester carbine in the rifle boot. George wasn't about to give up that prize, but it left no place for his own Henry rifle. There was no way he could get on the horse holding his gun, so he hung it from the saddle strings while he watched to make sure that Bennie didn't look back and see him. Bennie would think it funny that George couldn't mount without having to use both hands.

It took George three tries to mount, but he finally managed it by taking a good hold on the saddle horn and jumping and pulling on the horn at the same time and stabbing his toe into the stirrup at the top of his leap. It always bothered him that he was too short to get on a horse proper like most men. His usual method was to jump for his stirrup like he had then, but there were times when he used a stump or a handy porch to mount from. He had killed his first man for laughing at the way he had to mount, a Yankee drummer come to Texas to peddle laundry solvent that was supposed to take the worst stains out of any piece of clothing. He had snuck up on the laughing son of a bitch in his dove-gray suit and stabbed him in the kidney before he knew what hit him. Let him see if that soap he carried in his carpetbag would take the blood out of that suit.

"Did you hear me, Bennie?" George said when he quit reminiscing, and as he caught up to his brother. "You hear what I'm saying?"

"I heard you." Bennie looked at George, squint-eyed and his jaw working on the chew of tobacco like a machine. "I'll cut Clyde's guts out and show them to him. Promised myself that, and I don't need you reminding me of nothing. Time you shut up before you rile me."

George let their horses go a few more walking strides. The stirrups hung way too low for him, and he had to tiptoe to even touch them. It was an embarrassing feeling, and that made him all the madder. "Then why are you going the wrong way? Clyde is back there."

Bennie cast another look in the direction of the flat-topped butte screened from their sight by the thicket. He kicked his horse up to a trot.

"You ain't making sense," George said.

"I'm getting some distance between me and that hill. Don't like the thought of all this open ground and Clyde up there and likely looking for us in that rifle scope of his," Bennie said without slowing.

George cast a look behind him where Bennie had been looking, but only a quick look. He kicked the dun up to a lope and passed his brother. Bennie was a slow thinker and needed motivation sometimes, but maybe he was right for once. The thought of Clyde looking for them in his sights wasn't a pleasant one, and there was plenty of time to get him when things were right. Plenty of time. They had Clyde on foot and without supplies, and it was a long way to anywhere.

Chapter Fourteen

Red Molly was a woman used to keeping late hours and used to sleeping in of a morning. It was late, nearing midday before she came out of her tent, squinting at the sun and wondering what time it was and feeling she could have done with a few more hours of sleep if it hadn't been for the sound of those damned hammers.

The tent that was the Bullhorn Palace was only ten yards in front of her own dwelling, and a beaten path led from where she stood to the back door of the saloon. Instead of taking that path, she went around the saloon and hit the street and went up it towards the railroad tracks. She noticed that some of the North Fork people were already busy clearing the site of Irish Dave's burnt saloon as if they intended to do something with it, and another bunch was putting up a frame building along what had once been Ironhead's main thoroughfare. One of the carpenters began beating on a nail and Molly winced and put a hand to her temple. She thought about trying to buy the hammer from the man so she could throw it in the woods.

She walked on and was surprised to see another crew at work at the head of the street next to the tracks. There must have been ten men working there, with most of them unloading lumber off several freight wagons and the rest of them digging ditches for a foundation footing for some kind of building where the tent for the company store had once stood. The square they were laying out was large, and Molly assumed it was for the hotel she had heard talk of. Whoever was building it wasn't wasting any time.

One of the few remaining tents from the original camp, besides Molly's tent and the Bullhorn, belonged to Doctor Beauregard Chillingsworth, formally a surgeon for the Union army during the late war, Ironhead's only physician during its heyday, and its most talkative and amiable drunk. Molly was surprised that the doctor hadn't moved on with the rest of the camp. She could hear someone rummaging around in the tent when she neared it.

"Doc, you in there?" Molly said.

"Well you know it isn't burglars because there isn't anything in here worth stealing," said a voice from inside the tent. "Come on in."

Molly ducked through the tent flaps and found Doc Chillingsworth moving around the tent with surprising energy for a man of his weight and with his propensity for morning hangovers. Boxes and luggage were strewn around the front room of the tent, and all of the doctor's patient cots were folded and stacked in one corner. The doctor was gathering things and packing them with little regard for order.

"When are you going?" Molly asked.

"Train's coming up from Canadian any time now to get a load of rails from the warehouse," Chillingsworth said as he tried to force an armload of his clothes in a valise. The bag was too full to shut and the doctor put his foot on top of the clothes to compress them. "I aim to be on that train if I can get my things together in time."

"You aren't exactly a neat packer," Molly said.

The doctor turned to face her with a half angry scowl. His face was flushed and red, but then again, his face was always flushed and red. "I don't see you helping."

Molly arched an eyebrow at him.

At that moment, a young woman came from the back room through the partition wall that divided the doctor's hospital from his private quarters. She was a thin girl with long sandy hair that she wore loose, a narrow face, sharp nose, and freckles dotting her cheeks. She might have been twenty, or she might have still been in her teens. She never said, and the only thing certain was that she was young. A plain dress covered her bony frame and Molly noticed the pair of men's work boots sticking out from under the bottom hem of it. Dressed like that, and standing slumped as she was, it was hard to tell that Ruby Ann was once one of the most popular whores in Ironhead.

"Good morning to you, Ruby Ann," Molly said.

"Hello," Ruby Ann replied in a tight, quiet gush of air that came out more like a whisper, as if she were scared of the sound of her own voice.

Molly was shocked. As far as she knew, Ruby Ann hadn't spoken since she was the victim of torture and rape a month previous.

Doc Chillingsworth saw Molly's surprise. "She's a regular chatterbox now, aren't you, Ruby Ann?"

Ruby Ann didn't answer him, and instead, only looked down at her booted feet and nodded timidly.

"Did you get my bedding packed?" Chillingsworth asked her.

Again, Ruby Ann only nodded.

"Good girl," he said.

"Is she going with you?" Molly asked.

"I asked her to, but she won't," he said. "Poor thing's body has about healed, but I'm afraid it will be a long while before the rest of her is right, if ever."

Molly glanced at Ruby Ann to see how she reacted to the doctor's words, uncomfortable with such things being said in front of the girl. She remembered how Ruby Ann used to laugh, and how she was once so vain about that long hair. Hard to believe it was the same woman staring at her feet.

"What are you going to do, Ruby Ann?" Molly asked.

Ruby Ann never looked up at Molly, and rocked her weight from one foot to the other.

"I was hoping maybe she could stay with you," Chillingsworth said.

"With me?"

"Yeah, I heard you're staying to run Tuck's saloon. Ruby doesn't say much, but she's been good help around here," he said. "I don't know how I would have gotten through it when those bastard outlaws blew up the depot house if it wasn't for her helping me with my patients. She helped me stitch them up and bandage wounds and splint broken bones like a regular nurse."

Molly took a step forward so that she could see into the back room. "Where's that railroad man? The one that got shot during the bridge ceremony?"

"You mean Bert Huffman? I didn't think he would make it, but he pulled through the worst of it. Jay Cooke himself sent me a few telegraphs keeping himself appraised of Huffman's condition, and let me know that his personal physician would be coming to Ironhead to tend to his employee," Chillingsworth said. "Can you believe that? A tycoon like Jay Cooke corresponding with me? One of the richest men in the country, the newspapers say. Well, his personal doctor showed up three days ago, gave Huffman a quick once-over, pronounced him reasonably safe to travel, and then put him on a gurney and loaded him on a train bound for some hospital in Chicago."

"Is that so?" Molly was distracted remembering the day the Secretary of the Interior had come to the camp to dedicate the new trestle bridge spanning the South Canadian River, and how the drunks and the hard cases in camp, many of them Southern men with no love for the Reconstruction government, got out of hand and a riot ensued. And how that poor Huffman, an employee of the other competing railroad, the KNVR, took a bullet in the ensuing melee before the bushwhackers stormed the camp and tried to make off with the Katy payroll.

Chillingsworth nodded. "You would know this stuff if you came around more. I swear, you've become most antisocial as of late. I've truly missed partaking of an evening toddy with you and our fine conversations."

"Sorry, I've been busy."

Chillingsworth grunted as if he had heard that excuse before, but he seemed in too good of a mood to let that bother him. "I might add that Cooke's physician bragged on the treatment Huffman got while in my care."

"Oh, Doc, you're a fine one. Everybody knows that."

"Do I detect a faint trace of sarcasm in your tone, young lady?"

"Never."

"What about Ruby Ann?"

Molly looked to her. "How about it, Ruby Ann? Want to help working in the Bullhorn?"

Ruby Ann looked up then, and there was a hint of frantic fear in her eyes.

"No, that's not what I'm talking about," Molly said. "You can tend bar, or just help me run things and clean the place up. Whatever you feel like doing. How about that?"

Ruby Ann looked to the doctor who smiled encouragement at her. She paused for a moment as if unsure, but finally nodded at Molly.

"You can stay with me until we can find you something else," Molly said.

Ruby Ann gave no indication whether that was fine with her or not, but continued to stand there as if something were bothering her. She glanced at the doctor.

"Go ahead, ask her if you want to," Chillingsworth said.

Ruby Ann gave Molly a brief glance, then looked down at her feet again.

"She wants to know if Dixie is all right. She's been some upset since he left," Chillingsworth said.

"Far as I know, he's doing fine. Haven't talked to him since he went to Canadian," Molly said.

It didn't surprise her that Ruby Ann wanted to know about Dixie Rayburn. Never would she have picked the two of them for a match, but she was aware that they had become close during Ruby Ann's time with the doctor after her incident, and during Dixie's convalescence after the Arkansas Traveler tried to kill him. She had often seen the two of them sitting in chairs in front of the hospital tent watching the goings on in camp.

Molly gave the doctor a quick hug, and then motioned to Ruby Ann. "Come on down to the Bullhorn when you get your things packed."

Ruby Ann nodded and then turned and disappeared into the back room.

Molly nodded her head in the direction that Ruby had gone. "I've known Ruby Ann for almost three years. We always got along, even if we weren't close friends. You'd think she would talk to me."

"That sick bastard tore her up pretty bad. Give her time. You more than anybody should understand."

"Understand what?"

"What she's going through."

"I'm sick to death of everyone telling me how I feel or what I've been through. Not a damned one of you knows what I've suffered."

"Forget I said anything."

"Like you forgot your promise? I told you that we'd never speak of it again, amongst ourselves, or to anybody else. It's my business, and you damned well ought to give me that much respect."

"I never said anything to anyone, Molly. Promise you that," he said. "But I can tell you're still hurting. I wouldn't be any kind of a friend if I wasn't concerned for you."

"I've been hurt before, and I'll be damned if I'll let it turn me into what has become of Ruby. No man's going to break me like that."

Doc Chillingsworth shrugged. "No, I reckon not."

"Damn right." The anger in Molly's voice had softened and a quaver came into it. "I'm Red Molly, belle of the tracks, queen of the railroad from here to Chicago. You ask anyone."

Chillingsworth gave her a smile, but it was a sad one. "Goodbye, Molly. Look me up if you get to Canadian."

Molly realized that her face was suddenly flushed and that she had been talking too loud. She gave the doctor an apologetic look. "I'm going to miss you, Doc."

As she stepped out of the tent she heard the train coming up from the south, and she stood where she was, waiting to watch it arrive.

The train chugged slowly into the station with a hiss of released steam and the creak of the locomotive's wheel drivers and trunnions. It was a short train with only a locomotive and its tender car, three flatcars, and Superintendent Duvall's private Pullman on the tail end.

A crew of workers was riding on one of the flatcars and they immediately hopped off and went to the warehouse to begin loading railroad irons and other supplies and materials needed for work down the line. It was a good deal longer before two figures emerged from the Pullman. The first was Superintendent Duvall, and the second was a tall, slender blond woman in a fancy dress and hat. The superintendent stood at the foot of the stairs and took the woman's gloved hand as she stepped down to the depot decking.

Duvall unfolded a small lace parasol and handed it to her before the two of them headed Molly's way with the woman spinning the parasol over one shoulder and the bustle of her dress swaying like a treetop in the wind as she looked upon the desolate street with a slightly upturned chin. Molly was about to go to the Bullhorn, but the two were already close enough to her that she couldn't avoid them.

"Oh, look, dear, it's that Irish woman." The woman with Duvall said it with mocked pleasure, like she was some tourist taking a carriage ride through a city park and pointing out a quaint little squirrel begging for nuts, or some other novelty.

"How do you do?" Molly replied.

"Where are your manners, Willis? Tip your hat to the *lady,*" the woman continued in her New York accent and in an overly chipper way. And she emphasized the word "lady" as if there was something funny about it.

Duvall gave the woman an irritated look, as if to say there was no need for such politeness with a whore, but gave a slight tilt of his head to Molly and a half-hearted lift of his hat, anyway. "Hello, Red."

"Forgive Willis. He can be such a boor sometimes," the woman said. "Always with his mind on his railroad business. But you know how men are, don't you, Molly, dear?"

Molly caught the sharp jab meant by those last words, the same as she had the inference that she was no lady, but hid the irritation they caused. Helvina Vanderwagen may have been a rich gentlewoman, but she could be as snide as they came and her tongue was as sharp as Doc Chillingsworth's scalpels.

Molly looked her up and down from head to toe. Helvina was truly a rare looker with those blue eyes, skin like white porcelain, and that little dimple in her chin. Her corset was laced so tightly that it gave her a waspish waist, and the effect of it gave increased proportion to her chest. Molly knew Helvina was somewhere near her own age, but could have passed for a woman much younger.

Duvall shifted his feet out of impatience or boredom, obviously ready to be on his way. That movement caused Molly to take a step back, and Duvall noticed it for the flinch it was. A faint, gloating smirk formed on his mouth, and Molly stiffened and her chin began to quiver ever so slightly. The heat raced up her neck and to her face.

"I would have thought your *business* would have taken you to Canadian." Helvina leaned closer to Molly, and her expression was close to a conspiratorial wink. And she again gave a reminder of Molly's profession and how far below her own status Molly really was.

"I'm going to run the Bullhorn," Molly said.

"Do you hear that, Willis? She is going to run the saloon here," Helvina said. "Perhaps when we form a chamber of commerce you will invite her to join. We will need all of the fine, upstanding citizens and business people to participate if we are going to put Eufaula on the map."

"Have you purchased the Bullhorn from Mr. Tuck?" Duvall asked.

It was all Molly could do to stand so close to the man, and worse because she knew he recognized her discomfort and was enjoying that. She tried to steady herself. "No, I'm managing it for him, although, if things work out, perhaps I will make him an offer."

The thought that she might make an attempt to buy the Bullhorn was new to Molly, and she was surprised that she had said it.

"Running a business is no easy endeavor," he said.

"I can't imagine being a woman and running a saloon," Helvina said. "Having to deal with all those foul-mannered, drunken men, and with them pawing and leering at you."

Molly switched her attention to Helvina. The desire to slap the woman was something easier than trying to deal with the presence of Willis Duvall.

"I'm sure a *lady* like you would find a way to meet the challenge." Molly drug out the word "lady," exactly as Helvina had done earlier.

Helvina's face squinched tight, and her mouth made an ugly pucker, taking away some of her beauty. "Oh, I'm so sorry. You've taken insult, haven't you? You can't imagine how this embarrasses me. I assumed you meant to cease your former . . . mmm, profession. Pawing men must be old hat to you."

Molly's fists clenched, but she kept them at her side. "I will be running the saloon, and that's all."

Again, Molly's own words came as a shock to her. She didn't know whether she had let Helvina drive her to saying she would quit whoring, or if it was something that had been in the back of her mind all along.

"I'm sure Molly will do fine. She has always been a spirited girl," Duvall said, and there was that same smug smirk on his mouth. "Lot of fight in her."

If Molly had been wearing a gun then she would have killed him. But before she could do anything, Helvina placed one arm through the bend in Duvall's elbow and made as if to go.

"Did you notice the start of my new hotel?" Helvina asked.

"You're the one building the hotel?" Molly said, unable to hide her surprise.

Helvina gave a demure smile that was as close as she could come to modesty. "Oh, yes. Willis is building it for me as an engagement present. It's going to be quite grand when it's finished."

Of all the things that Molly had thought of Helvina Vanderwagen, her wanting to live in a backwater place like Ironhead wasn't one of them.

"Willis was going to name the whole town after me, but that was silly," Helvina said. "Although, this Eufaula thing might need to be changed. What will people think if we name the town with an Indian word? That's so heathen it's almost scandalous, and almost as bad as calling it Ironhead. People might not want to settle in a place with so little care for proper decorum."

"You use a lot of big words," Molly said.

"There are things called books and newspapers, and I must also admit to occasionally reading them."

"Bitch," Molly whispered through her gritted teeth.

"What's that, Molly? I think you are upset again. Perhaps you should go take your rest. The late hours you keep have worn on you. Sleep, dear, and I'm sure you will arise and feel a better woman." Helvina touched a dainty hand to Molly's forearm and then started Duvall off towards the hotel site. "Won't you pardon us? Willis is positively anxious to show me the beginning of my present. He's such a dear, isn't he?"

Molly squeezed her fists so tightly that her arms trembled with the strain.

"Oh, by the way," Helvina threw back over her shoulder. "How is your paramour?"

"My what?" Molly asked.

"How is dear Morgan? Is he around?" Helvina said. "Last I saw him he looked poorly."

"He left camp weeks ago." Molly knew that Helvina knew that as well as anyone did, but answered anyway.

"Poor Morgan. Such a handsome man, but always so predictable and boring. Flawed in ways that he can't help, and blind to all of them." Helvina spun her parasol with a flourish.

"Oh, you brazen, manky slag, what I wouldn't give for a wee clatter on that haughty puss you call a face," Molly said under her breath. It had been many years since Molly left Ireland and her speech had taken on a lot of the American, but her anger thickened her accent to the point she sounded like another woman, straight off the boat from the old country. "Prancing around like you're a real lady even though everybody knows how you're bulling for him and keeping his house. A hotel! Put on your fancy woman airs all ye want, but you earn your shillings on your back, same as the rest of us whores."

Helvina leaned against Duvall and giggled when they were farther away. When she spoke again it was meant to sound as if she was whispering to him, but purposefully loud enough to make sure Molly would hear her. "Can you imagine, Willis, a prostitute on a chamber of commerce?"

Duvall looked back at Molly over his shoulder, and the look he gave her wasn't at all humorous or flippant. It was cruel and hungry, and basking in the secret only he and Molly knew.

"You poxy, maggot bastard," Molly gushed, and spun on her heels and started down the street at a steady, determined clip, mumbling profanity to herself the whole way to her tent. She went inside and soon came out carrying the pearl-handled pistol Bill Tuck had given her. She marched through the back door of the Bullhorn Palace with the same determination and stride.

Ruby Ann had already arrived and was sweeping with a broom in the middle of the room, although what she was sweeping was lost on Molly. The Bullhorn had nothing but a dirt floor, and it was packed poorly. Clumps of dead grass and little rocks littered it amongst the wet spots from spilled beer, tobacco spit, and a roof that leaked like a sieve when it rained.

Ruby Ann looked at Molly, but said nothing. If she noticed the pistol, she didn't act like it. The man behind the bar appeared to be a little more skeptical about a woman brandishing a firearm barging into the tent.

Molly recognized him for one of Tuck's bartenders—a short

Italian that had busted his leg bone working on the railroad before Tuck had given him a job. Molly didn't know what his real name was, for no one called him anything but Noodles, a nickname given for the pasta he sometimes cooked for the free lunch the saloon occasionally offered its customers.

He took off his little round spectacles and began wiping at them with a bar towel, as if the lenses were dirty and he needed to clean them to make sure he was seeing what he was seeing.

"Are you all right, Molly?" he asked.

Molly said nothing, and marched across the room until she was at the front door. She pushed aside one of the canvas door flaps until a narrow view of the street was revealed. She shifted position slightly until she could see the hotel construction site. Duvall and Helvina were there with their backs to her, talking to one of their workers.

Molly cocked the Smith .32 and thrust it out the slit in the door she had opened. Her hand trembled with nervousness as much as it did anger, but she took a deep, ragged breath and aimed the pistol.

Chapter Fifteen

Molly tried her best to hold the pistol steady, but couldn't manage it. She grabbed up a nearby chair and dragged it over to the door. She sat down astraddle of it, facing backwards, and rested the pistol on the back of it.

She was aiming the pistol again when she felt Ruby Ann standing close against her. For a moment she ignored the girl, and focused on getting the pistol steady and pointed where she wanted it. But to her frustration, she found that the steady hold she wished for eluded her, even with the chair for a gun rest. It was a long shot, sixty yards or better, and the pistol's sights wavered and wobbled erratically across her target's back.

"He isn't worth it," Ruby Ann said in a whisper.

Molly looked at her, as much shocked that the woman had spoken again, and so many words, as she was angry to have been interrupted. "What he did to us can't stand."

Ruby Ann must have used up what little words she had for the day, and only looked somberly at Molly and shook her head as if the whole moment was the saddest thing in the whole wide world.

"Bollocks, girl, if we let him get away with it, then we don't matter at all," Molly said, and focused her attention back on aiming the pistol.

She experienced a steady moment and put her forefinger in the trigger guard, feeling gently for the trigger. Footsteps sounded behind her, and a hand grabbed the pistol around the barrel. The gun went off into the ground barely in front of the door, kicking up a little hole in the dirt of the road and ricocheting over the heads of the workers across the street loading a wagon with the debris from Irish Dave's burnt saloon.

Molly looked up and saw Noodles looking down at her. She tried to yank the pistol free, but he wrestled it from her grasp. She lunged to her feet and swung a wild fist at him and then another, but he dodged and turned his back on her and returned to the bar.

She watched him, breathing heavily. Her exertion brought on a fit of coughing, and she hunched over with one hand to her mouth. Someone pressed a handkerchief to her, and when she looked up it was Ruby Ann who held it. She took the handkerchief and held it to her mouth until the coughing subsided.

And then she glanced out the slit in the door and saw the commotion that her gunshot had caused. A crowd was forming across the street, and people were pointing at the saloon. She got away from the door, suddenly feeling conspicuous, even though she was sure none of them could see her. She looked at Ruby Ann, but only got that same sad look. She frowned at Ruby and went to the bar.

"Give me back my gun," she said to Noodles.

"No. Much trouble it make for you, I think," he said in his Italian accent, and he put the gun under the bar out of sight.

Molly was about to argue or take another swing at him, but the sound of someone outside her door stopped her. She turned in time to see the two federal deputy marshals barge through the door flaps. Both were tall men, with matching long mustaches, high-topped boots, and big hats.

"Who fired that shot?" one of them asked in no gentle way.

Molly was trying to think of an excuse when Noodles beat her to it.

"It was an accident." He pulled the pistol slowly from under the bar and laid it down on the bar top.

The sight of the pistol caused both of the marshals to put hands to their own sidearms, but they quickly relaxed when they saw the friendly smile and sheepish, ashamed look Noodles gave them.

"I was cleaning the *pistola* for Signora Testa Rosa, and it went off," Noodles said.

"Sig what?"

Noodles gestured at her. "Signora Molly. Her."

One of the marshals went across the room and took up the pistol. He gave Molly a frowning glance, moved that look on to Noodles, and then finally cracked open the Smith pocket pistol and unloaded it. He noted the one fired and empty case that he ejected into his palm, and then he smelled the end of the barrel as if to confirm it was, indeed, the gun that had been fired into the street.

"Is this your belly gun?" he asked Molly.

"No, it belongs to Bill Tuck. He doesn't like anybody to touch it, and he'll be mad when he realizes he left it."

The lawman took a closer look at the cartridges in his palm. "A .32 won't do you much good if you really need a gun. Not enough pop and not enough bullet to put a man down quick."

"I don't know much about guns," she said.

"That's right. If I remember correctly, you told me you didn't own one the last time we talked." The deputy marshal looked closely at her when he said that, as if looking for something in her reaction, then looked at his partner. The other lawman's expression was hard to read.

"If that's Tuck's gun, what were you doing cleaning it?" the marshal at the bar asked Noodles.

Molly butted in before Noodles could answer. "I spilled some water on it wiping the bar down, and asked him to clean it so that Tuck wouldn't be mad if he found it rusted up."

"You ought to be careful cleaning guns," the marshal at the bar said to Noodles. "Worst thing in the world is a loaded gun someone thinks is unloaded."

"I new to your country," Noodles said. "No so many guns in Italy."

"Well, at least you speak passable English. I can't understand half of what the other Dagos working on the line try to say."

The marshal put the pistol back on the bar top, along with its cartridges. He looked at Ruby Ann. "Is that the way it was? He was cleaning the gun?"

Ruby Ann didn't answer him, and went and took up her broom again and began sweeping.

"She doesn't talk," Molly said.

"You mean she's a mute?" he asked.

"I mean she doesn't speak much."

"We know her," the marshal by the door said. "We went to the hospital tent twice to question her, but didn't get a word out of her either time."

"Thought it might not hurt to try again," the marshal at the bar added.

Ruby Ann didn't seem to hear them, and kept sweeping. Molly looked from one marshal to the other. The wisp and scrape of Ruby Ann's broom was the only sound in the tent for a moment.

"Sorry to be a bother," Molly said to break the silence. "How about a free drink to square things?"

"No thanks," the marshal at the bar beside her said. You know we ought to haul you three in for peddling whiskey in the Nations."

"This saloon is on the railroad right of way," Molly said.

"Whether that matters is questionable. I could haul you in and let the court decide it."

"It would be a lot less trouble if you would let us buy you

two a drink."

The marshal by the door cleared his throat. "Miss O'Flanagan, you aren't going anywhere, are you?"

"Not that I know of. Why do you ask?"

"We might want to talk to you again."

"About what?"

"About the murder of Johnny Tubbs. There are still a few matters there that we aren't comfortable with."

"I told you all I know the last time we spoke. I knew the man's name, knew what he looked like, same as most in camp. But that's it. He was never one of my customers, and I don't know why you keep asking me about him."

"We're asking because somebody shot him full of holes while he was sitting in an outhouse."

"I'm sure you will get to the bottom of it."

"The outhouse or the crime?" the marshal by the bar said, and then chuckled. There was a twinkle in his eyes, and he tugged at one end of his mustache as if in thought.

"If Tubbs was the one who . . . the one who assaulted you and that woman there," the other marshal pointed at Ruby Ann, "then there are some that might say you had good reason to shoot him dead."

"You've said that before, and I've told you before that your assumptions of what happened to me are unfounded."

"Everybody in camp knows that you were beaten, and there are other rumors that . . ." the marshal stumbled over what he was about to say, obviously uncomfortable with speaking to a woman about her rape.

She felt the anger rising in her again. Lawmen or not, she hated them for digging into her own suffering, as if it were nothing more than another item on their list of duties or another piece of paper for the court docket. They thought she had motive, but what did they really know of motive? She had been on her own since she was twelve years old, and in that time, she had borne more than her share of wounds, inside and out, taking her licks, but survived in spite of it all. Truth be known, she had reason to kill a dozen men, and half that many women who had wronged or wounded her in various ways. There were two worlds out there, one for those that could afford it, and a nastier one for those that couldn't. Yet, she didn't complain, she didn't whine, and she didn't ask for help. She had learned early that no one cared and no one could fix the problems that mattered, and the ones that cried didn't make it long.

She had gotten Johnny Tubbs for what he did to her, handled it on her own. If the sorry little bastard had fallen off his horse and cracked his head there wasn't anyone in the world who would have cared or bothered to mourn for him. And yet there these lawmen stood, judging her and thinking only they or some court had the right to pass sentence on such a man. Crime? Tubbs dying was no crime. That was justice. What he did to her was the crime, and these prying lawmen poking around in the memory was another crime.

"If I was raped, don't you think I would report it?" Molly's voice rose considerably louder, no matter how much she told herself she needed to stay calm to fool them and to play their game and win. It was hard, feeling what she was feeling and thinking what she was thinking, only to say other things. Lying when she shouldn't have to lie. Talking about what she didn't want to talk about and as if it meant nothing to her.

The marshal seemed nonplussed, but patient. "Maybe you don't want to admit what happened to you out of shame. Maybe you wouldn't tell if you thought you had other ways to tend to the matter."

Molly gave a patient sigh. "From what little I knew of Mr. Tubbs, he was unpleasant and quarrelsome when drinking, and my thinking is that there might be plenty who he gave insult to."

"Well, he hasn't any enemies now. The one that did it made sure of that," the marshal said.

"I wish you luck," she said.

"What I always say about solving these kind of crimes is find the simplest reason and the person that reason belongs to and you've likely found your culprit."

The marshal at the bar laid a dollar on the bar top in front of Noodles. "How about you sell me one of those pickled eggs out of that jar yonder? I always did like a pickled egg."

Noodles took the lid off the jar and took one of the eggs out of it with a pair of tongs and handed it to the marshal. The lawman popped it in his mouth and chewed on it while he watched Noodles pull out the cashbox out from under the bar. Before the bartender could make change for him, the marshal reached over the bar and took a five-dollar piece.

"Thanks for the change," the marshal said, still chewing on the egg with his mouth open, and with dried yellow yoke meat stuck to his teeth.

Noodles was about to point out to the lawman that he had taken five dollars when he had only laid down a dollar to pay for the egg, but Molly caught his attention and shook her head at him to let it lie.

The marshal looked at them all while he sucked the egg off his teeth, as if daring them to say anything about his robbing the till. Apparently having made his point, he tipped his hat to Molly and Ruby Ann and then he and his partner disappeared through the door flaps.

Molly took a deep breath and then looked at Noodles. The bartender took off his wool cap and ran his fingers through his black hair while he watched the door. She saw him, too, let out a sigh of relief that the marshals were gone, and then heard him muttering something under his breath in his native language. She assumed it had something to do with crooked marshals, for the tone of it was a good fit, even if she couldn't understand the words.

"Thanks. I owe you one," Molly said.

"Signor Tuck, he say you run things, and now I work for you and him," Noodles said.

"Thanks, just the same. That bit about you cleaning the gun was quick thinking."

"Who was it out there?"

"What do you mean?"

"The one you want to shoot on the street?"

"I get to ask the questions while I run things." Molly gestured at a bottle of Old Reserve on the back wall. "Pour me one and let's see what you know about bartending."

He poured her a shot, then doubled it when she motioned for more.

"Those *poliziotti,* you think they will come back?" he asked.

"You mean those marshals?"

"Sí."

Molly turned her glass up and downed the whiskey in one swallow. She waited for the liquor to hit bottom, and felt almost instantly steadier when it did. "They'll come back."

"What will you do? They steal from Signor Tuck."

"I'll talk to Tuck and see how he wants to handle it. Don't worry about it for now. Those aren't the first coppers to put the squeeze on me, and they probably won't be the last."

She motioned to him to pour another double, and thought on her situation while she waited for the drink. The marshals' little shakedown operation wasn't what concerned her most about them. Those marshals were going to make what she had to do that much harder, and it was hard enough as it was. And she wanted to win just this one time.

She said his name, not out loud, but in her mind. Willis Duvall. Tubbs had only been the henchman, fetching flesh for his master and supping on the leftover scraps. Yes, he had raped her, too, same as his master had, but he was done for, and only Duvall remained. Only one piece of justice left undone.

The night Willis Duvall had called her to his private car she had assumed nothing would be different than usual, other than he had more money to spend than the usual John. And the thing that was hard to admit to herself was that she had stepped into the trap as blindly and foolishly as a youngling. She had been flattered by his attention, the rich railroad man, and the ridiculous amount of money he had offered to sleep with her. So flattered and so caught up in the thought of the money, she had put on her best dress. And then that Tubbs had come to fetch her and took her to Duvall's car. And he stood outside and guarded the door while Duvall showed her what he really expected for his money. A good honest hump wasn't what he wanted. He liked hurting women, and he liked hurting them bad.

She had known many men, good and bad, and most of them somewhere in between. And their lusts and their fetishes had long since ceased to surprise her. But Willis Duvall, he was another sort. Sick and twisted, he was. First poor Ruby Ann, and then her. And no telling how many more women he had defiled, and how many more were to come—those who had yet to learn about monsters.

Molly had known since she was a girl that monsters really did exist, and not under your bed or in your closet, or hiding in dark woods along lonely roadsides. They walked and talked amongst you, most times looking no different than anyone else. No different on the outside, but with the black hole of Hell carried inside them.

She tossed the second whiskey down, and it was bitter in her throat. She would be the victim no more. She promised herself that as she had a thousand times.

She went to Ruby Ann and took her gently by the arm. "Let's take your things to my tent, and then we can come back and get this place revved up and ready for business."

Ruby Ann gave her another one of those somber, unreadable looks, but went along.

"He's a monster," Molly said as they walked out the back door of the saloon. "You know that, don't you?"

"Don't do it," Ruby Ann said in a whisper so quiet that Molly had to lean close to hear her. "They'll hang you for it."

Molly put an arm over Ruby Ann's shoulders and hugged her close to her side as they walked towards the tent. "I'll get him. Not only for you and me, but for all of us."

A single tear rolled down Ruby Ann's cheek.

"Don't cry, Ruby Ann. Both of us know it doesn't do any good."

Chapter Sixteen

Morgan looked back behind him at the first light leaking up from the eastern horizon. He had made maybe twenty miles, maybe more, since slipping off the hilltop in the middle of the night, walking at a steady clip and following the river upstream. He had drunk his belly full and left the Salt Fork in the wee hours of the morning, aiming southwestwards and hoping to find more broken country, but still found himself on the plains with daylight rapidly approaching.

He wanted to sit down and rest, and he wanted to sleep, but the Kingman brothers were somewhere behind him, and the Traveler . . . who knew where he was? So, he pushed on, with his heavy rifle laid across both shoulders behind his neck. Often, he checked his back trail, and just as often he stopped to perceive some movement he thought he detected in the distance ahead of him. Each time he made such a pause, he knew he was giving the Kingmans time to catch up to him, if they were truly behind and had not passed him in the night.

The sun was almost directly overhead by the time he could see the ribbon of green marking some kind of watercourse ahead of him. He picked his pace up to a trot. Twice he crossed dry watercourses and gullies on his way towards that line of green, the dust at their bottoms torturing him with thirst and increasing his desire to reach the river ahead.

He could see what looked like red bluffs rising up the south on the far side of that line of green, and they grew in size as he neared them. Closer to them, his heart jumped upon seeing the shine of sunlight on water, and his raw throat could already feel the wetness, even so far away from it. An hour later he splashed into the shallow water spread out over a wide, sandy bed. He lay on his belly in the shadow of the bluffs and drank like a dog, sucking and lapping and dunking his head when his belly could hold no more. And then he waded across the river, his intent to climb the bluff to where he could look over his back trail. But instead, he lay down in a clump of willows and went to sleep. A short nap and another drink, and then he would move on again.

It was dark by the time he woke, and he went to the water and drank again. He had no canteen, but improvised. He took his powder flask from his shooting bag and emptied its contents into a rag he normally used for cleaning his guns. He tied the rag bundle at the top, put it back in the bag, and filled the now empty powder flask with water. He took a sip from the flask. The water tasted like sulphur and the flask held little more than three or four drinks, but it was better than nothing.

He topped the flask off with water, and drank again from the river before he rose to his feet. The moonlight lit the water like a sheet of glass, and he used that light as a guide to climb the bluff. Once more he moved southwestward, slower than before, stumbling in the dark occasionally, resting more and more often, but moving on, regardless. Distance is what he needed—distance and time to feed himself and perhaps find another horse.

Daylight came once more and revealed a change in the land around him. Instead of lush, grassy plains like those to the north, the vegetation and the terrain took on a more arid appearance. The only trees were a few, scraggly cedars growing along the gullies and other low brush barely the height of a man that raked against Morgan's body like old bones scraping over him. The buffalo grass became thin and patchy, and the bare spots revealed red earth. Scattered tumbleweeds and an occasional prickly pear cactus or yucca plant appeared, growing from the cracked and thirsty ground as if they had thrust it apart.

A line of scattered buttes or mesas rose up to the south, the tallest of them only a couple of hundred feet high. Most of them were as flat-topped as a dining table and their sides were of the same, eroded red earth as that beneath his feet. Even the wind blew red, bearing dust ground as fine as cornmeal, and dust that stuck to the rim of his eyes and worked its way inside his collar and to every joint in his body to rub him raw. The whole countryside hinted at nothing so much as an old, dry bloodstain, slowly blowing away.

He forged forward on aching and weary legs, his knee joints as hot and dry as the wind, and his eyes heavy-lidded. The rifle felt like it weighed twice as much as normal on his shoulders, pressing him downwards until he was sure that he would soon be absorbed into the blood red ground.

As he neared the closest butte, he thought he saw something twinkling on its side. He dropped to the ground in a panic, thinking that the sparkle was the flash of sunlight on the lens of a riflescope. Lying on his belly, and shoving back the brim of his hat, he brought the Moore rifle to his shoulder and searched the butte through the scope tube.

In a short time, he thought he realized what had caused the twinkling. The butte was banded in a couple of places with a thin line or horizon of what looked like white stone that was probably gypsum. Something in that white stone was reflecting sunlight, whether it was quartz or some other mineral, he could not tell.

Still cautious, he made another long search of the butte with his riflescope, but found nothing to hint of a gunman on its heights. He rose with effort, dusted his hat off on his thigh, shouldered the rifle, and started walking again. He aimed for a gap between the butte he had been watching and another, smaller one to the east of it. He knew next to nothing of the country, beyond bits of conversation he had overhead from men who had traveled through it. The river he had crossed the day before, he assumed to be the Cimarron. If so, then the chain of buttes before him should be the Glass Mountains. Perhaps the glint of light he had seen had something to do with their name.

He walked on, and was almost within the pass between the two buttes when he saw the rise of dust behind him between his position and the river he had left. It was not a dust devil he saw, but bigger than that. It was the kind of dust cloud stirred up by many hooves. It could be a herd of buffalo, or it could be horses. Horses likely meant that there were men on their backs.

He turned and started up the side of the biggest butte. He didn't want to be caught on level ground with no cover, and the dust cloud was rapidly coming his way.

The sides of the butte were steep on the south-facing slope, but he found a long ridge, like a chord of muscle stretching from the butte's top to the plain below, and used it to ascend. The top layer of the butte was made of the white gypsum rock he had seen from a distance, and when he reached the summit he saw that it was an almost solid sheet of the stuff littered with fist-sized chunks where wind and rain and freezing temperatures had shaped it and broken it. He picked one of the gypsum chunks up and saw that it was speckled with tiny crystals.

By the time he took a seated position on the lip of the butte where he could see to the north, the dust cloud had wormed its way across the plain to within a quarter of a mile of him. He took the last sip from his improvised canteen while he watched, and put it back in his shooting bag.

Shortly, he could make out the lead riders emerging from the dust cloud. They were Indians, and the more he watched the more he saw that there were a lot of them.

Behind the warriors in the lead, and between those riding at the flanks of the march, appeared woman and children, all mounted. Other horses without riders had an A-frame of long poles tied to their backs, and on that frame were bundles of their belongings and the tanned buffalo hides to erect their lodges. Dogs ran in and out of the procession, and a herd of loose horses trailed the procession, driven and herded by young boys.

Morgan watched the Indians come closer. He could see them good enough by then to pick out the flutter of feathers decorating the warriors' heads and to see that many of them carried rifles in addition to the bows and quivers protruding from their backs. Most of the warriors were all but naked, clothed only by the moccasins on their feet and a long strip of cloth, a breechcloth that ran between their legs and tucked into the front and back of their belt. The woman showed far less brown skin, and wore sleeveless buckskin dresses, many decorated with fringe or bead and quillwork. Morgan did not know what tribe they were, but could not help but be impressed with the sight of them.

All of the band before him rode like they were born to a horse, and he recalled the things he had heard about the prowess of the plains tribes when it came to horseback warfare . . . or any kind of fighting if it came to that. He looked back down the way he had ascended the butte and wondered what the odds were of them not finding his tracks if they continued their line of travel. He might hold them off for a while if they were inclined to make trouble for him, but there were enough of them that it would only be a matter of time before they overran him.

He checked the percussion cap on his Moore rifle and then lay down on his belly and put the scope's crosshairs on the

Indian warrior closest to him. The twenty-power telescopic sight had cost him a small fortune in his earlier life, before the war and before guns became a tool of his normal living. He turned the focus knob until the warrior jumped to life in the circular field of view that the optic afforded him. It was maybe a two-hundred-yard shot, and at that distance he could see the facial features of his target—an older man, his face seamed with wrinkles as if it were leather that had been folded and creased and then unfolded again. His hair was long, parted in the middle and worn in two braids over either shoulder. A single brown eagle feather was tied into one of the braids, and his dark eyes were like pinpricks of coal.

Morgan cocked his rifle, but did not fire. He watched and he waited, knowing that any advantage he may have had by keeping the Indians at a distance was rapidly disappearing, but reluctant to fire upon those who had done him no harm. The fear of what he had heard such warriors did to their captives made that a hard proposition, but he did not shoot.

As if they were drawn to him on a rope, the band headed straight for the same gap between the buttes that he had intended to pass through. He kept low and moved to where he could watch them pass virtually straight under his position, careful not to skyline himself. The band of Indians rode right over his tracks and none seemed to notice them, although several in the band did look up to the butte tops.

They were almost past him when one of the mongrel dogs with them stopped and sniffed where Morgan had started his ascent of the butte. The hair on its back stuck up almost straight, and Morgan could hear it growl. One of the warriors doubled back to see what the dog had found. He was young, and maybe not a true warrior at all, but rather an adolescent boy. He looked at the ground behind the dog while it sniffed farther up the slope, and then he said something to it that sounded like he was scolding it. Morgan let out a sigh of relief as he watched the boy leave to catch up with the rest of his people, and it was only then that he realized that he had been holding his breath.

He watched the Indians for a long while until they disappeared to the south behind another of the mesas there. He remained where he was after that, unwilling to move until nightfall and wanting the Indians as far away from him as possible before he moved.

It wasn't quite nightfall when he saw the glow of the Indians' campfires not two miles away. And then something else caught his attention. It was another tiny, flickering orange glow in the distance beyond the Indians' camp and a little to the southwest of it. Instead of multiple fires, it looked to be a single fire. From the Indians' position down on the plain, they probably couldn't see it.

Morgan wondered if that lone campfire belonged to the Traveler or the Kingmans. There was a chance that it was someone else, but the odds were against that. Only a white man would build such a fire so easy to see in unfriendly country, and if it were a party of buffalo hunters or soldiers the same odds said there would be a bigger fire or more than one. There had been a time when Morgan made his living speculating on what business ventures might succeed or fail and what investments might prove prudent and profitable. And business was so similar to gambling that there should be no distinction between the two other than the name. A good businessman, like a good gambler, always considered the odds.

He chuckled quietly. He was honest with himself enough to know that if he had been a good businessman he would still be in New York watching stock tickers and following the price of commodities instead of risking his life in the middle of nowhere. He wouldn't have lost every single dollar he had on the quick profit represented by five shiploads of Mississippi cotton. One storm and three sunken ships later, and he was broke without a single prospect to fix his situation. He had taken his first policeman's job after that, walking patrol in the slums of the Bowery or the Five Points. A failure as a businessman, maybe, but still, he was a man that considered the angles. He had to assume that lone campfire meant as little good to him as those belonging to the Indians. To do less could do far worse than break him. It could get him killed.

His stomach growled, as if it needed to remind him that he hadn't eaten in two days. He wondered how long a man could go without nourishment, and he looked to the Indian camp and considered that there was food there, as well as horses. A risky proposition, yes, but an opportunity for the man that could pull it off.

He waited several hours before he came down to the plain, watching the Indians' campfires while he walked. He wondered what the odds were of being able to keep those camp dogs from realizing his presence and barking until the whole camp was alerted. And he wondered what chance he stood of slipping into that camp and away again with a horse and with his scalp intact. He hoped he had got better at gambling since his younger days, and winced as he remembered that the last time he had played poker he had lost a month's pay.

His boots crunched over the dry ground, strangely loud to his ears as he neared the Indian camp.

Chapter Seventeen

Willis Duvall dropped the stub of his cigar to the depot decking and ground it out with the toe of his shoe while he waited for Helvina to climb the stairs up to his private railroad car. Her starched dress scraped on the steps and cast-iron bannister, and temporarily blocked his view up the length of the train towards the engine. When he could see again, the first thing he saw was the engineer leading a young black woman towards him. The engineer looked put out with something, but Duvall was too caught up in the young woman to wonder what it was.

She was probably somewhere in her mid-twenties, slim, and so feathery light on her feet that it dawned on Duvall that he had never seen a woman move so gracefully, even carrying the cheap carpetbag in one hand like she was.

"I done told her, Mr. Duvall, this ain't no regular passenger train," the engineer said.

Duvall barely heard the man. All of his attention was on the black woman and the way her fine cut cheekbones gave definition to the beauty of her face, framed inside a plain bonnet laced under her chin. Her skin was the color of oiled teak wood, and the hot day had given it a waxy shine.

"I told her the regular line ends here for now," the engineer added.

"I only want to catch a ride to Canadian Camp," the woman said. "I'll pay my fare. Wasn't trying to free ride on your train."

Duvall listened to the throaty way she spoke and watched the flexing of her long neck beneath the high collar of her dress. He had seen many black women, but they had never held interest for him until that moment. Somehow, instead of a poor negro girl, she struck him as exotic, and there was no denying the rarity of her beauty.

"You come on, now. This is the superintendent's private car." The engineer laid a gentle arm on the woman's elbow. "You come on, now. I got a schedule to keep."

"Hold on there," Duvall said.

He realized that the cigar butt was still smoking beside his foot, and ground it into the boards again as if he were angry at it. When he looked up, the woman had held her ground against the insistence of the engineer and was staring at him with defiant eyes.

"What makes you want to go to Canadian, girl?" Duvall asked.

Calling her "girl" brought a stubborn set to her little chin, and her full lips tightened as if she was about to snap at him. But she composed herself, pulled her elbow away from the engineer, and stood a little straighter while she smoothed the front of her dress.

Duvall barely suppressed a smile. *Oh, she was a proud one. Didn't like her place and thought she was above it.*

"My man is in Canadian," she said.

"Your man?"

"Yes, sir. I believe he works for you, Mr. Duvall. Saul Goldsby is his name."

The engineer saw the perplexed look on his boss's face and rode to the rescue. "I believe he's one of your cooks, Mr. Duvall."

"Ah." Duvall nodded his head, recalling the black man who had worked in the mess tent since they were first in Kansas. He couldn't remember the cook's face, but he did remember that the man cooked a good breakfast and made tolerable coffee.

"We are to be married," the woman added.

"Is that so?" Duvall said.

"I tried to tell her that there ain't no place for her to stay in Canadian," the engineer said.

Duvall noticed the way her dress top clung tightly to her breasts, and wondered if that flesh beneath it was as high and tight as it appeared to be and what her nipples would look like.

"Did you hear me, Mr. Duvall?" the girl said. "Saul and I are to be married. I've been working up at Fort Scott tending to a lady's children and keeping house for her for the past two years, but Saul wrote me nearly every month."

"You met Saul in Kansas?" Duvall asked.

"No, we've known each other since we were children. Been saving our money so we could be together. He's waiting on me, and expects me to be there today."

Duvall pulled his attention away from her chest and tried to act like he had been listening to her the whole time. "Saved your money, huh?"

"Yes, sir. I'll pay a fair ticket," she said. "I'm a hard worker and no freeloader. I intend to find a job in your camp as soon as I can."

"Let her ride," Duvall said to the engineer.

The engineer frowned, but pointed to the nearest flatcar loaded with a stack of chained-down rails and barrels of spikes. "You can ride up there if you can find you a place."

"No need for that," Duvall said. "She can ride with us."

The engineer had started to head for his place in the cab of the locomotive, but hesitated. He gave the superintendent a look that said he was shocked that his boss would let a negro girl ride in his private car. The look Duvall gave him back said that there would be no talk on that point. The engineer hustled toward the front of the train with a couple of backward looks.

Duvall offered his hand to help the woman up the steps and pointed at his private car with the other. "Please join us."

"No, sir, I couldn't," the black woman said.

"I thought you were bound and determined to go to Canadian," he said. "I am, but . . ."

"What did you say your name was? I didn't catch it."

"Hannah," she said. "Hannah Cole."

"Well, Hannah. Let's go to Canadian."

She was hesitant, but made up her mind with a brave sigh. "I thank you, Mr. Duvall. I surely do."

She put her foot on the first step, but the sound of someone clearing her throat stopped her. Both she and Duvall looked up and saw Helvina Vanderwagen standing on the platform. She had opened the door into the car but had not entered it. Instead, she stood there looking at them with no kind expression on her face and both arms crossed over her chest.

"What have we here, Willis?" she said.

He gave her a level look. "Why, this is Miss Hannah Cole."

"And why are you holding on to her?"

"She needs a ride to Canadian."

"And why can't she ride somewhere else?" Helvina looked Hannah up and down, and the tone of her voice was as cold as the prim set of her mouth.

"Because she works for me," he said.

Both women looked at Duvall with surprise.

"I do?" Hannah finally asked.

Helvina said nothing, and her cold stare had shifted to him.

"Yes, she's to be our new maid and cook," he said.

"Is she?" Helvina replied.

"You were just saying this morning how you wished for a better laundry service, and complaining about how filthy I kept the Pullman."

Helvina looked back at Hannah and gave a scoffing grunt.

She remained where she was for a long moment, arms still crossed and blocking the top of the steps. But, finally, she went inside the passenger car and closed the door behind her.

"Don't think anything of that," Duvall said to Hannah. "Helvina is slow to take to the help, that's all."

"We never talked about me working for you," Hannah said.

"Do you want the job or not? You said you were seeking employment."

"I . . . I . . ." she stuttered.

"Maybe you think maid's work is beneath you."

"No, sir, I . . ."

"You talk like you've had some education. Strange in a woman of your . . . uh, your people."

"You mean for a colored girl?"

"That's right."

"Well, Mr. Duvall, they've got schools for colored folk, too, now. I spent three years at the Freedman University at Quindaro."

"Did you now?"

"I did." Her chin lifted slightly.

"Where's this university at? Never heard of it."

"Kansas."

"And what did they teach you?"

"I went two years to preparatory school, and the last year I learned to be a teacher."

"Well, all I have is a maid's job to fill, but I assure you that you won't find a better job if you're dead set on coming to the camp to be with your fiancé."

"I'm not the least bit uppity. I worked at worse."

"Good. Now, are you getting on this train, or are you staying here?"

"What's this job pay?" she asked.

"A dollar and a half a day."

"How about two dollars?"

"I don't even know if you can cook."

"You don't know if I can do laundry, neither." She gave him a smile, and there was something in it that he was slow to recognize. And there was a look in her eyes that he finally realized said she wasn't as oblivious to his attentions as he had thought.

He stared at her until she looked down at the ground. He smiled at that, pleased. *Uppity negro flirting with him like she was white. Pretty thing, and used to getting her way with those smiles and a bat of her brown eyes and a wiggle of that dress she had bought a size too small.*

"Two dollars, then."

She looked up at the door leading into the car and bit her lower lip. He could tell what she was worrying about.

"Don't worry about Helvina. She's only mad at me, that's all. It's been a long day and she's tired."

"You mean to tell me you're going to let a colored woman ride in this fancy railroad car of yours? A rich man like you?" she asked.

He pointed at the door of the Pullman. "This is where I live, and you're my maid now."

"And if I didn't go to work for you? Would you let me ride in your car?"

"I'm from Indiana, Miss Cole. We pride ourselves on being quite a bit more civilized and sensitive to your plight than these Southerners you may have grown used to," he said, with a tad of impatience creeping into his voice. "You seem like a decent young lady."

Hannah turned on the steps and looked at where the construction crew was working on the foundation for the hotel. "They say you're building that for her."

"I am," he said.

She looked him up and down, as if appraising him. "You're a man used to buying things, aren't you, Mr. Duvall?"

Her question caused him to smile. "Why do you ask?"

"That lady I worked for up in Fort Scott had lots of money. Everybody said so. But she didn't pay me but a dollar a day."

"You get what you pay for, and I like fine things, Hannah. Always have."

"Fine things?"

"Fine like you."

She thought on that for a moment, her face expressionless. Then she gave him the same smile as she had before, giggled, and waved a hand at him as if to dismiss what he said. "I see you're a kidder, too."

He watched her go up the steps, her hips swishing her dress side to side in a fashion that would rival even the way Helvina walked. When she was at the top of the steps and at the door she stopped and looked back at him with that smile again.

"I'll take your job, Mr. Duvall."

"Good," he said as he followed her up and held the door open for her.

Bill Tuck came down to watch the train arrive in Canadian. The saloon owner scraped the edge of one hand against his shaved scalp and slung the sweat on it away. He leaned one shoulder against a telegraph pole and worked his gold toothpick around in his mouth while the train hissed and groaned like a tired old dragon and its running gear screeched to a stop. He made a habit of watching the arrivals to see who came and went. Knowing such things often came in handy, and information was always a kind of power few men recognized.

With lazy-eyed boredom he watched the workers climb down off the flatcar, and go to unbooming the chains that secured the loads of rails and other construction material. He was about to turn and walk back to the Crow's Nest when Willis Duvall and his New York woman stepped out of their passenger car.

While he enjoyed watching the New York woman, it wasn't her that caused him to pause and retake his stance against the telegraph pole. It was the black woman that came down the steps behind them.

The trio went towards the mess tent, with the black woman staying a couple of steps behind them. Twice, the New York woman turned around to say something to her. Even at a distance too far to make out what she was saying, he could tell by her expression that she was scolding the black woman or giving her some kind of orders.

When the three of them reached the mess tent, the superintendent and the New York woman turned and started back to their railroad car while the black woman stayed there. The New York woman never looked back, but Duvall watched the black woman until she disappeared inside the tent.

Tuck worked the toothpick to the other side of his mouth and his white teeth slowly showed themselves in a grin. "What have we here, Mr. Duvall? Are you at it again?"

Tuck started back to his saloon, as pleased as he had been in many days.

Saul was reluctant to let Hannah out of his embrace, but he finally quit hugging her long enough to push her to arm's length and take a good look at her.

"Lord, I'm glad to see you, girl," he said. "Thought you was never gonna git here."

"I'm here." Her smile was as big and bright as his own.

"I thought your train was comin' yesterday. Waited all day for you."

"The train put me off at Ironhead Station, but I caught a ride today with Mr. Duvall."

"The superintendent?"

"That's him. He gave me a ride in his private car."

"He didn't."

"Yes, he did."

Saul pushed her a little farther away, and looked closely at her face. "How come him to do that?"

"I'm going to work for him."

Saul let go of her. "You what?"

"He's paying me two dollars a day to cook and clean for him." She reached for him, but he dodged away.

"You ain't workin' for him. Thought we planned you was goin' to set yourself up doin' laundry for the camp like that Missus Bickford I told you about. She do well at it."

"Two dollars a day, Saul. You hear me? And it's easy work."

"I don't like you workin' for him."

"You work for him." Her smile disappeared and her tone changed.

"I ain't a woman."

"I told you he seems nice," she said. "Rich white man, but nice for all of that."

"I seen the way he looks at women. That man gots a rovin' eye, and probably rovin' hands if truth be known."

"Saul Goldsby, you jealous man. Don't you think I know how to handle myself? My momma was a house slave for most her life until she run off to Kansas. And I've been working around flirty white men since I was a girl."

"Ain't no woman of mine gonna . . ."

"What, Saul?"

"I won't have it."

She put both hands on her hips and leaned towards him. "I come here expecting you to be happy at us finally getting to be together, and now you are pouting like a baby and puffing out your chest and telling me what I'm going to do and what I'm not?"

He gave her a sheepish look, but the stubbornness came back in the set of his chin. "I is glad you's here, Hannah. Believe me I is. It just ain't what we planned."

She reached for him, wrapping her arms about him. "Two dollars, Saul. Do you know how much that is? That's sixty dollars a month. We can have enough money to move to that farm quicker than we ever thought."

He hugged her close and pressed his face into her neck, and it muffled his words. "I know, but the superintendent can be mean. I was only lookin' out for you."

"I don't think he's so bad."

"Maybe not. But you quit him if he's mean to you."

She pulled him closer. "Don't you worry. I can handle Mr. Duvall."

Chapter Eighteen

The Indian camp was quiet, and even the flames of their campfires had burned down to nothing but the lava glow of coals pulsing with each breeze like slowly throbbing hearts across the black plain from where Morgan stood.

He slipped closer, stopping often, partially out of caution, and partially to gather his courage. If one dog barked, if he stumbled or if he made too much noise and woke them, he was dead, or worse. He understood that an Indian could make a captive's dying last a long time.

The cloud that had granted him the cover of pure darkness passed on, and the revealed moon left him exposed. He stood there, not one hundred yards from the camp, a tall, stick thing with jointed bones made of whitewashed shadow, and the white of his staring eyes floating in the black nothing of his face like little moons themselves.

Whatever kind of Indians they were, they must have intended to move on with the dawn, for they had not erected their buffalo hide lodges like they would have for a semipermanent camp, and they had merely went to sleep in their robes around the various fires. Their baggage and their belongings lay heaped close to them, some still on the travois poles they had stripped from their packhorses.

One of the dogs bedded amongst its masters must have seen him or smelled him with a shift of the wind, for it growled deep in its throat. Morgan expected every one of the dogs to rise up and begin barking, and he waited and counted the moments by his heartbeats. And then the dog lay back down and quieted.

There was no way he was going to slip close enough to steal some food, so he moved to a safer distance from the camp and walked a quiet half-circle around it, listening and searching the moonlight-washed ground for sentinels, and most of all looking for their horse herd.

He heard the horses before he saw them—heard the scuff of their hooves on the dry grass, and the leathery snuffle of their exhales through their muzzles. And then they were shadow shapes before him, some rolling on the ground to scratch the dried sweat and matted hair from their bodies after a long day's journey, and he saw the dust floating off them like smoke in the moonlight.

He squatted and searched for those bound to be guarding and loose herding the horses, perhaps the boys that he had seen driving them earlier during the day. He saw nobody, and not knowing how many guards there were and where they were positioned was going to make every move he made from then a fool's gamble.

But he was a man that rarely turned back once he was committed to something, and he needed a horse. When he moved again he stayed so low to the ground that he had to often put out the palm of his free hand to support himself. He kept enough distance between himself and the herd that he thought he would be outside the ring of guards.

He came upon the creek bank blindly, and almost fell over the edge of it. Beneath him, standing in a pool of shallow water were some of the horses with their reflections cast on the mirror shine beneath them.

He glanced at the moon and wished another cloud would pass over it, but that was not to be. So, he waited where the creek bank dropped off, watching those horses.

After some time, three of the horses finished their watering and started up the bank directly at him. He had nothing to capture one or to hold one except for his suspenders, which he had taken loose from his pants. The first horse must have seen him squatted there or sensed him, for it blew through its nose in alarm and shied away from him. The other horse behind it trotted wide of him, but the third horse was less leery or observant. Morgan rose and placed a hand on the point of its shoulder, comforting it, and slipping the suspenders around its neck before it could flee. The horse did not pull against him, and he led it three strides away from the creek and swung up on its back without stopping it.

He didn't wait for the guards to spot him or to call out an alarm, for he drummed his heels into the horse's belly as soon as he had found his seat and was sure that he had a good hold on his rifle. The horse lunged forward, and Morgan hoped more than anything that the animal was broke to ride and would not buck him off.

He ran the horse straight at the rest of the herd, scattering some and driving others before him. He gave a wild scream like he hadn't since his days on the battlefield, as much to give him the courage he needed as it was to scare the horses running in front of him to greater speed.

Something hissed past his head, and without seeing it he knew it was an arrow. The shape of a man rose up from the ground in front of him, but the horse he rode was at a dead run. He thought he saw the flash of bare steel, maybe a knife or a tomahawk, and he kicked out with his boot. His foot hit the horse guard solidly, knocking him away, and then Morgan and his stolen herd were running free on the plain.

The shouts of the waking camp carried to him, and a gun blazed from near one of the campfires. He leaned low over the horse's neck and slapped one of its hips with the barrel of his rifle to urge it on.

He rode bareback with nothing but his legs squeezing the horse's barrel, and nothing to hold on to but the suspenders he had rigged for a rein or a handful of mane. The horse rose and fell beneath him, and twice he was almost unseated when it dodged around some obstacle or leaped and lunged over uneven ground, none of which he could see coming to have warning. And once he almost lost his hold on his rifle.

The thought of falling off was not a pleasant one, and he heard the Indians coming behind him far faster than he had hoped. There was no way they had caught mounts that quickly from the scattered herd he had left behind, and he cursed his stupidity for not assuming that each warrior would likely have a horse tethered close to him for such emergencies.

He let the horse run for what felt like a solid mile, and then coaxed it to a stop and turned it to face back towards the Indian camp, listening and trying to gauge how far away his pursuit was from him. The pound of hooves coming towards him told him that the Indians were closer than he had hoped and they were closing fast. They likely knew the lay of the land, and there was no way he was going to outrun them for long—not men born to a horse and used to riding bareback. He had no way to judge the quality of the horse he rode in the dark, and even the best horse for stamina and speed would eventually become too fatigued to continue on. And he only had one horse, and they, many. That would be the end of it, or the horse might trip and fall or go lame, or he might corner himself in some dead end within the looming silhouettes of the Glass Mountains he could see ahead in the distance. There were numerous things that could happen, and most of them bode him no good.

He turned the horse on its hocks and kicked it up to a run. It was too late to turn back, and all he could do was keep running. Often, he twisted at the waist and looked back, regardless if he could see anything or not. But soon, he saw the Indians behind him, the shape of their shadows and the moving legs of their horses so indistinct that they could have been black spiders crawling across the ground. And the same moment he realized that the horse he rode was not a fast one, and they would catch him in the next mile or two.

There was only one thing to do, and he tugged on the loop of suspenders around his horse's neck and guided it towards where he remembered seeing that other campfire burning to the south of the Indian camp. By feel or by luck he rode straight to it. Unlike the Indians' camp, this one belonged to white men and they had their fire heaped with dried buffalo chips and the flames reached high and danced in the distance ahead of him. He gave another wild war cry when he was close, and two shadow figures rose up beside the flames at the sound of it and the drum of the running horses' hooves approaching them.

The loose horses hit the camp at a dead run, and one of them sailed over the fire. The last thing he saw of the animal was the flash of its tail amidst a background of floating orange embers, and then it was gone, as if the world dropped off on the other side of those flames. The rest of the horses split to either side of the fire, and he saw the two men dodging and dancing among them to avoid being trampled.

And then he turned his horse hard at the edge of the firelight and headed west. Behind him, he heard the men's shouts of surprise and their cursing, and one of them fired a wild shot into the night.

When he had run the horse another quarter of a mile, he slowed it to a long, rocking chair lope. A little farther on, and he slowed it to a walk. He thought he had recognized the Kingman brothers rising up by their fire in the instant before he ducked out of there, and he hoped it was them and not some innocent souls. For whoever owned that fire was about to have some visitors that they weren't going to appreciate.

Chapter Nineteen

The buzzard sailed on a thermal wind high above the endless expanse of bare plain beneath him. He arched his outspread wings and tilted into a tighter circle while he cocked his head and peered at the tiny ant speck crawling slowly towards the west. That moving speck on the ground was two men riding double on a single horse, and the buzzard continued to watch them with interest. Such a bird was not intelligent by men's standards, but instinct and experience let it perform a certain kind of natural math without truly thinking. Two men on one horse, and one of the men slumping badly as if injured added up to death and a possible meal.

Texas George looked up at the buzzard and made as if to point his rifle at it. "I ought to shoot his ass out of the sky."

Bennie Kingman gripped his brother's waist from behind to keep himself on the horse's back, and looked up to see what his brother was doing. He saw the rifle George was about to aim, and then he squinted up at the buzzard.

"Put it down, you fool," Bennie said.

"Bad enough that those damned Comanche come on us in the night and like to have killed us, but now that corpse hawk up there is following us," George said.

"You don't know that they were Comanche. No way you could tell in the dark."

"I'm telling you they were Comanche," George said. "You call yourself a Texan and you don't know a Comanche from a hole in your head?"

"Well, whatever they are, they're still behind us somewhere, and liable to hear a gunshot unless you put down that blue blazer and get some sense about you." Bennie's voice was more a groan.

George lowered his rifle and looked behind him at the stub of an arrow sticking out of Bennie's right thigh and the blood soaking his pants leg. "That looks bad."

"You think?"

The broken arrow shaft pried at the wound and let out a burp of blood with every stride of the horse, despite the piece of rope they had tied tight above it for a tourniquet.

"We got to get that arrow out of you before you bleed out," George said.

"What we got to do is put more distance between us and those savages," Bennie said as he leaned his head between George's shoulder blades.

"I think we done lost them."

"You willing to risk your hair on that?"

George pulled the zebra dun to a stop and looked at the stretch of country behind them. Nothing moved upon it. No Indians, no dust clouds, and not so much as a jackrabbit showing itself. Nothing but nothing as far as he could see.

"Who was it you think put them Injuns on us?" George said. "They wouldn't waste time running a horse herd over us when they had us outnumbered bad like that. They could have rode right up on us easy like and slit our throats while we were sleeping."

"It was Clyde. Had to be." Bennie had let his head rest against George's back, and his voice was muffled.

"Figures. I thought I saw a man in a big hat riding behind them horses, but I couldn't make him out good." George squinted up at the buzzard again as if it represented everything that had gone wrong. "Just like Clyde to get someone else to do his fighting for him."

Bennie groaned again.

"Don't you worry, brother. We'll make it to Camp Supply. The army's bound to have a surgeon there to take that arrow out of you," George said. "Then when you're right again we'll find you another horse and go get our evens with Clyde, tenfold, I tell you. I'll hold the bastard for you and you can whittle him bloody with that knife of yours until he damned well wishes them Comanche had got hold of him instead of us."

"I ain't going to make it," Bennie said.

"You'll make it. Remember the time that you took that Yankee minié ball in the shoulder outside Shreveport? You were bleeding like a stuck pig, and you kept telling us you were going to die and to leave you before those Yankee patrols caught us all."

"This is worse."

"You quit talking like that. You'll make it fine." George kept telling himself that, even though he knew that the zebra dun horse that they had stolen from Clyde was too tired to do anything but walk after the long run they had put it through and the weight of them both on its back. They would be lucky if it managed to carry them all the way to the army camp, and even luckier if he could find their way to it. And luck wasn't something they had a lot of lately.

One moment he and Bennie had been sleeping beside their fire, and the next there were horses everywhere and Indians screaming war cries. Fighting when a man wasn't good and awake and shooting in the dark was difficult, but they had managed to hold off those red heathens long enough to get to their horses and make a run for it.

The Indians weren't having any more luck shooting in the dark than they were, but one of them did manage to kill Bennie's horse. Bennie got up on the saddle behind him, and it was a long chase after that. George thought they had pulled off a pretty slick escape about daylight when it seemed that they had lost those Indians, but it was then he saw the arrow sticking out of Bennie's leg like a little flagpole.

George stopped the horse. "To hell with it."

He lifted a leg up over the horse's neck in front of him and dismounted carefully, lest he cause Bennie to fall. As it was, he barely got his feet on the ground before he had to put a hand to Bennie to prop him up in the saddle.

"What are you doing?" Bennie mumbled.

"Let them Comanche come if they want to. We got to stop that bleeding."

He helped Bennie off the horse, and then he helped him lay down on the ground. He checked their back trail one more time.

"Them Injuns ain't going to come on us without us seeing them before they're anywhere near close," he said. "And if they do, to hell with them."

"Let me die."

"Don't talk that way," George said as he drew his Bowie knife.

Bennie had closed his eyes, but the sound of the steel sliding out of its leather sheath made him open them a little. "What are you doing?"

"I'm going to cut that arrow out of you. Roll over on your side."

"It's over, George. Go on and leave me here."

"I ain't leaving you."

Bennie gave a weak chuckle and closed his eyes again. "You always was dumb. I don't know why I ain't knocked you in the head long before now."

"Roll on your side. This is one time your big ass ain't in any shape to be threatening me."

Bennie didn't cooperate, and there was a stubborn set to his jaw.

"You listen to me, Bennie. I'm your damned captain, and I'm giving you an order."

"You never was no captain," Bennie said through gritted teeth. "You done told that lie so much you've started believing it yourself. You weren't nothing but a corporal."

"Well, that outranked your sorry ass. Roll over."

Bennie took two deep breaths and rolled on his side. "Give me something to bite on."

George unbuckled Bennie's pistol belt and gave him the end of the leather to clamp between his teeth. "You bite down on that hard when I go to work on you."

George examined the wounded leg, front and back. The arrow had driven in deep, but hadn't gone all the way through. The broken shaft was almost too short to get a good hold on, but he squeezed hard and gave it a yank. The arrowhead felt like it was set in stone, and George's hand slipped off the bloody shaft.

Bennie spit the leather out of his mouth, pounded the ground with his fist, and breathed like a panting dog. "Oh, Lord, that hurt."

There were only two things George could think to do, and Bennie wouldn't like either of them. He could cut a slit in Bennie's hamstring and push the arrow on through his leg, or he could hammer on the shaft and drive it through without cutting.

He picked up the gun belt and shoved it back between Bennie's teeth. "You hold still as you can, and I'll try to get it over fast."

Bennie nodded at him, with the yellow of his teeth revealed and the belt held between them pushing back the corners of his mouth. He tried to say something, but George couldn't understand a word of it.

George reversed the heavy knife, holding it by the blade so that he could strike with the fat of the handle, and then he reared back with it like he was swinging a hammer and brought it down on the stub of arrow shaft. Bennie bit so hard on the leather that it made his eyes bug out and he moaned. He spit the belt out and screamed when George hit the shaft a second time.

George heard a sound like a ripe tomato being squashed and the shaft disappeared. He wasn't sure if he had broken it off instead of driving it on through until he looked at the backside of Bennie's leg and saw three quarters of the arrowhead revealed with a ring of puckered, red flesh pushed out around it. He swiped at the flies swarming around the wound, put the tip of his knife behind the arrowhead, and pried it the rest of the way out. Bennie jerked and kicked like a brain-struck mule and almost knocked George clear of him. The hole in his leg was bleeding worse, and George cut a strip from the tail of his shirt and stuffed the improvised rag into the hole with his finger. Bennie howled again while George's finger twisted and pushed into the wound channel like a ramrod tamping a bullet down a barrel.

Bennie swung a fist that struck George flush on the temple and tipped him over backwards. He came to a sitting position with his bloody knife dangling in one hand. He sat like that and watched Bennie's body coiling and uncoiling with pain. The smell of raw meat and blood mixed with the smell of urine where Bennie had pissed himself made him want to puke.

After a while, he rose and fetched the canteen off the saddle. He brought it to Bennie and tried to get him to drink, but Bennie turned his head away. George examined the wound, and was pleased to see the blood flow had slowed. But he wondered what it would do if he loosened the tourniquet. Bleeding wound, or not, that belt was going to have to come off soon or it was all for nothing.

"You lay there a spell, brother. We got time." As soon as George said it he saw the dust cloud on the horizon. "I lied to you. Them Injuns ain't going to let us rest."

He led the dun beside Bennie, and it was all he could do to get his brother up on his good leg and then in the saddle.

"Leave me." Bennie's words were so slurred with pain and weakness that George could barely understand him.

"Like hell."

George picked up the bloody piece of arrow he had removed from Bennie's leg and closed Bennie's fist over it. "You hold on to that. Every time you think about quitting me you remember that arrow in your leg and how you're going to give it back to them savages what put it there. You get mean, Bennie. You hear me? Time to get mad dog mean."

Bennie nodded.

George swung up on the horse, this time sitting behind his brother instead of in front of him. He wrapped one arm around Bennie's waist and reached around him with the other to hold the bridle reins. He gave the dun a poke with his spur rowels, and the little horse started forward at a shambling walk. He kicked him again, and put him to a long trot. The dust cloud he had seen was still back there, but whoever was making it was moving slow.

"We might make it yet," George said. "Maybe they haven't spotted us, and we can give them the slip again."

Bennie said nothing in reply.

"You with me, Bennie?"

Bennie groaned, and slobber ran out of his mouth when he tried to speak.

"That's all right. You don't have to say nothing. You get hold of the saddle horn if you feel like you're about to fall off."

George continued to talk, and later in the long afternoon, he stopped the horse. The dust cloud had been gone for a good while, and only the buzzard remained with them.

"I think we're free again, Bennie. You hear me?"

There was no response from Bennie.

"We ain't had no damned luck at all," George said. "None at all, and it ain't looking no better."

George rode on, hugging his brother to him and shifting his course to the west. He hoped he could find that army camp, but it was going to be a long damned ride, whether he could or not.

He was in no mood for the buzzard when he looked up and saw it circling him. It could have been a different buzzard, but he was somehow sure it wasn't.

"To hell with it." He stopped the horse and shucked his Henry rifle from the scabbard. "You been laughing at me the whole time, ain't you?"

The draft of air beneath the buzzard's wings must have weakened, or else it wanted to circle lower for a closer look. Either way, it was a slow-moving target as it passed over George's head.

"Ain't nobody that laughs at Texas George."

George shouldered the rifle, rested the forearm on Bennie's shoulder, and fired. He was about to shoot again when a bullet tore through into his back. Both he and Bennie slid off the horse, and the boom of the gun in the distance sounded as their bodies slid from the saddle and thumped on the ground.

Chapter Twenty

Texas George lay on his back looking into the sun. His face burned and his eyes watered, but the rest of his body was strangely numb. He couldn't move his arms or legs, but after some effort, he managed to turn his head enough to see Bennie lying beside him facedown. Whatever had numbed George's body had also left his mind so foggy that he was having a hard time hanging on to his thoughts. Every time he managed to latch on to one, it slipped away, and he was slow coming to the realization that Bennie was dead. He considered that he, too, might be dead, but the thinking made him tired. It was easier not to think at all.

He didn't know how long he had lain like that, but it seemed a long time. He continued to track the sun across the sky, until it was low on the horizon. Staring so long at it had blurred his vision to the point he wasn't sure it was a real sun he was looking at anymore.

He heard the crunch of footsteps behind him, and soon a man carrying a scoped rifle and leading a black horse with nothing but a blanket on its back stepped into his field of vision. He was a little man, even smaller than George. He wore a pair of scuffed and scratched cavalry boots that had once been black, with his pants tucked into the tops of them. Above that he wore a butternut-colored shirt, and cinched around his waist was a beaded Indian belt bearing his knife on one hip, and a Dance revolver high on his other. A sweat-stained, narrow-brimmed black hat with a round-topped crown sat on his head, and the hat and the way the man had his chin tilted down cast his face in shadows.

At first, George thought he was an Indian come to finish him off, especially with those two long braids of hair hanging one over the front of each shoulder.

The little man with the big rifle squatted down on his heels at George's feet. He studied the wound in George's chest while he worked a chew of tobacco around in one cheek. "Busted you plumb center, I did."

The man tilted his head back to reveal his face, and George saw that he had blond hair. His skin was tanned and brown enough to pass as an Indian and he had a hooked beak of a nose and bony cheekbones like some of them, but the eyes that looked back at him were white man blue.

"Help me," George gasped.

"What's that?"

"Help." George thought he got the word out, but he wasn't sure.

The man rested his rifle across his thighs and looked over at Bennie. "I ain't never took two with one shot. Course, I didn't know there was two of you, so I reckon that don't count."

The revelation that the man before him was the one that had shot them came as little surprise to George, for it had been that kind of day. The only thing he couldn't figure was why he couldn't move. The ground must have knocked the air out of him. Soon as he had time to rest a little he would get up and settle the matter.

The man stood and went to Bennie and looked at the wound in his back, and then rolled him over and checked the exit wound. "Clean through the both of you. Wouldn't have thought it."

The man bent over George and reached for his chest with his

free hand. George wanted to flinch, but couldn't. All he could do was watch as the man's hand disappeared out of view. When it reappeared, there was blood and tiny white bits of bone up to the first joint of the three fingers he held before George's face for him to see.

"You got a big, wide hole in you." The man brought his bloody fingers closer to his own face to examine them, and flicked something off one of them. "Can't see how you're still alive. I figure you're half turned to juice on the inside."

George didn't hear him. He had noticed something pass high above and behind the man standing over him. It sailed by again, and he realized it was the buzzard.

The man standing over him must have noticed he was looking elsewhere, for he half turned and shaded his eyes with his bloody hand and peered up at the sky.

"Shoo, bird," George whispered. "You get on out of here."

"Bothers you, don't it?" the man standing over him said. "Knowin' it won't be long until that bird is picking the meat off your bones? They go for your eyes first."

"Unlucky."

The man leaned over George, closer to his mouth so that he could hear him better. "What's that?"

"Never had no luck. Not a one of us boys."

The man wiped his fingers on George's shirt, and then straightened and looked at the zebra dun gelding standing nearby. "Can't argue with you there, boy. You two are the second time I thought I was shootin' somebody else. Must be slippin'. First time I shot his deputy that was wearin' his coat, and now this. You boys were too far away to make out that you weren't him, but I seen you was ridin' my horse. Damned unlucky for you any way you look at it."

The man's talking had given George time to grab hold of a few more thoughts, and he had come to believe that none of it was real. Nothing but a weird dream, like the one where you were sitting in the schoolhouse naked and everyone was looking at you, or where you were trying to fight or run from something and your body wouldn't work right. Any minute now he was going to wake up, and the little demon talking to him wouldn't be there anymore. And Bennie wouldn't be dead.

The man looked to the west. "I don't suppose you're in any shape to tell me where you got that horse? I'm supposin' you stole him from the man that stole him from me."

George continued to stare at the dream sky, but the mention of Clyde caused his eyelids to flutter.

The man with the big rifle saw that reaction. "Clyde. That name gets your blood boilin', don't it, boy, same as me? I seen you two in Ironhead and I know you had trouble with him. But he got the best of you, didn't he? Figure you and your brother were most likely out here after him."

George's eyelids spasmed again.

"You wouldn't have killed him, no ways," the man with the rifle said. "And I would have killed you if you had. He's my meat, and I won't have nobody ruinin' my sport."

The buzzard drifted across the dream sun again, and George imagined he could hear the wind in its feathers like the scrape of brittle fall tree leaves under your feet; like rat feet rustling through dead corn stalks. He wondered why feathers would sound like that, and if in his dream, it would be the bird or the rats that came for him.

"That Clyde, he's more like me than he knows, but he won't admit it," the man continued like he was used to carrying on conversations with nobody but himself. "And me and him got us a history. First time I seen him he was up on this hill and I was hid amongst a boulder pile. That was back in the war, when a good man with a rifle gun could really shine at his callin'."

"Anyways, I seen him up there. Seen him through my riflescope, and he was lookin' back at me through his. Then the cannons started rainin' hellfire down around me before either of us could take the other's meat. I hoofed it out of there right quick before they cratered me. Got me three Yankee officers there on that hill, and the sharpshooters with me got a couple of more before those shells started fallin'. But alls I could think about was that Yankee sharpshooter I seen wearin' the green uniform coat. One of Berdan's boys, I figured, and they had them a big reputation as long shooters for the Federals."

The man paused long enough to pull the thoroughly masticated wad of tobacco out of his cheek and pitch it away. "Most men got no edge to 'em nor no skill. Meat and nothin' more. But that green jacket, he spotted me where I was hidin', and might have took me given time and if he was able to keen the wind and find the proper elevation. If you know anything about shootin', then you know that's no sure thing. Man workin' long range can miss easier than he can hit. Gotta know what you're doin', and how to bring the magic. That what I calls it, the magic. Only word I know to explain what there ain't no explainin' for."

The man hunkered down again and set his big rifle butt-down before him and leaned against it before he continued. "Anyways, I thought on him all night, and you can imagine my surprise the next day when I seen him again. I had taken me a stand on the second floor of this big house where I could see down on the battlefield while our boys was trying to take that ridge the Federals had dug in on. Worst bloodletting I ever seen, 'less it was Sharpsburg. Reckon you heard about Gettysburg, but it don't matter none. The dead don't forget a day like that."

A shiver seemed to run through the man's body, and he shook his head to chase away whatever chilled him and rocked his head side to side like he had a stiff neck. "What I was tellin' you

The man paused to look at the horses before he continued. "You see, boy, there's plenty that will pay me lots to put a bullet in someone, but it ain't money that gets the juices flowin'. Not to me. Those that pay, they're only meat, same as the ones they want killed. It's the hunt that matters. Choosin' the slain through the glass, that's magic better than between any woman's thighs, or the thunder booming over the church steeple."

The man sighed and scratched at the back of his neck with one hand. "Don't know why I wasted my time tellin' you such. Meat don't understand. Never will. You're probably lyin' there thinkin' how I'm tetched in the head, or what an evil thing I am. But there ain't none of us innocent. I know that cause I seen what men can do to other men. Seen their natures stripped bare to the marrow bone."

The man bent over him, blocking out the sun. George felt a slight tickle in his nose. It didn't itch much, but he wished he could see what the man was doing to him.

"There now," the man said as he admired whatever handiwork he had performed on George's nose. "You're just about a step from Hell's door, and when you meet old Lucifer I want him to know who sent you. Left my mark on you, but you go ahead and tell him the Traveler sends his greetin's."

The man rose and went to Bennie one last time, and bent over him the same as he had done to George. When he was finished, he mounted his black horse and rode over to the dun and took up its bridle reins.

"Shame you can't tell me where you seen that green jacket. Might have saved me some trouble," the man called over his shoulder as he was riding away.

George listened to the retreating sound of the horses' hooves whisking through the burnt grass and was glad that the demon was gone. The flapping of wings startled him, and he looked out of the corner of one eye and saw the buzzard standing on the ground a few yards from him, watching and waiting. And then another buzzard landed beside it, and then another. He wanted to shoo them off, but he was too tired to make the effort.

Maybe he dozed off, but when he looked again the buzzards were closer. One of them waddled on its scaly legs towards him, neck low, and those black eyes burning into him like coal fire. He thought he could smell the carrion reek on it, and knew in that instant that it was no dream. He took a deep breath, watching the hooked beak reaching towards his eye, and when air rushed out of his crippled lungs one last time a white feather floated away on the wind.

Chapter Twenty-One

Dixie Rayburn worked his way to the west edge of the camp, having looked most everywhere for Superintendent Duvall's crane operator, and he spent most of a morning in the search. No one seemed to have seen the man. Although all he had questioned hinted that there was something about the man that they thought everyone knew, they were unwilling to say exactly what that something was. And none of them were shocked that the crane operator was missing work.

The campsite had been chosen on the site of a Choctaw trading post. At the foot of the little timbered mountain above camp laid a two-room cabin built Texas style, with a porch the length of it, both front and back, and a breezeway through the middle separating the two rooms. The Indian man that ran it was a bachelor, and he lived in one room and used the other for his store.

Dixie had heard that the old Choctaw was making the best of the construction workers that had invaded his homestead, and was selling homemade whiskey off his back porch. According to Duvall, the crane operator's problem was worse than a thirst for cat whiskey, but Dixie thought it wouldn't hurt to ask the Choctaw trader if he had seen the crane man. He was about the only one left that Dixie hadn't asked.

Bill Tuck's big bouncer, the one Saul had called the Hilltopper, was sitting in a wicker-bottomed rocker in the middle of the front porch when Dixie got within sight of the store. His eyelids were ringed with black and so deep-set in his skull that Dixie felt like a corpse was watching him

Two other men, both Indians, sat in a pair of chairs at the far end of the porch in front of the door to the room that served as the owner's personal quarters, but Dixie had no clue which one of them was the proprietor of the establishment, if either. Dixie stopped a few yards in front of the weathered and sagging oak plank steps leading up on the porch, and he and the Hilltopper stared at each other. He noticed that the giant had one hand wrapped around a quart Mason jar, the kind of glass jar that women used for preserving vegetables and canning jelly and such. Only, it wasn't vegetables that were in the jar, but a clear liquid.

The Hilltopper put the jar to his lips and took a sip of cat whiskey. Dixie started to go up the steps, but the big man's chair sat at the top of them in the way.

"What you looking at?" The Hilltopper's voice was deep and his words came slow and lazy, as if the moonshine he was imbibing had slowed him to a crawl. A blue jay was fussing in the treetops above the cabin.

"You tell me," Dixie said.

"Got a smart mouth on you, don't you?"

Dixie put a boot on the first of the porch steps. "You going to move, or do I have to move you?"

The Hilltopper, instead of being annoyed, gave a deep-throated chuckle. "You and whose army, little man?"

Normally, Dixie would have taken insult to such talk, but he let that slide. He was barely shy of six-foot tall, but everyone was little compared to the big man looking down at him from the porch. Nothing good would come out of a fight with the giant, and he had other things to attend to.

The Hilltopper rocked the chair, once, twice, and the wood in it creaked so loudly that Dixie thought the furniture was going to bust apart under such weight.

"Who you looking for, law dog?" the Hilltopper asked.

"Who said I'm looking for anyone?"

"You're skulking and sniffing around like a kicked dog."

"Are you going to get out of my way, or am I going to have to whip your big ass off that porch?"

"Bold talk. That badge has made you brave."

"I got no idea why you're on the prod, but you feel froggy, you jump."

The Hilltoper chuckled again. "Feisty, ain't you? How about you give me that Rebel cap and we'll be friends?"

"I'm partial to my hat." Dixie put his right hand on the top of his thigh as he took another step, as if to brace for the steep ascent, but really as an excuse to have it closer to the brass-framed Confederate Navy pistol sheathed in his holster at a cross-draw on his other hip.

"Makes me sick to see a secesh wear a badge. That don't fly up in Taney County where I'm from." The whiskey had caused a sweat to break out on the Hilltopper's forehead, and a streak of it ran down one side of his temple while he glared at Dixie like a dumb bull.

"You lettin' me pass, or are we goin' to do it the hard way?" Dixie said.

"Nothing hard about handling you."

"You and me tangle, you'll know you've been in a fight. Now get out of the way."

The Hilltopper took another sip of whiskey from the jar and gestured with his other hand at the narrow space between one side of him and a porch post. "Me? I ain't stopping you."

When the Hilltopper put his hand back down Dixie noticed that it came to rest on the handle of the big knife he wore across his belly. Dixie judged the big man's reach and imagined the kind of edge that knife was liable to have, and then he went up the steps. He passed so close that he brushed against the Hilltopper's shoulder.

"I'll give you ten dollars for that cap just so I can take a shit in it," the Hilltopper said as Dixie went by him.

Dixie didn't stop and turned towards the end of the house that served as the store. Dixie was barely inside the room when he heard one of the Choctaws coming along the porch behind him.

The room had a single window in the back wall, with a short counter to one side of it. The other two walls had shelves from the floor almost to the ceiling. A cast-iron wood stove sat in the middle of the room, with its stovepipe streaked with rust where the rain had leaked down it.

Dixie ducked under a string of steel traps hanging by lengths of chain hung on a nail in the rafters, and he dodged around two salt-cured hams hung with string in much the same way. The blankets and other goods on the store shelves were covered in dust, and the room smelled like cat urine and rotten wood.

The culprit that had contributed to the piss smell came out from under the counter and rubbed against the Choctaw's legs, purring loudly. He was a yellow tabby with a scarred face and one ear half gone, and his potbelly sagged close to the floor.

The Choctaw storekeeper looked down at the cat, shoved it towards the door with his foot, and at the same time called out something in his native language to someone outside.

It wasn't long before there was the sound of scrambling toenails on the porch, and a little spotted terrier slid around the corner and into the room wagging his bobbed tail. The little dog immediately saw the cat, and the cat was just as quick to spot an enemy. The cat's back arched like an Indian bow about to launch an arrow, and the hair on its spine stood straight up. The dog growled twice and then charged like a white blur. The cat stood its ground long enough to hiss and spit and swipe a paw across the terrier's face, but sprung for the door as quickly as the blow landed. The two animals went outside in a wild chase.

Dixie walked back to the door to see how the scrap turned out, and saw the tomcat up a tree in the front yard. His tail swished his displeasure as he looked down at the barking dog gnawing tree bark and barking and bouncing like a spring. Dixie thought it was probably an old game between the two, and while the dog had the passion, it was the tomcat who had the brains.

"That cat, he's gonna get too old one of these days, and that dog's gonna catch him," the storekeeper said.

The storekeeper was a short, stocky man, dressed in a collarless white shirt, and a pair of work pants and lace-up boots. His black hair was cut straight across at shoulder length and parted in the middle to frame the thick features of his face. His skin was dark, like many of his tribe, and Dixie guessed that he was a full blood Choctaw. That was rarer than it once was, for many within the tribe had intermarried with whites and blacks long before they moved to the territory.

His English was good, but that didn't surprise Dixie any, even for a full blood. The majority of the Indians in the eastern side of the territory were bilingual, and there were many of them that were educated as good or better than their conquerors.

The Five Civilized Tribes—Choctaw, Cherokee, Chickasaw, Creek, and Seminole—had been forcibly removed from their original lands in the Southeast. Many of them were already dressing like white men and had turned Christian long before the Great White Father in Washington, in his all-seeing wisdom and kind concern for their well-being, aided greatly by his wanting their lands, ran them out at gunpoint and moved them to the Indian Territory.

Despite the harsh treatment, those tribes had adapted and

done well in the new country, and before the war, they had built good homes, churches, and schools. They raised cattle and hogs, farmed cotton and corn, and tended fine garden crops. They formed their governments modeled on a blend of tribal and white law, and the Cherokee had their own written language and newspapers. Some of the more well-to-do members of the tribes ran extensive plantations and owned slaves. Those slaveholders fought with the Confederacy, and many of their pro-Union opposites did the same for the North.

"What can I do for you?" the storekeeper asked.

"My name's Ben Rayburn, but most call me Dixie." He tapped the badge on his vest. "Railroad police."

"I heard about you."

"Don't believe half what you hear."

The Choctaw grunted and smiled. "I don't believe much of what any of you white men tell me, but some of you aren't too bad. Name's Harold Moshlatubbi."

"Glad to meet you."

"Same."

Dixie jerked a thumb at the door, towards the porch. "You do know it's illegal to sell spirits in the Nations, don't you?"

"Thought you was railroad police and not a Federal."

"No business of mine, just curious."

"Them Federals and the Lighthorse make it their business. They'll bust your still in a heartbeat, confiscate your whiskey, and haul you to court. My cousin was sentenced to a whipping last year."

"Risky business . . ."

"I don't sell whiskey," the storekeeper said. "I wake up in the morning and somebody might have left a jug or two in an old hollow stump up the mountain. People come to my store and I tell them they look like some exercise might do them good and they ought to take a walk. They go around back sometimes and find those jugs in that stump and get them a drink. Before they leave they might buy one of my painted rocks for a dollar or two."

The storekeeper pointed to a low-sided wooden box on a table beside the door. Inside it was a bunch of various-sized rocks with paint slapped on them. It was obvious that no attempt had been made at creating some kind of trinket or souvenir, only chunks of creek stone crudely painted with a brush.

"I don't sell whiskey, only rocks, and those deputy marshals ain't never caught me doing otherwise. When the law comes, I don't care if they find a jug or two up the hill, and I tell them I don't know where it came from. When they leave, I might wake up in the morning and find somebody left a couple more bottles in that stump again, and I make sure I've got plenty of painted rocks."

Dixie laughed. "Those marshals or your Indian police haven't ever wondered why your rocks are so popular?"

"It's Indian art. Spirit rocks I call them, if you get what I mean. Tourists love that stuff." The storekeeper winked and laughed, too.

"Well, Mr. Moshlatubbi, I'm wondering if you might have seen the Katy's crane operator around here. Blasingame is his name."

One of the storekeeper's eyebrows cocked slightly. "What's he look like?"

"Regular height, they tell me. Got curly hair and missing a couple of fingers on one hand."

"White man I take it?"

"Yep. Swede. Smokes a crooked pipe and wears a red cap."

Again, the storekeeper gave him that look. "What do you want him for?"

"He's missed work, and the superintendent needs him. From

the way you're looking at me, I'd say you have an idea where he is."

"I might."

"Well, don't make me wait too long."

"You going to buy a spirit rock? Big medicine. Indian magic. Make you happy."

"Believe I'll pass." Dixie grinned. "Get too many rocks in my pockets and I might not be able to make the walk back to camp."

The storekeeper motioned for Dixie to follow him out on the porch. When Dixie went out the door he saw that the Hilltopper was gone. He followed the storekeeper down the porch to the other Indian sitting in a chair, a young man, probably in his teens. The storekeeper said something in Choctaw to him, and the young one nodded his head.

"My son says he will take you to where he last saw the man you're looking for."

"How come he knows where Blasingame is?"

The storekeeper frowned and pointed off the end of the porch at a footpath winding through the woods. "There's a woman that's got a cabin a little ways down that trail. She's not a good woman."

"What's that mean?"

"She has a lot of company, and most all of them are men."

"You mean she's gone into business?"

"Seems like it."

"White woman?"

"Choctaw. She used to be a good woman, but now she drinks too much and won't listen to her grandmother. Shames herself and her family."

"And this Blasingame fellow has been keeping company with her?"

"Saw him come through here yesterday and he took that trail."

"What shape was he in? He didn't stop and buy any of your rocks, did he?"

"He was in bad shape, like always. I don't know what kind of spirits he's carrying, but it isn't whiskey."

The storekeeper's son was off the porch and was waiting for Dixie.

"Thanks for the information," Dixie said to the storekeeper.

"Think nothing of it. Maybe you'll come back around when you learn to appreciate primitive art."

Dixie went down the steps and to the boy at the head of the trail. He looked back at the storekeeper. "Tell him he can stay here. Looks like I can follow that trail easy enough, and if Blasingame is there and tanked up, it might get rough. I don't want your boy in the middle of that."

"I speak English as good as you," the son said.

"Probably better," Dixie replied. "I only went to school through the fifth grade, until the teacher got sick of me mangling the King's English and losing my reading primer, and Pa got tired of me not helping him with the farming. Seems like neither of them took me for the scholarly type."

"Take him with you," the storekeeper said. "She herself is hard to deal with sometimes, but he can usually talk sense to her."

The young Indian led the way along the trail, and Dixie followed him. The footpath wound through open hardwoods and a few scattered pines until it dipped down into a shallow draw on the mountain slope and passed through a briar patch and over the rock bed of a dry branch barely one hundred yards from the store.

"Her cabin is only a little farther," the young Choctaw said. They were climbing up out of the dry branch when he held up a hand to motion Dixie to stop like he had. "Somebody's coming."

Dixie listened, and after a moment he heard footsteps crunching through the leaf bed and rattling rocks. The Indian moved forward a few steps, and Dixie followed him, moving as quietly as he could. As soon as he did he saw a crude little one-room cabin with a shake roof and gaps between the unpeeled logs where the chinking was either missing or the owner had never bothered to weatherproof it. An Indian woman wearing nothing but a moth-eaten blanket wrapped around her was standing in the doorway watching a man walking away from the cabin.

The man leaving her was none other than the Hilltopper. The big tough wasn't following the trail, and was taking a straight line towards the construction camp. Dixie and the young Indian hid behind tree trunks until the Hilltopper was out of sight.

There was a little clearing in the woods where the cabin stood, and it was littered with old stumps bearing axe marks and a few brush piles. An empty hog pen lay on the far side of the clearing, and two black shoats were rooting up acorns under a post oak not far from the pen.

The woman spotted them, but neither waved nor said anything in greeting while they walked up to her door. She was neither young nor old, pretty nor ugly, caught somewhere in between, but the hard living on her face was plain to see. Her black hair looked like it hadn't been combed or washed in a long time, and her hands were as dirty as her mud-stained bare feet. She was also obviously drunk, for she stared at them belligerently and staggered slightly when she straightened from where she had leaned against the doorjamb.

She gave the young Indian only a cursory glance and a tiny frown, but she managed a bored smile when she looked at Dixie and said, "Four bits."

"What's that?" Dixie asked.

"I said it's four bits if you want to lay with me." The blanket wrapped around her had come loose a little in the front, but she hadn't noticed or didn't care.

The young Indian with Dixie turned away so he wouldn't see her nakedness, and Dixie took one look at the brown skin revealed through the open slit in her blanket and then he looked up and kept his attention on her puffy face and glassy brown eyes.

"If you ain't got the money, then you go on. Git. No credit here," she said.

"I'm not here for you." Dixie tried to see around her inside the cabin.

She stuck a bare leg out to block his view, and giggled. "What's the matter? Don't you think I'm pretty?"

Dixie was three good steps from her, but he could smell the must and sour sweat on her. "I'm looking for Bill Blasingame."

She was beginning to realize that she wasn't going to get any money out of him, and she frowned. The downturn of her mouth made her look uglier and more pitiful than before. "How about whiskey? I'll trade you a piece for a bottle."

The storekeeper's son hung his head, and Dixie could tell that he wanted to leave more than anything. Dixie wondered if the young man was related to the alcoholic whore in the doorway.

Dixie was a man that appreciated an occasional drink of liquor, but he began to rethink his stance on the government's prohibition of ardent spirits in the Nations. The woman standing in front of him wasn't the only Indian he had seen brought down by alcoholism. There were plenty of white drunks, always had been, but for some reason the whiskey problem was worse within the tribes.

"Is Blasingame in there?" Dixie asked, wanting to get it over with.

"What's the matter, white man? You don't like squaw loving?" she said, and he noticed that one of her front teeth was missing.

She tried to strike a seductive pose, but only managed to stagger again. She burped and showed the missing tooth in another smile meant to cover her failed attempt at awing him with her womanly wares. "I'll hump you real good."

She was so short her head barely came to his chest when he pushed past her into the cabin, ignoring her cry of protest. She tried to punch him in the back when he went through the door, but she was too drunk and the wild swing of her arm only resulted in her falling down.

Something glass rang against his foot, and he looked down at the empty whiskey bottle he had kicked across the floor when his eyes adjusted to the windowless gloom. Two more bottles lay scattered on the floor, and another one lay on the dining table amidst the dirty dishes and a cast-iron skillet half full of cornbread with green mold growing on the top of it. A cockroach skittered across that table and disappeared in the shadows as Dixie moved further into the room. The stove door had broken sometime in the past, and he walked wide around the overflow of old wood ashes that had spilled out of it.

There was a man lying on the bed, sprawled on top of a crumpled quilt and dressed only in his red long johns. He was apparently asleep, and one of his arms was flung out and hanging off the bed like a limp noodle.

Dixie noticed the red wool cap hanging off one of the posts on the bed's iron headboard, and he noticed that there were two fingers missing from the man's hand that dangled over the dirt floor. He studied that hand.

He bent over Blasingame and tried to shake him awake. "Get up. You're late for work."

It took a good shaking to wake Blasingame, and when he did come awake his eyes were as shiny as the Indian woman's had been. It seemed like he was having a hard time focusing, and then a slow, lazy smile spread across his mouth. When Dixie tried to get an arm under the man's shoulder blades and lift him up, he found him as limp as a rag.

"Leave me alone," the man said, and the smile wouldn't leave him.

"Duvall's going to fire you if you don't show up for work."

"To hell with work. I'm fine right here." The man laughed a crazy laugh. "More than fine."

Dixie could tell that Blasingame was so loaded up with the dope that he was no good for anything, and spending any more time trying to get him on his feet was a wasted effort.

Beside the bed on a small table was a round, dark brown ball with a chunk torn out of it lying atop a piece of some kind of paper that had once been wrapped around it. Beside the object was something that looked like a lamp globe, and inside that globe was some kind of kerosene burner with a little heating pan on top of it.

Dixie thought on what the contraption might be while he picked up the brown ball. It was neither overly soft nor firm, having somewhat the feel of resin or hard beeswax, and when he held it under his nose it smelled faintly sweet. He studied the missing chunk in the side of it where it looked like bits of it had been pinched or pried off.

He smelled the ball again and then put his nose over the opening in the end of the glass globe. The smell there was the same, only stronger, like burned syrup or molasses.

Dixie knew next to nothing of opium, other than third-hand talk and scandalous rumors and innuendos written in the newspapers. Some called it the Chinese Tears, Dragon Smoke, or Turkish poppy. He studied the ball of opium and the little cooker inside the glass globe and guessed that an addict like Blasingame put a bit of the dope on the tiny cook plate over the burning kerosene wick and put his mouth to the opening in the globe to inhale the smoke. Pipes were used in the Chinese opium dens in California, but the contraption on the nightstand ought to work much the same.

He wrapped the ball of opium back in the paper and tucked it away in his vest pocket. Blasingame was watching him the whole time with a dreamy expression, and when he smiled again Dixie could see bits of brown in the man's teeth. Was he eating the stuff, too? He gave Blasingame a disgusted look, and then went outside.

The woman was lying naked on the ground, too drunk to get on her feet. She glared up at him as he passed her. "You going to bring back some whiskey?"

The storekeeper's son left with him, and never looked back at the woman.

"Me and you have good time," she called to Dixie as they were walking away.

"She didn't used to be like that," the young Indian said when they were halfway back to the store. "It's the whiskey that did it to her."

"Is she kin to you?"

"My aunt."

Dixie left him at the store, waved at the storekeeper, and went back to the camp. He saw several of Tuck's doves leaving the Crow's Nest as he neared it. They were in some kind of a hurry, and passed him by, headed for somewhere across the camp towards the railroad tracks. Dixie was headed in the same direction, and saw more people streaming that way as he went. Everyone seemed excited, and Dixie wondered what was going on.

When he came in sight of the tracks, he saw a small crowd gathered around the blacksmith's shop. As he got closer, he saw the blacksmith standing behind his anvil with a heavy, short-handled shop hammer in his hand. The Hilltopper stood on the other side of the anvil, and it was obvious that the two men were having words. The Hilltopper's deep voice carried to Dixie, and he sounded angry. The blacksmith didn't seem too stirred up, but the way he held the hammer told Dixie that he had it ready to use it on the Hilltopper.

Chapter Twenty-Two

The blacksmith shop wasn't really a shop, being only an open-faced tent with a forge and an anvil stand in front of it. A line of hitching rails for tying the horses and mules to be shod fenced off one side of the approach to the tent, and a pile of railroad iron and scrap steel walled off the other. The crowd had blocked off the way, and Dixie had to shove through them to get close enough to the forge to see what was taking place.

"You say it, and I'll leave you alone," the Hilltopper said as Dixie cleared the crowd.

Dixie reappraised how big the Hilltopper actually was and wondered why he had such bad luck to have run across the man twice in a single day. And then he looked at the blacksmith.

Most of those who made their living at the blacksmith trade were strong men, made that way pounding red hot steel and iron to shape, standing under horses nailing on shoes, or wrestling wagon wheels and such. But the man on the other side of the anvil from the Hilltopper wasn't a burly man.

Dixie had known Hank Bickford since their days together in Ironhead Station. The Missouri blacksmith had worked for the Katy since it was still in Kansas, and his wife lived in the camps with him and added to the family coffer doing laundry for the railroad workers. Most in the crowd knew Hank, and that knowing and the reputation and sheer size of the Hilltopper is what had drawn everyone not working out on the line to the argument.

While Hank might have not been a big man, he was known to be especially strong. He was a decent wheelwright, and Dixie had once seen him lift the rear wheel on a big freight wagon that he had repaired and set it in the back of a wagon bed by himself. Those who worked around him had other such tales, and nobody had ever seen him lose an arm wrestling or a leg wrestling match. It had gotten so back in Ironhead that the gamblers couldn't get anyone to try him.

Incredibly strong for a man of his stature and weight, and at the same time he was normally a mild mannered, quiet type. And while the Hilltopper was glaring at him and talking his talk, Hank said nothing and stared calmly back at him.

"You made your brag," the Hilltopper said. The moonshine Dixie had seen him drinking at the store had added a little swagger to him, and there was a slight slur to his speech. "I been hearing how you said you was the strongest man on the line."

"I didn't say anything of the sort," Hank said in a quiet voice.

"I been hearing it," the Hilltopper said.

"You didn't hear it from me."

"That's a damned lie."

Hank took a deep breath, but said nothing in reply.

The Hilltopper stepped a little closer to Hank, and looked down at him. The size of him dwarfed the smaller man. "You made your brag, and now can't back it."

"I don't have time to play your fool games," Hank said. "I've got work to do."

"Who you calling fool?" The Hilltopper stepped closer and put both hands on the anvil face and leaned against it. There wasn't two feet between the two of them.

"I'm not calling you a fool. You're drunk." Hank started patting the shop hammer he held in the palm of his free hand. The pat of that hammer was as steady and even as the stroke of a clock.

The hammer caused the crowd to whisper more, for every one of them thought he was going to use it on the Hilltopper and then all hell was going to break loose. Dixie started forward and put a hand on his pistol butt.

"You say you're the strongest, then you're the strongest," Hank added.

"I could bend you in two without breaking a sweat," the Hilltopper said, and leaned farther over the anvil.

"You come across there, and I'll put a dent in that big head of yours," Hank said as quietly as ever and as if, hammer or not, the thought of combat with the giant bothered him not in the least.

The Hilltopper turned his head and looked at the crowd, a slight sneer on his face. Dixie knew that he was going to swing on Hank or grab for him the instant he turned back around. He was only playing to his audience, or trying to distract Hank and catch him off guard.

Dixie drew his Navy .36 and fired off a round into the air. The crowd melted back several feet, giving him room, and the Hilltopper quit leaning over the anvil and looked over his shoulder at Dixie.

"There won't be any trouble here," Dixie said.

"No trouble, Dixie," Hank said, still patting that hammer in his palm.

The Hilltopper said nothing, and was looking at Dixie like he was thinking on how long it would take him to cross the ground between them and shove a pistol down a certain policeman's throat.

Dixie cocked the Navy again. He didn't aim it at the Hilltopper, but close enough for him to get the point. Regardless of the threat of the gun, he could see that the Hilltopper wasn't going to take being shown up in front of the crowd. He was obviously a man who enjoyed his reputation as a tough. And Dixie was under no impression that a bullet, or even two, was certain to be enough to stop the giant when he came at him.

"You two want to see how strong you are, I got a better idea than you cracking each other's heads and gouging eyes," Dixie said.

"What's that, Chief?" somebody in the crowd asked.

Dixie struggled to come up with an idea, as he had only been buying time when he suggested an alternative to the bloodletting. And then it came to him. He holstered his pistol and went past the Hilltopper to a rack of horseshoes inside the tent. The Hilltopper's coon-ringed eyes tracked him the whole way, and he straightened and took his hands off the anvil.

Dixie came back to him carrying a horseshoe. It was no ordinary horseshoe, but a large, thick one, Number four sized, and made to go on the hoof of a draft horse. He held it out over the anvil between Hank and the Hilltopper.

"What are we going to do with that?" the Hilltopper asked.

"I saw a circus strongman one time that could straighten a horseshoe with nothing but his hands. Let's see which one of you can do that."

Hank looked at the horseshoe, but didn't reach for it. He did, however, quit patting the hammer. The Hilltopper looked at both of them and laughed. Then he looked at the crowd and took the horseshoe from Dixie at the same time.

"Ain't no way he can bend that shoe cold," someone in the crowd observed.

The Hilltopper glared at the crowd and looked for the one that had said that. The crowd went quiet.

He took hold of the sides of the horseshoe with both hands, braced his feet wide apart, and began to pull in opposite directions. Even with his shirt on, you could see the muscles in his arms and shoulders expand, and the chords in his neck and the veins in his temples stood out like shallow tree roots. His face turned red with the strain and his whole body trembled. But the horseshoe didn't change shape.

Once more, he looked to the crowd, and then he changed his hold. He put one leg slightly in front of him, braced one hand against his thigh, and began to pull with the other. His face turned a deeper shade of red, and his knuckles went white, so tightly did he grip the shoe. A grunt and then a great groan issued from his chest, and the crowd began to whisper again. Slowly, the shoe bent. And after more grunting and tugging, the Hilltopper relaxed and let go of the shoe with one of his hands, letting it hang beside his leg.

He waited for a moment, panting like he had been running a foot race instead of tugging at a horseshoe, but when he looked up at the crowd, he gave them a devilish, gloating grin.

And then he held the horseshoe up for all to see. The iron of it no longer was bent back on itself in a sharp curve. Instead, it was nearly a straight line. Some in the crowd clapped, some cheered, and a few of those gathered only looked at Hank Bickford to see what he would do.

The Hilltopper was thinking the same, and he turned around and showed Hank what he had done to the shoe. "Your turn, little man."

Hank patted the hammer a couple of times, and his expression was unreadable. He looked at the shoe and then he looked at the Hilltopper. "All right."

"All right what?" the Hilltopper asked.

"All right, you're the strongest."

The Hilltopper looked at the rack of horseshoes, and nodded at it. "You ain't even tried."

"No need to. You're the strongest."

The Hilltopper glared at him, and then at Dixie. Dixie moved his hand closer to his Navy, not quite sure how it was going to turn out.

"All brag, wasn't you?" the Hilltopper said to Hank. "Can't do it, can you?"

"You're the strongest."

The Hilltopper looked to the crowd to make sure they had heard what Hank said. "Which one of you says I ain't the strongest man on the line?"

Nobody answered him.

"Which one of you wants to try your hand on one of these shoes? Huh?"

Again, he got no takers. Several in the crowd were looking like they would rather be elsewhere.

"Guns, fists, or knives, I'll take any one of you."

"That will be enough of that." Dixie had taken hold of his pistol butt while the Hilltopper was glaring at the crowd.

The Hilltopper whirled on him.

"You've won. Now let's break this up," Dixie said.

The Hilltopper looked like he enjoyed the winning, but he still wasn't liking the fact that Hank had the hammer and that Dixie had hold of his pistol.

He looked at Hank. "That little old hammer wouldn't have done you any good. I'd have shoved it up your skinny ass."

Before Hank could answer, the Hilltopper turned on his heel and walked away. The crowd began to break up.

Dixie looked at Hank. "Can't you find a smaller fellow to pester? That Hilltopper is nobody to trifle with."

Hank put down the hammer. "He caused the trouble, not me."

"You didn't make things better patting that damned hammer in your palm."

Hank put a hand to his lower back and arched his spine. Then he looked at the work horses tied to the hitching rail waiting to be reshod, and at the pile of wagon wheels and other work ready for him to finish. "I'm about done with this camp. Tired of working for this railroad, and tired of people like that big ox working for Tuck."

"Hard to buy your bread unless a man has a job."

"I've saved some. I know that's hard to believe with the skimpy wages Duvall pays, but I've done it. Not much, but some."

"What about Lottie? Ain't she doing all right with her washing business. By the time this railroad gets to Texas you two might save more."

Hank shook his head. "She's tired of this, too. You know Lottie. A Bible thumper like her gets offended with the goings on in a railroad camp. And there's my kids to think of. This is no place to raise children. My son asked me over breakfast this morning what a bawdy girl was."

"Are you going back to Missouri?"

"Maybe, but we've talked about giving Ironhead a try."

"Don't tell me you're buying all that talk about a town."

"Don't need a big town, but a blacksmith might do well with the wagon traffic that comes through the crossroads. Might take up a little farm on the side, and Lottie took a liking to that preacher out at the mission school. He's asked her to help him with some of the Indian children and intends to build a church in town."

"There ain't a town there, yet."

"Got to build it first."

Dixie scoffed. "Rumors. If I had dollar for every rumor I've heard in my lifetime that wasn't true, I'd own this railroad and you'd be working for me."

Hank smiled and took up his hammer again. "You ought to come with us, Dixie."

"You ain't an Indian. How are you going to get around that if you want to settle in Ironhead?"

"I can get a license for the blacksmith shop, and I talked to a Choctaw fellow about some farmland. He's willing to lease me the ground I need."

"I wouldn't want to put my sweat into a place that I didn't own."

"I'm thinking it won't be long before the government breaks up the tribal holdings and opens them up to the public," Hank said. "The land is too good, and there's too many of us wanting such for the growing of things and a place to build and raise our families. Do you really think the politicians are going to leave all this country in the hands of the Indians? Never have before."

Dixie started to argue with that, but knew that Hank was likely right. It was only a matter of time. The government had forced the tribes out of the Southeast for the very same reasons, the hunger for land, and there was nothing to make him believe they wouldn't do it again. There never had been a treaty with the Indians that amounted to more than the paper it was written on. And the Indians and the government allowing white businesses places in the territory and white men to lease ground from the tribes was simply the first step, and there would be no turning back.

Dixie sighed and shoved up the back of his hat and scratched at his head. He liked to stick to the simple things that you didn't have to think on too much. And he was steadily feeling more and more alone, as if the whole world had gotten too complicated for his understanding. It was like everyone he knew had gone crazy. First Morgan going off to fight the Traveler, and now Molly and the Bickfords all of a sudden wanted to be town builders.

Hank went to his blower and began to turn the crank to breathe some life into the coal fire in his forge. He paid no attention to Dixie, and studied the glowing coals intently. He was a hard worker, and not a man to be talkative while he was busy.

"See you later, Hank," Dixie said as he headed for the tracks.

Hank only nodded and kept cranking up his fire.

Dixie reached the tracks, crossed over them, and climbed up on the end of Duvall's private car parked on a siding he had built for it. He knocked twice on the glass window in the door and waited.

"Come in," Duvall's gruff voice sounded from within.

Dixie opened the door and went inside. As usual, the superintendent was at his desk, but this time the New York woman was sitting on a parlor couch at the side of the room. She sat with her legs drawn up on the couch beside her with shoes off, and had a crystal goblet perched in one hand, with that elbow resting on the arm of the couch. She looked like nothing so much as a woman posed and ready to be painted by some artist. Whatever liquid was in the goblet sparkled and fizzed with tiny bubbles.

"Care for some champagne?" she asked, and found something funny in her asking that by the way she pursed her mouth.

Dixie had never drank champagne, nor had he ever seen anyone drink it. He had no idea what it was other than the name, and the sight of someone who was supposed to be a lady openly drinking spirits in front of a strange man bothered his sensibilities. But he knew enough about Helvina Vanderwagen to know she wasn't exactly your normal lady. She put on certain airs, always reminding everyone of her rich family and how New York was the only civilized place in the whole wide world, but it was common knowledge that she was Duvall's kept woman. Whether she had somehow fallen from grace, or actually liked being a mistress, he didn't know.

He still couldn't see how she and Morgan had ever ended up married. Dixie knew that Morgan hadn't always been the same man as he had come to know him, and he suspicioned Morgan had once been wealthy himself. Maybe he had liked such women when he was still in New York and before the war took him away. The Lord only knew when it came to affairs of the heart or the urges people took. For the little Dixie fathomed about New York women, they all might all be like Helvina.

"Don't believe I will," he said.

"Hors d'oeuvres?" She pointed at a silver tray and a bowl of some kind of tiny food on the low table in front of the couch.

"What?" There were crackers and some kind of little black beads. A bottle of whatever she was drinking lay in a bucket half filled with chipped ice.

"It Beluga caviar," she said when she noticed him looking at the black, beady stuff.

"Caviar?"

"Russian fish eggs, Mr. Rayburn," Duvall said from his desk. "They come from the sturgeon fish in the Caspian Sea. A rare delicacy. I had a few tins shipped here from New York, along with Helvina's champagne."

"Willis positively spoils me," she said and batted her eyelashes at the superintendent. "I do so love this wild, boisterous territory, but such rustic pleasure does not lend itself to the finer tastes. A little touch of civilization reminds us of home, don't you think, Mr. Rayburn?"

"I believe I'll pass on the fish eggs, same as the bubbly stuff." Dixie crossed the room to Duvall's desk, taking care to walk around the Persian rug. He still couldn't get used to walking on the fancy thing. A rug was for wiping your boots on before you went in your house, and not supposed to be something so pretty that it looked like it cost more than a man made in a year's work.

"What brings you, Mr. Rayburn? I assume you have word of the whereabouts of my crane operator?" Duvall said.

"I found him," Dixie said.

"Where?"

"Laid up with a . . ." Dixie hesitated and looked at Helvina.

"Go ahead, Mr. Rayburn. The man was laid up with . . . ?" she said.

Dixie blushed and looked back to Duvall to gather himself. "He was with this woman."

"He's been missing work to spend time with a prostitute?" Duvall reared back in his chair and threw up his hands in exasperation. "That cuts it. It really does."

"Positively scandalous," Helvina threw in, taking a dainty sip from her goblet and smiling coyly at Dixie.

"Well, how come you didn't drag him back here for me to talk to him?" Duvall asked.

"He couldn't do you any good with the shape he's in." Dixie reached in his vest pocket and pulled out the paper-wrapped ball he had taken from the cabin. He laid it on Duvall's desk.

"What's this?" Duvall unwrapped the paper and studied what was inside it.

"Is that what I think it is?" Dixie asked.

Duvall nodded. "I believe you are correct. It would seem my suspicions were not misplaced. Did you find who it is that's peddling opium in my camp?"

"I saw that giant Tuck has working for him leaving the cabin where I found Blasingame right as I was getting there," Dixie said. "The Hilltopper, they call him. Don't know what he had to do with it, if anything, but I wouldn't put anything past Tuck if it's crooked and there's a dollar in it."

"But you have no evidence that Tuck is involved? You've heard no rumors of such?"

"Nothing, but Tuck's the most likely candidate. I don't see the Hilltopper as the kind to swing such. He's muscle, that's his game. Tuck's the kind that could organize the supply, and it fits with the booze and the . . . the ladies, and the gambling. Right up his alley, if you ask me."

"I'll speak to Tuck. Fact is, I've been meaning to talk to him. In the meantime, you keep looking. If you catch whoever is selling the stuff, you let me know."

"You don't seem as fired up about this dope as you were the other day."

"Forgive me for that. The crane operator had me in a foul mood," Duvall said. "But that's not to say I don't want this stuff gone from my camp. I want to make an example of whoever is selling the stuff. You hear me? I'll loan you some of the rougher men from my crews should it come to that and you need the help."

"I think I get what you're saying. You talk to Tuck, but don't take him at his word."

Duvall gave a condescending, crafty smile. "I've know many men like Tuck, and sometimes they need reminding of their place and lot in the grand scheme of things."

"Whatever you say, but don't fall for his talk. He's a crafty one." Dixie reached for the ball of opium.

"Leave it."

"Right."

"And one more thing," Duvall said. "I want you to escort Helvina to Ironhead tomorrow. She wishes to oversee the hotel construction, and I've had her a tent pitched so that she will have a place to stay until it's completed. You will take the train tomorrow."

"Try not to look so glum," she said to Dixie. The corners of her pouty lips had a way of folding like the corners of a cat's mouth when she frowned. "You can be such a gloomy sort sometimes. No wonder you and my late husband were friends."

"Late husband?"

"Oh, I only meant my ex-husband. Silly me. I'm sure Morgan is alive and well and spending his time doing all sorts of manly things."

Dixie headed for the door.

"Are you sure you wouldn't care for some caviar, Mr. Rayburn?" Helvina asked in that same coy voice.

Dixie glanced at her long enough to see her pop a cracker pasted with the black fish eggs into her mouth and make a show of chewing it. He opened the door without answering her.

"Goodbye, Mr. Rayburn. Always so nice to swap pleasantries with our esteemed and debonair chief of police," she said as he closed the door behind him.

He heard her giggling as he went down the steps. New York women.

Chapter Twenty-Three

Morgan worked his way westward, riding bareback on the stolen horse. He stopped once to fashion a bridle out of his suspenders and strips of leather cut from his boot tops. The strips of leather became a noseband of sorts, and the suspenders made the headstall and a single loop rein. It wasn't much of a bridle, a crude copy of a Mexican braided bosal and mecate setup, but it served the purpose of guiding and handling a horse that had been trained with nothing but a strand of rope through its mouth and under its bottom jaw, Indian-style.

After making the bridle, he rode throughout the day, rarely stopping, and alternating between a fast trot and a walk. He wanted to keep the horse in good condition should his life suddenly depend on the animal being sound and ready for all occasions, but he also wanted to put distance between himself and the Indians likely looking for him. When he camped, he made no fire, only curling up on his side in the bottom of a gully with his suspender rein clutched in his hand and the horse standing practically on top of him.

He woke hungry and feeling little rested, and knew his exhaustion was mainly due to having nothing to eat for almost four days. He let the horse graze on the end of the rein for an hour at first light, while he sat on the top of the gully bank and kept watch on the surrounding plain.

Farther to the northwest, he could see what looked like the country rising up above the plain, and when he mounted he headed in that direction. Somewhere before noon he entered more uneven terrain, littered with gypsum rocks lying on the ground and exposed ledges of it forming rimrocks on the sides of cedar brush canyons. He crossed over a wide, flat tableland, broken often by narrow canyons and drainage valleys.

It was in this country that he began to see his first buffalo in greater numbers. He had heard tales of herds so big that it took a full day to watch them pass, but that was not what he saw. Instead of traveling and grazing in mass, or in a singular herd, the buffalo were found in smaller groups. There was only a handful in some places, and a hundred or more in others. But, had you put all of the buffalo in a few square miles together, there truly would have been thousands of them.

Morgan needed food badly, and his immediate intent was to down one of the great beasts for its meat. The sound of a gunshot was going to carry a long ways, but he had to eat or die, no matter if there was a chance it would alert his enemies to his location.

He soon found a bluff overlooking a shallow valley following the winding of a sandy stream, and dotted everywhere with the shaggy beasts. He sat his horse high above it all like a lost sentinel, planning his hunt, and at the same time, soaking in the vision that lay before him, rapt with it all.

The spring breeding season was all but over, and the animals were slowly grazing northwards. The spring calves bucked and played around their mothers, their reddish color standing out in stark contrast to the darker wooly hair coats of the adults. An occasional old bull bellowed to show he was the boss, or in his frustration at not having found some cow still in need of companionship and yet to receive his affections. He watched two of those bulls battle each other with their great foreheads and hooked ebony horns butted together and their grunting and pushing stirring up clouds of dust. All over the valley were little dust clouds where other buffalo wallowed and rolled on the ground to scratch the fly bites on their skin or to scrape away their shedding, itchy winter coats.

And he knew then what had caused the numerous small craters he had come across, like scooped-out pits of powdered earth. The whole country he rode through was littered with such depressions, what the plainsmen called buffalo wallows. Some of them were waist deep to a man, and he wondered how many buffalo such a hole represented, and how many times their kind had to wallow in the same place to rub away the earth.

He gauged the wallows by their depth and breadth, like counting the rings on a tree stump to determine its age. And in his mind he envisioned them, all the buffalo that ever were or would be, masses of oversized, wooly heads and chin beards swinging in synchronized stride, lumbering in their odd, hump-shouldered gait, bawling and grunting deep from their leathery lungs, calling to each other to reassure themselves that they were a part of the herd; always grazing, always moving, a slow rolling cycle of birthing and rutting, living and dying, the original nomads; the greening of the grass beckoning them on like the moon pulls the ocean tides; north in the summer, south in the fall, hooves lapping and lapping over the same rutted trails, ages and ages of migration, an infinity of buffalo passing over the same sea of sunburnt grass.

And he saw more, some things only in his mind, and others truly coming to pass before his eyes, and all of it somehow like a dream, so new it was to him. Tickbirds danced from back to back and beast to beast among the herds, flitting like butterflies through the dusty haze. Ground squirrels gave their cricket call, so small in their scamperings as to often go unnoticed, and prairie dogs, their bigger cousins, piped their alarms and flicked their tails as a rattlesnake slithered by their burrow holes. There were mule deer, whitetails, and pronghorn antelope staring back at him atop the mesas and hillsides with their thin legs silhouetted like stilts with the sun behind them, and bounding high in a flash of tail and pale underbelly when they fled.

He saw coyotes and big loafer wolves prowling along the outskirts of the herds with stalking strides and their long noses low to the ground. Their flanks were hollow with constant hunger, and their predator eyes continually searched for the foolishly young, the old, or the weak straggler from the herd. At night, their yaps and howls were as forlorn and lonely as anything he had ever heard. The vibrato of that wolf song was otherworldly and new to him, yet at the same time, familiar.

He felt an outsider, yet strangely, he knew he somehow belonged to it all, as sure as the endless sky overhead went on and on. Live or die, and despite the hard journey that had brought him to the moment, he was glad that for once he had ridden such a wild, unspoiled land, for he was sure there would come a time when it would be as it was no more.

To the east were restless men and women eager for a new land, homesteaders, pioneers, and adventurers, ready to go forth and multiply, to conquer and reshape. They would come, of that he had no doubt. They would come seeking not only places to raise their children, but grass for their livestock, timber and stone to build with, and minerals to make them rich. And when that time came, there would be no more buffalo, and no more wolf songs.

Morgan took one last look, wanting to lock away the picture of how it was in his mind for all times, and then rode down off the high point with his rifle laid across the horse's withers. He crossed the valley at a slow walk, looking for a good place to take a stand where the setup and the distance of the shot at one of the buffalo would ensure he made a clean kill.

He saw such a place where he could approach downwind of

one bunch of buffalo and get within a hundred or so yards of them and hidden behind the sloping foot of a butte that fingered out into the valley. He was riding towards that point when something else appeared.

There was a small copse of elms and cottonwoods in the bend of the creek bed, the valley otherwise void of anything resembling a tree other than the dark green patches of short, twisted cedars growing on the hillsides and rocky bluffs. And working their way towards that grove of trees on the creek was a flock of turkeys, probably feeding their way back to their roost before nightfall. They were only a short dash ahead of him, yet to take alarm at his presence, and still a good two hundred yards from that roost. And he saw them for what they were, a chance to take meat without firing his gun.

He kicked the horse and was soon charging across the flat bottom of the valley at a run, intending to get between the turkeys and the grove of trees or to run one of them down before it could reach there. Half of the flock took flight when he closed on them, flapping with hard-beating wings for the high limbs of those trees and making hard work of it, for they were poor fliers and preferred keeping their feet to the ground. The others stretched their necks out like racehorses and ran before him with a fleetness that surprised him.

He shifted his grip on his rifle and took hold of it near the end of its barrel. The horse was right behind three of them, and when they scattered before him he singled out his victim and leaned from the horse's back with the rifle reared back like a polo player with his mallet. He swung the rifle as the turkey came alongside him, and was rewarded by the solid whack of it striking the bird in the head and a scattering of bronze-tipped feathers. He was pulling on the reins and looking back at the downed bird when the horse stepped in a prairie dog hole with one of its front legs.

The horse was still at a high lope when it went down in the front end, and its hindquarters lifted high until its whole body turned end over end. Morgan was thrown through the air and landed in a jarring, rolling heap that knocked the wind out of him and the rifle from his hands. He came to his feet, relatively unhurt except for a few scrapes and bruises, and saw the horse trying to get up. He could tell from its struggles that it was likely crippled.

He found his rifle and went to the animal, hoping he was wrong. The horse had gotten to its feet, but was hobbling on three legs. One of its front legs was broken at the cannon bone below the knee. The poor animal was in such pain and so shook up that it fled from him when he tried to catch it, hopping in pitiful, slow lunges with that maimed leg flopping and swinging limply. When he caught hold of the rein and stopped it, he saw the white of bone showing through the busted skin. He patted the horse's neck, talking soothing nonsense, apologizing. And then he drew his pistol, cocked it, and placed the muzzle of it close to the horse's forehead, a little above the line of the eyes. The pistol shot rang off the bluffs, and he listened to it carry into the distance, the crack of it slowly fading.

The Arkansas Traveler, the man once known as Erastus Tuck, had struck the Cimarron River that morning. He was following its channel upriver with an eye out for the tracks of a barefooted horse crossing its red sand bed when he suddenly pulled his horse up hard and cocked his head and listened. He gave a slow nodding of his head when he was sure that it was a gunshot he heard, as if it confirmed what he already suspected. The shot had come from somewhere to the southwest of him, in the gypsum hills he could see there.

"Headed for the rough country, ain't ya? That's where I'd go," he said to himself. "Are ya lookin' for a place to lay up and wait for me, or are ya runnin', Green Jacket?"

Since regaining his zebra dun, he had been alternating his riding between it and the black Kiowa mare, covering more ground that way without running either of the horses to the ground. He was a patient hunter, but had expected to encounter Clyde long before then. However, he felt he was close to Clyde now; felt it in the marrow of his bones. And he could also feel the jitters and the impatience rising up inside him like a boiling pot rattling its lid, and knew he had to fight that down lest it cause him to make a bobble. The hunting of men, especially dangerous men like Clyde, didn't tolerate bobbles.

He could have killed Clyde back on the Salt Fork instead of toying with him, but he wanted Clyde to know that they had found each other and that the dance had started, and he wanted to put the fear in him, to let him know the only way it could end. Wanted him to know that he wasn't good enough to match the Traveler.

But it was time to finish it. No more playing. It was time to find Clyde in his scope glass. Find the green jacket, see him true, and kiss the trigger. Finish what he had started all those years ago.

So long coming, a hunt longer than any he had known, but he had to work slow. Clyde might take a stand on some high ground where he could see for a long gunshot and wait for him to ride into his field of fire. A man not careful, not sniffing the wind and keeping careful watch for such likely places, might ride himself into a bullet, might find himself the meat. And then there were the Kiowa buffalo hunting parties. Twice he had come across them and barely avoided being seen. And they knew that there were white men in their country and would be on the scout for such.

The Traveler had hunted with the Cherokee as a boy, and they taught him much of what he knew about tracking and hunting, and the art of concealment and patience, so he knew a little of how an Indian could read sign. It was only a matter of time before one of those hunting parties ran across the tracks of either him or Clyde. He needed to get it over, and get it over soon.

It was in the Glass Mountains, riding in the darkness two nights earlier, that he had chanced on to the campfires of the Kiowa camp, and then spied the other, single campfire burning in the distance a few miles away. He had made his way towards that single fire and camped on the buttes above it, waiting for the dawn and wondering if he had run down Clyde.

He was watching that campfire and waiting when the horses charged the camp below him, with the Kiowa soon behind them. He could make out little other than the sounds of gunfire and running horses, but that was enough to keep him in hiding.

By the next morning, the Kiowa warriors had returned empty-handed from their pursuit, and the whole band broke camp and moved on. He came down off his high place when they were gone. The ground was so torn up from the multitude of horses that he could make little from the tracks around the ashes of the campfire, and the Kiowa had already poured over the camp for anything of use to them—all but his diaries, which he found pitched under a bush.

He had picked up the little black books, gave them a close examination, then stuffed them inside his shot bag and moved on. He kept the buttes between himself and the way the Kiowa had gone, and headed in the direction that the warriors had returned from that morning.

He hadn't gone far before he found a dead horse. There were skid marks in the ground beside it, and he took that to mean that it had bore a saddle before the Kiowa took it. Five miles later, beyond the point where the Kiowa's tracks turned back, he came across the tracks of two horses, both headed in the same direction, but not traveling on the same line. One was his own zebra dun. He could tell by the shape of its shod hooves, for he knew them as well as the look of his own hands, and the other set of tracks belonged to an unshod horse.

Late in the afternoon he saw a tiny cloud of dust on the horizon. Closer still he could make out the faint hint of movement, and when he dismounted and kneeled with the Whitworth to his shoulder, that blur of indistinct movement contained a flash of tan that he knew was his dun horse. He had remounted and ridden wide and fast ahead, until he closed the distance and took a stand belly down on a low swell of ground. He was still far away, that time, but closer and near enough that he could make out that it was the zebra dun and it had a man riding it. He steadied the rifle until he was sure he had made the magic, and then kissed the trigger.

And then he had ridden across the flats only to find it was the Kingmans he had killed, not Clyde. The disappointment had been raw in his throat for a while, but the more he thought on it the more he knew that it wasn't meant to be that easy. And a thing worth the doing was a thing worth savoring.

And so, he hunted on another day, following the tracks of the unshod horse, losing them and finding them again, and always pausing to look squint-eyed at the distance ahead, trying to guess how it might all play out and where and when.

And now, he sat his horse and looked at the gypsum hills to the south once more, and stroked the stock of his Whitworth rifle. "Is the fear on ya, Green Jacket? Has the hunt broken ya and got ya runnin', or are ya out there crafting me? Drawing me in like an old spider with his feelers on the web?"

He turned his horse and started it towards the direction of the gunshot he had heard in the distance, and gave a crackling, wet chuckle. "Let's go see what you're made of, Green Jacket. Let's see who's the meat and who's got the magic."

Chapter Twenty-Four

It was well after noon when Molly came out of her tent and went through the back door into the Bullhorn. She had slept poorly and woke up in an irritable mood because of it. Noodles was behind the bar, leaning on one elbow with his chin resting on his hand while he watched the man across from him nursing his mug of beer. Business had been slow so far, and the sight of the Italian bartender's lazy stance and the single customer in the poorly lighted tent put Molly in a worse mood. Her world seemed to have slowed to a crawl, and the room stood as an example of that.

She went behind the bar, took up a towel, and began wiping the bar top. Noodles was oblivious of her presence until she knocked his arm out from under his chin with a swipe of her cleaning hand. He gave her a surprised look and was about to say something until he saw the mood she was in.

"Open those door flaps wider and let some light in. It's like a root cellar in here," Molly said more harshly than she intended.

He went around the end of the bar to do as she said, and made slow progress limping like he was. That, too, angered her.

"Don't you dare hurry," she said.

He stopped at the door, looked down at his crippled leg, and then back at her. He gave an apologetic shrug. "This leg, she don't bend no more, she don't. Bastard rails they drop on me, they fix it so my knee, she stiff like a board."

He showed her a fist and a flexed forearm as if to emphasize how rigid his game leg was, and then he smiled.

"What are you smiling about? I'm being mean to you, and you smile?"

"I open the door wider. Plenty of sunlight, you see," he said and smiled again.

The fact that she could get no reaction out of him other than that apologetic, goofy smile made her madder, even though she knew she was taking a bad morning out on him.

The whisk of a broom made her realize that there was someone else in the saloon, and she turned and saw Ruby Ann sweeping at the floor.

"Can't you find something else to do?" Molly said. "You can sweep that floor all you want to and it's still nothing but dirt."

Ruby Ann put the broom aside and gave Molly a bland look. She stood there unmoving and seeming at a loss for what to do next.

"Quit staring at me. You want to do something, how about you figure out a way to stir up some business in here?"

Ruby stayed where she was.

"I said quit staring at me. Why don't you fix us a pot of coffee?"

Ruby Ann moved to the stove in the center of the tent and filled a speckled graniteware mug from the pot already warming on one of the burner lids. She brought the mug to the bar and set it before Molly.

When she bent over, Molly could see the scabbed, dotted scars of two cigar burns below her collarbones where her dress top hung away. And Molly remembered seeing those wounds when they were fresh and wet, right after some men had found Ruby Ann lying in the woods and brought her to Doc Chillingsworth's hospital tent, half naked and battered, with rope burns on her wrists and other wounds so bad she couldn't walk on her own.

Molly took a sip of the coffee and scowled. "That's awful. Tell me you didn't make that."

Ruby's eyes shifted to where Noodles was fumbling with the door flaps.

"Don't you Italians know how to make coffee?" Molly said to him.

Again, he gave another shrug without looking away from what he was doing. "These men . . . these Americans out here, they like it strong."

Molly took another sip and made the same face. "You could peel paint with that."

She looked at the single customer again, making a long go of finishing his beer. The sight of him brought her anger back. There wasn't going to be much business on an early weekday morning, not in a two-bit crossroads like Ironhead, but they hadn't had a busy night yet since she took over.

Noodles finally got the door flaps tied back, and the sunlight spilling into the middle of the room soothed her a little. She stared out the door and said nothing for a long while. Noodles hobbled behind the bar and was about to start dusting the stock of whiskey bottles.

"Forget that. I want you to take an inventory of the liquor we have. Beer, too," she said. "And look at the pickled stuff, too. Those salty eggs and pigs' feet put a craving on a man for something to drink."

He gave her a bewildered look.

"Inventory. Count all of the stock and let me know what we have."

"*Sí,* Signora. I count good."

"You call me that again, boyo, and you're fired. Red Molly is my name, and you better remember that. I don't know what a Signora is, but I'm pretty sure I've never been one."

Noodles looked at the whiskey bottles on the shelves behind

the bar as if he were at a loss.

"There's a ledger book and a pen and inkwell under the counter. You do know how to write, don't you?"

"Sí, Sig—" he cut himself off, and gave that apologetic shrug again. "Sí, Red Molly. I count good."

She was beginning to think that "good" was the only English word he was really comfortable with. She went back to staring out the door while he took the ledger book out from under the bar.

"But I don't write the English," he added.

"Copy what you see written on whatever you're looking at, or your best guess. I'll look over the accounts later," she said. Her own literacy skills were limited, but she wasn't about to let him know that. And she told herself she was going to have to learn some new things.

"What we need is to put up a false front on this place. Make it look like something," she said, thinking aloud. " 'Twill still be nothing but a tent with a dirt floor, but it wouldn't look so much like one from the outside."

"And I need to hire a girl or two. The men will come if they know there are pretty women here. Once those blokes are here they'll buy drinks. Simple as that."

"We need a dealer to work the faro layout. Maybe hire one on for a cut of the winnings. I know a few up the line that might do, but I don't know any of them would want to come to a two-bit place like this. The good ones are going to want somewhere with more action."

Molly felt Ruby Ann staring at her again, and noticed that the woman had never moved since bringing the coffee. "Oh, I know what you're thinking, even if you don't say it."

Ruby Ann shook her head. Molly didn't know what that was supposed to mean, so she went with her best guess.

"You think I'm a fool to be considering what I'm considering, and that this place isn't ever going to amount to anything. You're saying I ought to get myself up to Sedalia or down to that new camp and go back to lying on my back with my legs in the air for any hairy-arsed chap with a few quid in his pockets."

Ruby Ann placed a hand on top of Molly's on the bar top. She shook her head again, and her big eyes were somber and sad like they had been since she had gotten well enough to first get out of Doc Chillingsworth's sickbed, and the bruises and broken bones knitted enough for her to go around staring at everyone like some phantom haint.

"Don't you give me those eyes again. Don't you dare," Molly said. "I won't apologize to you. I won't, or to nobody else for what I'm thinking. I come all the way from County Kerry with my brother when I was but a lass. Twelve years old I was, and my brother not much older. The bearing of me took our mother, and the whiskey and then the fever took our no-good piker of a father. And all the people in the village looked at us like you're looking at me right now. They said who are those silly orphan children thinking they will go across the ocean and have a go of it? To the church orphanage is where that lass ought to be, and that boy indentured to someone with a trade for his keep.

"Tell me I haven't seen a thing or two in my time, and I won't apologize for none of it. I'm standing here, ain't I? Made it all this way, and don't owe anybody for the doing of it." Molly jerked her hands out from under Ruby Ann's, and her face was turning red with the remembering and her accent became stronger, even though her voice remained quiet.

"And that manky old money lender up in his cottage on the hill looking down on all that owed him rent. Him, his lecherous self, trying his best to get a hand under me skirts every time he thought no one was looking. Me, a girl of twelve, and him whispering to me to forget about going to Canada or America and keep his house for him. Said if I was a good lass he would forgive my father's debt and let my brother, Michael, stay in our home. And that with him old enough to be my grandfather and with a nasty eye and a rutting goat's ways about him, so that I could tell what he was and what he wanted even with no more than I knew then.

"You know what I did?" she asked. "You know what I did, Ruby Ann?"

Ruby Ann shook her head, no different than she had numerous times before, and unclear as to whether she wanted to hear more or didn't.

"Well, I'll tell you. The captain of that ship had posted in all the villages around that he would be sailing back to Quebec and taking on passengers for forty shillings apiece. Forty shillings you say? That's not much to some, but it was a fortune to us. We had nothing but a rented cottage with holes in the thatching big enough to put a milk cow through and a little field of weeds and dead potato plants, and no horse for the plowing of it. And that with our owing of the landlord, that money lender his miserly self.

"Michael was a shipwright and said he would find work to come up with the price. But there was no work with the whole county and all of Ireland starving or leaving for other parts.

"So, I let that money lender run his hand up my skirt, and I let him whisper in me ear when he cornered me off the street and out of sight of everyone in the village. And I went up to his house one night when he asked me to again, only I didn't do like he wanted. I tricked him into undressing and crawling under his covers, and then I took up his shillelagh, you know, a good stout stick for the walking or for the beating of a barking dog on the roadside, and I gave him a smart one on the head. He wanted to fight, but he was old and thin and his bones brittle, and when I smacked him again he told me where his coin was hidden under a hearth stone."

"What happened? To you . . . after that, I mean," Noodles asked.

Molly didn't know how long he had been listening, but she gave him an irritated look. She felt a little ashamed that she had said so much, but she was caught up in the telling of it all, caring not whether they heard her and only thinking back to the way it had been and to another girl in another place so far away and so long ago that it was all as if a dream.

"Me and Michael legged it all the way to Tralee in the dark. Made it in one night, though it was a far piece to travel riding nothing but shank's mare."

"The *poliziottos,* did they catch you?" Noodles asked.

"No, the High Sheriff didn't catch me, or I wouldn't be here now. Would I? Only thing worse than a big-talking Irishman without two pence in his pocket is a Dago bartender with a banjaxed leg and too many questions."

"Pardon me."

"That ship they were advertising was hardly a ship at all. Not for the carrying of passengers, mind you. No sleeping berths, and only a captain with a mouth like a bilgewater on him and trying to make some extra pounds going back empty across the ocean to load more wood. For seven weeks, we slept below the decks in the cargo holds, and then on the top decks when some of the other passengers got the fever and we wanted to be away from them. Three cups of cask water a day the crew gave us, and a slab of dried cod and a piece of moldy bread that you had to pick the bugs out of in the evening.

"Still, all and all, we had eaten worse before, I promise you we had, swear it on the name of Saint Christopher I do, and the thought of somewhere we could get us a start was a fine thing. Fine enough to do what it took to get there."

Molly noticed that the customer at the end of the bar had set down his half-finished beer and was turned toward her and listening.

"Buy another beer if you want the rest of the story. I don't give anything away for free," she said to him.

He was wearing coal-sooted overalls and a sweat-stained derby hat, and she assumed he was a worker on one of the trains, maybe a firebox tender from the black filth on him.

"You'd charge for a story? It ain't costing you nothing to tell it," he said, but motioned for Noodles to bring him a beer while he was saying it.

"Cost me nothing? You listen to me and you'll hear how it cost me, or you're more the fool than you look," she said. "There were other ships loaded with poor Irish, so many that they lined the big river for a mile when we got to Quebec. The typhus was bad on all the ships, the fever, and the government was quarantining the sick on a little island down from the city. Everyone coming into port had to get a doctor's examination, and you were likely to die waiting your turn with them.

"The captain he let me and Michael off on the shingle a ways downriver. Said we were healthy and not to let anyone we met know we were fresh off the boat and without our inspection, especially not the soldiers. Said he wished he could get rid of all the God-awful sick Irishmen on his ship, but it wasn't to be. Said there wasn't any more work there for poor, dumb Irishers, but we might make it if we followed the road upriver to Montreal and then crossed into the States to Pittsburgh where they built many things and a young man like Michael might find work."

"That captain left you, just like that?" The man in the overalls finished his beer, and took up the second one.

She nodded. "And maybe an act of kindness it was. The typhus was running bad, and there were other ships dumping their dead into the river, and the inspection hospitals were so crowded that even the doctors were taking sick.

"So, we set out on the road to Montreal like the captain said, with everything we owned in two packs on our backs and Michael carrying his carpenter tools in a handbox he built for them. Everywhere we walked there were other Irish walking, too. Seemed like the whole of our people had come across the ocean and landed there. Some of them were sick and all of them were hungry, and some so bad they were lying on the side of the road. Many of their landlords back in Ireland had promised them that they would be paid a small amount to get them started in their new place once they landed in Canada or the States, but that was all a lie to get poor Catholics out of the country.

"And we worried about the money we carried hidden in our packs. The money I stole from the landlord, it was, and forty pounds of it left to give us a start and to feed us until we found our way in the new land.

"We camped with an Irish family from County Cork the second night on the road, a man, his wife, and their two grown sons. They were worse off than we were, and Michael wanted to help them. He gave them a bit of the food we had bought in a tavern that afternoon, and thought he was doing a kindness. But I saw the way they looked at us when he told him where the food came from. Saw them speculating on how we could afford the price of a meal in the tavern and if we might have other coin or more food hidden in our packs.

"Not that they were bad people, but I saw how the hunger and the hard times had put them to a place they never thought they would be. You get to that point, and all you can think about is surviving and taking care of your own. Two strange kids on the road don't matter when it's like that, and Michael should have seen that, he should've. But he didn't, and they set on us in the night. Killed him with a rock and tossed me around until I gave them the coins."

"You're lucky that they didn't kill you, too," the train man said.

Noodles made the sign of the cross on his chest in the Catholic way, and mumbled something in his native tongue that none of them could understand.

"Lucky? Me brother was dead and I was alone in a strange land with no food and not a single pence to my name. I had nothing to bury Michael with, so I sat with him for two days. I begged others coming by to help me tend to him, but nobody would. After a time, I walked to the next tavern down the road and begged for something to eat. The tavern keeper's wife fed me and gave me a room in the back to sleep for the night, and I was thankful I had found such as she, a kind, Christian woman she seemed."

"Right kind of her," the train man said after he took a slurp of his beer.

Molly frowned at him, and then she saw Ruby Ann nodding at her as if instructing her to go on, and as if she knew the next turn of the story before it came. Molly wondered how Ruby Ann had gotten so wise after what had been done to her. Molly had suffered many things, but felt none the wiser for it, only weary and a lot more cautious and mistrusting.

"When I woke up I found that the tavern keeper's wife had locked me in the storeroom. I screamed at her, but she didn't answer me and she didn't feed me for two days. When she finally did open the door, she had a pot of water and a rag, and told me to clean myself and to try to look presentable. When she came back she had a plate of food and a man with her. She said if I was nice to him I could have the food, and then he came in the room with me and she shut the door behind him."

Ruby Ann's hand reached out to touch Molly's again. It was only a brief touch, not like before, light as a butterfly touching your cheek. And then she pulled it away and drew it to her own chest, kneading it with her other hand like bread dough; like some of the misery of Molly's story had gotten into it and she needed to rub it away.

The train man looked uncomfortable with what he had heard. He put some coins on the bar top and motioned to Noodles to make his change without looking at Molly again.

"What's the matter? My story too much for you to stomach?" Molly asked. "Does it shame you to hear a whore talk this way? To hear how the kind of woman you buy for a few dollars comes to her place?"

The train man shook his head, took his change and pocketed it, then started for the door. "Train should be here before long, and I've got to relieve the tender. Hate to lose my job."

"If I could take it, then so should you," she threw after him.

When he was gone, she poured a slug of whiskey into the coffee mug, left the bottle unstoppered on the bar beside her, and downed half the measure in a single drink. Then she cleared her throat and went back to her story.

"That tavern keeper and his wife used me that way for a while. Sold me to every man that wanted me for whatever they could afford to pay. Fur trappers and river men, and half-breed Indians and soldiers, sometimes for a dollar and sometimes for less than the price of a cup of whiskey. Some of them were crazy for any kind of a woman, and the others, the worst kind, enjoying most that I was only a girl.

"Then the law came asking the tavern keeper about how he'd heard of a slave girl being kept in the tavern. The tavern keeper and his woman denied it, but they sold me to some river men the next morning. They used me, same as before, all the way to Pittsburgh, and then they got drunk and I ran away and hid from them in the city.

"There were plenty of Irishmen in Pittsburgh working in the

mines and the iron works and the glass factories, but none of them took pity on me. I slept where I could, and stole what I could to eat until the coppers caught me. I thought they were going to take me to jail or to some orphanage, but they took me to this house up on a hill above the smokestacks. A lady met us at the door and they showed me to her like I was some little pig caught and brought to the feast. She pulled back my hair and looked at me in my filthy rags. And then she said I'd be pretty enough when cleaned up, and she paid those coppers a handful of coin for me and put me to work. The men called her Philadelphia and the place where they took me was Philly's House, but her real name was Elizabeth Preston and the big white two-story home was her bawdy house.

"At first, she only put me to work cleaning and picking up after the doves that worked for her and helping cook for them and doing their laundry and the like, but one day she came to me and asked me if I'd like to make some money instead of working only for my room and board. Said a girl with pretty red hair like mine need never go hungry as long as she was brave and smart. Said all women suffered from men in one way or another, and the best way she had found was to get paid for the trouble. I knew enough then to understand what she wanted me to do, but I wasn't sure about the other things she told me, not for a long time.

"It wasn't easy at first, not with all them coal-dust Welshmen and dumb-talking Germans from the glassworks and tin shops hot and heavy to try the new girl. And the Irish boys were the worst, and it shamed me for my own countrymen and Catholics to see me like that and know me for the Jezebel I was. But Philly, she looked out for me as best she could, and she taught me the trade. Taught me how to handle the johns, and how to keep myself clean and dressed better than the rest.

"And then they started building a railroad up at Allegheny

City, and Philly took me and some of the girls, 'cause she thought how those railroad workers would be short of women and nothing to spend their payroll on. I think she was also sick of the smoke and stink of the city and having to give a cut of her profits to the coppers and the councilmen."

Molly cleared her throat again, then looked at Ruby Ann and then at Noodles. "How come you two are looking at me that way? Here you stand staring at me instead of working."

Neither of them moved.

"This railroad, it was good for you?" Noodles said.

"The work wasn't any different, but Philly was right. There weren't any coppers to put the squeeze on you, and I liked seeing new places. Philly, she got tired of the camp life, and went back to Pittsburgh and then back east. I heard she caught the clap and died. Maybe she always had it and it only got worse. Anyway, I never saw her again to ask."

"And you?" Noodles asked.

"Me? I stuck with the railroad, first one line and then the other. Don't know why, but the life got in my blood. Ended up in Memphis during the war, and that's where I met my husband. A handsome one he was, straight off the riverboats working the shills at any kind of gambling they were game for, and sporting his fancy coat and hat and smiling like he was worth all the Queen's treasure . . . like he knew something nobody else did.

"We went to Sedalia when they were building the line there, and then he said he wanted us to try this Kansas cowtown he had heard about. He drug me to Baxter Springs saying how wonderful it was going to be, but he was already turning mean by then. The whiskey and the late hours always put him on edge, and then his luck at the tables failed him and I was the only one to take it out on."

"What happened to him?" Noodles asked. He had poured himself a beer and the head on it had left foam on his nose.

Molly pointed at his nose, and continued while he was wiping it off. "He stole from the wrong man and got himself killed for it. I knew the Katy and the KNVR were building line towards the Indian Territory, so I packed my kit and went there. I've spent a good part of twenty years working one line or the other. Sometimes it feels like the only life I've ever known."

Molly sniffled, and when she looked at Noodles again her face was flushing red as it had earlier. "How about your story, Italian? How'd you end up here?"

His eyebrows raised above the top rim of his eyeglasses, and there was still beer foam on the end of his nose. "Me? I don't have no story."

"We've all got a story. No way you get from one place to another without one, and it's the story that makes us who we are," she said. "Who are you, Noodles? What's your real name?"

He set the beer mug aside and straightened himself and brushed the front of his vest smooth. He cleared his throat before he said, like he was introducing a grand duke or something, "Salvatore Finocchiaro. And I am Sicilian."

"What did you say your name was?"

He said it again.

"No wonder they call you Noodles. I couldn't pronounce that if I had to."

She went to the front door and looked out upon the street. Already, whoever had cleaned up the site where the Bucket of Blood had once stood had their frame building almost completed on the outside. She had heard that the storekeeper at the old Indian town of North Fork a couple of miles to the east had torn down his mercantile and was moving it to the tracks. Apparently, that rumor was true.

Up the street opposite from the depot and beside the tracks, the white lumber framing of the hotel was already rising up like bones stacked on bones. Before long, the old camp was going to look different. Not a real town, but the start of something better than it had been. Nothing fancy, but still raw and real and built for purpose more than pretense—the kind of place where your past wouldn't matter as much because everyone was starting from scratch.

A train whistle sounded, and as the railroad man had told her, there was a train pulling into Ironhead from the south. Molly watched it come to a stop, and it wasn't much later when she saw Dixie Rayburn walking down the street carrying two armloads of luggage and being led by Helvina Vanderwagen towards a brand-new tent that the hotel crew had put up not far from the construction site and back under the shade trees at the edge of the woods.

Molly's eyes narrowed as she watched Helvina strutting down the street with the long feathers in her fancy hat waving like cavalry sabers and her chin up like her feet didn't touch the dirt like the rest of the people.

Molly felt Ruby Ann and Noodles both close behind her, looking past her at the same thing she was looking at.

Molly pointed at Helvina. "If she can do it, why can't I?"

"What thing will you do?" Noodles asked when he saw that Ruby Ann wasn't going to say anything.

"Build me something," Molly answered. "Quit moving on. Take a hold and make a place for myself."

"You want to build a hotel?" Noodles said.

"No, you fool. I don't know anything about a hotel. But a new town is going to need a good saloon."

"You have a saloon."

"No, Bill Tuck has a saloon. In fact, he's got two of them right now, but I aim to have one of them."

She turned and started for the back door.

"Where do you go?" he asked.

"I'm going to catch that train if it's going back to Canadian.

And then I'm going to find Bill Tuck and buy this place from him if he'll have my deal."

Ruby Ann turned and looked at her. There was a tremble in her jaw, and Molly wondered if it was because she had latched onto her like a beaten dog that had finally found somebody to be nice to her and feed her scraps, or if it was because she didn't like what Molly was about to do.

"I'll be back, girl. Wipe that look from your face. He'll take my deal and be happy about it, or I'll build my own place," Molly said. "I'm sick of it all and I want a change."

She almost made it out the rear of the tent, but stopped one last time. "One thing Philly taught me was to always have a stash of coin hidden back to get you by in the hard times, and the other was that a full cunning woman is something to be reckoned with."

Chapter Twenty-Five

Bill Tuck moved through Canadian Camp with a purposeful stride, as if anything or anyone that got in his way would get stepped on without so much as a bit of hesitation on his part. He always walked like that when he had worries on his mind or a definite chore to attend to. The stub of an unlit cigar was jammed in one corner of his mouth as solidly as if it had been thrown like a knife and stabbed there, and the Colt Open Top .44 flopped on his right hip in rhythm with every step. The pistol itself was unusual, for Tuck rarely wore a belt gun. The Hilltopper strolled behind him, and the bored, sleepy expression on his undertaker's face was in contrast to his employer. Everybody gave them wide berth, both recognizing Tuck's mood, and wanting no part of the giant heel-hound following in his wake.

They reached the tracks and Superintendent Duvall's private railcar, and Tuck stopped and pitched his cigar stub to the ground and scowled as if it suddenly became distasteful. The look he gave the door to Duvall's Pullman made him frown worse.

"Son of a bitch thinks I'm at his beck and call," he said. Then he looked at the Hilltopper and thought he saw him smirk. "You seem in an unusually fine mood this morning."

"No business of mine," the big man said.

"Well, it's my business, and I don't care for it one bit. Mr. High and Mighty railroad superintendent sends for me and thinks I'll come running just because he orders it."

"Seems like he was right," the Hilltopper said.

Tuck gave him a cold look. "Careful there. It's my coin jingling in your pocket and my whiskey you're swilling down every night while you're laid up with my whores. Best you don't forget that."

The Hilltopper shifted his booted feet on the roadbed, and the sound of the chat gravel crunching beneath them grated on Tuck's nerves like fingers raked across a chalkboard.

"You seem to be forgetting a lot of things lately," he added and turned and faced the Hilltopper. There was nothing in his stance that showed he recognized that his henchman outsized him by a considerable margin. He took a step to close the distance between them. "I'm the one man in this camp that isn't afraid of you. You get cross with me and I'll tear you down to the quick."

"All right," the Hilltopper said, but there was that same, smug boredom written all over his face that Tuck couldn't put a finger on.

The Hilltopper was always hard to read, but normally a dependable man who knew his place. Slow but steady, and loyal as long as his appetites were fed. You used him like a tornado that you could control. Gave him plain instructions for whatever unpleasantry you required, who you wanted scared or maimed, and the thing was as good as done the instant you said it.

But there was something different about the way he was acting then, almost defiant, and a version of himself that Tuck had not seen in a long time. The story of the Hilltopper's confrontation with the blacksmith and his bending of a horseshoe with his bare hands was the talk of the camp, and Tuck wondered if that notoriety had the Hilltopper momentarily full of himself. Maybe he had kept the reins too loose on the Hilltopper as of late. The man had been so long in his employ that he rarely gave him thought anymore and took him for granted.

And Tuck knew that you took nothing for granted. He told himself he was going to have to get his head back in the game, pay attention. The details were always what mattered, and if you knew the details you were rarely surprised. If you knew more than the other man, then you were likely the one who ran things. It was best he clamped down on the Hilltopper for a while, and reminded him who was boss. Details.

He studied the Hilltopper carefully, wondering if he had been dipping into the product that he was supposed to be selling. But he didn't show it if he was. The man's eyes looked as they always did, the same cadaver's stare since the first time they had met.

That first encounter was during the last years of the war on the riverfront in Memphis, when Tuck stood there in the middle of the fighting pit crowd, alone in the circle of space they had formed. And then that press of human flesh had parted to let the Hilltopper into the ring, a man so big that he towered over them all.

Tuck gave a grim smile, in part to make the Hilltopper uncomfortable, and in part because of the memory. He remembered how that crowd had stared so smugly at him, waiting to see his reaction upon seeing what he was about to face. And he remembered how the quiet swagger of the gamblers had changed to boast and all-out calls for bets and any takers at high odds who thought the stocky, shaved-head whoremonger could best the giant they had brought from upriver to take him.

Then, as now, the Hilltopper was truly the biggest man that Tuck had ever laid eyes on, and a man born with something missing inside him. The kind who could bend you and break you and listen to your bones snap with no more compunction than a wicked child watching an insect as he tore its wings off. And on that long-ago day, the Hilltopper had stripped out of his shirt, flexed his oxlike muscles, and stared at Tuck with that same flat, dead expression, as if his new opponent were no more than the next bug to cripple.

But Tuck had been a younger man then, in his prime, and already so often a victor down on the river docks that he rarely fought his own matches anymore, instead, pitting his stable of fighters against the other gamblers and making a regular profit through his shrewd betting. Sometimes, he made his money by being able to judge who was the toughest man, but the real windfalls weren't so simple, for there were other men with sound judgment and a cautious purse. But a crafty man, a man who knew how to manipulate things, could still find a way. Sometimes all it took was ordering his own fighter to take a fall and having his henchmen place many small bets against him on the sly, but occasionally, you could bring in a ringer that the locals didn't know. It was the same with roosters and dogs as it was with men. Either find a fighter who didn't look the part, or get someone to take a large bet in favor of their fighter before they had a chance to see what you were putting against them.

The instant the men across from him stepped aside to let in the Hilltopper, he knew that they thought they had found themselves a ringer. No wonder they had worked so hard to convince him to fight himself, and no wonder they seemed so confident when he handed the bet holder a stack of Yankee greenbacks thick enough to choke a horse. Fools, did they think this was a new game to him? Did they think they had reeled him in, hooked like a fat catfish on the end of a baited line?

The fighting pit was not truly a pit, but rather a bare strip of flood silt and dark sand gently sloping to the edge of the water between two boat docks jutting out into the murky river. Men normally busy at work loading and unloading the riverboats and wrestling goods back and forth from the riverfront warehouses sat on the edge of the docks looking down at him with their legs dangling. Others below them on the riverbank had formed a tight circle between the dock pylons that would serve as a fighting ring for the two combatants. There were other kinds among the river men: soldiers in their sweaty blue uniforms, gamblers from up town in their tall hats and fancy coats and scraping the muck from their shoe soles with their walking canes, and whores and sneak thieves looking for a pocket to pick. All of them, ready to see the giant from Missouri put Bill Tuck in his place. There were many there that had reason to dislike Tuck, and they were already gloating over what was surely to come.

Although Memphis on the banks of the Mississippi was a decade ago and three hundred miles away, Tuck inhaled and he could still smell the river that night with its strange mix of rotten mud and dead fish, and the man stink and tobacco smoke mixed in so thickly that it would almost gag you. And the pitch pine torches held high by some to light the ring, with the soot tendrils of resin smoke and sluggish flames casting hell shadows on the leering faces around him.

Tuck had watched the Hilltopper and thought how the ring would tighten once the men began to cheer the fighters and tried to position themselves to see the action, and how as the fighting space shrunk it was going to be hard to avoid the Hilltopper's big arms. The thing to do was to get it over fast.

And Tuck had stripped his own shirt off, and then bent to take up a handful of that stinking silt to rub between his palms to dry the nerve sweat from them. He had barely straightened and stood upright when the Hilltopper charged him. The giant obviously intended to take his adversary off guard, and the span of his hairy arms spread wide to engulf the smaller man. But Tuck had learned to fight in the logging camps of Minnesota, where no-holds-barred and root, hog, or die was an understatement. And his whole life had been a fight, from wean infant to grown man, spent bare knuckle and skull, kicking and gouging and whatever else you had to do to get ahead and keep from being put under someone else's boots. The Hilltopper's move was an old tactic as such things went, and he was obviously overly confident with too many easy victories over lesser men who feared him.

Tuck was not afraid. He hooked two short, hard ones into the Hilltopper's gut as he closed, and then he drove the top of his shaven head under the giant's chin. Tuck's bare scalp was marked with a half-dozen tiny scars from such blows, and that head-butt struck the Hilltopper so hard that everyone heard his teeth clack together like glass. When the giant staggered backwards and spat the blood from his mouth, one of those teeth flew through the torchlight.

Tuck had closed then, with the Hilltopper tottering on his heels, stunned with pain and all but finished on his feet. And Tuck had chopped at him, one hard fist at a time, enjoying the solid feel of each punch landing home and the meaty thud of those licks like he always had. The Hilltopper only managed a feeble defense, and that, too, was gone before long and it was only a slaughter.

He had punched the Hilltopper until his own knuckles split and the blood of them mixed together, slick and hot. And then he put the boots to him when his arms became too weary to lift. He punished him bit by bit, even though the giant was done for and there was no need for such. None of the crowd tried to stop him, but even they, used to bloodshed and violence, stepped back some, wanting no part of it. Tuck glanced at them out of the corners of his eyes, enjoying reminding them who he was and the cost of trying him. They were going to remember, and that remembering meant power for him.

He beat the Hilltopper until the sweat poured off of him and his lungs heaved for air. And then he looked down and saw what he wanted—saw the one meat-raw and bloody eye staring back up at him and recognized the defeat there. Only then was the brute's pea brain beginning to fathom that he was truly beaten.

He wrestled the Hilltopper to a sitting position and grasped his head in both hands. He hooked two fingers inside one corner of Hilltopper's mouth, pulling back hard towards his ear and stretching the skin of his face back until his jaw teeth were revealed in a death grin. The river men called that fighting move the "fishhook," and many a man who had been fishhooked bore the scar on his cheek where the skin had been split from the corner of his mouth halfway to his ear. The "Mississippi Smile" some called such a scar.

The thumb on Tuck's other hand pressed into the corner of the Hilltopper's right eye, pushing a little harder and harder until it bulged from its socket. The Hilltopper moaned.

"Say it." Tuck leaned close over him, cheek to cheek, and hissed in his ear.

The Hilltopper only moaned again and his bulging eye laced with red vein roots circled wildly and tried to focus on Tuck. Only a little more pressure and it would pop free from its socket.

"Say it," Tuck said again.

"Please." The Hilltopper's plea was slurred with his mouth distorted and gargled with the pink drool choking him, but everyone heard him good enough to know that he begged for his eye and for his life.

Tuck had let him go and backed away after that, but not with the exhausted rage the onlookers suspected, rather with a calculating measure of his victim and what he had done to him. He watched the Hilltopper flop over on his side, limp, and with his breathing coming slow and in great shuddering sighs like a horse ran to the ground and wind broken. Tuck swiped the sweat from his eyes and nodded at the beaten, bloody heap of man flesh before him. The Hilltopper was going to know who was master. The extra beating had not been a thing of rage, but with that in mind. However, the Hilltopper was a big, tough man, and with one like that you had to tear them almost all the way down. He would be lucky to survive it, but if he did . . . well, he might prove useful.

After that, Tuck had the Hilltopper brought to his saloon, stashed him in a back room, and assigned one of his whores to attend to his wounds. It was two weeks before the Hilltopper was on his feet again, and another month before he was anywhere close to being healed. There came a day when Tuck called the big man to him and said it was time to repay his room and board. And the Hilltopper had only blinked at him while the slow cogs of whatever mind that drove him turned and spun, and then he nodded and did as he was told.

Never once had the two of them talked about their fight, not in all the years they had known each other. And almost every day of their time together, the Hilltopper had been a silent shadow always lurking at hand, doing what was bid of him without question and without opinion. So, it had come with some shock and a great deal of displeasure on Tuck's part when almost two years ago the Hilltopper had disappeared while the rest of Tuck's operation was going to Texas with the Katy, saying only that he was going back to his home in Missouri for a while. When he returned and rejoined Tuck at Canadian he said nothing of why he had come back, but there was a rope burn around his neck that he tried to hide with a kerchief wrapped over it. Tuck didn't ask, and the Hilltopper didn't say, how that hanging mark had come to be there.

"What are you thinking?" the Hilltopper asked, and his boots ground the gravel beneath them again.

Tuck gave a thin, grim smile again, for he knew that the Hilltopper was also remembering the same day on the river and all the pain and the months it had taken him to heal, no matter how dumb and unreadable he tried to keep the expression on his face. A man beaten like that never forgets it, nor did he forget who did it to him, like a whipped dog growling his displeasure but also tucking its tail in submission.

Had the Hilltopper been any smarter and more experienced it might have been Tuck who had taken the beating that day, but that was not the case. And as long as he remembered how Tuck had crushed him, he would always have at least a sliver of belief that it could be done again. Hatred, yes, maybe, but the doubt made it easier to keep such men in line. Cruel understood cruel, and power respected greater power. Tuck knew that was why the Hilltopper had agreed to work for him and had stuck with him so long since.

Tuck straightened his shirt and made sure it was tucked in his waistband neatly, and then went up the steps with the Hilltopper following behind him. He knocked on the pane of glass set in the door, and then entered the Pullman car when there was an invitation from within. Willis Duvall stood on one side of the room looking at a map he had tacked to the wall between two windows. He kept his attention on the map, as if he hadn't heard the two men enter. Tuck took two more steps into the room, and the Hilltopper stayed beside the door.

"You wanted to meet with me," Tuck said.

Duvall looked at the map a little longer, but finally pointed at his desk without turning towards it. "Tell me about that."

Tuck went to the desk and saw the ball of opium half covered by the crumpled wad of brown paper. He picked it up and turned to face Duvall. "You obviously know what it is."

Duvall looked at the Hilltopper and then turned to Tuck. He pushed his rolled-up sleeves back above his elbows and walked the length of the room as if pacing in thought.

"What I want to know is if you're selling that stuff in my camp," he said when he stopped behind his desk.

Tuck started to deny it, but Duvall already knew better. "If I remember correctly, you gave me sole rights to any and all vice within the construction camps. You agreed to that so I would tend to a certain railroad competitor you needed put out of your way. The same railroad fellow that ended up with a bullet in him."

"I gave a monopoly on the saloon business in my camps, and no more," Duvall said.

"Happy men work harder, and that's where I come in. Whiskey, women . . . a little gambling, I make money and your railroad gets built and you make money. Both of us win."

"I've had a man that I needed not show up for work, and another one was so messed up on that stuff he overheated a boiler yesterday and almost blew my whole crew up. My foreman says he admitted he had let one of your soiled doves cook some of that stuff and inject it in his arm with a doctor's syringe."

"Whiskey or opium, what's the difference? Some men can't handle their medicine, and some don't know how to mix work and pleasure. You've fired drunks before, so get rid of them and hire someone else."

"This is different. And those federal marshals are still snooping around Ironhead. They're turning a blind eye to your saloons because of my railroad's influence and the right of way it holds, but you're pushing it too far with this opium. And I don't need the newspapers putting out any more articles about me and the MKT, not after what happened in Ironhead."

"Nothing in the books says opium is against the law."

Duvall ran a hand through his slicked-back hair oiled with tonic. "You, sir, seem to be under the false impression that it is you who owns this railroad."

"You gave your word."

"My word to a two-bit whoremonger and whiskey trader?"

Tuck looked at the Hilltopper and then back at Duvall. "I hear that Huffman, that KNVR man that bothered you so, is on the mend. They say he was talking and in fair spirits when he left for Chicago."

"Another reason that I owe you nothing."

"I'm thinking that Mr. Huffman might like to know how you wanted him murdered."

"You wouldn't dare. You'd be admitting your own guilt."

"Oh, no. I would tell him how you tried to hire me, and then how I turned you down."

"Try it, and I'll see to it that it's you that hangs."

"Oh, I'd do more than try, but that's not how it's going to be. The thing about knowing nasty little details about each other is that it demands a certain civility between us, if that is the word for it. Cooperation and compromise, Mr. Duvall. You tend to your rat killing, and I tend to mine." Tuck held up the ball of opium again. "This is my rat killing."

At that moment, a young black woman came through the door from the back room wearing a new yellow dress and carrying a tray of food. She hesitated when she saw the Hilltopper and Tuck in the room with Duvall, and Duvall gave her a sharp look as if trying to gauge how much she had heard.

"Go ahead, Hannah," he said. "Leave my food and then go about your business."

She set the tray down on the desktop, but never took her eyes off the two strangers.

"Go on, now, girl," Duvall said.

"Mr. Duvall. You remember you promised me I could have the afternoon off," she said. "Today's the day I'm getting married."

"Yes, yes. You've brought my lunch, so go have your afternoon. But I'll expect you back with my dinner this evening, wedding or not. This railroad is a seven-day-a-week proposition, and you'll get no special treatment." He nodded his head in the direction of the door she had entered by, and waved her off with a lift of his hand.

She threw one last look over her shoulder at them as she was leaving. When the door had closed behind her, Tuck smiled.

"Like them young and pretty, don't you?" he said. "But I never knew you went for the colored girls."

Duvall's cheeks pinched in and his eyes narrowed. Tuck instantly regretted having said that. And the other secret he knew about the superintendent was best kept to himself and saved for another day when he should have need of it. A little at a time, that was the proper way of it. Hold some of his blackmail material back for a rainy day.

"You, sir, have gone too far." Duvall jerked open a desk drawer and his hand darted inside it.

Tuck put a hand on his pistol butt, but didn't draw it. "I wouldn't do that Mr. Duvall. I'd hate to have to shoot you. There's no profit in it for either of us."

Duvall froze, but kept his hand inside the desk drawer. His face was flushed, but he was calmer than Tuck expected.

Tuck smirked again. Things were going well. Time to put the condescending bastard in his place. The instant the superintendent had asked him to hire someone to kill Bert Huffman was the same instant he had begun to own the man. At first, he had thought that the Traveler's failure to put a killing shot on the KNVR man might be a loose end that could come back to bite him, but now it was working out quite the opposite. Duvall couldn't claim Tuck's involvement without admitting his own guilt, and even if he did, he couldn't prove it. That was blackmail fodder, and that was leverage.

Huffman himself had been in Ironhead hoping to cause problems for Duvall. The Katy had been stalled out for months trying to cross the South Canadian River, and Huffman hoped that perhaps his own company could get the contract to build the rest of the line should the Katy have a few more mishaps with Congress and the newspapers constantly pointing out the Katy's construction setbacks. He had paid Tuck and a gang of Missouri bushwhackers a healthy sum to see to it that all hell broke loose at the very moment that the Secretary of the Interior was giving his speech to the crowd from the rear of Duvall's private car, and he had also paid to have those same men attempt to blow up the Katy's railroad trestle. Only Morgan Clyde's interference had stopped the destruction of the bridge.

At the same time Huffman was hiring him, Duvall, being an equally unscrupulous man and seeing his rival, Huffman, in his camp, paid Tuck a healthy sum to see to it that Huffman was killed before he could cause any trouble. There had been a large crowd at the ceremony to inaugurate the completion of the Katy's bridge over the South Canadian River, and nobody knew that it was the Traveler's bullet that had struck Huffman when so many were popping pistols in the air to celebrate. The common belief of those that were there was that a stray bullet from some drunken reveler had struck Huffman.

Tuck kept his hand on his pistol butt. "Now, why don't you let go of that pistol you have in your desk and listen to how it's going to be."

Duvall surprised him then, for when he removed his hand from the drawer there was only a bottle of whiskey in his hand. And he smiled in a way that instantly started little bells going off in Tuck's head.

"Again, Mr. Tuck, you prove that you're a problem I don't need and can't afford," Duvall said. "Did you truly think you could blackmail me? That you could come in here and threaten me with that gun you are wearing? A businessman fights with his brains, not guns and knives."

It dawned on Tuck then, and only then, that the opium wasn't the reason Duvall had called him there. And it dawned on him that he had caught on to that far too late.

The sound of a cocking pistol and the press of cold steel against his neck below his ear was even more of a surprise. He looked sideways and could make out the Hilltopper behind him and the Dragoon pistol he held.

"What the hell?" Tuck said.

Duvall poured himself a glass of whiskey, put the bottle away, and when his hand came out the drawer a second time it held a little Cloverleaf Colt pocket pistol. He laid the pistol on the desktop, as if to prove he didn't really need it. He was gloating, and Tuck knew then that the whole thing had been planned way in advance.

"Your big friend here is now in my employ, in case you haven't figured that out by now," Duvall said with apparent pleasure.

"Go ahead," Tuck said. "I suppose this is the part where he busts a cap on me and then you tell everyone how I was trying to assault you or rob you, or some other such excuse."

Duvall nodded. "So bloody, Mr. Tuck, but that's the general idea."

Tuck was thinking of ways to stall, buying time for a moment when the Hilltopper's pistol wavered the least bit. "You don't care so much about the opium, do you?"

Duvall shrugged. "A minor annoyance that could have been worked out in other ways, had I chose to."

"It's all because I have the dirt on you? Is that it? Cleaning up a few loose ends, are you?"

Duvall pulled back his desk chair and lowered himself into it. He took a sip of whiskey. "By now my men are on their way to your saloon. They will, of course, find your stash of opium, thanks to the Hilltopper here."

Tuck turned his head to look at the Hilltopper, pushing

against the cold steel of the pistol muzzle.

"Oh, don't look so shocked, Tuck. He appreciated the pay raise, and I've also handed over a working interest in your operation to him and a position as one of my railroad policemen as a side bonus," Duvall said.

The Hilltopper pulled his vest aside and showed the badge pinned on the breast of his shirt under it. A grin creeped across his face so slowly that Tuck could see where his lips were stuck together and peeled apart.

"By now, and if they haven't already, my men, along with your other people that I have bribed or bought, will have found that stash," Duvall said. "Imagine, Mr. Tuck, how that will look. Why, it will be no shock at all that a man who would traffic in such scandalous contraband would also attempt to burglarize my personal train car. And of course, be caught in the act by my new policeman."

"You . . ." Tuck started to say.

"Oh, but I will, and I have," Duvall interrupted him. "It might seem immodest for me telling you all of this, but what fun is winning if the man you've bested does not know how you've bested him?"

Tuck cut his eyes to the side at the pistol held to his ear, but the Hilltopper held the heavy Colt's Dragoon like it weighed nothing.

"You see, Mr. Tuck. You have proven to be a most distasteful and untrustworthy man with your threats to blackmail me and your double-dealing with Huffman and that Missouri riffraff that tried to rob my payroll. Oh, yes, I know about that, too. Saddens me that you thought I was so dumb as to not notice your crude machinations," Duvall said. "But you have also proven that your operation can be quite profitable. The only liquor sales in the whole territory that the tribal police and the federal marshals haven't pursued, as long as you're within the

200-foot swath of my right of way. Now, that's something, especially when my railroad is experiencing . . . well, difficult times, let's say, and my personal fortunes have suffered equally."

"You intend to run my saloon on the sly, don't you? Have the Hilltopper here act as a shill for you so your railroad board or anyone else doesn't know you own it," Tuck said.

"Slow, Mr. Tuck, but it's finally soaking in for you. The addition of your business and that little nest egg you've stashed in your safe will do little to help the company, but it will fluff my personal books somewhat, at the very least. What is it they say? Ah, yes, every little bit helps."

Duvall got up out of his chair and rolled down his sleeves and buttoned them. He watched Tuck while he tied his string tie and smoothed his hair back and donned his hat. Tuck tensed, but the Hilltopper pressed the pistol tighter into his skull and stopped whatever he had been about to do.

Duvall went past them to the door, opened it, and let the sunlight hit him full in the face. "Such a beautiful day to build a railroad, don't you think?"

"To hell with you," Tuck said.

He heard Duvall turn back to him and felt his gaze on his back. He saw the Hilltopper exchange glances with his new boss.

"Don't use the pistol on him. The sound of a shot mightn't give you time to place his body where it is most beneficial to our cause, and a blade is much more discreet. Don't you think?"

Tuck heard the door close behind Duvall and the sound of him descending the stairs. Then he heard the rasp of the Hilltopper's blade sliding out of its sheath.

"Say it," the Hilltopper said as he leaned closer. "Say it."

Chapter Twenty-Six

The Hilltopper's breath was as rancid as rotten meat as it washed across Bill Tuck's cheek. The cold press of the pistol steel was still there against the point of his jaw, and the knife in the Hilltopper's other hand pressed its needle point against his kidney.

"Say it, and maybe I'll make it quick," the Hilltopper growled. "This here knife is real sharp. Slit your throat like cutting hot butter. Won't hurt at all if you ask nice."

Tuck swallowed once and could feel the blood trickling down the side of his thigh where the knife point had pierced his flesh. Not deeply, but enough to hurt and enough to bleed him—a hint of what was to come, but no more. The Hilltopper was taking his time, enjoying the moment.

"Say it," the Hilltopper repeated.

"Puh . . . Puh . . . Puhlee . . . ," Tuck said.

The Hilltopper smiled and the pressure on the knife blade eased for an instant. Tuck spun into the big man and away from that pressure. The long, sharp edge of the blade slid across his side, and the pistol rolled off his neck. He was reaching for his own pistol when the Hilltopper's Dragoon roared and searing flame scorched his neck.

Tuck was blind with pain, but to quit moving, to quit fighting, was to die. There was no room to swing a fist with the two of them pressed against each other, so, as he had so long ago, he squatted and then drove upward with all the power of his legs and slammed the top of his skull under the Hilltopper's chin. The giant fell backwards and crashed against the wall, and his pistol roared a second time. The bullet flew wide of Tuck and only shattered one of the windows. Tuck turned and dove over the desk. When he came to a crouch, he got his pistol out of its holster. He did not rise up to where he could see the Hilltopper, but remained below the cover of the desk and merely stuck the gun above it and fired two blind shots in the general direction of where he thought the Hilltopper stood.

The Hilltopper roared with rage, and kicked the desk into Tuck, knocking him sprawling once more. Tuck rolled onto his back, saw the Hilltopper looking over the desk, that big knife in one hand and the smoking Colt's Dragoon in the other. Greasy strands of hair had fallen across his face, and he swung the knife with a fury. Tuck barely managed to duck in time, and the blade slashed the air over his head.

Tuck scrambled backwards towards the door leading into Duvall's personal quarters in the end of the car. He managed to get a hand on the doorknob, jerked it open, and was lunging through it when another bullet splintered the doorjamb beside him.

He made it to his feet, fell again over Duvall's bed, then rolled off the other side in a tangle of bedding. He hit the far door with his shoulder and it crashed outward against his weight. Behind him, he could hear the Hilltopper stomping after him. He fired behind him without looking, and then put a hand to the railing on the train car's rear deck and swung himself over it to the ground below.

He landed in a heap, rolled, and came up running, headed down the tracks. His pistol dangled at the end of one arm, and his other hand was pressed to his bloody side. The Hilltopper struggled to pass his width through the mangled door, battered it out of his way, and staggered out onto the rear deck. By then

Tuck was fifty yards away.

A bullet scattered gravel beside Tuck and then ricocheted with a nasty whine off a railroad iron. The blood was so heavy on his knife-cut side that it sagged his pants and shirttail, and he knew he was getting weak with the loss of it and wasn't going to run much farther. Already, he was stumbling and breaking stride. But there was one thing keeping him moving, and that was the train pulling out of the station headed south.

There was a flatcar on the tail end of that train, and it was only a few more strides ahead of him. The train was slowly creeping up to speed, churning and grinding, and ever so slowly building momentum. It seemed to Tuck as if he was never going to catch up to it. He dropped his pistol and reached out for the end of the flatcar.

And then that hand found a hold and he locked onto it with all the strength remaining to him. Unable to keep up his race, he stumbled and was drug along the roadbed, his toes skidding furrows in the ground. He let go of his side and took hold with both hands, straining to pull himself up on the car by his trembling arms. Another bullet ricocheted off the steel beside him as he got his belly over the edge of the flatcar and rolled onto it.

He pressed himself flat to the wood decking and looked back down the tracks. The Hilltopper stood on the platform of Duvall's car with his pistol aimed. Tuck closed his eyes, but no more shots came his way. Beneath him, the flatcar clanked and swayed. He opened his eyes again, and Canadian Camp was slowly fading out of sight as the train went around a bend.

Somewhere, sometime later, he rose to his knees, picked a likely spot, and fell from the flatcar to the roadside. He was too weak to stand, so he crawled on his belly into the brush and lay there for a long time.

Red Molly rode her own flatcar into Canadian, sitting atop a wooden crate beside Dixie Rayburn and watching the countryside roll by. She had never been one to wear her hair up high and braided or curled according to what was proper or stylish for a lady, usually letting her thick mane of dark red hang to the middle of her back or simply gathering it loosely at the back of her head with an ivory-backed clasp or a piece of cloth to bind it and keep it out of her face. She liked the way the wind whipped through it, and she felt freer than she had felt in a long time.

Maybe it was the wind in her hair, or maybe it was what had brought her to Canadian that gave her that feeling. A little pit of nervousness lay in the hollow of her belly at the thought of what she was going to ask Bill Tuck, but she had made up her mind and there was no turning back. She put her face to the wind once more and squinted at the sun hitting her face.

The work train pulled into Canadian, and when it rolled to a stop Dixie climbed down and helped her to the ground. He gave her an uncomfortable look, then cast his gaze at her feet, squirming a little, restless-like.

"What's on your mind? I told you I have business to attend to," she said.

"You better take some time and think on what you're going to say to Tuck," he said. "I know you aim to buy him out on the fair and square, but he's a touchy man that doesn't give up what he claims easily."

"I've made my mind up, and that's all there is to it."

"I know you have, but what's your hurry? That's all I'm saying."

"No, I know you. What else is on your mind?"

He kicked the ground he was watching so intently and then looked at the sky as if it might rain, although there wasn't a cloud to be found. It always amused her how bashful he was around women, even whores.

"I was thinking you might go with me to a friend's wedding," he said after whatever ritual he required to get the words out.

"Dixie Rayburn, are you courting me?"

"No, ma'am, I only thought you might like to come. Remember Saul from the cook tent back in Ironhead? Well, he's getting married today. There's not likely many to come other than that colored tie-cutter crew and maybe a few others, and, well . . . Oh, hell, I thought you might like to go with me. Maybe you remember Saul, and maybe it would be something to get you out of the funk you've been in."

She gave him a naughty wink. "And what is dear sweet Ruby Ann going to think of you two-timing her?"

"It ain't like that, and you know it. Besides, me and Ruby aren't sweet on each other."

Molly looked at the camp, anxious to wade through it and find Tuck, and anxious to have her say with him. But she held her arm out and let Dixie take the crook of her elbow.

"Lead the way, sweetheart," she said.

He adjusted the Rebel cap on his head and started along the tracks towards the biggest tent they could see.

"I hope we aren't late," he said after a few strides. "It's supposed to start at one o'clock. The superintendent is letting them use the mess tent after dinner time."

Molly was hard-pressed to match his strides. While not an overly tall man, his lanky legs were the longest part about him. She looked up at him, about to tell him to slow down, but thought better of it. His neck and smooth-shaven face were already blushed simply from the touching of her.

"You know, you're kind of handsome in a homely sort of way," she said. "I can see what Ruby Ann likes about you."

He blushed more, but finally grinned at her. "I know I'm nothing to look at, but you ain't heard me sing."

Before she could respond he broke into a song that was unfamiliar to her, and in a baritone voice that was surprisingly strong and clear. "Oh, Apple cider, and persimmon beer, Christmas comes but once a year. Ginger puddin' and pumpkin pie, gray cat kick dat black cat's eye. Oh, Jenny get ya hoe cake done, my Jenny. Oh, Jenny get ya hoe cake done, love! Oh, Jenny get ya hoe cake done, my Jenny. Oh, Jenny get ya hoe cake done, love!"

While he sang he did a little jig beside her in time to the lively tune he was singing. He took two strides after he was finished before he gave her a shy grin.

"Why, Mr. Rayburn, I never would have thought you a musical man," she said.

"My old mama, when I left the farm to go to war, she said I was gonna make a fine sodger boy," he said. "She said, Ben Rayburn, my son, you got the rhythm in your knees, you do. All that marchin' is goin' to suit you plumb fine."

"You're full of the blarney today, you are." Molly laughed, and it felt good.

And he heard her laugh and saw the smile on her face, and he began to dance along with his skinny legs bowed out and his knees and feet high-stepping to the shuffle of his chant.

"The Massuh and the Missus promise me, when dey die to set me free. Now dey both are dead and gone, left ole Silas hoeing their corn. Oh, Jenny get ya hoe cake done, my Jenny. Oh, Jenny get ya hoe cake done, love!"

They were still giggling and making small talk when they reached the mess tent. Inside the tent and under its flapping canopy was a small crowd that included the other black cook that worked with Saul, a few other colored men from the tie-cutting crew, and the blacksmith, Hank Bickford, and his wife and two children. Dixie and Molly slipped to the back of the group.

Saul and his bride to be, Miss Hannah Cole, stood at the front of the group, side by side, and she was every bit as pretty in her yellow dress as Saul had said she was. Saul wore a brand-new pair of overalls and a new white shirt with a celluloid collar buttoned on it and closed with a string tie. The pair of them fairly beamed at each other.

A preacher in a black dress coat and tie, despite the heat of the day, faced them with a Bible laid open in one palm. Dixie couldn't imagine where they had found a preacher, but guessed the man was a circuit rider or from one of the mission schools or Indian churches scattered about the east half of the territory. Many of the Indians thereabouts were strong on religion.

"And, do you, Hannah, under the watchful sight of the Almighty, take this man, Saul Goldsby, to be your lawfully wedded husband? Do you solemnly vow to have and to hold from this day forward, for better, for worse, for richer, for poorer, in sickness and in health, to love and to cherish, to honor and obey until death do you part?" The drawl in the preacher's voice was decidedly Texas.

The young woman looked up into Saul's face and nodded. "I do."

"Saul, place your ring on her finger and repeat after me," the preacher said.

One of the other black men from the tie-cutting crew produced a wedding ring from the bib pocket on his overalls and handed it to Saul. Saul held the ring to the tip of Hannah's finger.

"With this ring, I thee wed," the preacher said.

"With this ring I thee wed," Saul repeated, and then slipped the wedding band onto her ring finger.

"Then, in the name of our Lord and the sovereign and holy sacrifice of his son Jesus, the Messiah, and the powers vested in me by man and church, and the great state of Texas, I pronounce you man and wife," the preacher said.

The small group of onlookers gave a ragged cheer and a few clapped their hands as the newly married couple turned to face them. The men began to pat Saul on the back or hug the new bride.

"Congratulations," Dixe said as he shook Saul's hand. "She's every bit as pretty as you said."

Saul pumped Dixie's hand and beamed, and the woman beside him gave a nod of her head to Dixie meant as a curtsy to his compliment.

"You watch old Dixie here," Saul said to Hannah. "He's a sly old fox, and lettin' him 'round the women folks is like lettin' the fox in the henhouse."

"And you're a bald-faced liar, Saul Goldsby," Dixie said. "But I was thinkin' how if you could find a woman like this, then there might be hope for an average fellow like me one of these days."

Saul and Hannah laughed, but it was apparent that they had their mind on leaving.

"What? You ain't leaving yet. Not while we've got time to celebrate," the other black cook said as he came up with a fiddle in his hands. "We got us a good hour or so before we got to get supper ready. Plenty of time to have some fun."

Dixie grabbed hold of Saul's arm. "That's what I'm thinking. It's not every day we have a wedding in camp. I'm going to go get my banjo."

Dixie gave Molly a jerk of his head that indicated he was going to his tent to retrieve the instrument, and then he left her standing alone with the newlyweds.

"What say you, Mrs. Goldsby? How 'bouts a little wedding jubilee?" Saul said to Hannah.

Hannah smiled at that, but looked at the men around them, all of them strangers to her before the ceremony. "You sure, Mr.

Goldsby? We don't have much time together. I've got to serve the superintendent his supper this evening."

"You told me you got the rest of the day off, and ain't got to work no more for the superintendent 'til the mornin'. That's what you said."

Hannah glanced again at the strangers gathered around. "He wants his supper, and he'll get mad if I don't bring it."

"There's plenty of time for him to get his feed. Don't tell me you can't dance a little," Saul teased. "Maybe that uppity school you went to didn't teach such things and all that money the superintendent is paying you done gone to your head and you done forgot how to be ordinary folks."

"Husband, I can still dance the legs off any old farm boy," Hannah threw back at him.

Dixie returned carrying his banjo, and he and the cook found each other. Another man, a Chickasaw Indian with a pock-marked face and a guitar, joined them, and the trio put their heads together and agreed on a song. Shortly, they began to play, with Dixie leading off on the banjo and singing. The tune was sprightly, and the metallic plunk of the banjo strings and Dixie's voice rang under the tent.

"Old Dan Tucker was a fine old man, washed his face in a fryin' pan. Combed his hair with a wagon wheel, and died with a toothache in his heel. Get out the way, Old Dan Tucker. You're too late to get your supper. Get out the way, Old Dan Tucker. You're too late to get your supper."

The fiddle player broke in as smoothly as if they had played together before, with the guitar player strumming harmony. A couple of the long, wooden mess tables were pushed out of the way and a space made for dancing. Hannah acted shy at first when Saul led her out onto the improvised dance floor, but she was soon lost in the music, dancing with a grace all her own and laughing and giggling like a schoolgirl. The men around them slapped their legs in time with the music and cheered them on. Molly found her own foot patting the ground to the beat and rhythm of the song.

"Old Dan Tucker come to town, ridin' a billy goat, leadin' a hound. The hound dog barked and billy goat jumped, landed ol' Tucker astraddle of a stump. Get out the way, Old Dan Tucker. You're too late to get your supper. Get out the way, Old Dan Tucker. You're too late to get your supper."

Some of the men began to take turns stealing Hannah away from Saul, most times rarely getting to dance a single verse with her before another of them stole her away. In turn, she danced with them all.

Dixie sat aside his banjo and let the other musicians play on while he went to Molly and danced around her.

"What's the matter, Molly? Got no rhythm in your knees?" he said.

He held out his hand to her, and when she took it he spun her like a top, then caught her up again. Their dance was not one that was recognizable by any single style or type, but they simply did what felt good and what Dixie led her to, sometimes a wild, almost-waltz, and sometimes individual moves taken from square dances and quadrilles. Dixie was a good dancer, even if a little improvisational and backwoods in his maneuvering, but Molly was not to be outdone. She pulled away from Dixie to give herself space, and began a high-kneed Irish step dance, holding her dress out to the sides while she danced, springing high and pointing her toes in front of her, and making complex twists of her feet and stomps of her heels.

Dixie stopped dancing and cheered her on, clapping his hands. The fiddle player picked up the speed. Molly was already light-headed from the exertion, and the stab of pain in her chest came like a lightning bolt. She quit dancing and raced out of the tent with a hand held to her mouth. She grabbed hold of a stake rope once outside, and bent far over at the waist, coughing until her eyes watered and the knife stab of pain in her lungs felt as if another cough would split her chest in two.

The coughing spell lasted a long time, and when she was finished with the worst of it she felt a hand lay lightly between her shoulder blades. She wiped her mouth with a handkerchief she carried for such spells before she looked around at Dixie standing over her.

"Are you all right?" He asked like it was nothing, but he was looking down at the bloody phlegm she had spat on the ground, same as she had seen there.

"Oh, quit looking like that. I'm all right," she said as she straightened and pulled away from him.

"I've suspected you were a lunger for some time," he said.

"I never got over that croup I caught last winter. All that dancing brought on the cough," she said. "Bring me a glass of water or cup of coffee."

He went back in the tent, and she coughed a few more times and dabbed at her mouth to make sure it was clean while he was gone. He returned shortly with a mug of coffee.

"There's no shame in being sick," he said. "I don't know why you're acting this way."

"What do you know about shame?"

"I'd say a thing or two."

"Like what?" Molly reached inside her wrist purse and pulled forth her bottle of opium tincture. She took the coffee from him, poured a jolt of the tincture in it, and sipped at it and grimaced at the heat of it.

He eyed the bottle dubiously while she glared at him and dared him to say something about it.

"You ever been a cheap, lunger whore? A Jezebel with a taste for the dope?" She broke into a coughing fit again, slopping the hot coffee on her wrist and cursing the pain between her hacking and wheezing.

He shook his head. "No, but I had an older brother. Me and him went off to war together, and he was the brave kind, you know. Did things without thinking that most men would have to build themselves up to. He was like that since we were boys. He was the fastest one, the toughest one, and smart as a whip. No wonder my folks doted on him so.

"You would have thought he was the one that would come home from the war, but that wasn't the way of it. Our company was working its way up this hill, Little Round Top they called it. Horrible fight with them Yankees dug in on the high ground. Ask Morgan about it sometime. He was there on top. He'll tell you if you can get him to talk about it. Most men won't when it comes to a thing like that."

"What happened to your brother?" she asked as she leaned against the taut tent rope and clutched her chest with one hand and her coffee mug with the other. Her face had gone pale as death with the shortness of air and the pain of it.

Dixie pointed at the missing lobe of his left ear. "I got a bit of meat shot off me fighting through this old peach orchard, and then a bullet busted my ankle as we were skirmishing up that hill. My brother, Big Dixie they called him, he come to me across the battlefield. I told him to leave me lying there and to look out for himself, but he threw me across his back and carried me down the hill like he was toting a sack of grain. Never paid no mind to the bullets cutting the trees around us and the mortars shredding everything.

"I wouldn't have done that, I tell you. Don't think I have the courage to do it, even for him, my own flesh and blood, but he did. Carried me to safety without a thought for his own. And then when it looked like he had us in the clear a shell burst close to us and he dropped me. I crawled to him, thinking he had only tripped or was stunned by the concussion. But he wasn't stunned, he was dead. Him that had come through half a dozen fights, always running at the front and never a scratch on him, and not a single piece of that shrapnel so much as touched me."

"That's a terrible thing, Dixie, but no fault of your own. No shame in it at all." Her voice was quiet, barely above a whisper, as if she didn't have the strength to speak at a normal volume.

"Those army surgeons wanted to cut off my foot, so I snuck out of the hospital tent before they could do it. Snuck out of camp and hid in an old house. Laid up like that for weeks while two widow ladies living there doctored me and fed me. Me hiding in the root cellar of that house every time a Yankee patrol come by. Me hiding from my own side.

"You might be thinking that I'm ashamed to have run from those surgeons, but I ain't. I wanted to keep my foot. I'd seen too many men left missing their limbs, and the sight of them that way marked me something fierce. What I'm ashamed of is that I didn't go back to my company and rejoin them when my ankle was better. That was the same as spitting on him that saved me. There was no way I could go back home and look my folks in the eyes after that. No way I could deliver the news to them with me standing there a deserter and a coward, and the man that their favorite son had given his life for. So, I went to Texas, and now I'm here. Maybe a better man than I was then, and maybe not."

"Dixie . . ."

It was his turn to pull away from her touch. "You didn't used to get mad so much, Molly. You didn't used to let your problems get you down like you do. Everybody has got something that eats at them. Things they can't ever really let go of. You think Morgan doesn't have his shame? What about that woman that left him, Duvall's uppity slut, and the same that took Morgan's son and run off with him while he was gone to war? They had them a baby girl that died while he was away. Did you know that? Did you know she had the Pinkertons put on him when he tried to find them?"

"I know it," she said. "He says her name sometimes in his sleep or when he's been drinking too much."

"You think he's proud of everything he did in the war? He's got his secrets same as me and you, and so does everyone else you know. You don't hide everything from your friends, and you don't think you're so big that you don't need any help. Everyone needs help sometimes."

She wiped at her mouth again, fought off the cough caused by the tickle in her chest, and took a gulp of air. "You know, you talk pretty good sometimes."

"I always talk good. Problem is getting some people to listen to me."

He looked again at the opium bottle she was holding. "You know that can be habit forming, don't you?"

"That's what they say."

He was about to say more when gunshots sounded from somewhere near the train tracks.

"Are you all right here by yourself?" he asked her. "I can get Saul to come help you if you need it. Might be best if you went back inside and set down for a while and got your air back."

She shook her head. "Where are you going?"

He jerked his head towards the train tracks and the sound of the guns. "Duty calls."

"I'll be all right," she said.

He hitched up his gun belt and started for the tracks, not even noticing that she and the rest of the wedding party were following close behind him. Others from the camp fell in with him, all of them curious as to what the gunfire was about.

When he neared the tracks, he saw Bill Tuck crash through the door of Duvall's private train car and leap to the ground.

He motioned the crowd behind him to get back, and at the same time he drew his brass-framed Navy pistol. Bill Tuck was running down the tracks, hunched over at the waist and obviously wounded, and the Hilltopper appeared on the platform of Duvall's car with a leveled revolver in his hand. He fired twice at Tuck, but missed. Somehow, Tuck managed enough foot speed to catch hold of the supply train headed out of camp. The last Dixie saw of him he was lying on top of the flatcar, maybe alive, or maybe dead.

He looked to where the Hilltopper stood, glaring at the retreating train, and with a bloody knife and a smoking pistol held in either hand. Dixie wasn't looking forward to what he had to do next, and he wondered how many shots the Hilltopper had left in his pistol.

And then he realized that Molly was standing beside him, one hand clutched to her bosom, all but wheezing for air, and looking at the train disappearing around the bend in the distance.

"I don't guess you'll be having to worry about Bill Tuck anymore," he said.

She, too, looked like she was wondering whether Tuck was dead or alive. And then she looked a question at Dixie, as if wanting him to confirm it one way or the other.

"Looks like you might have inherited a saloon," was all he said.

Chapter Twenty-Seven

Morgan Clyde made his way through the gypsum hills, carrying his rifle in one hand and the dead turkey in the other. When he stopped atop a high piece of rolling ground and looked behind him, he guessed he had walked near two miles as the crow flew since losing his horse.

And the sun was low on the horizon when he came to a narrow canyon blocking his way to the north. The sides of the canyon were choked with cedars, and below the rimrock of it, he could see the tops of oaks and other kinds of trees lining the drainage at the bottom of it.

The way he took down the canyon side was steep, and littered with rock and loose earth, and he was hanging on to the twisted trunk of a small cedar and lowering himself down the roughest stretch of his descent when he saw a dark shadow to the side and below him. The farther down he went, the more it looked like the rimrock, some forty or fifty feet thick, was undercut into a large overhang, and such a place might be a good one for a campsite.

He slid down the last few feet to the bottom, and worked his way towards the black mouth of the overhang. He worked his way along the dry streambed he had landed in until he was directly in line with the overhang, and then climbed over a jumble of rock to it.

He was almost there when a black cloud of squeaking, flapping creatures streamed from under the overhang and passed over his head. He hunkered in surprise with one hand up to shield him from above, and then felt silly when he realized it was only bats flying out at sunset to hunt for the night. They went on and on, and he saw other clouds of them lifting to the sky from other points along the canyon sides.

When the stream of bats had thinned to a few occasional stragglers, he stepped under the massive slab of stone above him and saw that it was no overhang he had found, but a large cave. The mouth of it was at least thirty feet wide, and the ceiling loomed some eighteen feet above his head. It was made of pale gypsum rock, smeared in places with browns and oranges and pinks. He reached out to touch one side of it, rubbed his fingers firmly there, and felt the weird softness of the stone. Alabaster was what some called it, gypsum to others.

He dropped the turkey and went to retrieve wood for a fire. When he returned, he was carrying an armload of dead limbs and a bundle of dry grass, along with whatever other fuel he could break free or pick up off the ground.

He couldn't tell how far back the cavern went, but laid his campfire makings on a flat shelf behind two large boulders that had broken off from above and partially blocked the opening. He knelt there, wadded a double handful of the dead grass before him, and then leaned a few small sticks and strips of cedar bark over it like an Indian's tipi. He lit the ball of grass with a match taken from the tin in his pocket, and pressed his face close to the ground and blew on the smoldering bundle until it blazed up. He knelt there for a good while, feeding more wood on the fire as it called for it, and watching the sunlight fade to a dim gray out the cave mouth.

When he was sure that his fire was all right to leave alone, he left the cave and went to the dry creek bed in front of it. A little walking and he found a pothole of water. It was stagnant and a little buggy, but he skimmed the worst of it away with the edge of one hand. He lay on his belly and drank his fill, and then washed away the worst of the grime on his face and neck.

It was dark by the time he returned to the cave, and he skinned the turkey by the light of his fire. The heart, liver, and gizzard organs he laid on a flat rock against the fire to cook slowly, and then ran a cedar limb through the carcass and held it over the flames.

He was so hungry that he didn't wait for the bird to cool properly, and he blew on his fingers and smacked his lips against the burn of the grease and juices as he picked away the meat a bit at a time. It was undercooked and lacked any seasoning, but never had anything tasted so good. All but one of the legs and back meat was gone by the time he had his fill.

Amongst the pile of wood he had carried in was a gnarled, dead trunk of cedar that he had pulled from the ground. It still contained a wad of its brittle root ball, and he held that end to the fire. Once it was burning on its own, he held his torch high and moved farther back in the cavern.

The torch provided little light, but he began to fathom that the cavern went farther back than he had guessed. In fact, it appeared to open up into a larger chamber ahead of him. And there was a sharp, bitter odor on the air the farther he went into the canyon side. He felt something soft under his feet, and scuffed his boot against it to feel it again. Instantly, the odor became stronger, so strong that it burnt his nose and watered his eyes. Bat dung. Guano they called it.

He retreated back to his fire and away from the worst of the smell. He took up the remaining turkey leg, leaving the organ meat and what was left of the carcass for breakfast, and went to the mouth of the cave and squatted there. He watched the stars through the treetops and listened to a pack of coyotes yipping somewhere above him.

Later, he pitched the turkey bone aside and went out into the darkness to gather more wood and to take another drink. When he returned to the cave, he built his fire up and lay on his side, half-curled around it. He was asleep almost as soon as his body hit the ground.

And he dreamed of the woman who had left him, the son whom he hadn't seen since he was a small boy, and the daughter he had never known, died while he was away to war. And he dreamed other restless things, as he often did, of guns and men with guns, and of a face seen once across a smoky battlefield and framed in his crosshairs so long ago. Only a glimpse of him with long blond hair and eyes more intense than should belong to any man, but the face of the phantom the same, and the old nightmare that came more than the rest.

Morgan awoke clutching his side, hand atop the old scar over his rib bones, and it took him several blinks of his eyes and twice that many heartbeats to realize that the pain wasn't real anymore, nor had it been for many a year. He shook off his dreams and reached out and fed a few sticks into the feeble coals that were all that remained of his fire.

The wood was slow to light, smoldering, and through the smoke he could see that it was already light outside, the sunlight trickling down through the treetops and spilling halfway to where he lay on the floor of the cave. He wondered how he had slept through the bats' return to their roost, but perhaps he had been sleeping too soundly, for he had been as tired as he had ever been.

He was still drowsy and only half awake, and the boulders blocked a portion of the cave entrance, so he was slow in seeing the white piece of paper pierced on a stick set in the ground a few feet outside the cave. And he took two steps towards it, almost outside before his mind registered what it was, and he turned and dove back towards his fire.

A split-second later a bullet shattered pieces of stone from the cave wall where he had stood. He lay behind one of the boulders and listened to the sound of the rifle shot echoing down the canyon.

The Traveler adjusted his folded jacket padding the forearm of his rifle where it rested on rock before him. He lay on his belly and wiggled some to get more comfortable and steady behind the rifle stock. The mouth of the cave was barely visible in his scope lenses through the little hole in the tree limbs he had found.

Once again, he had let Clyde slip away. Placing a page from one of his diaries on a stick to lure Clyde had been a crafty thing that gave him much pleasure, but Clyde had understood what it was meant for a little too quickly, and he had missed a short, easy shot.

No matter. He had Clyde cornered in that cave. All that was left was to wait and to make the next shot count when Clyde lost his patience or starved out. Only a matter of time, and he was good at waiting.

He had found Clyde's dead horse with its broken leg the evening before, and the sign was fresh. But he hadn't found Clyde by the time nightfall came. He had been riding in the dark and looking for a likely spot to lay his head down and wait for morning when he came to the lip of the dark canyon. He smelled wood smoke almost immediately, but could find no sign of a fire's flame anywhere in the canyon bottom. After a long search for such a fire, he had ridden west toward the head of the canyon, and where it was so narrow and shallow you could almost jump a horse across it. He went around the head of it, and then rode the half mile back to a point on the north side of the canyon and opposite from where he had smelled the wood smoke.

It only took a quick search for him to spy the glow of a campfire flickering from inside that cave mouth like a candle in some kid's Halloween jack-o'-lantern.

So, he had ground-tied his horses and waited, watching the glow of that fire, until it dimmed to almost nothing. And then he had gone back to his horses and taken out one of his diaries. He started to tear out a page at random, but another thought crossed his mind and he struck a match to see by, shielding it in case Clyde should be awake and watching. It took him four matches to find the page he wanted for his bait. Perhaps the meaning would be lost on Clyde, but it tickled the Traveler immensely. It was all a part of the magic, and another sign that it was meant to be.

He had slipped down to the cave mouth, moving like a cat, so little noise did he make. And he had stuck that stick in the ground there with the page from the diary stabbed through at the top of it. Then he had moved back up the canyon side and waited.

Waiting as he was now, with an easy shot missed and his trick failed. He stared at the cave mouth, frowning his displeasure and anxious for Clyde to show himself again. He wouldn't miss the next shot.

Chapter Twenty-Eight

Morgan dragged his rifle to him and kept low behind the boulder that sheltered him. His greatest fear was that the Traveler would keep firing into the cave and try to cut him up with ricochets. The cave was big enough to lessen the chance of that some, but he still worried about it.

And there was no way that he was going to show himself in the mouth of the cave. The only place the Traveler could be was on the far side of the canyon, directly in line with the cave. That was the direction the shot had come from, and that was the only way he could have seen into the cave well enough to have taken the shot.

Morgan searched through the treetops, trying to find any hint of where the Traveler might have taken his stand, but he could make out little of the far side of the canyon, especially high up where the Traveler would likely be.

The daylight got brighter and the day slowly heated up. But Morgan was cool enough in the shade, only he was already thirsty. His two trips to the buggy waterhole had quenched his thirst for a time, but he knew that he was still a long way from rehydrating his body, so long had he been without water since leaving the Cimarron River and running across the Indians.

And he also knew that the Traveler would wait however long it took. The drygulcher would have water and he would have food, and he would have all the time in the world.

Morgan took up the turkey gizzard off a rock beside the fire and popped it in his mouth and worked it around between his jaw teeth. Gizzards were always gristly, but that one was overcooked and as tough as it was dry. And it only made him thirstier.

He chewed slowly and watched the angle of the sun change where it hit the cave floor. An hour passed, and then two.

And then a strong gust of wind blew into the cave, and he heard the rustle of paper. He looked beside him and saw the piece of paper that had been on the stick fluttering past him.

He turned and watched it until it was lost in the shadows. And he stared into that darkness and knew that there were only two things he could do. He could wait for dark and try to slip out of the cave, but the Traveler might move down close to the entrance and be waiting for him to try that. The only other option was to explore the cave and see if he could find another way out. He had a suspicion that the bats had entered the cave elsewhere, for he was quite sure that no matter how tired he was, he would have woken up if they had flown over him on their return to their roost at daylight. If they had entered elsewhere, then that might mean a place he could escape from.

He took his knife and cut off one sleeve of his shirt, then cut it in long, thin strips. Next, he took a dead oak limb and split the end of it down a few inches. The strips of cloth he slid down between the split, then wrapped the excess around and around the stick, tucking the ends under each other when he was through. There was a tin of brown grease in his shot bag, and he smeared a thin film of it over the cloth knob on the end of the stick. Satisfied with his work thus far, he emptied one of his powder flasks, the same one that he had used for an emergency canteen earlier, onto a flat stone. He touched the greasy knot of rags to the pile of black powder and rotated it and rubbed it until most of the powder was adhered to the torch head he was making.

He needed to move farther back in the cave before lighting it, for the sight of a burning beacon would quickly draw a shot from the Traveler. But first, he cut the other sleeve from his shirt, split it into two halves, then fashioned it into a sling for his rifle. He slung the rifle across his back to free his hands, took up his unlit torch, and moved deeper into the cave.

H crawled on his belly at first, and then on hands and knees. He hadn't gone forty feet when the gloom around him became so dark that he couldn't see, and the smell of bat dung became stronger than ever. A thought crossed his mind as he reached his hand out to feel his way, and it wasn't a pleasant thought. Putting his hand on top of a denned rattlesnake was the last thing he wanted.

The thought of such made him look back toward the light at the mouth of the cave, and he decided he was far enough away to try and light his torch. He took his tin of matches from his vest pocket, but fumbled the lid and spilled the container and the matches. He moved his free hand blindly along the cave floor feeling for the matches, and stuck his hand in some kind of loose fluff. Immediately, he knew it was the bat dung, but he kept feeling for the matches.

Instead of matches he felt a piece of paper, and he knew it was the paper that the Traveler had used as a lure at the mouth of the cave. He crumpled it and stuffed it in his vest pocket, and then felt again for his spilled matches. After a panicked moment of groping, he laid hand to two of them.

The first match sparked when struck against stone but wouldn't light. He said a quiet prayer and struck the second match. It flamed up brightly, and he held it to the head of his torch. The black powder flashed white, sizzled, and then the grease and cotton cloth caught flame. It was a smoky dim light at first, but it burned brighter after a while. He had no idea how long the torch would last.

Deciding that he had better move while he had light to see by, he gathered the tin and the few matches he could find and rose to a crouch. Beneath his feet, the bat droppings were knee deep, and in some places, they were piled as high as his waist and cured down to a fine white powder. He shuffled through and over that litter, holding the torch high before him. Overhead, he could see the dim shapes of the bats clinging to the ceilings, sometimes in small clusters, and sometimes in numbers that he couldn't begin to guess at.

Before long, the ammonia smell of the detriment beneath him became too much, and he tied his bandanna over his nose and behind his head. Still, his eyes watered in places when he kicked through an especially deep layer of the stuff.

As he had suspected, the chamber he was in grew wider where he stood. He lifted the torch higher and leaned back his head and saw that the roof was gradually sloping lower the farther he went, which might not bode well for the passage continuing much farther. And already, his torch was half burned away.

On he went, past weird formations of rock eroded and shaped by who knew what forces, and long stalactites hanging from the ceiling like dragons' teeth. In those same places the gyp rock had its wildest colors, with swirled veins of pink, yellow, and black flowing along the rock face like molten metal on its way to the mold. Tiny crystals or some kind of mineral within the stone sparkled like diamonds, much like he had seen in the Glass Mountains. In other places, the weak torchlight flickered on smooth walls that appeared to be hollowed out by water flowing through and over them.

The torch was only a dim glow by the time the cave narrowed down to passage barely six feet wide and where the ceiling only cleared his head. His feet splashed into water, and when he knelt down he saw that he was walking in a flowing stream running above his ankles. The water felt cold, and he was tempted to scoop up a handful. But the memory of the bat droppings he had passed through earlier made him afraid the water was tainted. A little farther on, there was water dripping and trickling from the ceiling. His parched mouth all but begged him to stop and have a sip.

The torch went out at a point where the passage narrowed even more, and he was left alone in the pitch black. For a moment, it felt as if the walls were closing in on him, and the fear set in. He fought off the urge to strike a match to see, for he had few matches left to him.

Placing his hands against the stone walls to either side of him, he moved forward. When he came to a wider point in the passage and lost that touch, he guided himself by the splash of his feet in the stream. The flow of the water seemed to be following the main channel of the cave, if that's what it was, and he could think of no other way to navigate.

But suddenly, he took a step forward and there was no more water, as if it had disappeared into a crack beneath him. And, at the same time the smooth floor of the cave ended, and it felt like he was crawling through a crack between leaning boulders. He had lost all sense of direction, but was sure that he was going up instead of down. His eyes strained in the darkness, wanting more than anything to see a ray of sunlight that meant he had found some kind of opening.

Twice he struck precious matches, but their meager flame showed him little. He was down to two matches when he finally saw light ahead. The climb became steep, as if many boulders had spilled down from above to fill a narrow chute. He moved from one to another, and always up that chute and toward the sunlight. Soon, he could see a dagger-shaped slit in the solid rock high overhead, and a little more climbing brought him to a small chamber directly below it.

The floor of the chamber was relatively flat, and he was bellying himself onto that ledge when he came face to face with a grinning skull. He rolled and pushed himself as far away from it as he could, not stopping until his shoulder blades butted against solid stone and he could flee no farther.

Once his racing heart slowed, he gave a cautious study to what he had found. In the single bright patch of sunlight in the center of that chamber lay the skeletons of a man and his horse. The man's rib bones and torso were cased in a steel breastplate of a kind Morgan had only seen in history books. It was old, Spanish armor, such as worn by the conquistadores like Cortés, Pizarro, Coronado, and other conquerors who had come to the New World some three hundred years earlier in search of gold and other riches. The grinning skull that had startled him was still inside its steel helmet, and the wispy remains of a beard clung to its lower jaw like dried moss. When he touched the helmet, strands of those whiskers fell away like dust.

A long, wooden lance shaft with a great, forged steel blade on the end of it lay in the bone pile, as well as a dry-rotted leather saddle. Morgan looked up at the dagger-shaped skylight some thirty feet overhead and envisioned what had happened to the Spanish soldier and his horse. The skylight was likely a sinkhole, and the Spaniard had fell into it unawares. Even if he had survived the fall, there was no way to climb back up, for the solid stone walls of the chamber were smooth and almost vertical. Morgan hoped that the man had died instantly after his plummet, for what a terrible thing it would have been to have to lay there crippled staring up at the patch of sunlight.

Morgan sat there for a good while, resting and thinking of what to do next. The last thing he wanted was to return down the chute into the darkness, but that was where he had to go. Adjusting the rifle on his back, he started down, and before long he was in the dark again.

His greatest fear was that he would fall or trap his leg or

ankle in some crevice and cripple himself. All he could do then was stay where he was and die, much as the Spaniard had. How long would it be before someone found his bones, if ever?

His feet splashed in water again, and he was pretty sure he had returned to a point near where he had started his ascent up the chute. He reached out ahead of him in the dark and moved in shortened steps, feeling with his boot toes as much as his hands. He expected any moment to find again the point where the stream disappeared into the cave floor, but the water got deeper instead of disappearing. He was soon up to his knees.

He ran his face into stone, not hard, but enough to make his nose hurt. The passage he seemed to be following made a few tight twists and turns, and once more, he had no sense of direction other than he seemed to be going gradually down.

Another rivulet of water spilled from somewhere overhead. He had become too thirsty to think about what the water might be contaminated with, and put his mouth beneath it and drank greedily. Maybe he would regret it later, but the water tasted as sweet and pure as any he had ever drunk.

Somewhat refreshed, he moved on. Twice the stream passed under large slabs of stone, and he had to climb over them, never sure that he would find the watercourse guiding him to wherever. And at times he had to stop and stand in place for long periods, fighting off the feeling of the darkness closing in on him and that he was lost and never to see daylight again.

And then the stream became shallower and shallower, until he couldn't feel its pull against his feet anymore. He kicked and heard no sound of a splash, and then knelt to feel with his hands. Only a thin sheet of water flowed across his fingers when he pressed his palms to the floor, and when he reached forward his hands struck a solid wall of rock, as if the water issued straight out of it.

He stood and began to turn, reaching out for the feel of

anything. The panic in him grew, for he felt nothing. How many times did he turn a circle? He swore that he could feel the darkness spinning about him. And then his hand felt a leaning slab of smooth rock, and when he reached with his other hand, he felt another slab leaning in the opposite fashion. Into that V he climbed. The bottom of it was too sharp an angle to let his feet pass, so he braced his legs against one slab and his back against the other. In that fashion, he crabbed sideways.

The V passage ended after only a little distance, and he was once more back on a level floor. When he moved his feet, he could hear the dust scuffing beneath them. And the farther he went, the more light he found, until he could see well enough to tell that he was traversing a narrow hallway sloping downhill a little. He passed around a gradual bend and sunlight spilled into a smaller version of the amphitheater he had originally started from. He almost cried he was so glad to see the little opening ahead leading out into the real world of sunlight and fresh air.

The opening was no more than ten feet wide, and maybe four feet tall, overhung by a rock ledge. He stopped just shy of the opening, and peered out into the canyon. It seemed much wider there, wherever it was that he had come out, and he guessed that he might be farther down it and near to the mouth of it where it spilled out onto flatter, more open country. A thicket of low growing, scattered cedars was all that was in sight, and no more of the oak trees where he had entered the caverns.

The Traveler could be anywhere out there. Morgan had no idea how far he had come, or where he was right then. Everything was only guesswork. The opening before him might be a mile away from the one he had entered by, or it could be ten feet away. And the instant he stepped outside one of the Traveler's bullets might take him.

The smart thing would have been to wait for nightfall, but he had all of the cave he wanted. He pushed outside and ran for the nearest clump of cedars. No shot came his way.

The way down the canyon provided the fastest, easiest going, but he went up the side of the canyon, instead. High ground was what he needed, where he could see the Traveler before he saw him. Where he could, he kept behind the cover of the cedars growing precariously on the steep slope and sometimes right out of what looked like sheer rock. He took a zigzagging path, using rocks and eroded cuts both to find purchase for his feet and hands, but also to cover him where there were no trees or bushes. And above all, he went slowly. Never more than a step or two at a time, watching and listening for any sign of movement that might be the Traveler.

The sun was maybe an hour above the western horizon when he climbed over the rimrock and stood on level ground again. He looked towards the head of the canyon, and thought he spied the point where he had entered it the evening before. If that was the place, he guessed that he traveled at least three quarters of a mile in the cave system, and perhaps twice that far with all his twistings and windings and false turns in the dark. Over half a day he had spent lost inside the earth.

He unslung his rifle from his back, examined it for damage, then glassed the far side of the canyon. Once he thought he saw the flick of a horse's tail in a clump of large cedars, but when he sat down and rested the rifle on one upraised knee he could not spot that flash of movement again. Maybe it had been a horse, or maybe it had only been a deer moving through the brush or the flitter of a bird from limb to limb.

Rising up, he moved east, winding his way through the labyrinth of cedars. The canyon side soon ended in a broad point of land that jutted over a broad flat stretch of rangeland. The north side of the canyon opposite him continued farther on, the two walls that had once ran parallel now growing apart like the bell of a funnel.

He sat on the ground at the highest point he could find on that great outthrust of tableland, and watched the opposite rim, and all below him. He assumed the Traveler was somewhere on the far side, and perhaps farther up the canyon, still waiting on him to appear from the cave where he went in. To the north and east of his position the land gradually broke into a vast plain after passing through a few scattered buttes. If he came down off the tableland and headed that way, he was going to be out in the wide open. He decided to stay where he was, and hope that he might spot the Traveler or catch him moving before the sun went down.

His stomach growled and he thought of the turkey bits he had stuffed into one of his vest pockets. When he reached in that pocket, his hand found the piece of paper the Traveler had left for him. He unfolded the crumpled sheet, and saw that it was what he thought it was, a page from one of the Traveler's diaries.

The sun was so far down that it was barely enough to read by, but he squinted at the paper, anyway.

July 3, 1863—I seen one of those green jackets today shootin at our boys through a hole in a rock fence. Studied him some and was sure it was the same one I seen two days ago. Seed him true and clean through the cannon smoke rollin' over the hill and made my calculashuns. Just a hint of a crosswind from the west. Used my iron sights on the 1,000 yard notch for a locatin shot. Held upwind a smidgen. Shot high and didn't play the wind right. Used my scope for the second shot and dialed the back ring adjuster to my scratch mark for 800 yards. Held half a body length upwind on him. Second shot was high and I knowed I was too ankshus. But I found the range and windage by then and swabbed my rifle bore and reloaded. Waited for a gap in the smoke and found that green jacket clear in my crosshairs again. And then he rolled over and looked at me. No way he could see me where I was hid, and no way he should have knowed I was shootin' at him. Fair gave me the chills and I knowed then he had the sense on him. He knowed he was about to die, same way the hogs know when it is butcherin time. I kissed my trigger and saw my bullet take him in the middle and watched him squirmin' like an old worm pulled out of the ground. And then he didn't move no more. Nothin but meat.

Morgan crumpled the paper in his fist, squeezing and squeezing, and crushing the memory of it. Reading about his own wounding brought back more of that day than he cared to remember, and the heat ran along the roots of the long scar on his side until he could feel the tracing of it without laying his fingers to it. And then he looked over the canyon in the fading daylight. It was time to end it, one way or the other.

Chapter Twenty-Nine

Dixie was still weighing how best to approach the Hilltopper when Superintendent Duvall came through the crowd and walked right up to the car platform. The Hilltopper put away his weapons at Duvall's arrival, and the two of them held a quiet discussion. They ceased whatever they were saying when Dixie eased up close to them, his own gun still in his hand.

"That damned saloonkeeper tried to rob my safe," Duvall said to him when he noticed him.

Dixie looked from one of them to the other, trying to figure out what was really going on. While he wouldn't put robbery past Tuck, burglary wasn't normally his style.

"Tuck's your boss, ain't he?" he asked the Hilltopper.

"This man is in my employ," Duvall said.

"Your employ?"

"Yes, my employ. Only recently I became aware of certain rumors that someone was plotting against me, and I thought it prudent to hire this man."

"Swap loyalties kind of quick, don't you?" Dixie was still looking at the Hilltopper.

Duvall didn't let the giant answer. "This man came to my train car to discuss with me the terms of his employment, but found me gone. Before he could leave, he heard someone rummaging around inside and investigated the matter."

"And he caught Tuck red-handed, did he?"

"Quite so. Mr. Tuck then brandished a weapon, and my employee was forced to shoot."

"That so?"

The Hilltopper nodded.

Dixie looked to Duvall. "You don't think it odd that Tuck would break into your car right after you hire his man away from him?"

The Hilltopper tensed at that, and Dixie was careful to note how the big man's right hand eased up toward his belt.

Duvall held out a hand to the Hilltopper as a signal not to do whatever it was he was thinking on doing. "I'm quite certain that there was no arrangement between the two of them, as you seem to be thinking. In fact, it was this man who initially warned me of Tuck's plans to rob me."

"Regular concerned citizen, aren't you?" Dixie said.

"Only doing my job," the Hilltopper answered.

"You two keep talking about this job," Dixie said.

Duvall nodded to the Hilltopper, and the giant's mouth creased a little in what Dixie thought was meant to be a shit-eating grin. The Hilltopper slowly pulled back his vest to reveal the railroad police badge under it.

"You are too perceptive, Chief, and I must admit that I haven't told you the whole truth," Duvall said.

"Well, by all means, please do."

"This man has been working undercover for me for some time now," Duvall said while the sight of the badge was still soaking in on Dixie. "That was why you saw him leaving the cabin where you found my crane operator."

"You hired him as a policeman?"

"Unbeknownst to you, there have been several threats to my person since the difficulties back in Ironhead. I also had my suspicions, same as you did, that Mr. Tuck was behind much of those difficulties. Although, I didn't give voice to those suspicions at the time, thinking it more prudent to hire someone on the inside of his operation to find the truth of the matter."

"I'll agree that Bill Tuck was a lot of things, but I don't see him foolish enough to risk trying to rob your safe in the broad daylight."

"It seems that you were wrong."

"Mind if I have a look?" Dixie gestured to the Pullman.

"Suit yourself, but I think you could holster your pistol now."

Dixie squinted at Duvall, and then at the Hilltopper. He took a long time thinking that request over, but finally shoved his pistol back in its holster as he stepped past them and up into the Pullman.

He found nothing inside the car other than signs of a fight. The safe behind Duvall's desk was closed and unmarked. Dixie tried to imagine how Tuck thought he could break into it on the quiet, unless he had somehow procured the combination or a key. And he couldn't help but think that the deal had been something that was cooked up between Tuck and the Hilltopper—a something that had gone very wrong for Tuck.

He came back outside and stood on the rear deck, looking at the crowd that stood at a distance. He could see Molly there amongst them, shading her brow with the flat of one hand and looking anxious. He took out his pocketknife and cut a chew of tobacco off the plug he always carried, and gave the crowd one last look before he went down the steps. Duvall and the Hilltopper were waiting for him.

"Well?" Duvall asked.

Dixie pressed the blade of his pocketknife against the back of his leg and folded it closed while he nodded at the Hilltopper. "I'm not working with him."

"In case you haven't noticed, Mr. Rayburn, I run this railroad," Duvall said.

"Let me fix that attitude of his," the Hilltopper said.

Dixie kept plenty of distance between himself and the Hilltopper, but ignored the threat and focused on Duvall. "You run this railroad, true, but you hired me as your police chief. That means I pick my men."

"The Hilltopper will travel with me as my personal guard. Consider him a special agent, and the badge only gives him some needed authority in that capacity. You will still attend to your normal duties and have charge of law enforcement along this line," Duvall said.

"You want a bodyguard, I'd advise you to let me hire you one."

"I'm quite satisfied with his performance so far. Where were you when Tuck was in the act of robbing me? And what if Tuck wasn't trying to burglarize my car at all, but rather wished me bodily harm and was waiting for me to return?"

"You've hinted a couple of times about that. What did Tuck have against you?"

"I have had unpleasant conversations with Mr. Tuck on several occasions, and I'm quite sure some of the directives I've given him in regards to his conduct in my construction camps did not set well with him," Duvall said. "I also sent word to him yesterday that I wanted to speak with him about the opium you found, something you might well remember."

"Maybe so, but I wouldn't trust this one as far as I could throw a bull by the tail." Dixie nodded again at the Hilltopper.

The Hilltopper stood a little taller, and his hand had somehow come to rest on the handle of his knife without Dixie noticing it until then.

"He insults me again, and I'm going to pinch his little pin head, no matter what you say," the giant said.

Dixie took two steps backwards, ready to pull his pistol and wondering if he could get it out in time before the Hilltopper had at him with that knife.

"It is you, sir, who is acting most uncivilized," Duvall said to

Dixie. "I don't know what your personal dislike of this man is based upon, but I expect you to forget the matter right now and act like a gentleman and a peace officer."

Dixie and the Hilltopper continued to glare at each other.

"I told you I won't work with him," Dixie said.

"You won't work at all if you don't get on your horse right now and go find Bill Tuck," Duvall said.

Dixie hesitated, but finally spat a stream of tobacco juice on the ground between himself and the Hilltopper, and then turned and headed for the company corrals. The Hilltopper made to go after him, but Dixie stopped and turned back to them.

"I go alone. You're nothing but the bodyguard, remember?"

The Hilltopper looked to Duvall, and the superintendent took a long moment before he nodded his agreement.

"I want Tuck found, you hear me?" Duvall said as Dixie walked away. "You bring him back here alive, or hanging over a saddle, I don't care which."

Dixie passed by Hank Bickford's shop on the way to the horse corrals. The blacksmith left his forge and fell in beside him.

"What was the deal with Tuck?" Hank asked.

"Duvall was gone, and his new man caught Tuck prowling around in his private car," Dixie said without breaking stride.

"His new man?" Hank gave Dixie a perplexed look.

"Oh, haven't you heard? Duvall has pinned a badge on the Hilltopper. That's his special detective and personal bodyguard." Dixie shot another stream of tobacco juice to the side of them as a sign of his disgust.

"So, Tuck's hired man is now Duvall's hired man?"

"Curious, ain't it?"

Dixie kept walking, but Hank stopped.

"I'll tell you what's more curious," Hank said. "I saw the

Hilltopper and Tuck going into that Pullman on my way to the wedding."

That stopped Dixie in his tracks. "You don't say?"

"I do. What are you going to do about it?"

Dixie looked at the rope-fenced horse corrals, and then at the train tracks leading south out of camp. "I reckon I'll do what Duvall wants and go find Tuck. He might have some interesting things to say if he's still alive to do any talking."

Chapter Thirty

Red Molly was the last of the crowd to leave. The rest of the onlookers had their walk around the Pullman and a gander at the scene, and then went about their business murmuring whatever rumors about the event they were already forming. She soon stood there alone, suddenly unsure what she was going to do next.

Feeling conspicuous and awkward standing there like that, she walked through the camp until she located Tuck's new saloon. If anything, it was even uglier than the Bullhorn. It was too early for good business, and when she went inside she found that she was the only one in the room beside the two bartenders behind the bar, and one of the faro dealers sitting at his table idly shuffling cards while one of Tuck's soiled doves sat across from him and watched him practice.

Molly recognized one of the bartenders, the one everyone called Pork Chop, and went over to him. She stood there awhile before he finally put down the newspaper he was reading and gave her a bored up-and-down glance.

"What will it be, Molly?" he said as he adjusted one of the suspenders that held up his checkered pants. He was a heavy man, and if it weren't for those suspenders his belly wouldn't tolerate a pair of pants.

"Pour me a beer, Pork Chop."

He took a brown bottle of beer from the back shelf and set it before her. "Are you here for business or for pleasure?"

"Thought I might talk to Tuck. That's all." She sipped at the lukewarm beer and stared at him over the bottle.

"Guess you haven't heard," he said.

"Heard what?"

"About Tuck."

"I saw the end of that fight as I was coming over here. Do you think Tuck's dead?"

"Maybe. Didn't see it myself, but from what I heard . . ."

"I needed to talk some business with him. You know he left me to run the Bullhorn for him."

Pork Chop tugged at his suspenders again and gave her a strange look. "Tuck lost more than that fight with the Hilltopper."

Immediately, Molly knew there was more going on than she knew. "How's that?"

"The Hilltopper's running things now. Guess you'll have to talk to him."

"Is that so?"

He looked around the room, as if checking to make sure that there was nobody eavesdropping. "I guess I can say this to you. You know how Tuck was. Mean and stingy to work for. Can't say he didn't have it coming, and maybe it won't be so bad for us."

"This Hilltopper is the one I saw shooting at Tuck, isn't he? The big one? Should I know him?"

"Don't know how you could forget a man as big as he is if you ever saw him once."

"I don't remember him from Baxter Springs, or anywhere on the Katy line."

"He used to work for Tuck in the old days, and he joined back up a week ago."

"And he took things over? Hard to believe he could outfox Tuck."

Again, Pork Chop checked for eavesdroppers, and then said in a quieter voice. "I didn't tell you this. You hear me? Don't need no trouble."

Molly nodded at him solemnly.

He leaned close to her over the bar top. "Wasn't long after Tuck left here that some of the railroad boys showed up armed to the teeth, six of them. Wasn't nobody here but us this early in the day, and they made a lot of noise claiming Tuck had been selling opium. Claimed that it had made some of them sick, and that another man had died pumping that stuff in his veins. They shook the place up some, saying as how Bill Tuck was going to be lynched if they caught him."

"Was that after Tuck was shot or before?"

"You tell me." He shrugged. "See that faro dealer over there? He's new, too, same as the Hilltopper. Tuck thought a lot of him for some reason, but as soon as those railroad men showed up he took them right to Tuck's safe."

"Tuck wouldn't have told anyone the combination to his safe."

"Nobody but the Hilltopper and Tuck could get in it, but that dealer learned the combination somehow, and he opened it up for those railroad toughs. They sacked up everything in it and claimed it was evidence for the railroad police. Threatened us a little more, and then they left. Didn't even bother with my cash drawer. Said that the Hilltopper would be around soon to tell us how things were going to be from here on out, and that Superintendent Duvall had hired him for the railroad police."

Molly looked around the room. "Nobody seems too upset about it."

"Like I said, Tuck wasn't very lovable. He's gone, and none of us want to fight his battles for him if he's gone for good, especially not if it's the railroad police we're fighting. Nobody has forgotten how Duvall brought in the army back in Ironhead. You can't buck the big shots, and that's a fact."

She gave him a scornful look. "You let them rob the place."

He lifted both hands in appeasement. "Oh, I know. Maybe it's a rotten deal, but it is what it is."

Molly took another sip of beer. "So this Hilltopper has the backing of the railroad?"

Pork Chop looked over her at the door and then picked up a bar rag and started wiping the bar top, moving away from her. "I ain't saying anything else, and I doubt you'll find anybody who will."

A large shadow cast over her, and she turned to see what had frightened the bartender away. The Hilltopper stood just inside the doorway, and he was even bigger than he had looked from a distance when she saw him at the tracks.

"You come looking for Tuck?" His voice was deep and his speech was especially slow.

"I did. I'm Red Molly, and I run the Bullhorn at Ironhead."

"I know who you are." He looked around the room and gave a grunt, whether because he was pleased with what he saw, or disgusted by something, she couldn't tell.

"They say you're running this place now," she said, unsure what else she could say.

He looked back to her. "I am, and I'll be paying you a visit at Ironhead before long. Want to look over my holdings."

"Your holdings? Tuck *sold* you the Bullhorn, too, did he?"

He grunted again, something closer to a chuckle that time. "Got a smart mouth, don't you?"

"Maybe, or maybe I'm trying to understand how things are."

"Well, I don't like whores running my businesses, and I don't like smart-mouthed whores at all." He stepped closer to her as he said it, so close that she could smell him.

It took all that Molly had not to move away from him, and to keep looking up into his face. "Well then, you ought to sell me the Bullhorn."

"I suppose you want to buy it with the money Tuck left you to run it," he said.

"No, with my own money."

He stepped around her, passing so close that he brushed against her and caused her to move a little to keep from being knocked down. Pork Chop handed him a bottle of beer without being asked for it, and then went back to the far end of the bar.

The Hilltopper rested one hand on the bar top, and turned up the beer with the other. He drank it down in a single pull, never taking his eyes off Molly. When he was through, he set the bottle down before him and rested his other hand there, leaning on his arms with his huge shoulders hunched together. "When are you going back to Ironhead?"

"Today if there's a train. You sure you won't rethink selling to me?"

"Not a chance. You come down here for whatever and see that Tuck is finished. A crafty one might think she had a chance to get something for free."

"That's not the way it is. I came here to make the same offer to Tuck, but now it seems I'm dealing with you."

"You're not dealing with anybody. The Bullhorn is mine. Tuck left it to me, the same as this."

"Left it to you? I'd say you killed him or pretty close to it."

"I was his right-hand man, and he owed me money. You show me a will that says it shouldn't go to me to square things." He looked around the room. "Anybody here question who owns this place?"

None of them said a word. Molly felt her anger rising as she stared at his hairy chest hanging out of his unbuttoned shirt and the dark brown ring of scar tissue around his neck. "I don't suppose you could show me a title to the Bullhorn or its contents, could you?"

His fingers gripping the wooden top of the bar squeaked as he contracted them. "And I don't suppose you could show me one, either."

"No," she said. "But for the sake of argument, say I give you five hundred dollars for it all. The Bullhorn Palace, lock, stock, and barrel. No questions asked. I give you the money and you write me a bill of sale. If Tuck comes back and makes an issue of it, then I've lost five hundred. If he doesn't . . . well, you're all the richer and you can tend to the Crow's Nest here and the next place down the line. Easy money, and no trouble."

"Bitch . . ."

She hated that word, always had.

"Bitch, Tuck ain't coming back. I don't know who you're used to talking to, but it ain't me, I guarantee you." He leaned closer to her, so close that she could feel his breath on her face and smell the rotten teeth and beer on it. "Let me tell you how it's gonna be. I'm going to send a man with you back to Ironhead, and you're gonna open the safe there. Hell, I may go myself."

"And if the money Tuck left me is still there?"

"Then I'll take it, and you and me won't have to talk anymore."

"What if I've really got five hundred dollars? What then? Have we got a deal?"

"If you had five hundred dollars, you wouldn't be advertising it around to a man like me. No, I'd say you're lying to me, and I don't like liars any more than I like a sassy whore."

It was growing dark outside, the last of the sun looking straight into the tent door.

She straightened at the bar, hating how his size and the way he was staring down at her made her feel small. "I'll be going now."

"Like hell you will. You keep your ass right here until I tell you it's time to go. Supply train won't leave until this evening, or maybe early morning."

He didn't have to say what he would do if she didn't. She searched the room, but none of the others would even look her way. They wanted no part of her trouble, and weren't going to lift a hand to help a crazy whore that had twisted the Hilltopper's tail, any more than they had tried to stop him from taking over their former boss's saloon.

She wished she had a gun, and she wished she knew where Dixie was. She thought about yelling for help, but she didn't. Dixie was brave enough and a little on the salty side, but he was no match for the Hilltopper. In fact, she had always thought he was a poor fit as a lawman.

She had been around tough men and violent men for a lot of years, and she knew that all she would do was get Dixie hurt or killed. He didn't have the mean streak that Morgan had. Morgan was a good man in most ways, yes, but there was a cold streak that ran down his middle, and he walked far closer to the line that divided the good from the bad than he probably realized.

Dixie wasn't like that. He was a happy, talkative man, content to while a day away telling stories. He talked about how much he hated farming, but a lot of his stories went back to his boyhood behind a plow. A man that talked that much about something missed it.

She knew he had fought in the war and worked a brief stint somewhere in Texas as a sheriff's deputy, but she had a suspicion that he had only accepted Morgan's offer to be one of his railroad policemen because he felt he owed him. She still remembered when Dixie was a laborer for the Katy, right up to the time he had gotten into a fight with one of the steam engine mechanics, and Morgan had shackled him to one of the posts that served as a jail in Ironhead. It was Morgan's offer of a job that had got him set free, and Dixie was beholden to that favor and the fact that Morgan had seen enough in him to trust him, even if he was reluctant to admit it, same as how he wouldn't admit that he might just miss farming a bit.

No, she wasn't about to call for help and have him or someone else get themselves hurt or killed trying to pull her fat out of the fire. It was her problem for the moment, and she would wait things out a little and see how it played out. She would reconsider her options when the time came.

She looked down the bar and waited until she caught Pork Chop glancing her way. "Hey, bring me a whiskey, will ya? Old Reserve if you've got it."

Pork Chop poured her a glass and brought it to her, being careful not to get any closer to the Hilltopper than he had to. She took the whiskey and started across the room.

"Where do you think you're going?" the Hilltopper asked.

She took a chair at one of the tables against the far wall of the tent where she could face him. "I'm going to sit down if it's all right with you."

"I think I'm gonna have to go up to Ironhead with you myself," he said. "Maybe I'd enjoy it. Tuck always said that there wasn't a wench on the line that could make a man as crazy for her humping as you can."

"I wouldn't hump you for any price."

He came around the bar, and she thought she had gone too far with her talk. He stopped in the middle of the room, and made a show of looking her over. "I like a whore with big tits."

"Is that a fact?" Molly said as calmly as she could.

"Maybe you ought to come to work for me. A whore that wants to buy a saloon likes her money, and you could make plenty here. You talk real sweet and I'll give you a cut of the drinks you can sell, and a good tent for you to put your bed, same as Tuck used to do for you."

"No thanks. I'm independent."

He started for her, but the sound of cocking gun hammers stopped him. Pork Chop had a double-barreled coach gun laid across the bar top and leveled on him. A twelve-gauge it probably was, but the two holes in the end of it looked bigger than that, even all the way across the room.

"That'll be enough," Pork Chop said. He was a little shaky, but the shotgun was steady enough to do the job.

"You put that scattergun down, or you're gonna wish you had," the Hilltopper said.

"Molly ain't done nothing to you. Leave her be."

"Put that gun away or I'll feed it to you."

The Hilltopper was mad and talking tough enough, but Molly saw that despite his talk, he wasn't going to try that shotgun. But he also knew that Pork Chop wasn't going to shoot him unless he made a move for him or her, and he sought to frighten the man with the threat of retaliation later.

The other whore in the saloon got up and ran out the back of the tent, and the other bartender that had been lighting the lanterns shook out his last match and did the same. The Hilltopper watched them go, then looked at the faro dealer.

"That fat bartender pulls those triggers, I want you to put a bullet in his skull."

The faro dealer nodded, and he had one hand under the table like he was trying to take hold of a gun.

"Lynch!" Pork Chop said, and he shifted the shotgun halfway between the two men. "You hold on there, or I'll put a load of buckshot in you, same as I will the Hilltopper."

"You think you can get both of us?" the Hilltopper said.

"I got a barrel for each of you. Two for you if Lynch gets that hand out from under the table." Pork Chop's face was sweating more than it should have been in the shade of the tent.

"You put that shotgun down and I'll let you walk out of here," the Hilltopper said. "You put it down and I won't come over there and take it away from you. I won't take this here knife I'm wearing and cut you wide and deep."

Molly was beginning to think that she was wrong, and that the Hilltopper was really going to try to buck the shotgun. But at that moment a man came into the saloon. He was slow recognizing the situation, but stopped when he saw the shotgun Pork Chop held. He started to back out of the room, but the Hilltopper wheeled around to face him.

"Superintendent Duvall said he needs to talk to you," he said to the Hilltopper. "Caught me on my way to my tent and said I should come fetch you."

The Hilltopper watched the man slowly back out of the room, keeping a close watch on Pork Chop's shotgun.

"He said to tell you, and I told you," the man said when he was at the door. "Reckon I'll be going now."

As quick as that, he was gone.

The Hilltopper gave a glance at Pork Chop, and then at Molly. "You," he said to her, "had better be here when I get back. And you," he looked back at Pork Chop, "better be gone."

The Hilltopper went out of the saloon at a brisk walk, not looking back once. Molly looked at Pork Chop and saw he still held the shotgun, and then at the faro dealer.

Pork Chop shifted the shotgun until it was aimed right at the faro dealer. "Lynch, let it be."

The faro dealer brought his empty hand out where Pork Chop could see it and began shuffling his cards again. "The Hilltopper won't forget what you did."

Pork Chop kept the shotgun aimed at the faro dealer, but he looked at Molly. "What are you waiting on? Get out of here."

She stood and started to go, but hesitated. "What about you?"

"I won't be far behind you. I want to make sure Lynch there doesn't change his mind."

"How about you come with me to Ironhead? You used to be a pretty good faro dealer, from what Tuck told me, and I might could use one at the Bullhorn."

He lifted one hand. "Got the arthritis in my hands. Can't handle the pasteboards like I once could."

"There's a job for you if you want it."

"You run along. I can fend for myself."

"I owe you one."

"You owe me more than that. Get gone."

She went out of the saloon, walking fast in the darkness and keeping a close watch for the Hilltopper. She was nearing the train tracks when she saw the glow of a fire, and then she heard somebody scream.

Chapter Thirty-One

Willis Duvall was slightly drunk, as had been the case more and more recently, and he was alone in his private car with his socked feet propped up on one corner of the desk and a whiskey glass in his hand. His shoes lay on the Persian rug where he had tugged them off, and his hat was thrown haphazardly on the couch.

The whole room, once so pristine and stately, looked ragged, courtesy of the Hilltopper's fight with Tuck. There were bullet holes and splintered trim, a broken window that let the mosquitos in. But he couldn't find it in him to care. The day had started so good, and then that damned Tuck had escaped. And now this latest piece of bad news.

He frowned at the yellow piece of paper pinned under the weight of the decanter of bourbon on the desktop before him, the very same telegram that had been handed to him no sooner than the Hilltopper and that pain-in-the-ass police chief left him. He took another sip of bourbon and debated on reading the telegram again, but didn't. The message wasn't going to change. The board was sending a new man to take over, and that was that. He had sent a flurry of his own telegraphs back up the line, but it was late in the day and he doubted he would get a reply before morning. No matter, they had their minds made up, and he was wasting his time trying to tell them otherwise.

"Fools," he said, as if there was someone in the room to hear him.

For months, they had been complaining and threatening to replace him, as if they knew a thing about what it took to build a railroad, to actually build it instead of talking about it. A railroad didn't get built by drawing pretty lines on a map. It got built with blood and sweat and nastiness, and he had the damned thing done halfway across the territory already. Who were they to judge him, and who were they to begrudge him picking up a few scraps off the food pile for his efforts?

Everything he had was sunk into landing his position as the superintendent and his minority share of the line, his big chance. He had begged, borrowed, and scraped to come up with the money. Bribe the ones who could be bought. Kiss their pompous asses if you couldn't buy them. No pride for once, willing to do what it took. Play the game. Fight for a place.

And what did that get him? A paltry salary, and then a two percent share if he brought the line through on time and according to the contract. Another two percent more he had bought for himself on the sly after he had purposely spread rumors that the Katy was going broke to drive the share prices down. He might have bought more, but that was all his bankers would lend him the money for. He had no doubt that he would be hearing from them as well, and soon, when they found out he was fired.

And he had added another percentage point, more shares he bought with money he embezzled from the company. Months of altering the books with tedious attention to the details, overblowing expenditures, taking and giving kickbacks from the contractors and subcontractors. All according to his plan, but in the end, all of it for nothing. The damn moneymen were firing him.

He was over budget and behind schedule, and there were

questions about his accounts. That was what they were claiming and had been for the last two months, as if the lot of them weren't working their own deals, and as if they were truly honest men. His own lies were no worse than theirs—all their big talk and promises of how there would be sections of land granted to the Katy along every mile of completed track, and town lots to sell and a thousand other ways to make money. And they promised him he was going to be an integral part of it. Oh, he had heard it all, their conceit and the bluster of how they had men in Congress to make it so. Hadn't the Union Pacific and the Central Pacific built the first transcontinental line that way? Why not again? And he had gambled that it would be like those other railroads, as much graft and corruption as it was construction—the kind of project that made ordinary businessmen into millionaires and tycoons. Vanderbilt had done it, and so had Gould and Huntington. All railroad men, and every one of them as much a crook and a tyrant as they were entrepreneurs and visionaries. There was no other way if you wanted it all.

But the damned politicians had reneged, and there were to be no land grants other than the two-hundred-foot right of way—one hundred feet to each side from the center of where the tracks were laid—because the land belonged to the heathen Indians according to some treaty written almost four decades ago when there wasn't a white man in the world that wanted to live in that country. Indians, of all things. Nobody cared about the Indians. The whole territory would be opened up as soon as the politicians in power saw it to their advantage. It was all about money and power, and who could blame him for trying to get his?

He tossed down the last of the bourbon in his cup and set it down so hard on the desktop that it knocked a dent in the swirled grain of the lustrously polished mahogany. He was barely sober enough to realize that he was feeling sorry for himself, and he abhorred a whiner.

Hadn't he pulled himself up in the world by his bootstraps for fifty-five years, starting with nothing but a decrepit side-wheel steamer on Lake Erie that his father had left him? He had turned that into three ships before he sold them all, then a contract for the concrete work on the suspension bridge over the Ohio River at Wheeling, West Virginia. And then more bridge work along the growing web of railroad lines in Pennsylvania and Ohio. Every time, he took the fortune he amassed, or what was left of it, and gambled it all on his latest venture. Sometimes he lost, and sometimes he won, and that was what he needed to remember now. He had been broke before and survived it to come back again. The thing to do was to have another drink and figure out how to make the best of it. Any general knew that there were victories to be had, even in retreat.

He was quite drunk, and the room had long grown dark by the time he finally lit the lamps and took count of the money he had in his safe. There was five thousand dollars of railroad money there, not much, but something. He cursed himself for not seeing the writing on the wall sooner and giving himself time to sell off what he could to help fund his traveling stake.

But there were the four brown leather sacks that his men had brought to him from Tuck's saloon right after he had received the telegram. There was more than twenty thousand in hard coin and paper money in those sacks, and he was quite surprised that a man like Tuck had managed to accumulate such a healthy nest egg. He lifted his whiskey glass in toast to those moneybags. Things were looking up already.

He put all the money in a large valise with stout leather handles, along with some documents. He used three other similar valises to pack his clothes and some personal belongings. Then he sat down with the last of his bourbon and contemplated his next moves.

According to the Hilltopper there were two small wooden crates filled with the heroin that Tuck had been selling, and he would offer that and complete ownership of the saloon to the Hilltopper for a discount price.

He heard the work train rolling into camp from the south, and went out onto the platform at one end of his railcar in time to catch the last of his workers getting off the train and passing by his car headed into camp. He yelled until one of them answered his call. When the man came over he instructed him to tell the Hilltopper he wanted to see him tonight.

He was barely back at his desk when someone knocked on his door. He mumbled a reply, and Hannah came into the room carrying his supper. He watched her come to him through half-lidded, heavy eyes, noticing the sway of her hips beneath her dress and the lithe, lean grace of her shoulders and neck. Drunk as he was, he felt the hunger slowly come over him. Not a hunger for the food she carried on a tray before her, but a hunger that he had not fed in a while.

There was so little time for a man of his position to indulge in the finer things. Nothing since he had left Missouri but boring whores, and so little time with them and no proper place to really enjoy them.

That bitch, Helvina, for all her looks was nothing but window dressing. Her family name and social graces were helpful to his cause, but no more than another expense to him beyond that. He had often thought of what it would be like if he could show her what really pleased him. How shocked she would be to be forced to crawl and to call him master; how delightful to bruise that unblemished white flesh and feel it shiver under his touch?

Or would she be shocked at all? There had been that bit of scandal in Kansas City, but no one had really believed the whore who had made the claims against him, not a man of his stature. A little bribe and a quiet payment of her doctor bills, and the charges were dropped and no one heard from her again. Did Helvina know of that? Did she have any suspicions about the two whores back in Ironhead? A brief letdown of his guard, that last bit, same as Kansas City had been, but his urges had grown stronger of late. No matter, Helvina would be gone as quickly as she heard there was no more money to be sucked from him, and she would never say what she might think for fear that the taint of it might stick to her.

"Good evening, Mr. Duvall," Hannah said to him.

His eyes opened wider, taking in the vision of her. The thought of what she would look like with her dress off wouldn't leave him. He had never lain with a black woman, and that made the wondering a sweeter potion; made the itch down deep inside him need scratching all the more.

"I said good evening, Mr. Duvall. Were you asleep?" she said.

He recognized then what the smile she gave him meant, and wondered why he hadn't realized it for what it was earlier. She wanted it, same as him. Smiling and flirting with him all the time. Teasing him and daring him like they always did.

Instead of answering her, he pulled her onto his lap as she bent over to set his meal on the desktop. She struggled against his arms wrapped around her waist, and kicked out with her legs against the desk. The good ones always struggled.

"Mr. Duvall!" she cried.

He felt the press of her round bottom on his crotch, and felt himself growing harder the more she squirmed and fought him.

"Don't play-act with me girl," he hissed with his face against her throat. "You know you want it. You've been asking for it since you came to work for me."

"Let go!"

"Fight if you want to," he said. "Go ahead. I like it when you fight me."

She bucked and twisted and tried to dig her fingernails into one of his forearms, but he threw her against the wall.

"Go ahead, scream," he said as he staggered towards her.

She turned to him, and there was blood on her mouth. She pressed her back to the wall and stared at him with her eyes wide and frightened. He could smell the fear on her. Lovely girl. Lovely fear.

"Not the screaming type, huh?" he said as he reached for her. "Well, you will. I promise you will."

She dodged to one side, and all he managed was to get a hand inside the throat of her dress. The cloth ripped like paper against his drunken grip, revealing one brown breast and a dark nipple. It was the sight of that breast that gave him pause, and in that moment, she laid hand to the lamp at the end of the parlor couch and struck him in the face with it. The blow was not that hard, only shattering the thin glass globe of it. But he was so drunk he could barely stand, and he staggered and fell to one knee against his desk.

She was running out the door by the time he righted himself, and he stared dumbly down at the lamp base lying on its side in the middle of his Persian rug. Kerosene had spilled across that rug, and creeping, burning fingers of it slowly spread outwards. Instead of seeking something to smother the fire, he simply leaned against the desk and watched it grow, fascinated with the flames.

He took the ledger books from his safe and threw them into the fire, and then he took up another of the lamps and busted it on the floor. Let whoever they sent to replace him sleep in a tent, damned them.

The Hilltopper knocked open the door, and looked through the flames at him. Duvall then realized how truly ugly the man was with the glow of the fire lighting his face. An ugly, dumb, brute.

"Help me get my things," Duvall slurred, and plucked a piece of glass from his bloody eyebrow.

The Hilltopper leapt through the wall of fire, shielding his face with one forearm held before it. He gave the flames another look, as if there might be something done to smother them, but the blaze was too far along by then.

"Help me with my bags," Duvall said again.

He took up the handles of the bag containing the money, and the Hilltopper took up the others. They moved away from the heat and through Duvall's bedroom, but not before he took another lamp and slung kerosene over his bed covering.

"Light it," he said to the Hilltopper.

The Hilltopper gave him a questioning look, but didn't argue. He took a match from his vest pocket and held it to the covers until they were on fire. The two of them went out the door and down the steps, and they hadn't gone but a little way from the burning Pullman before Duvall staggered and had to lean against the Hilltopper.

"Shit, damn!" he said. "Go back in there and get my shoes."

The Hilltopper looked at the glow visible through the windows. Glass popped from somewhere inside, and then a window shattered and the smoke and flames gushed out.

"What have we got here?" Duvall laughed after he said it.

The Hilltopper thought that the drunken superintendent was laughing about the burning railcar, but then he heard the pounding footsteps coming towards them. And when he turned away from the fire he saw the man charging at them with a meat cleaver raised over his head.

Chapter Thirty-Two

The white of Saul's eyes and the gleam of firelight on the silver steel of the meat cleaver he carried was all that was visible as he charged out of the dark. So enraged and focused on Duvall was he that he didn't even see the Hilltopper.

Saul never stopped running as the meat cleaver slashed down in a high arc aimed for Duvall's chest. But the Hilltopper stepped in front of the superintendent and caught the blow on the luggage he held in one hand. His other hand drew the Colt Dragoon, and the nearly five-pound revolver struck the side of Saul's head with a sickening crack.

Saul fell limply to the ground, the meat cleaver clattering away. He rolled onto his back with a groan as the Hilltopper cocked the pistol and stepped astraddle of him, aiming at his face. Duvall staggered over, lost his balance and caught himself against the Hilltopper's shoulder, and looked down at Saul.

"My woman . . ." was the only thing Saul managed to say before his eyes twitched and his head jerked, and a slow last gasp of air hissed out of his mouth.

The Hilltopper uncocked his horse pistol. "He's dead."

"Dead? Did you say dead?" Duvall staggered again.

"Busted his head, I reckon," the Hilltopper said.

By that time, the fire had drawn people from the camp. Many of them were forming a bucket brigade from a water tanker parked on a siding near the burning car, but others simply stopped at the edge of the firelight and stared at the dead cook and the two men standing over him.

Duvall pushed himself away from the Hilltopper and spun in a circle with his valise full of money windmilling on the end of his arm, as if he were surrounded and trying to see everybody at once.

"What are you looking at?" he said to the onlookers.

No one answered him. The Hilltopper took hold of his arm and tried to move him away, but he jerked free.

He pointed down at Saul's body, and then at the bloody side of his face. "He attacked me with a knife. Tried to kill me."

Again, no one said anything.

"Tell them," Duvall said to the Hilltopper, and then lost his balance again and fell on his knees.

Hannah appeared in the crowd, clutching her torn yellow dress to her chest, and staring quietly at the shadow of Saul's body. Those beside her noticed the condition of her dress and the tears streaming down her cheeks. And then she began to sob and her knees buckled, and those same onlookers held her up for a moment.

The Hilltopper showed the crowd his badge. "Railroad police. You all go back to your tents. Let us handle this."

No one moved, and the Hilltopper didn't like what he saw on their faces.

"Some of you men carry this body to Doc Chillingsworth's," he said.

But again, they didn't move.

"Come on," the Hilltopper said, and took hold of Duvall's arm and tugged him to his feet.

The murmur of the crowd was growing louder over the crackle of the fire. The Hilltopper practically drug Duvall up the tracks and away from there, brandishing his pistol and maintaining a close watch on the crowd.

"That nigger tried to kill me," Duvall called back to them,

but whatever else he was going to say was cut off when the Hilltopper jerked his arm.

Hannah tore away from those supporting her and ran towards her husband's body with outstretched arms. She was wailing by then, and she fell to her knees beside him and took one of his hands in hers. The crowd moved then. They formed a ring around her, some patting her on the back or giving her consoling words, but others watched Duvall's and the Hilltopper's retreat.

"Somebody tore her dress," someone in the crowd said.

"She's the cook's wife, ain't she?" asked another one. "Somebody said they were only married today."

The bucket brigade was having little luck putting out the burning Pullman, and the scorching heat of the blaze had become too much. Volunteers carried Saul's body farther away from the fire, with Hannah walking alongside and still holding his hand as they moved him.

Another group had splintered off from the crowd, standing alone, and their talk grew more pointed.

"Maybe that cook was wild on the whiskey. I've seen Indians go crazy on the stuff, and I don't reckon a darkie is any different," someone said. "Got drunk on his wedding night and beat his woman and run her out on the street. Could be the Hilltopper and the superintendent tried to stop him."

"I knew Saul," someone else said. "Worked with him in the mess tent back in Ironhead. He didn't drink. Christian man and a kind sort."

"The superintendent was the one that was drunk. You all saw him," said another.

"Can you believe that the superintendent put a badge on the Hilltopper?" came a different voice. "First, he shoots Tuck in that Pullman, and not a little while later it's on fire."

"And now this," said the first one who had spoken.

"I'd say the Hilltopper has got out of hand, and maybe the superintendent, too."

Men grumbled their agreement.

"Nobody is above the law, that's what I say."

"Might be that we ought to ask a few more questions of the superintendent and his new policeman," came another voice in the dark, followed by a thoughtful draw on his pipe, visible by the cherry glow of it.

"He won't like that." That voice was followed by several worried murmurs.

"Doesn't matter if he likes it or not. I need a job as much as the next man, but there's been two men killed here today and a woman hurt. Who's going to do anything about that? We saw who he's got wearing a badge now, so who's going to make it right? I don't know about you, but I don't want to see things get like they were at Ironhead again. I got a family back home."

The argument went on, and the bucket brigade, having given up on the fire and confident that it wasn't going to set anything else ablaze, added their numbers to the group. A quarter hour later, someone suggested that they retrieve some lanterns, and those that had a gun ought to go get those, too.

The Hilltopper drug Superintendent Duvall beside him until they were beside the work train that had arrived from the south earlier in the evening. He stopped there, and looked back towards the fire.

"Find me a place to sleep," Duvall said.

"If we go to sleep, the both of us might wake up with a hanging noose around our necks," the Hilltopper said.

"What?"

"That crowd back there is working themselves up to come after us. We better be gone before they make their minds up."

"We'll claim self-defense. He had a knife."

"Did that colored gal have a knife?" The Hilltopper pushed him against one of the boxcars. "You listen, you stay here if you want to. Me, I'm gonna make myself scarce."

Duvall blinked a couple of times, then looked back at the crowd near the fire. "They wouldn't dare. There's not a man there that doesn't work for me."

"Like hell they wouldn't."

"I'll fire every one of them."

"You tell them that when you're standing on your tippy toes and they're about to stretch your neck. I done been down that road, and don't care a damn for it."

"Get some men together to stand them off until they cool down and will listen to reason."

"What men? I've got maybe two that would stand with us, but the rest of the men you're talking about are the ones down there right now figuring out what you did and what they ought to do about it. And they'll be the first ones to pitch the rope over your head."

"I don't even have any shoes on."

The Hilltopper ignored him and waved over two men he saw passing down the side of the train. One of them held a lantern, and the other one was carrying an oil can. The Hilltopper recognized one of them as the engineer.

"What's going on back there?" the engineer said. "We were going to help with the bucket brigade, but there seemed plenty and the engine needed tending to before we left it."

"Somebody set fire to Duvall's car," the Hilltopper said.

"It was my maid. She did it," Duvall interjected.

The Hilltopper shoved Duvall back against the boxcar and out of the way. "Mr. Duvall here is injured, and wants you to take him to Ironhead to see a doctor."

Both the engineer and the other man with him stepped to the side a little where they could see around the Hilltopper and down the tracks where the Pullman was burning. Then the engineer held his lantern high and close to Duvall's face so they could see the bloody cut on his temple where Hannah had struck him with the lamp.

"You're right, that's going to need a few stitches," the engineer said. "But Doc Chillingsworth is here in camp now. No doctor in Ironhead anymore. Nothing there at all worth mentioning."

"Mr. Duvall said he wants you to take him to Ironhead." The Hilltopper grabbed hold of Duvall's shirt and shook him. "Ain't that right, Superintendent?"

Duvall mumbled something in reply that none of them could understand.

"There now, you heard the man. Fire this train up," the Hilltopper said.

"Wouldn't take a bit to stoke a fire up," the man with the oil can said. "And the boiler is still warm."

The engineer looked around the Hilltopper again and at the people gathered by the burning Pullman. "I don't know."

The Hilltopper took hold of the engineer's hand holding the lantern and pulled it close to his chest. He flipped back his vest and showed them the badge on his chest. "I'm the law, and I say you take us to Ironhead."

"You're railroad police?" the engineer asked, and then looked to the superintendent to confirm it.

Duvall said nothing, and appeared to have passed out standing up.

The Hilltopper drew his Dragoon and shoved the barrel of it under the engineer's chin. "You crawl your sorry ass up into that locomotive and get this train moving."

"Fifty dollars . . . fifty dollars apiece, and I won't fire you if you get me to Ironhead," Duvall slurred.

The engineer nodded as much as he could with the pistol

barrel pushing his chin up too high. The Hilltopper uncocked the pistol and shoved him ahead of him. The other man was already trotting toward the locomotive.

The Hilltopper grabbed Duvall and pulled him along in his wake. When they reached the cab of the locomotive, he let the engineer climb in first, and pitched their bags in behind him. He had to practically pick Duvall up to get him up the ladder. The tender was already pitching chunks of wood in the firebox.

"How long 'til she's ready to go?" The Hilltopper stopped halfway up the ladder, looking into the cab at the engineer.

"Ten minutes. Maybe less," the engineer said.

Duvall had taken a seat on the floor against the wall of the cab, or maybe he had fallen there.

"Are you awake?" the Hilltopper asked him.

"Of course I'm awake, you fool." Duvall pulled his carpetbag up on his lap and hugged it to him.

The Hilltopper took another look back down the train at the crowd by the fire, and then he jumped to the ground.

"Where are you going?" Duvall asked.

"I'll be right back. Have you got a gun?"

"You're leaving me?" Duvall fumbled around with his carpetbag and finally found a little Cloverleaf Colt pistol. His legs scrambled on the floor as he tried to stand, but only made it halfway up the wall before he slumped back to the floor. "They're coming, aren't they?"

"There's something I've got to get," the Hilltopper said.

"You're leaving me, aren't you?" Duvall asked.

"Do you think you're sober enough to stay awake?"

"What do you want me to do?"

"You keep that pistol pointed at these fellows and make sure they keep feeding that fire," the Hilltopper said as he holstered his pistol and walked away.

Chapter Thirty-Three

Red Molly stopped far back from the fire, taking watch in the darkest place she could find against the side of one of the tents. It was Saul's scream she had heard, and she arrived within sight of the burning Pullman in time to see the Hilltopper standing over his body with a pistol aimed at his head.

She saw it all from that point on: saw Hannah weeping over Saul's body, the bucket brigade working frantically to put out the fire, and most of all she saw what the Hilltopper was capable of and that he worked for Duvall.

She was still standing there after Duvall and the Hilltopper were long gone, and it was then that the dim glow of a kerosene lantern far up the work train caught her eye. By the time she moved closer through the tents, the lantern light had moved inside the locomotive cab and she thought she could hear the sound of fuel being thrown into the firebox.

If the work train was making a night run to the north, she intended to be on it before the Hilltopper found her. She searched the dark line of the train for a likely place to ride. The best thing would be for nobody to see her climb aboard.

But somebody did find her as she moved closer to the train. In fact, she ran right into him. It was Hank Bickford, the blacksmith.

"Thought that was you I saw," he said.

"Get out of the way, Hank."

He didn't move. "Where are you going in such a hurry?"

"I'm going to catch that train."

She could make out the side profile of his shadowed face as he looked back towards the fire. "You saw all of that?"

"Enough, and I want no part of it."

"Bad thing, that. And then there's what happened to Tuck. Bloody day."

"Get out of my way."

"You aren't the only one that wants out of here," he said.

"I bet you don't have that Hilltopper looking for you."

"Did he threaten you?"

"That he did, but if he wants to find me he's going to have to come to Ironhead."

Hank took a gentle hold on one of her arms. "I don't know what's going on with you, but if the Hilltopper's after you, you better wait. I saw him and the superintendent go up the train. Best you give them time to move on elsewhere."

She jerked away from him, for she had had her fill of bossy men for the day, but what he said gave her pause.

"If Duvall or that giant of his did that to Saul's woman, do you think that one of them could've been the one who hurt that woman back in Ironhead?"

"What was her name?" he asked in a quiet voice.

"Ruby Ann."

"That's her."

She didn't ask, but she wondered if Hank knew about what had happened to her, too.

"No place to raise a family. The Missus tried to tell me that, but I wouldn't listen," he said. "I'm thinking I'll go fetch her and the kids and send them with you."

"I'm not waiting."

"There's time."

"I don't want to chance it."

They could hear the crowd by the fire growing louder.

"Nope, this is no place to be tonight," he said. "Liable to get ugly. Look over there. They're passing a whiskey bottle around to help them make up their minds. Working up their courage."

He guided her towards where they would have a better view of what was transpiring. And true to the sound of it, there must have been forty men gathered in a group by the firelight. Duvall's Pullman had burned down to the frame by then, and someone must have taken Hannah and Saul's body elsewhere. The group was passing a bottle around, exactly as Hank had said, and they were steadily becoming more rambunctious.

"You wait here," Hank said. "I'll go fetch my family and Saul's wife if she wants to go. She'll be right in the middle of it all if she stays here."

"She won't leave her husband's body."

"I'll bring Saul up to Ironhead for burying, as soon as I can, but you might ought to come with me and talk to her. You've seen a mob before and know how they get. And that poor woman has seen enough already."

She was about to answer him when a horseman rode into the firelight.

Chapter Thirty-Four

Dixie had ridden nine miles down the track, most of that at a high trot or a slow lope, following the way the work train had gone that had carried Bill Tuck out of the camp. He knew that the Katy had line built for fifteen or so miles past Canadian, and fully expected to find Tuck when he got there. The railroad crew down there would have him or would have seen him. Either way, he ought to find him before dark if his horse could hold the pace, and there was plenty of time to think on things.

He needed a job as bad as the next man, but working for Willis Duvall was about more than he could take. Any man that would hire the Hilltopper as a policeman wasn't the kind you wanted to work for.

Morgan had once told him that sometimes the worst part about being a lawman was the people you answered to and the ones that paid your salary, whether that be some city council, or marshal, or a railroad boss like Duvall. According to him, the trick was to act like you listened to them and then do what you thought you ought to do, regardless of what they said. And he was pretty sure that Morgan would have already told Willis Duvall where he could shove his badge. Hell, he had hinted to Dixie not to take the job in the first place.

Granted, giving Duvall a piece of his mind had its merits, but Dixie hated to quit a thing he had started. He would have already quit if it weren't for that and if it hadn't felt so much like failing. His first job as chief, and he hadn't lasted a few days.

You start a furrow, you plow it to the end. That was what his pa had said back in Alabama. There was a time when not much his pa had told him made any sense, but the older he got the more he was beginning to think his old pa was wiser than he had any right to be.

The horse was getting a little winded and sweating hard, and Dixie slowed him to a walk. The thing to do was to find Tuck, bring him or his body back to Canadian, and then either he or the Hilltopper had to go. Nobody could say then that he had quit in the middle of a hard task.

He wrapped the tail of his bridle reins around his saddle horn to free both hands and took a harmonica out of his vest pocket. He was still trying to get the hang of the new instrument, and as a result he played snippets of several songs but never a whole one. He was making a fair attempt at the beginning bars of *Dixie* when he rode into sight of the work train. The tracklaying crew was at work about a hundred yards beyond it.

He passed along the train and asked the brakeman and the engineer and his fire tender if they had seen Bill Tuck, but none of them had. They had heard some gunshots as they were pulling out of Canadian, but weren't even aware that Tuck had gotten on one of their flatcars. He rode on past the train, further down the line to where the new track was being laid.

The track laying was old hat to him, but he still enjoyed seeing men work together like that. It was hard, sweaty, brutal labor from daylight to dusk, but there was also a certain beauty to it like a dance all its own. One crew laid down hand-hewn wooden crossties taken from a wagon beside them, working on the roadbed ahead of the rest of the construction crew. And then came the tracklayers.

A crew at the flatcars offloaded lengths of railroad iron, or rails, onto a small car. A single horse in harness with long trace chains or simply a long rope hooked to the car pulled the load down to the end of the tracks at a fast trot and sometimes at a gallop. As soon as it got there, two men grabbed a hold of the end of a rail and started dragging it off the car. As it slid off, other pairs of men took hold of it at intervals and helped carry it to the end of the last rail laid down. At the foreman's signal the rail was laid carefully in place, and behind them, other teams were carrying more rails and dropping them down end to end in the exact same fashion, until the car was empty. And as quickly as that car was unloaded, the crew heaved together and turned it over on its side so that the next horse could come flying up with its fresh load. While the new car was being unloaded, the empty car was stood back up on the tracks behind it and taken back to the train to retrieve another load. Over and over the process was repeated.

Another team butted and bolted the rails together, with a gauger using his template to make sure the tracks were the proper width apart. The spikers swung their sledgehammers in a steady rhythm that went on all day—three licks per spike for a good spiker, ten spikes to a rail, four hundred rails to a mile, twelve to fifteen hours a day, seven days a week in heat and cold, for three hundred miles across the territory to Texas.

Dixie had got his initiation to the railroad business on such a tracklaying crew for the Katy not many months before in Kansas, and before he moved on to the crane crew doing bridge work. He didn't miss the backbreaking work, but he did miss the camaraderie and the pride looking back down the line at the end of the day and seeing what he had helped build.

"Swing them hammers, boys. Let 'em ring," Dixie said in imitation of an old black spiker he had once worked with.

One of the spikers paused his hammer at the top of his stroke and gave Dixie a wry look. "Why don't you get yourself down off that horse and show us how you can make this old hammer talk."

Dixie grinned and shook his head. "Not me. This lawman work has done spoiled me, and I fairly break out in a rash just looking at those hammers."

The crew laughed and teased him some more while they worked.

"Don't suppose any of you have seen Bill Tuck down here?" he asked them.

None of them had. Dixie had fully expected to find Tuck lying dead on the flatcar he had rode out of Canadian, but it appeared that Tuck had gotten off the train somewhere between there and the camp.

He turned his horse around and headed back towards the train. It was going to be a long ride back to Canadian, going slow and looking for any sign of where Tuck might have fallen from the train or bailed off of it. He couldn't for the life of him understand why Tuck would have left his ride, unless he was scared of something or hurt so badly he wasn't thinking straight. And the feeling he had back in Canadian that there was something wrong about the shootout between Tuck and the Hilltopper grew stronger.

He pulled out his harmonica again, and tried out the chorus of *Oh, Susanna.* He blew a sour note or two, but was proud that he had somewhat played it through.

One of the tracklayers called out to him as he was passing. "What's that you're screeching on, Chief?"

"A little music helps pass the miles," Dixie said.

"Maybe so, but I'd hate to be your horse," the man threw back at him, and his remark caused the whole crew to laugh and make some more witty comments about Dixie's lack of skill with the harmonica.

Dixie lifted a hand to them in a mock wave goodbye, and then made another try at *Oh, Susanna* to let them know he didn't care about their lack of appreciation for his musical talents.

The construction crews had several spare wagon horses standing ground-tied alongside the tracks, and he swapped his saddle over to one of those work horses and left his weary mount behind to be brought into camp later. He was only halfway to Canadian by the time it was dark and the work train passed him by on its way back.

He had hoped to come across some sign of Tuck along the roadbed, but he had no skill as a tracker. If there was any sign, he had missed it, and now it was pitch dark. The only thing left to do was to come back in the morning and look some more. Maybe he could hire one of the Indians hanging around the camp to scout for him.

He was another hour reaching Canadian, and the glow of a fire was what he saw first. The next thing he saw was a group of loud-talking men standing outside the mess tent. Several of them hailed him as he rode into the firelight.

"What happened here?" he asked them. He recognized most of them as the tracklaying crew that he had seen working earlier. Good men for the most part, but something other than the burning Pullman had them worked up.

"The Hilltopper killed Saul, that darkie cook, and we think him or the superintendent roughed Saul's woman up, too," one of the men answered.

Several of the men were drunk, or working their way to it, and he also saw that one of them had a club in his hands. And he spotted two others with rifles milling around at the back of the crowd and trying to hide them from him. They were Irishmen and spikers on the track gang.

"We were just about to go hunting them when you rode up,"

the one that had first spoken to him added. "Thought we'd question them. Get to the bottom of this, one way or the other."

"Question them, hell." It was the man with the pick handle in his fists that said that. Dixie had arrested him for fighting back in Ironhead once, and he was a worse hothead than the two Irishmen with the rifles.

"You men need to tone it down," Dixie said. "Let the law handle this."

"Meaning you?" the man with the pick handle said.

"Meaning me. You men fall out," he said. Dixie looked down at them from his horse, trying to come to a conclusion about how close they had worked themselves up to a lynch party. He wanted to ask more details to find out what it was all about, but they weren't going to give him that much time.

"What are you going to do about it? Duvall owns that badge, doesn't he?" The man with the pick handle took a step at him.

Dixie spurred his horse forward, knocking him down and to the side, and scattering the rest of them.

"Nobody owns my badge." He didn't draw his pistol, but he turned the horse slowly around so that he could look at them all, one by one. "You go to your tents like I said, and I'll find the Hilltopper."

"And the superintendent, too." The one Dixie's horse had knocked down had gotten back to his feet, but he kept his distance.

"You can't take the Hilltopper alone," someone else said.

"Maybe, but I'm the one wearing the badge. My job," Dixie said.

"You catch them, you bring them to us," the man with the pick handle said.

"If I catch them and think they've done what you said, I'll take them to Fort Smith to Judge Story." Dixie pushed his horse closer to the man with the club, making him give ground.

"You've got my word on that, and I'll take you with me, too, if you give me any more lip."

Dixie had seen Morgan bluff men down, and he was hoping his own act would hold, although he was well aware that they weren't going back to their tents. He would be lucky if they let him have his try and didn't interfere.

One of the men pointed across the camp. "I just saw the Hill-topper going into the Crow's Nest."

"Are you sure?" Dixie asked.

"Too dark to see real good, but nobody but him is that big."

Dixie started his horse along a lane through the tents leading to Tuck's saloon. He shucked his Spencer carbine out of his saddle boot and propped it on one thigh. He passed in and out of the streaks of lamplight leaking out of an occasional tent door, and the sounds of his horse's hoof falls were soft on the grass.

Ahead of him, the Crow's Nest was the brightest lit place in camp, with lanterns hung from the trees around it, and more kerosene burning inside it. He could see the Hilltopper's shadow cast on the tent wall, and then it was gone.

Dixie dismounted and dropped a rein, checked that a cartridge was loaded in the chamber of his Spencer, then moved towards the front entrance. He stopped in the opening between the tied-back door flaps. The Hilltopper was bent over behind the bar, but there was no one else in the room. The rest of them must have gone to see the fire.

Dixie took care to walk quietly, and crossed the room with his carbine pointed at the bit of the Hilltopper's back he could see above the bar. He was almost all the way there when the Hilltopper straightened and saw him. Dixie wasn't sure if he had heard him, or simply finished what he was doing. A metal cashbox was held in the crook of one of his arms.

"Keep your hands away from your pistol." Dixie cocked the

Spencer. "And that pigsticker, too."

"You think you're arresting me?" the Hilltopper said.

"That's right. I said lift them hands."

The Spencer's muzzle wasn't a foot from the Hilltopper's belly, but instead of lifting his hands he merely stared at Dixie.

"I said lift them hands," Dixie repeated.

"You ain't getting my gun."

"I'm getting it or you're getting a bullet in your gut."

For a moment, Dixie thought the Hilltopper was going to try him, but he slowly reached for his pistol and took hold of it with only his fat thumb and one finger.

"Easy now." Dixie pushed the Spencer's muzzle closer to the big man's middle.

The Hilltopper slid the Colt's Dragoon out of its holster and laid it gently on the bar top. Dixie's attention was drawn to the revolver for a split second, and in that same instant, the Hilltopper drew his knife with his left hand so fast that Dixie barely recognized what was happening. The blade was the length of a grown man's forearm, and it slashed through the air in a backhand swipe at Dixie's throat.

Dixie bent far over backwards to avoid the cut, and at the same time he pulled the trigger. But the Hilltopper had already grabbed the barrel and shoved it aside, and the bullet only shattered a whiskey bottle on the back bar. The Hilltopper tugged the Spencer hard towards him, and Dixie was pulled against the bar and closer to him. The knife slashed again, and Dixie barely ducked it. The Hilltoper was coming over the bar wanting to close with him, and Dixie's vision latched onto the Colt's Dragoon lying there on the bar top within inches from his hands. He grabbed for the gun, but before his right hand could reach it the Hilltopper stabbed down with his knife. The broad blade pierced completely through his hand, back to palm, and sunk into the wood with such force that the steel flexed.

Dixie screamed. The Hilltopper was over the bar, and he kept a hand on the knife and his other hand grabbed Dixie by the forehead and bent him back until they were looking each other in the eyes.

"Hurts, don't it?" the Hilltopper said.

Dixie tried to pull his hand free from the blade, but he was pinned and the pain made him scream again.

The Hilltopper kidney-punched him once, and he dropped to his knees with his arm outstretched and bent over the bar where the knife held him. The Hilltopper kicked him in the ribs, then took up his Dragoon and backed a few steps away, letting go of the knife handle and admiring his handiwork.

Dixie clawed for the pistol on his hip with his left hand, but the Hilltopper gave him another boot in the elbow. Dixie could feel the knife edge slicing a wider hole in his flesh and the grate of it against his hand bones.

"You stupid son of a bitch," the Hilltopper said. "You pull a gun on me you'd better pull the trigger in a hurry."

Dixie reached for the knife handle, wanting to pull it out of the wood, but the Hilltopper slapped him across the side of his head. A slap, maybe, but his open palm cracked like a bullwhip and drove Dixie's head against the bar.

"I wipe my ass with tougher men than you." The Hilltopper spit on him and then bent over and picked the Rebel cap off the floor.

Again, Dixie grabbed for his holstered Navy, but he was hurt too badly and moved too slowly. The Hilltopper yanked the pistol away and slid it down the bar out of Dixie's reach.

He also stuffed Dixie's Rebel cap behind his belt, and leered at Dixie as he did it. "I told you what I'm going to do with this secesh cap of yours, didn't I?"

Dixie gathered his knees under him, but couldn't find purchase for his feet and slipped down again.

The Hilltopper cocked the Dragoon .44 and placed the muzzle of it to Dixie's ear. "I'm going to take it with me, and the next time I need to shit I'm going to take it in it."

Dixie groaned and tried to get up again. The Hilltopper looked down at his pistol and noticed the missing lobe of Dixie's ear.

"You got an ugly ear." He let the hammer down on his Dragoon and holstered it, then took hold of the knife. "Think I'll balance you out and make both sides match."

Dixie screamed for a third time when the Hilltopper jerked the knife free. He would have slid all the way to the floor, but the Hilltopper held him sitting up. The knife blade contacted the top of his good ear, and the edge was so sharp that only the touch of it started the blood flowing down the side of Dixie's head.

"Changed my mind," the Hilltopper said. "Think I'll cut both your ears off and keep them with your hat. I got a cigar box full of ears I cut off of secesh trash and bushwhacker scum during the war."

The Hilltopper laughed and was about to make his first cut when the sound of running men outside the saloon stopped him. The lantern lights of the lynch mob were visible through the canvas walls of the tent.

The Hilltopper let Dixie fall to the floor clutching his wounded hand, and then he ran to the back doorway. He stopped there and looked back at Dixie.

"You ever want this hat, you come get it," he said. "You come get it and I'll finish trimming your ears."

With that, the Hilltopper disappeared through the door flaps at the same time the lynch mob came through the front door. While they were helping Dixie to his feet and trying to stop the bleeding of his wounded hand, the Hilltopper was running for the train.

Chapter Thirty-Five

Red Molly and Hank walked Hannah between them towards the train. The young black woman all but sagged against the support of their arms.

"I promise you, I'll bring Saul to Ironhead on the next train going north," Hank said.

"It isn't right to leave him," Hannah said.

"He would understand," Hank said.

"You want all those men asking you questions?" Molly asked. "You want to stay here when that Hilltopper might be looking for you and wanting to make sure you don't talk?"

Hannah shook her head that she didn't and let them lead her on. "Still isn't right."

"Nothing about it is right, girl," Molly said. "But Duvall and the Hilltopper will get theirs before the night is through, if I don't miss my guess."

"I just want my Saul back." Hannah started sobbing again.

Molly was at a loss as to where they would ride once they reached the train. Behind the locomotive and the tender was almost nothing but flatcars, but Hank led her farther down the line and showed her the single boxcar near the end of the train. He slid the door open, and set Hannah's bag inside the car, and then took her by the waist and lifted her up to join it.

"Nobody will check in here," he said. "Nobody cares about the supply train. It's not like trying to steal a ride on a regular run."

"Have you got a gun that you could lend me? I'd like a gun." Molly said.

"No gun," he answered. "But you'll be fine. Me and the engineer are old friends, and I'll find him and let him know what the deal is."

"What about your family? I thought you were sending them with us?"

"Lottie said she wasn't going without me, and when that woman makes her mind up there's no changing it," he said. "If you ever met her you'd know what I'm talking about."

Molly vaguely remembered Hank's wife, a fussy, heavyset woman who did laundry back when Ironhead was the end of the line, and led the hymns and sang the loudest when the preachers held church in one of the tents.

"Me and Lottie will keep the children close tonight, and then we'll come along tomorrow or the next day," he said. And then he put a hand on Hannah's where she sat in the door of the boxcar. "Might give me time to build Saul a coffin. I'm a fair hand with woodwork, and I saw some pretty red cedar lumber yesterday over at that Choctaw sawmill that's been cutting timbers for the Katy."

Hannah sniffled. "Saul would like that. He was partial to woodwork when he was younger. I remember him saying how he loved the smell of cedar."

Hank started to lend Molly a hand up, but she was already climbing into the boxcar on her own. He slid the door closed behind them, and Molly led Hannah to one end of the car and listened to the sound of the latch falling in place.

Hank had only gone two cars up the line towards the locomotive when it started rolling out of camp. He broke into a jog and yelled at the engineer, but the noise of the huffing engine and driver was too loud for him to be heard.

He was still jogging towards the locomotive when the Hilltopper came out of the camp ahead of him at a run. Hank looked in the direction the Hilltopper fled from and saw lanterns' lights following after him.

The Hilltopper leapt onto the ladder on the side of the locomotive, hauled himself up, and then Hank saw the flame of a pistol shot from the cab and heard the boom of the Hilltopper's pistol.

Twice more, the Hilltopper fired at the lynch mob as the train slowly worked its way out of camp. Somebody in the mob fired at the Hilltopper, and Hank saw the spark of a bullet striking the engine's cab.

Hank skidded to a stop and turned back to the boxcar. It was upon him quickly, and he reached for the door latch but missed it. He got a hold of it the second time, but the latch had been bent sometime in the past and it was stiff and heavy. He was a short man, and with the train moving, he couldn't get a proper hold to open the door. By the time he tried again, he was jogging to stay even with the boxcar.

And then he couldn't keep up, and the last thing he saw of the boxcar was Red Molly jerking the door open and looking back at him.

Chapter Thirty-Six

Morgan waited for full darkness before he came down off the mesa, moving quietly through the moonlit cedar brush. He struck the Cimarron River once again, and spent half the night there satiating his thirst, eating the cold remains of his turkey, and sleeping in short stretches before he rose to listen to the night and to watch the shadows.

There was still several hours of darkness left when he waded across the salt-crusted, red sand shallows and headed north. The tracks he left behind on the sandbar were plain for anyone following him to see, and that was exactly what he intended.

He had hunted men in the war, and since, and dealt his share of death, same as had the Traveler, but he had no taste for it, found no pleasure in it. He knew he wasn't a good man, but he was also certain he wasn't a bad man, caught somewhere in between like most of humanity.

There were some who might have said he was a killer, but let those who would judge him harshly. They didn't know what it was like on the darker side of the world beyond the civilized trappings of city and society they draped themselves in, a false world of streetlights and courtrooms, and lawyers and judges who frowned and argued their jurisprudence, as if words carved into stone tablets or scrawled onto law books were what built monuments and kept men from each other's throats. Those same men locked their doors at night and never realized that laws and punishment do not deter the wicked, nor do they defend the just. Words could be fine things, but they were poor substitutes for sword and shield against those who could understand nothing else.

He had walked the slums and dark alleys of New York, Five Points, and the Bowery; strode across battlefields into the musket smoke of the enemy; and ridden the wild country of Kansas, Texas, and the Indian Territory. Almost a third of his life spent in places where the only respect a man had was what he made for himself, and the only law that often mattered was what he carried in his holster. No jury to pass sentence, and no judge to decide your fate. If a man pulled on you, you put him down or you died, simple as that. And good man or not, he was a man that valued his life, same as he valued those words that men should live by. And he would not give over his portion of the world, the space he stood in, to those that would take it.

And the Traveler was a man who wanted to take his life. A wicked man so twisted that the sane and the just would never understand him; a man who understood nothing himself but the most primitive laws of survival, and would have it no other way. And out beyond the gas streetlights and outside of locked rooms and law books there was but one way to survive such a man.

Morgan struck out across an open plain, keeping the line of red hills to the east of him. His first inclination had been to keep to the broken country and wait for the Traveler to make a mistake, but he was without food and the danger of what faced him would grant him no time to hunt or gather. He would grow weaker and weaker, and starvation and the land would kill him as sure as the Traveler could.

What he had to do was get it over, and get it over quickly. And to do that, he needed to draw the Traveler in. He needed to set him up at a place where he least expected it, and at a place that allowed a good clean field of fire. He had no idea what that place would look like, but hoped he would know it when he found it.

He walked five miles, then six, out onto that stretch of flat country spreading before him into Kansas, looking often behind him. He had little time to find what he sought, for the Traveler on horseback would outpace him once he saw where Morgan had crossed the river.

The sun was almost straight up in the sky when he came across the dead buffalo. Slaughter, there was no other word he could think to describe it. Strewn before him along the prairie were the carcasses of buffalo, at least fifty of them. The men that killed them had taken the animals' hides and left the rest of them to lie there, and the meat of them and the bone-white glare of revealed tendons and ligaments stood out on the brown grass like beacons with the hot sun beating down on everything. Crows and buzzards waddled on the ground, too full from their scavenging to take flight at his arrival, and a potbellied coyote slinked among the carcasses and eyed him warily.

He passed amongst the dead buffalo, noting their bloated bellies, and fanning his face against the swarm of flies and the stench of it all. Not a single steak or any other part had been butchered from the dead. Only their hides and tongues had been taken, and the only hair left on them was that on their wooly heads and what lay beneath their knees and hocks. It was a pitiful sight. Three dollars a hide was what that man back on the Salt Fork had said, and Morgan would have paid twice that not to see the results of that market.

It was white hide hunters that had killed them, for no Indian would have been part of such waste. On a slight swell of ground 150 yards beyond the carcasses, he found the mashed-down place in the grass where the shooter had lain and saw the holes pressed into the ground where he had used a crossed set of shooting sticks to rest his rifle on. An empty brass cartridge case that the shooter had forgotten, a 50-70, probably out of a Sharps rifle or a Springfield, lay in the grass along with two cigarette butts.

Morgan also saw the white lines of wagon-wheel marks in the grass where the skinners had loaded and hauled the hides away. He could follow those tracks and find their camp.

He shook his head, as if holding a conversation with somebody else instead of only in his mind. No, it was time to end it, and finding the hide hunters' camp wasn't going to change anything.

He looked back at the ground behind him, and it came to him then. This was where he was going to make a stand. This was the place, and a more fitting place there never was. A killing ground.

Chapter Thirty-Seven

The Traveler sat the black Kiowa mare and glassed the flat before him through a pair of binoculars, and on his second pass over the prairie with them he saw the buffalo carcasses far ahead of him. There was nothing but those rotting carcasses and grass for as far as he could see, yet he hesitated to ride farther. He couldn't say why, but he felt danger. And he was a man who had long trusted his gut feelings.

He could make out no place where Clyde might take a proper stand against him, but he had been suspicious ever since Clyde's tracks had led out onto the plain. Such a thing made no sense for a man on foot if he wanted to run, and no sense for a man with Clyde's craftiness. The line of gypsum buttes and more broken country headed in the same direction, and Clyde could have easily stuck to them. But he hadn't. Either the fear was on him and he wasn't thinking straight, or he had a plan. The Traveler was almost sure it was the latter.

Every time he thought he had Clyde, the man managed to slip away. Stealing his horse and then finding another way out of that cave in the dark proved he had guts as well as craftiness, and such a man might pick the least likely place to make his fight. If Clyde was out there somewhere on the plain, there was no way the Traveler was going to ride up within shooting range of him without Clyde seeing him first. Such a fight would be a thing of distance and a matter of who could shoot the truest—who could make the magic. And the Traveler hoped he was right. In fact, he longed for it more than anything. There was no other way it should be. Finish the thing like they had started it so long ago, a sharpshooter's fight, and let their rifles decide who was truly the hunter and who was the meat.

And when he passed his binoculars over the prairie one more time he paused on a spot beyond the killing ground. It was nothing but a slight hump in the prairie, and a place where the grass grew a little taller. But there in the midst of it, if the weak magnification of his binoculars and his own eyes didn't lie to him, was someone bellied down in that grass and ready for a shot. Clyde.

There was nowhere for the Traveler to run, and nothing to take cover behind except for his horse. He fully expected a shot to be fired his way while he was dismounting, but none came.

He stood behind the mare for a long while, peering over the saddle and trying to make out if indeed it was Clyde out there. And then he pulled his zebra dun to him by its lead rope. One of the reasons that he was partial to the stripe-legged, line-backed little horse was that he had so much time invested in him. And true to that training, the gelding responded to the cue he gave it and folded its front legs and lay down. He took a prone position against the horse's back and with his Whitworth rifle resting on its ribs. The black mare stayed where she was, and he aimed his rifle under her belly and through her legs at the little knoll in the distance.

Again, he guessed the range at six hundred yards, or maybe a smidgen further. The wind whipping through the grass was going to make the shot twice as difficult as it ought to be. A hard shot to make, for sure, but never had he wanted to strike true so badly.

Through his scope lenses he could make out Clyde's black hat in the grass, and the more he watched the more he was sure he could see the dark line of Clyde's rifle pointed at him.

But why hadn't Clyde fired by then? Was the range too great for him to be sure he could hold his mark? Was the sun blinding him out there in the grass, or the gusting wind giving him the fits? A thousand factors came into play trying to send a bullet that far downrange and make it hit where you wanted, and any one of those factors could be causing Clyde to hesitate. Maybe Clyde wanted him closer before he took the shot, and failed to realize that he had been spotted before his quarry took to the ground.

The Traveler grinned and dialed the elevation screw on his rear scope ring to the proper mark. Nothing but his head and the rifle showed above the back of the horse, and Clyde had nothing out there to cover him. The Traveler cocked his hammer and found that black hat in his crosshairs. And then the pad of his pointer finger caressed his trigger.

The Whitworth recoiled against his shoulder in a cloud of smoke and a dull boom, and the 530-grain hexagonal, .45-caliber bullet cast from hardened lead, patched with a piece of felt, and backed by 100 grains of black powder, launched its way toward Clyde. The instant he kissed the rifle's hair trigger he knew that he had made the magic and that the bullet was going to fly true as lightning. But after the rifle settled again and he found Clyde in the crosshairs once more, he saw that something had gone badly wrong.

Morgan tightened the bandanna across his nose, and retched once at the smell of the buffalo he laid behind. The dead bull was large enough that its hairy head and the high swell of its bloated ribcage hid him totally. Only the valley of its neck between its head and shoulders provided him a view of the prairie to the south of him, and his Moore bench rifle was rested in that swag.

He was barely settled in behind the dead bull when the rider appeared on the horizon. It was several more moments before it was plain to Morgan's vision that it was indeed a man astride a horse and leading another one. And it took longer for Morgan to be sure that it was the Traveler.

And Morgan rolled on his side and looked back across the killing field behind him to the grassy knoll where he had left his hat and shirt fitted over the rear leg he had cut off a cow buffalo. The crude setup would never pass for a man up close, but maybe it would appear that way at a distance.

He turned back to watching the Traveler ride closer, and he held up a brass stadia range finder to estimate the distance between them. The range finder was of the kind that artillery crews calculated ranges with, and a model that sharpshooters on both sides of the fight during the war had quickly adopted for their own use. It was simply nothing more than a rectangle of brass with a vertical V slot cut inside it. A sliding aperture could be moved up and down over that V cut, and the operation was simple. There was a string attached to the bottom of the stadia, and you held the end of the string to the bottom of your aiming eye and moved the stadia away from you and towards the target until the string tightened to achieve the proper perspective. The size of the stadia aperture was calibrated for an average height of six feet for a man, and you slid it up or down until the man you were aiming it at perfectly filled its opening. The outer rectangle of the stadia was marked with lines for different yardages, and you simply read off the mark that the aperture's position corresponded with.

The Traveler came closer, with Morgan watching and taking multiple readings: first a thousand yards, then seven hundred, and then four hundred yards. Morgan was about to ready his rifle when the Traveler stopped. Sunlight flashed on glass, and Morgan guessed the Traveler was searching the prairie with a set of binoculars.

Morgan settled the Moore rifle to his right shoulder and found the proper weld of his cheekbone to the stock. He wanted to take the shot then, but it had been long since he had tried to hit anything at such a distance. He had fired the Moore rifle only three times since the war, and all three of those were practice shots he had taken back in Ironhead to check the rifle sight in. And none of those shots had been at such long range or aimed at a real man—a real man who was likely to shoot back, not the same at all as punching holes in paper targets.

He adjusted his scope, cocked the rifle hammer to make sure the primer underneath it was in place on the nipple, and watched his crosshairs rise and fall over the Traveler in time with the beat of his heart. But he did not shoot. He might get only one chance and needed to make it count. The closer the Traveler came, the greater the odds that his rusty skills could make the Moore rifle shoot true. That was the whole purpose of the decoy he had built, to possibly distract the Traveler into a long rifle shot while he was actually hidden much closer to him.

And then the Traveler dropped off his horse and stayed behind it. Morgan moved his crosshairs, trying to discern his enemy behind the black horse but couldn't. He watched as the Traveler's zebra dun moved closer to the black, and knew in the instant the dun laid down that the Traveler had spotted either him or the decoy.

Having the horse lay down for a breastwork was a trick Morgan had never seen, but one that he had heard some cavalry troops trained for. A man on his belly behind a horse like that provided little target for his enemies, especially at four hundred yards away.

Morgan moved his crosshairs again, trying to find the Traveler in his scope. The black horse stood directly in front of the dun down on the ground, and he was aiming under the black's belly when he saw what he was almost sure was the Traveler's head and rifle peering over the dun's side. He hated to risk shooting either horse, but he had no other choice.

The black stomped its leg restlessly against the bite of the flies pestering it, and he waited for a moment when it stood still. And then that moment came and the Traveler's head was visible again. As before, Morgan watched the crosshairs rising and falling with each of his heartbeats, and he took a deep breath and let a little of it out until his aim steadied as much as it was going to. He shifted the vertex of the crosshairs a man's width upwind of the Traveler's head and put the very end of the pad of his finger on the trigger. The double-set trigger works on the Moore rifle were honed smooth and set to break at half a pound of pressure, and you simply thought about squeezing it to fire a round, rather than actually squeezing it.

But before he could think the shot downrange, he saw the powder smoke blossom out of the Traveler's gun and was sure he had waited too long to fire and was about to die.

Although he never saw the Traveler's bullet strike the decoy beyond him, he knew that the Traveler wouldn't have missed that badly and must have taken the bait. The Traveler's black horse had been frightened by the gunshot and ran some distance away, leaving only the dun horse on its side to hide the Traveler. Morgan fully expected the Traveler to disappear behind the dun while he reloaded, but he didn't. It seemed he was too busy watching the decoy. And then his head rose a little higher behind the horse's side until all of it was revealed in Morgan's scope.

It was an impossibly small target to hit for a man that hadn't practiced the art in almost a decade, and even in his prime days of rifle marksmanship Morgan had rarely hit such a small target at that kind of distance with the first shot. He told himself that as soon as he fired his rifle he needed to duck below the buffalo carcass and reload fast.

Again, he went through his ritual of steadying the rifle,

engaged the set trigger, and found his hold. The trigger pull was so light that recoil of the rifle surprised him, and he waited for the smoke to drift away so that he could once more see downrange.

He fully expected to see the Traveler aiming his own rifle back at him, but when his gunsmoke cleared, the Traveler had disappeared from sight. Morgan kept watch on the dun horse while he fitted the false muzzle to the end of his rifle barrel. It took him a couple of minutes to pour a powder charge from one of his quick-load tubes, seat a patched bullet home, and place a fresh percussion cap on the nipple. And yet, in all that time, the Traveler never appeared above the dun horse.

Morgan waited for what seemed like an hour, sweating behind the dead buffalo and breathing its rancid stink until he could taste it. The blowflies lit on his face and crawled with tickling legs across his skin, but he wouldn't risk swatting them away, so focused was he on staying behind his rifle optics and keeping watch for the Traveler to rise up from his horse.

But it wasn't the Traveler that finally moved. It was the dun horse. The gelding stood, shook the dust from its hide, and nickered at the black horse off in the distance. The black answered it, and soon the dun trotted away towards it. Morgan closed his aiming eye to squeeze the tears from it and to try and relieve the strain of staring through the scope for so long, and when he opened it again he saw the Traveler lying flat on his face on the ground. And he knew that there was no kind of ruse where the Traveler would have given up the protection the horse had offered him.

Morgan stood and started through the buffalo carcasses, ready to drop back to a prone position if the Traveler should show signs of life, and he altered his course to a wide arc, circling to the Traveler's right to force him to shift position to track him if he should be only wounded.

But the Traveler never moved, not even when Morgan stood over him, and not when he was rolled onto his back. Morgan looked down at the Traveler with the Whitworth rifle still clutched in his dead hands and a bullet hole in his forehead.

Morgan stared at that face, every detail of it, wanting to see it for what it really was and not the vision of Old Death he had carried for so long. And truly, lying there like that, the Traveler didn't look like a demon that stalked men in their nightmares, not ominous at all, but simply a petite, weathered little man with missing teeth, bad skin, and long blond hair with bits of grass and other debris tangled in the braids it was gathered with.

"You've come a long way from your Arkansas hills to wind up here, Erastus Tuck," Morgan said.

He went and retrieved the Traveler's horses and walked them back to the body. Then he took the Traveler's Dance cap-and-ball revolver, and stuffed it in the saddlebags on the dun. There was no shovel to bury the dead drygulcher, so Morgan simply scraped a hole in the ground at the Traveler's head with his hands, and set the Whitworth rifle butt down in it and packed the dirt back around it. He left it standing upright like a tombstone as he swung up onto the saddle on the zebra dun. He reached into the saddlebags once more and took out the Traveler's diaries, and then took the one out of his vest pocket that he had carried with him since the Kingman brothers had attacked him back on the Salt Fork. He pitched all of them down on the Traveler's body, and then rode away across the killing field.

He wasn't yet out of sight of the Traveler's final resting place when he dropped his Moore rifle to the ground. He kept on riding, never once looking back at either the gun he had dropped or the man he had killed with it. And the wind blew one of the Traveler's diaries open behind him, and pages began to rip loose, one by one, and flutter slowly through the grass.

He rode into the buffalo hunters' camp on the morning of the next day under a gray sky and a steady drizzle of rain. The men around the smoking, damp fires and crouched under their wagon beds put their rifles to hand and watched him ride up to them with a wary readiness.

He stopped a short distance out from their camp, but did not hail them or ask for an invite to share their fires, simply setting slumped on the dun horse he rode and staring at them. And the hunters were equally slow to greet him, for they weren't quite sure what to make of him. But finally, one of them waved him in.

"Light and set, stranger," that one said when Morgan rode up to the nearest fire.

Morgan dismounted slowly, and kept to the offside of his horse. He studied the men over his saddle in the same way they were studying him.

There were at least twenty of them, all rough-looking men. Three double freight wagons and a lighter chuckwagon were parked up in a rough U shape. Two of the freight wagons were heaped high with bundled and dried buffalo hides. "Flint hides" were what some hunters called them due to how hard they cured. And more hides were pegged out to ground around the camp to be scraped and prepared when the rain clouds moved on and the sun showed itself again. A small herd of work oxen, a handful of mules, and some saddle horses were loose, herded on the prairie not far from the wagon under the watch of two mounted men.

He kept hold of the Henry rifle in his hands when he walked out from behind the horse.

"Cautious sort, ain't you," said the man who had first spoken as he crawled out from under the wagon that had sheltered him. His clothes were filthy with bloodstains and dirt from longs days of skinning buffalo, and his beard reached halfway to the top of his chest. But the Remington Rolling Block rifle cradled in his arms looked to be in tip-top shape.

And Morgan saw how they were all looking at him, and then he looked down at himself and chuckled. He had lost at least twenty pounds since he had left Ironhead, and he and his clothes were as tattered and filthy as those the hide hunters wore. Standing there in his mutilated boots, and missing his shirtsleeves, he must look a sight. He ran a hand through his beard and grimaced.

"You boys keep looking at me like that and you're going to embarrass me," he said. "I guess you haven't ever seen such a sharp dressed and comely man."

That brought a round of laughter, and most of the men seemed to relax a little. The man who did the talking for the hunters up to that point set his rifle butt down on the ground before him and leaned on the barrel.

"We haven't seen town in a while ourselves, but damned if you don't look like you crawled out of a cave somewhere," he said.

Again they laughed, and Morgan laughed with them. He really laughed, like he hadn't in a long, long time.

And when he rode away from their camp he had a belly full of hot coffee, soggy beans, and buffalo steak almost too tough to chew, and he had traded the Traveler's Dance revolver for instructions on how to hit the nearest railhead at Newton, Kansas, by following the Chisholm Trail north, and had enough supplies in his saddlebags to see him there.

Chapter Thirty-Eight

The pain in Dixie's hand had lessened, and all he felt was nausea. Twice he had to stop and vomit on his way to the telegraph operator's tent after Doc Chillingsworth had cleaned and bandaged the wound. And each time, the lynch mob waited for him to finish before they followed him on.

Again, they stopped and waited while he went inside the tent, and were still there when he came back out. Several of them had retrieved saddled horses, and a wagon had been readied for those who hadn't been able to procure a mount.

He wanted nothing more than to lie down somewhere, and the look he gave the crowd was a bitter one. Behind him, from within the tent, came the clicking sounds of the operator pecking away on his Morse key.

"Where the hell do you think you're going?" Dixie said to the crowd of men.

"We're going with you after them," one of the men carrying a rusty Parker shotgun said.

"None of you are going anywhere," Dixie said. "I've wired ahead to those two deputy marshals at Ironhead, and if they're still there, they'll stop the train and arrest Duvall and the Hilltopper."

"You're going up the line, aren't you?"

"I'm going."

"You're going to need some help," said another man.

"What I need is for you men to sleep off your whiskey and

then get up in the morning and go back to work."

"You don't know that those marshals are still in Ironhead, and you couldn't handle the Hilltopper by yourself the first time," came a voice from the back of the crowd that caused heads to bob in agreement with him.

"And none of us are going to catch them if those marshals aren't there to stop the train," Dixie said.

"So what you're telling us is . . ."

Dixie cut off the man with the shotgun before he could finish. "What I'm telling you is that I'm going to pursue them. I'm hoping those marshals are there to stop the train at Ironhead, but I'll go on up the line if they don't. Those two can't outrun the telegraph, and they'll be arrested before too long, one way or another."

"You can say what you want to, but some of us are going with you, at least as far as Ironhead," said the voice from the back of the crowd again. "That colored gal was the third woman that's been mistreated in our camps, and we're nothing but damned cowards if we stand for it."

"That's right," another man in the crowd said.

Dixie saw how they were looking at him with no confidence in him to handle the matter. And he couldn't blame them. He felt as weak as a sick cat and he was sure he fell far short of appearing as a commanding figure standing there with one hand bandaged and supported in a sheet sling across his chest.

He asked himself what Morgan would do, but gave it up no sooner than he had started. He wasn't Morgan Clyde, and the more he wore a badge the more he decided he didn't want to be.

In the end, about half of the mob went with him. Someone brought him his guns, and then he climbed into a wagon with about ten of his unofficial posse and started up the Texas Road to Ironhead. A half-dozen more men headed in the same direction, some of them on saddle horses, and the rest on a handcar they pumped along the train tracks.

Dixie wanted to lay down in the back of the wagon, but for the sake of appearance and his official capacity as a Katy policeman, he roughed it out slumped over on the jostling wagon seat beside his driver. Someone offered him a drink of whiskey to help with his pain, but a slug of it made him sick again.

"Get up," the Hilltopper said to Duvall.

The superintendent had fallen asleep, and only mumbled and pulled away when the Hilltopper shook his shoulder.

"I said get up," the Hilltopper repeated. "We've got trouble."

Duvall managed to gain his feet after two tries, still clutching his valise to his chest. He leaned his head out the side window of the cab and looked at a tiny red dot of light up ahead. That dot could be nothing other than a red lantern hanging on the hook post in front of what was left of the Ironhead depot house. Such a lantern instructed the engineer to stop.

"What's the problem?" Duvall rubbed at his face trying to get fully awake and in the moment.

"Could be they've got passengers or freight that needs a ride," the engineer said as he slowed the train.

"There's no through trains, and this one wasn't supposed to be here to pick up rails until the morning," the Hilltopper said.

"Could be that the tracks are washed out or something else wrong somewhere past Ironhead," the engineer said.

The Hilltopper shoved his Dragoon in the engineer's side. "You throttle this engine back up, and you do it now."

"I'm getting off here," Duvall said. "I have things I must attend to in Ironhead."

"Have you thought that the first thing that mob would do was to wire ahead of us?" The Hilltopper leaned his head out the opposite window for a closer look at the depot ahead.

While still groggy, the rest seemed to have sobered Duvall some. "They can wire up the line to any of the stops."

The Hilltopper started to argue, but didn't. Instead, he thought out loud. "Maybe the best thing is to chance it here instead of going on. The soldiers could be waiting for us at Gibson Station, and there's the Lighthorse and an occasional marshal usually hanging around Muskogee."

"And there's not much of anybody left in Ironhead," Duvall said with more than a little condescension.

"Yeah, but that red light bothers me something fierce. You got any idea if those two marshals that were snooping around Ironhead have left yet? Could be that light is their doing."

The fact that Duvall didn't answer him told him that he hadn't thought of that at all.

"The thing to do might be to chance it here and strike overland for Fort Smith. Or maybe find a good place to lay low for a while." The Hilltopper took his horse pistol out of the engineer's side, but didn't holster it.

"What's it going to be?" The engineer had his hand on the brake lever. "I'm running out of room if you want to put the whoa on this train."

"All right. We're stopping."

The engineer slowed the engine and added some brake.

"If I see something I don't like, you better be ready to pour the throttle to her," the Hilltopper said to the engineer. And then he turned to the tender. "And you better be chunking the wood to that box like the Devil boiling water."

The tender opened the firebox below the boiler, and the fire inside it shone a light on his nodding head. He hadn't said a word since they had pulled out of Canadian with the lynch mob's bullets rattling off the locomotive cab.

Ahead, the locomotive's lamp beam lit up the new white framing where the depot house was being rebuilt, and the two-story hotel across the street from it. Nobody was visible on the depot's platform decking or along the tracks, but that didn't ease the Hilltopper's mind. He shifted sides in the cab to stand beside Duvall and to be nearest to the depot when they pulled up beside it.

"You still got your pistol?" he asked.

"I've got it," Duvall answered.

"If I start shooting, you take that pistol and make sure this train man isn't slow letting off that brake," the Hilltopper said.

The driver wheels creaked and screeched against the tracks, and little by little the locomotive slowed to a crawl.

"You roll on past the depot a ways before you stop," the Hilltopper said.

The engineer nodded.

The locomotive crawled past the depot and came to a stop fifty yards beyond it with the train behind it even with the platform. The engineer opened a valve and bled off the rest of his steam pressure.

"You first." The Hilltopper shoved the engineer towards the door.

The only opening into the locomotive's cab was on the opposite side of the tracks from the depot, and the Hilltopper went down the ladder right behind the engineer. At his urging, the tender and then Duvall got to the ground after him. The Hilltopper marched the pair of train men around the front of the locomotive with his pistol held at their backs.

He paused under the engine's headlight to peer at the depot house, and purposefully let his hostages get a little ahead of him while doing it. If there was anyone waiting for him, the appearance of the train men might draw them out.

But nothing moved in the ruins of the depot building, and the Hilltopper took a few quick strides to catch back up to his hostages. Duvall stumbled over the rails after him.

"Hold up there!" came a command from somewhere inside the depot.

The Hilltopper didn't stop. He shoved the engineer toward the sound of that voice, and then he was running down the rutted street that led away from the tracks and passed between the hotel site and the depot. His Dragoon pistol bellowed with a lance of flame, once, twice, and a rifle barked from the depot house. The engineer fell to the ground, either because he was hit or because he didn't want to be. Duvall leapt over him, and then went after the Hilltopper in an awkward run with his shoeless, tender feet giving him problems on the rough dirt road and hugging the carpetbag full of money.

A bullet kicked up dirt in front of Duvall, and he weaved towards the hotel. The Hilltopper was already headed that way, still firing his pistol at the gun flashes winking inside the depot framing.

The hotel provided some shelter from the fight. The carpenters had managed to raise the second-floor framing, roofing it with corrugated sheet iron, and in places the board and bat pine siding was in place. But there were still large gaps where the stud walls were exposed and their ambushers' bullets flew through the open rib bones of the structure without meeting much resistance.

The Hilltopper was crouched inside the front doorway behind a sided section of wall when Duvall went past him. Duvall didn't stop when he saw him, but kept running towards the back of the building. He ran into a partition wall and fell.

There was a lull in the gunfire, and again someone shouted from the depot house. "Federal marshals! Throw down your guns and come out!"

The Hilltopper answered that command with a gunshot, and then shifted his position to a window opening farther down the wall a moment before two bullets splintered holes in the pine plank siding where he had been.

Duvall scrambled to his feet, found a way out the back, and sprinted towards the tent he had erected for Helvina at the edge of the woods. There was lamplight glowing from within it, and Helvina was sitting wrapped in a robe in a chair at the far end of the room when he charged inside. She held a Colt Root side-hammer pocket revolver aimed at the door, and didn't lower the dainty, .31-caliber weapon when she saw it was him.

"You've got to hide me," he said. "Hurry."

She looked at the valise he clutched and at his own pistol dangling at the end of one arm. More gunshots sounded from up at the hotel.

"Put that thing away," he said to her. Her pistol wasn't even cocked, and he was sure her holding it was meant as nothing more than one of her usual antics to irritate him.

She continued to hold the gun aimed at him. He ignored it and began rummaging through the paperwork atop the wooden desk to one side of the tent.

"Where's the money I left you?" he asked, scattering papers and yanking drawers open.

"Do you mean the money you left me to start on the hotel?" she said.

"Get it."

"I paid the carpenters with it, and I paid for material with it," she said in a calm voice.

"All of it?"

"All of it. In fact, I intended to wire you for more funds so that I could order the finish work."

He looked frantically around the tent. "No matter. I've enough to see us through. As soon as this blows over we'll take a wagon overland to Fort Smith, then catch a steamer there to Little Rock."

"To Little Rock? Dear, whatever would I want to go to

Arkansas for?"

"We have to go."

"No, you have to go."

He looked at the doorway, listening to the sound of the continuing fight. "Is that the marshals out there?"

She nodded. "Your roving eye has got you in a bit of trouble this time, hasn't it, Willis? But a black girl? Really. So scandalous."

"Move so I can hide under your bed," he said.

She didn't move. "I will if you give me what's in that valise you're holding."

He remembered only then that he too held a gun, but the Hilltopper shoved into the tent at the same time. The appearance of a giant man brandishing a pistol caused no change in the expression on Helvina's face, but she did shift the pistol to cover them both.

"What have we here?" she said. "Another outlaw fleeing the long arm of justice?"

"Put that gun down and shut the hell up," the Hilltopper said as he peered out of the crack of the door flaps toward the hotel. "Shut her up or I will, and put out that lamp."

"Helvina, do as he says. We'll have time to discuss this later," Duvall said.

Helvina cocked the little pistol, and the sound of it made the Hilltopper look over his shoulder at her.

"The money you're carrying, and I'll do my best to hide you both," she said to Duvall.

"Helvina, you blow out that lamp right now," Duvall said. "Or I will . . ."

"Or you'll what? Lose your job? Withhold funds for my hotel? Ruin my reputation?" she said.

Duvall thought to bring his own pistol to bear on her, but the Hilltopper's voice stopped him.

"She shoots that pistol and those marshals are going to be all over us quicker than you can spit," the Hilltopper said.

"Helvina, this behavior is beneath you," Duvall said. "Now put down that gun and put out the light."

"The money, Willis. Perhaps, I would even settle for half of it. Half might do to see the hotel built, and to keep me from having to grovel before my father for another loan from him. You know, times are quite hard right now, and he can be so difficult when it comes to his dwindling fortune."

Duvall reached for the pistol she held.

"Help!" Helvina screamed. "Help! Marshals, they're over here."

Duvall froze, but the Hilltopper whirled to face her. He saw that her pistol had shifted its aim to him.

"Woman, you better hope we never meet again," he said.

"I'm counting on it," she said.

The Hilltopper hesitated only a moment while he thought about trying her, but was out the door almost as quickly. Duvall was left alone with her.

"Go ahead, Willis, put down your luggage and run," she said. And then she looked at his feet with their torn socks and nothing else covering them. "Such a poor outlaw you make. Almost as poor as your business schemes. My father warned me that you were a man who would never amount to much."

"Helvina . . ."

"Go on, Willis, set your bag down and run, before I decide to shoot you. I'm quite a good shot, you know," she said.

"You said only half."

"The price has gone up," she said. "Truly, if I were the witch you thought me to be I would have already killed you. After all, who would question a terrified lady defending herself against a known abuser of women who barged into her tent?"

He made as if to go, still clutching his valise. She fired the pistol, not at him, but into the wall of the tent beside him. He gave her one last look, then placed the bag on the floor before he left. He had no clue where the Hilltopper had gone, but thought he could hear crashing footsteps in the brush behind the tent. He plunged blindly into the thick woods after them.

Helvina was waiting outside the open door of her tent in the lamplight when one of the marshals appeared out of the dark. She made sure to tremble appropriately and to rub her eyes hard enough before he arrived to cause a tear to two to run down her cheeks.

"They went that way," she said and pointed into the woods behind the tent.

"Are you hurt?" the marshal asked.

"No, but they threatened me with all manner of vile things before I fired at them," she said.

"Lucky you were armed," the lawman said as he flipped back one door flap with his rifle barrel and checked inside the tent.

"I only did what you told me to do when the wire came from Canadian. I stayed in my tent just like you said."

"Yes, ma'am. You did fine. Was there two of them?"

"I don't know. I think . . . Oh, it all happened so fast."

"I know you're shook up, ma'am, but were there two of them?" The marshal put a hand to her shoulder to support her as she swooned against him. "Steady now. You're safe."

She sniffled and regained the strength of her legs. "Forgive me, Marshal, it seems my feminine nature isn't up to the task of such heightened excitement. Yes, there were two of them. My fiancé and some other man. A big fellow with long hair."

"That's the Hilltopper, all right. Thought we had him back at the depot, but he opened up on us when we called for his surrender."

"I hope you catch him, oh, I surely do."

The other deputy marshal came up, breathing hard after his run and also carrying a rifle. "I wired the army at Fort Gibson, and the Creek police at Muskogee."

"Good," his partner said. "We'll run them to ground one way or the other."

"I never would have guessed such horrible men existed," Helvina said. "Thank goodness, you brave souls came to my call."

"That Hilltopper is a new one on me," the second marshal said. "But I would guess he's got papers on him somewhere. Man like that usually does."

"He . . . he threatened me," she said. "He . . . he said if I didn't hide them he would do to me what they did to that colored woman and her husband in Canadian."

"They admitted to that?"

She sniffled again and nodded. "It all seemed so preposterous when you came to me and told me that Willis and this . . . What did you call him?"

"The Hilltopper," the second marshal said.

"Yes, that's it. When you said that you had received a wire informing you of their crime and that Willis might seek shelter with me in Ironhead, I must admit to not believing you. Who would ever have imagined him to be . . . oh, I would never have imagined any of it. How could I? It's all so heinous." She sagged against the marshal beside her again, and made sure to press herself against him when he moved to catch her. "How could I know he was like that?"

"Some of the worst ones put on the best act," the marshal holding her said.

"Yes, I suppose so," she said. "But that makes me feel no better for having been engaged to such an animal."

The marshal holding her upright moved her into the tent and sat her down on her chair.

"Please don't leave me," she said. "What if they are close by?"

"They're making tracks away from here right now, I assure you, Miss Vanderwagen," the marshal said. "But if it will ease your mind, I'll have someone sit with you."

"Oh, would you?"

When the lawmen were gone, Helvina straightened her robe and smiled. She rose and tied the door flaps shut before she pulled the valise out from under her bed. She opened it long enough to see that it held money as she assumed it would—a great deal of money—and then she put it back and took a seat in her chair. She was tempted to smile again, but the marshals might return and she would need to look the part of the distressed lady-in-waiting.

Chapter Thirty-Nine

Although she couldn't see any of it from her place inside the boxcar, Molly guessed who else had decided it was a good time to get out of Canadian when the lynch mob fired on the train as it rolled out of Canadian. And her guess was confirmed when the train stopped at Ironhead.

She waited until well after the gunfire was over before she led Hannah from the boxcar. The young black woman had said nothing to her since their departure from Canadian, only occasionally crying and sobbing, and the gunfire on both ends of their journey hadn't helped her situation any. Molly herself was more than a little jittery.

They could hear men talking over by the hotel, and not wanting to chance who she might run into in the dark, Molly stayed off the main street as she took Hannah to her tent. Ruby Ann met them there and held back the tent flaps while they entered. Molly sat Hannah down on her bed and then went back outside with Ruby Ann.

"Did you see any of it?" Molly asked.

Ruby Ann shook her head, and Molly could barely make out the shadowed movement of her answer.

"I'm guessing that somebody wired the marshals that Duvall and that Hilltopper were coming," Molly said.

Ruby Ann made no gesture in response that Molly could make out.

Molly quickly told Ruby Ann what had befallen the crying

black woman inside the tent, filling in the unknown details with what she surmised about the affair. She also told her about her run-in with the Hilltopper and what had happened to Tuck. Again, Ruby Ann took the news in silence.

"I want you to set here with her and make her comfortable as you can," Molly said. "I'm going over to the saloon to get us a gun."

Ruby Ann stepped in front of her, barring her way.

"Duvall's somewhere in this camp, and so is that Hilltopper," Molly said. "Maybe those marshals will do us a favor and catch them before the night's over, but I'd feel some better if I had us a pistol to sit with."

Molly went around Ruby Ann and slipped in the back door of the Bullhorn. Noodles was there with a single lamp set on the bar top beside him. She noticed the cot and a rumpled set of blankets behind the bar.

"Have you taken to sleeping here?" she asked as she joined him behind the bar.

"Nowhere else to sleep, Molly. I don't sleep in no woods. Not for you. Not if you want me to work this place," he said.

"Have you got any idea what's going on out there?" She pointed to the front door when she asked it.

"I know something. The marshals, they was in here a little while ago, looking for that railroad big shot, Signor Duvall, and some other man," he said. "They tell me to stay here and not let no ones come in here without I tell them."

She bent below the bar top and found Tuck's nickel-plated pistol on a shelf where Noodles had left it. She snapped the pistol open, saw that it was unloaded, and then rummaged around on the dark shelf feeling for the cartridges for it. Noodles watched her load the gun.

"You done got in trouble with that pistol once," he said.

"If you had been through what I've been through this evening you would be wanting two pistols instead of one," Molly said.

She went to the front door and looked out of it at the street. The new storekeeper across from her was on his porch and talking to two men. She shoved the gun down the front of her dress between her breasts and lodged the barrel of it in the top of her corset, then she moved across the street.

There was enough light coming through the front windows of the store that she could see that it was the two marshals the storekeeper was talking to. All three men quit whatever they had been saying and turned to her.

"What's with all the shooting?" Molly asked. "A woman can barely sleep around here."

"I thought you already went through all the tents," one of the marshals said to the other.

"I did," came the reply.

"Ruby Ann said you'd come by while I was at the privy," Molly said. "Thought I would come over here and see what the fuss was about after she told me."

"There's two fugitives on the loose," one of the marshals said.

Molly was having a hard time telling who was talking, but said nothing about it. "Fugitives?"

"Willis Duvall, the railroad superintendent, and another man," said one of the marshals.

"What did they do?"

"Don't know for sure yet, but the police chief at Canadian wired us that there had been a man killed down there and a woman hurt. He requested we apprehend those two and hold them for questioning."

"Doesn't look like you're doing any apprehending here on this porch."

There was a moment of silence before one of them answered her. "The man with Duvall put up a fight, and the pair of them ran off in the woods."

"Well then, why aren't you in the woods chasing them?" she said. "Or do you prefer accusing innocent women of crimes they didn't commit?"

Again, there was silence, followed by a sigh. "Why don't you go back to your saloon and let us attend to our business? There's a posse on its way here from Canadian Camp, and another one helling it here from Fort Gibson. Those two won't go far afoot, and we'll run them down by tomorrow morning if I don't miss my guess."

"You had the drop on them and you missed," she said as she started back across the street.

"Opinionated woman, that one," she heard the storekeeper say when she was almost too far away to hear him.

She passed by the Bullhorn, went around back of it, and then ducked inside her tent. Ruby Ann was sitting on the bed beside Hannah trying to coax her into eating some kind of soup from a bowl. Both women looked up at her as she came through the door.

Molly dragged her rocking chair to where it faced the door, and took a seat in it. She dug in the top of her dress until she had a hold of the pistol and pulled it out and laid it in her lap. Both women looked at the pistol, and then at her.

"I'm finding that there's other advantages to being well endowed," was all that Molly said about the pistol.

"Did Mr. Duvall and his man follow me here?" Hannah asked as she shoved aside the bowl of soup.

"No, I'm thinking we only had the misfortune to ride on the same train with them," Molly replied.

Hannah seemed steadier, and Molly thought it was a good sign that the woman had finally decided to talk a little. But she knew you didn't force such things, so she waited.

"Are you women . . . Are you . . . ?" Hannah made a show of

looking around the room instead of at either of them when she tried to ask whatever she was fumbling to find words for.

"Yes, we're whores. At least we were," Molly said. "Don't act so shocked. If it helps your sensibilities, then I'll tell you that both of us have recently retired."

Ruby Ann looked a question at Molly.

"Well, we're working on retiring," Molly said.

Hannah looked around the tent some more. "Will that blacksmith really bring my Saul to me?"

"I imagine you can take him at his word. I never heard of him lying before."

"I told him I wanted to stay, but he wouldn't listen. Told them all to let me be so I could sit with my Saul."

"It's best you came here, unless you wanted to answer all the questions that mob would have put to you about what happened. My guess, same as Hank's, was that it would be good for you to have a little quiet time to yourself. Hank's a rare man to understand that."

"Mr. Duvall tried to have his way with me," Hannah said. "He was bad drunk, and I fought him off. I was going to hide it from Saul, but he come in our tent and saw me crying and with my dress torn up before I could change it. I tried to tell him that Mr. Duvall was only drunk and didn't mean anything by it. Told him to let me handle it. Told him I would tell Mr. Duvall I quit the first thing in the morning."

Molly took a deep breath, and let it out slowly. "You aren't to blame. I know it doesn't seem like it now, but you aren't."

"I never should have told Saul. I knew what he would do."

"Your Saul had a right to know."

Hannah dabbed at her eyes with one hand. "I saw it all. Saul wasn't a fighter. Never was. He was a gentle man that liked to make people laugh and to see them enjoy his cooking. But that big man he didn't care about that. He laughed after he killed

Saul. And Mr. Duvall didn't care, either. Mean drunk, he was."

"The marshals are looking for them. I suspect they'll have them caught before long."

"And what will they do when they catch him? The law won't hang a rich white man for what he done to two black people."

Molly was about to tell Hannah she was wrong, but couldn't bring herself to tell the lie. Her guess was that Duvall was in real trouble this time, but there was no certainty of justice. She had known that herself after what he had done to her, and it was a part of the reason she hadn't gone to the law then. She envisioned all the lawyers Duvall would hire, and how they would twist things enough to convince a jury to let him off, if the crime ever made it to a courtroom.

"Those marshals told me there's a posse coming up from Canadian," Molly said. "Seemed to me like they believed you, and I don't think they will listen to Duvall's lies."

"The law is in on it now," Hannah said. "The marshals won't let a hanging happen."

"Best you get you some sleep now, if you can," Molly said. "It will be a long day tomorrow."

"I can't sleep. All I can think of is my Saul."

Molly rose and poured a glass of whiskey and held it out to Hannah. "Drink this. It will help you sleep."

"I don't drink."

"Won't hurt you this once, and we won't tell."

Even Ruby Ann agreed with that, and she nodded and gently pushed the glass towards Hannah's mouth.

"Drink it fast," Molly said. "There, now, that's the way."

Hannah made an awful face at the taste of the whiskey and coughed once, but Molly cajoled her into a second glass, and then laid her down on the bed and pulled the covers up over her. Ruby Ann crawled into the bed beside her, and put an arm across her.

"My Saul, he didn't deserve to die like that," Hannah said in a quieter voice. "We were going to move to a farm in the Seminole Nation with my brothers and my cousins as soon as we saved enough money. I was going to teach school and Saul was going to put in some cotton and maybe a garden big enough to sell some greens out of until we were settled in and making a go of it."

Molly let the woman talk on, telling of her childhood on an Arkansas plantation near Little Rock, and how she and her mother had been freed when the Yankee army had taken over the state capital. She told of how they had later migrated to Kansas, of the boarding school there, and how Saul had found her after the war while he was working on the railroad.

Hannah talked for half an hour, sometimes only fragments of memories about she and Saul, and sometimes only mumbling to herself about things Molly couldn't make out. But Molly understood that Hannah needed to talk, and simply sat in her rocking chair and listened.

Late in the night, Ruby Ann fell asleep, and Hannah wasn't too far behind her in succumbing to slumber. Molly rose again and looked down at the two of them for a moment, at the way Ruby Ann hugged Hannah to her, and then she adjusted the covers over them and went to her dresser.

She poured herself a small drink of whiskey, adding a couple of drops of the opium tincture she took from her wrist purse. When she was finished with her drink she went back to her chair and laid the pistol in her lap.

And she rocked that chair while she listened to Ruby Ann's soft snoring. And she rocked that chair when she heard the mob from Canadian arrive in the camp. And she was still rocking it when the sun came up, wondering if this was the day Willis Duvall would get what was coming to him.

Chapter Forty

Bill Tuck awoke with a faint buzzing sound in his head and an ache in his side. He looked around him at the briar patch and sumac bushes he lay in, then the treetops rising above him, and tried to remember where he was at or how he had come to be there. With some difficulty, he propped himself up on one elbow and could see the sunlit open ground of the railroad right of way not far from where he lay. The instant he moved the buzzing sound grew louder.

He turned his head slowly and saw the snake not much farther than an arm length from his face. It was a coon tail rattler, as big around as his ankle at its middle and maybe six feet long. Its wide head was reared up at eye level with him, its fork tongue flicking out, and the rattle on the tip of its tail vibrated an angry warning.

He wasn't sure he could move if he wanted to, and even when healthy there was no way he could dodge the viper's strike. He remembered once seeing a man playing with such a rattlesnake, letting it strike his boot, and the milky venom left there and the fang marks pushed halfway in the cowhide leather. That much venom struck right between his eyes would kill him for sure.

The rattler continued to buzz its tail, and its vertical pupils stared back at him with an intensity he could feel crawling down his spine. He held his breath and tried not to blink, fearing that even so little a movement on his part would cause the snake to strike.

After what seemed like an eternity, but was actually only a matter of seconds, the snake lowered its head and turned away from him. He watched it until its diamond-patterned hide slithered out of sight behind a deadfall log, and then he let out his breath.

He fell back on his shoulder blades and stared up at the sun shining through the treetops. When he finally decided to get up, he found he was so weak and stiff it took him three tries simply to get to his knees. One side of his shirt was plastered to his ribs with dried blood where the Hilltopper's knife had cut him, and his neck on the same side was blistered and blackened with powder burns. His head throbbed with a terrible, dull ache, and his mouth was dry and tasted of chalk.

He stayed on his knees for some time, and then he managed to take hold of a low limb and pull himself to his feet. He hugged the maple sapling the limb was attached to, and waited for some strength to return to his legs.

He walked on wobbly legs out of the edge of the woods and onto the railroad right of way. He vaguely remembered falling off the train, but had no clue how far he had ridden the flatcar. The end of the line was supposed to be a little more than ten miles south of Canadian, and that gave him some idea of where he was, even if he wasn't familiar with the countryside.

To go back to Canadian likely meant fighting the Hilltopper again, something he was in no shape for, and to go south to the end of the line meant he would run across the Katy's construction crews. Surely Duvall had put the word out about him, and the workers there were liable to be as dangerous to him as the Hilltopper.

He was weighing which option he disliked the least when a wagon came rolling towards him from the south. It was driven by a plump Choctaw man wearing a big hat with a turkey tail feather stuck in the hatband and a brightly colored shirt decorated with ribbons.

Tuck felt for the pistol that should have been on his hip, but found only his empty holster. Instead of drawing a weapon he smiled when the Indian was near, smiled like he was a man simply out for an afternoon ride and had been bucked off his horse, instead of a half-gutted, desperate man, as crazed with the need for revenge and to take back what was his, as he was with the sight of the Indian's Winchester rifle leaning against the wagon dashboard.

Willis Duvall hunkered under the creek bank and waited for the Hilltopper to come back. The place where he hid had been undercut by periodic high water, but was barely big enough to permit him to sit up inside it. A tangle of exposed roots from the tree directly above him partially screened the eroded hole he sat in.

He could hear the sound of breaking brush and men calling to one another in the distance as the posse looking for them searched the woods. The Hilltopper had crawled out of their hole at daylight and climbed the creek bank to try and get his bearings on where they were and to get an idea if they were being pursued. Duvall knew he was still on the creek bank above him, for he could occasionally hear him moving around in the dry leaves up there.

Those same leaves rustled more loudly, and the Hilltopper appeared in front of him and pushed his way beside him. Both of them sat facing the creek, and listening.

"I'm going to run for it as soon as they're past us," the Hilltopper said after a while.

Duvall had no clue where the man thought he would go, even if he avoided capture by the posse. But he didn't say that. He was too tired to say much of anything.

Duvall watched as the Hilltopper cocked his head this way and that, listening to the sounds of the men searching for them.

"I say we surrender ourselves to their custody," Duvall whispered.

"You say what?" the Hilltopper asked in a whisper of his own.

"We give ourselves over to those marshals. I'll explain this whole misunderstanding to them."

The Hilltopper grunted. "You will, will you?"

"I am a man of some standing, but if my word does not suffice, then I will hire us proper counsel when they take us to Fort Smith for trial."

"What makes you think they'll take us to Fort Smith for trial?"

"Is that not the closest court?"

"I'm not talking about Fort Smith. I'm asking you why you think we'll get a trial."

"Why, of course we'll get a trial."

"The quickest way to a necktie party in these parts is to get caught bothering a woman," the Hilltopper said. "And you don't know that it's those marshals out there we're hearing. You think those men back in Canadian aimed to take us to Fort Smith to hand you over to some judge?"

"They've had time to cool down. And those marshals are nearby. I doubt even such a mob would turn vigilante with officers of the court present."

"Keep your voice down, or I'll strangle you myself."

"Do you intend to make a fight of it if they find us?"

"I do, if it comes to that."

"Surely you don't think you can best so many men."

"No, but I can take a few of them with me. Beats letting them put a rope around my neck."

"You'll get us both killed."

The Hilltopper grabbed Duvall and put a hand across his mouth. “Quiet.”

Duvall struggled briefly, but quit when he heard someone walking down the creek bank. In time, the footsteps in the leaf bed were directly above them. Whoever was up there stopped, obviously looking down into the creek bed and the briars and the brambles along its course for any sign of them.

Duvall looked at the Hilltopper’s big boot prints mashed into the fine gravel at the edge of the water and at the mouth of their hiding place. He was sure that the man above them would see those tracks. But whoever it was moved on. They could hear other men close now, and once they got a glimpse of a man on horseback riding down the far side of the creek.

The Hilltopper removed his hand from Duvall’s mouth and let him go when the posse had moved well past them. He ducked low and crawled out of their hole, his pistol ready in his hand.

“Are they gone?” Duvall asked.

“For now.”

“Where are you going?”

“I’m going to walk to North Fork and see if I can steal a horse.”

Duvall remained in the hole, looking at his own legs stretched out before him. His socks were in shreds and the soles of his feet were bruised and lacerated. “My feet are so sore I doubt I could walk another mile.”

The Hilltopper squatted down where he could see Duvall. “You don’t get this at all, do you?”

“I’ve got money . . .”

“You let that woman take it from you.”

“Not all of it. I still have some emergency funds in a bank in Chicago that I can lay hands to. You bring me a horse and I’ll see you’re well paid for it.”

"Chicago might as well be on the moon."

"Name your price."

"The only thing I want is a fast horse." The Hilltopper disappeared as he climbed the creek bank.

Duvall listened to him walking and then that sound, too, was gone. He told himself that the next time he heard the posse nearby he would call out to them, and he practiced the words he would say as they took him into custody. And he was still sitting in his little cave on the creek when the sun tipped over in the sky well past midday.

Chapter Forty-One

Red Molly went to the Bullhorn and cooked a breakfast and brought it back to Hannah and Ruby Ann, then she went back to the saloon. Noodles was up from his cot by then, and the two of them nursed mugs of coffee and watched the street through the open front door.

An hour later a party of Creek Lighthorsemen rode past the saloon, and she counted ten of the tribal lawmen, all well-armed. She went to the door in time to see them headed east down the road to North Fork, the same way the marshals and the posse from Canadian had gone at daylight.

She puttered about the saloon until noon, doing little of use, but helping her pass the time. When she heard the train being readied, she sent Noodles down to the depot to find out if it was going back to Canadian. And if it was, she wanted him to go with it and help Hank Bickford bring Saul's body to Ironhead.

Noodles and the train were barely on their way south when the posse from Canadian rode back into Ironhead. Dixie was riding in their lead, looking tired and slumped in the saddle, and with one arm bound in a sling. She waited for him in front of the saloon.

"I'll be back to see you soon," he said as he rode by her.

And so she waited for another half hour until she heard his horse once more outside and he entered the saloon carrying a shotgun and some tools in one hand.

He laid the shotgun down on one of the tables and took a seat there. She brought him a mug of coffee.

"Wouldn't happen to have anything to eat, would you?" he asked.

"I'll fix you something," she said as she went to the stove.

She fried him some bacon, and heated up a pot of beans and a loaf of bread left over from the previous day. While she cooked, she watched him.

He took his arm from the sling hung around his neck, laid the shotgun across his thighs, and pinned it awkwardly there with his forearm, making sure to keep his bandaged hand out of the way. With his good hand, he began to saw at the shotgun's barrel with the hacksaw.

She brought him the food, set it before him, and took a seat across from him. "How's the hunt going?"

"Not worth a damn," he said. He was having a hard time with his work on the shotgun, being practically one-handed like he was.

"Oh?"

He paused his work long enough to pick up a piece of bacon. It was still too hot to eat, but he took a bite anyway and smacked and moved the piece around in his mouth.

"Farmer found us an hour ago and said the Hilltopper stole a horse from him," Dixie said after he washed the bacon down with some coffee. "Sergeant Harjo's Indian policeman went to the crossing to head him off, but we think he was already across the North Canadian."

"Maybe the army from Fort Gibson will catch him."

"Maybe." He spooned up a mouthful of beans, and took hold of his saw and the shotgun again.

"Let me help you with that," she said.

He let her take the shotgun. She laid it across her own thighs.

"What about Duvall?" she asked while he sawed.

"No sign of him yet. Hold it still."

She looked down at the gun she held for him. It had a shotgun barrel that ran out from a can-shaped hump in front of the single hammer. "Odd-looking fowling piece."

"Roper shotgun. Got a revolving magazine inside it," he said between his strains and grunts as he worked the hacksaw back and forth. The blade was halfway through the barrel and screeched a little with every new bite into the steel. "Traded my Spencer carbine and fifteen dollars to one of those Creek Lighthorse for it and a sack of reloadable cartridges it uses."

"You bought it and now you're cutting it in two?"

"Want it where I can handle it one-handed," he said as the end of the barrel fell free to the floor.

He took the gun from her, propped it up on its buttplate, and pinned the shortened barrel between his knees. He traded the hacksaw for a file on the table and began to smooth the burrs from the fresh edge at the muzzle.

"What are you planning on shooting one-handed?" she asked.

"Thought I'd ride up to Checotah and then cut over to Webbers Falls."

"You're going after the Hilltopper?"

"Maybe."

"You're in no shape for it. What happened to your hand?"

"He done it. Killed Saul and then he put a knife through me." He pitched the file aside and laid the shotgun back in his lap. "I had the drop on him and let him do that to me."

"There's plenty of men out looking for him," she said. "Let them handle it."

"My job." He untied the drawstring on the canvas sack on the tabletop and plucked a steel shotgun cartridge from inside it.

"At least get some sleep, and maybe let me look at your hand."

"I'm not tired." He opened a hinged flap on top of the

shotgun and cocked the hammer.

"How bad is your hand?"

"Hurts worse now than when it happened." He poked a shell in the shotgun, and then let down the hammer and cocked it again.

"Best you let me look at it. That bandage is dirty, and you don't want the infection setting in."

He took another shell and shoved it in the gun. "I'm all right."

"If you're determined to go after him, won't you take some men with you?"

"Who says I'm going alone?"

"Don't lie to me."

"I never said one way or the other." He loaded two more shells in the shotgun, then laid it on the table and began eating the rest of his meal.

"I never saw a shotgun that held four shots," she said.

"Me, neither. That's why I bought it," he said around a mouthful of beans.

She saw how pale his skin was, and the way the sweat was pouring off him even in the shade of the tent saloon.

"Hannah's in my tent," she said.

He sopped the last of his bean juice with a heel of bread and stuffed it in his mouth while he watched her.

"I thought it best to get her away from Canadian for a while. You know, let her get her legs back under her before you and everyone else goes to prying her with questions."

"Good," he said as he stood and took up the shotgun. He didn't bother with putting his sling back on. "When Sergeant Harjo or one of those marshals comes back, you tell them where I've gone. If they don't have Duvall and the Hilltopper with them, you ask them to send a party down to McAlester's and wait at the trading post there to see if they can catch them slipping down the Texas Road."

She followed him out and watched him shove the shotgun in his rifle boot and mount his horse.

"You don't have to do this. You aren't Morgan," she said.

"No, I'm not, and I don't care to be," he said as he turned the horse and rode away.

Chapter Forty-Two

Two days came and went in Ironhead, and none of the posses found Willis Duvall or the Hilltopper. Hank Bickford brought his family on the morning train, along with a varnished red cedar coffin containing Saul's body.

They buried Saul in the cemetery on a sunny afternoon, with only Molly, Ruby Ann, and the Bickfords in attendance to comfort Hannah. Euless Pickins, the Methodist preacher and Indian agent from the nearby Creek Ashbury Mission School at North Fork, rode over and preached the burial service. He was a gangly, awkward man in his dusty black suit coat and the crooked glasses perched precariously on the sharp bridge of his nose. But his voice carried strongly up through the limbs of the water oak trees shading the cemetery, as he read from the Bible he held open in his hand before him.

Hank and the preacher remained to cover the casket while the women went back down the hill to Molly's tent. They were passing down the street between the Bullhorn and the new general store when Molly noticed the man sitting in a chair under the shade of the store's porch roof. The sight of him caused Molly to scuff her feet and stumble a little, and the women with her stopped to see what she was looking at.

"Who's that?" Hannah asked.

"Go on and get some lunch fixed," Molly said to Ruby Ann. "And if those marshals come around bothering Hannah again, you let me know."

Ruby Ann and Hannah went on, leaving Molly standing in the street alone. She took another look at the man on the porch, then went inside the saloon. The posse from Canadian had left Ironhead and returned to work the day before, but a handful of infantrymen had arrived from Fort Gibson to supposedly help with the manhunt. Right then they were bellied up to the bar, and Molly didn't understand how the army thought that foot soldiers were going to be of help running down fugitives over hundreds of miles of horseback trails. But at least they brought business to her saloon.

Pork Chop, the bartender from the Crow's Nest in Canadian Camp, sat at a table in the back end of the room playing poker with two of the soldiers. She hadn't a clue when he had arrived in Ironhead, but she intended to talk to him later. There was still the setup for a faro bank and layout stacked against one wall, and she could use his skills in that department.

She checked with Noodles to make sure he was getting along with their recent surge in business traffic, and then she went back to the front door and looked across the street. The man was still sitting on the store's porch, looking right at her as if he had expected her to reappear.

She started to turn back into the saloon, but instead, she marched rapidly across the street holding her dress up out of the dust, and stopped at the edge of the porch boards in front of him. He said nothing, but simply stared at her as he had before.

She had known many men, and a few good ones stacked amongst them, although they were rare as diamonds. But the one before her was no good man. Far from it. He was another kind altogether. Of the bad ones she had known, some she simply had no use for, some she despised, and some she hated. But truly, he was the only man she ever feared. You knew how dangerous he was without him doing or saying anything, the same way you walked through a zoo's exhibits and knew that the predator stalking on the other side of the cage bars would eat you in a second if given the chance or the need. Simply to be around him made her instantly want to be somewhere else.

He was not a big man nor a small man, average in all appearance except for the fine sharp bones of his face and the delicate, almost feminine working of his hands. And even less daunting was his physical appearance sitting there as he was then, so pale and sickly thin to the point that his white shirt sagged over his shoulders and chest sitting slumped like he was with his legs stretched out before him. A bandage was wound around his throat from his sharp chin to the collar of his shirt, and a new flat-brimmed, straw boater with a ribbon band sat on his head tilted down over his brow. But she saw those languid, burning eyes, regardless of how the hat brim shaded them. His eyes were the only things about him that appeared alive. The rest of him was like a corpse, cold as death itself.

"What do you want here?" she said to him.

"Does this place belong to you now?" His voice, once so deep and marked by a Southern gentleman's manners and diction, was now cracked and broken by the wound in his throat beneath the bandages until it was barely a hiss. "I would say you have come far in the world, Molly, if that be true."

"I thought you were dead. Hoped it."

He put a hand to his throat and gave a painful grimace when he swallowed. "Not far from it for a time, but we are all closer to Hell's door than we like to admit, aren't we?"

"Don't give me any of your preacher blather, Deacon," she said. "I see right through it."

"No preaching from me, sister," he rasped. "I have ever been a sinner, but my convalescence with the good preacher Pickins at the mission has given me time to reflect on my sins and to realize the hypocrite I have been."

"You're about as close to godliness as a snake."

"True, sister, true. And that's why I've come here today. Took conveyance with Brother Pickins when I heard he was coming here to preach a funeral."

"What do you want here?"

"I came to talk to him. To ask his forgiveness for the wicked I did him."

"No, you came hunting him, didn't you?"

"Maybe that's what I would have done before I saw Heaven's light shining at me from the dark pit of death."

"You're always spouting scripture when you're drunk."

"I'm stone-cold sober, truth be told. Haven't taken a drink since he did this to me."

It dawned on her then that he was sober, and that he wore no pistol at his waist. But a snake was a snake, no matter how you dressed it or how it talked like a real man.

"Well, you've came a long way for nothing. He's gone. Has been for almost a month," she said. "So, you can slither back in the hole you came from."

"Gone." His voice was so weak that she could barely hear him. "But the knight errant will always return."

"I don't think he's coming back."

He stood then, with a grate of his chair legs on the rough sawn oak planks of the porch, slightly stooped where he had once stood as straight as an arrow. A hot gust of wind came down the street and ruffled the clothes covering the bones of him.

"When he comes, you tell him I want to talk to him," he said so quietly that it was as if he had used the last breath of him to say it.

With that, he moved stiffly down the porch steps with one hand on his light straw hat to keep it from being blown off, and started up the street to the cemetery hill where the preacher and Hank were still at work filling in the grave. The rumor was that the Deacon had taken three bullets in the fight between him and Morgan and the Kingman brothers, and a knife cut so deep into his throat that Doc Chillingsworth had to stitch his windpipe back together. And he, indeed, walked like a man whose body was far from healed, a shell of the vicious killer and pistol murderer he had once been.

Deacon Fischer, bushwhacker and outlaw from the old Quantrill and Clement's tribe, gun for hire, and a man so crazy and feared that Jesse and Frank James themselves were said to have ousted him from their gang because of it.

She watched him walk up the hill to the grave, and wasn't fooled by his condition. Shell of his old self or not, there was still the same chill about him as there had always been. And as much as she needed otherwise, she hoped Morgan Clyde never came back to Ironhead.

Chapter Forty-Three

Morgan Clyde stepped off the train at Muskogee Station wearing a new black frock coat, despite the heat, and a new black Stetson hat with a broad, flat brim shaded the pale sides of his head where a barber back in Kansas had shorn the hair above his ears almost to the skin. His face was shaved smooth except for his mustache, and a fat cigar was jammed in one corner of his mouth.

He adjusted the Remington on his hip under his coat, stepped down from the passenger car, and walked down the train towards the stock pens and the loading ramp there for livestock. That loading ramp was the sole reason he was getting off the train where he was, for no such conveniences were to be found, yet, farther down the line. And the dun horse was too good of a mount to risk breaking its legs jumping it from a stock car. He would make the rest of his trip horseback from there.

Two railroad workers slid back the stock car door, and he led the lightning-branded dun horse down the ramp, then returned to the car and retrieved his saddle. Since the coming of the railroad, the sleepy settlement along the Arkansas River and not far from the old army post at Fort Gibson seemed to have grown overnight. In addition to the new livestock shipping pens, the pale, unpainted sawmill lumber of new buildings lined the main street, and everywhere he looked people were going and coming, as many white men and black men as Indians, and most of them dressed so much alike that he could barely tell the difference. And he was more sure than ever that the territory wouldn't belong to the Indians much longer, not since the railroad had come.

He was saddling his horse when he saw a man standing beside the passenger car. He was holding up one hand to block the sun and watching Morgan intently.

Something about the man was vaguely familiar. He wore a pin-striped suit, and a shock of bushy dark hair curled out under his hat brim. Morgan continued saddling the horse, but kept his eye on the newcomer. He saw the man pull aside the conductor for a brief conversation. And he saw the conductor, in response to whatever the conversation had been, turn and point at him. The gentleman in the suit came down the side of the train towards Morgan at a brisk walk. Morgan was on the far side of his horse, and he made sure to flip his coat behind the butt of his Remington before he stepped around it to meet the man.

"The conductor tells me that you're Morgan Clyde," the man said. He had very narrow set, large eyes, and an intense way of looking at you, as if he was fighting to keep those eyes from crossing or to keep them focused in the same direction.

Morgan nodded. "He told you right."

"Bert Huffman." The man offered his hand.

Morgan shook his hand, but still wasn't sure who he was.

"I saw you a few times in Ironhead," Huffman said, "but I still wasn't sure it was you when I saw you saddling your horse."

"You have me at a loss," Morgan said.

"Bert Huffman, formerly of the KNVR and several Union Pacific ventures before that. I was in Ironhead for the bridge inauguration."

"You're the one that was shot, weren't you?"

"You are correct," Huffman said and put a hand to his chest and gave a fake wince. "Though I could do without remembering it. The doctors tell me that I am fortunate to have survived such a wound."

"Glad to meet you, Mr. Huffman."

"I had hoped to run across you," Huffman said. "Imagine my surprise when I see you the first place I get off the train."

"What can I do for you?"

"I've brought you this," Huffman said and held out the thin wooden box he carried. It was made of finished walnut with a brass clasp holding it closed. "This is a token of the MK&T's appreciation of your dedication and service during the attempted robbery of our payroll this past spring. The Secretary of the Interior himself chipped in on its purchase."

"I thought you were Jay Cooke's man," Dixie said. "KNVR and the Union Pacific, and all that."

"I no longer work for Mr. Cooke, and have taken a position with the MK&T. I will be its new construction superintendent replacing Willis Duvall."

"Duvall got the axe, huh?"

"Yes, and on top of that I was informed on my journey down here that Mr. Duvall has gotten himself in a bit of trouble with the law, which, frankly, doesn't surprise me. I will be attending to his dismissal and thorough audit of his operations once I reach Canadian Station."

Morgan opened the box and found that the inside of it was lined in red velvet. And lying inside indentions formed into the wood and velvet was a new pistol, ornately engraved and with a pair of one-piece ivory grips. It was of a kind he had not seen before. It was similar in look to Colt percussion revolvers and cartridge conversion pistols, but had a sturdy top strap that connected the frame above the cylinder, much like his Remington. He took out the pistol and weighed the feel and balance of it.

"That is Colt's newest invention," Huffman said. "A .45-caliber cartridge loader."

The rimmed ends of six brass cartridges stuck up out of a line of holes below where the pistol had lain in the presentation box. Morgan noted that they were not rimfires, instead having a primer in the center of their case heads to ignite the powder charge.

Huffman noticed the way Morgan was admiring the gun, and added, "Colt hasn't yet offered them to the public. Several prototypes were manufactured for the trials the army is holding to choose a new service sidearm, and the MK&T was fortunate enough to procure one of those pistols, with the Secretary of the Interior's help, of course. He was quite impressed with your efforts in defense of his party, you know."

"Was he, now?"

"Yes, indeed. He wanted to thank you personally, but you were still resting your wounds and indisposed when he had to leave the camp," Huffman said. He pointed at the pistol. "The Colt gunsmiths did some custom work on it per our request, and assigned their very best engraver to it."

Morgan studied the fancy scroll engraving on the blued steel of the barrel and the color-case-hardened frame, and also noticed the stars engraved into the cylinder.

"It's one of a kind, I assure you," Huffman said. "Not another one like it, or will there ever be."

Morgan pulled one of the cartridges out and examined it. Heavy, roundnose lead bullets protruded from the brass cases.

"I have four boxes of cartridges for it in my luggage," Huffman said.

Morgan barely heard him, for he was intent on the thin silver plate in the shape of a badge recessed into the bottom of one side of the ivory grip. The wording engraved into it read, *MORGAN CLYDE, MK&T RAILROAD POLICE.*

"I hope you will accept the pistol, as well as the company's thanks for your contributions to this project," Huffman said.

Morgan put the pistol back in the box and closed the lid. "It's a beautiful weapon, but in case you don't know it, I no longer work for the Katy."

"I'm aware of that, and it is something else I hoped to talk to you about," Huffman said. "I would like to hire you back."

Morgan gave Huffman a hard look. "I don't see where you come in. You were Cooke's man, and now you swap over to the Katy?"

"Mr. Clyde, there are two kinds of railroad men. Some think of a railroad and they think of stocks and bonds and nothing more than an idea to sell. And then there is the second kind."

"What's the second kind?" Morgan asked.

"A railroad to the second kind isn't a thing on paper, nor a thing to be sold and traded. It's a thing you can put your hands on. It's miles and miles of road and ribboned steel built piece by piece with brains and sweat. I'm the second kind of railroad man, and I needed a railroad to build, simple as that," Huffman said. "Mr. Cooke, unfortunately, wanted me to be the first kind of railroad man, which I must admit, I'm poorly suited for."

"You'll have to build your railroad on your own. I've had all I want of working for the Katy," Morgan said.

"I assure you that I am a different man than was Willis Duvall," Huffman said.

"That may be, but I'm not your man." Morgan offered the pistol box back to Huffman, but the new superintendent refused to take it.

"Keep it, Mr. Clyde, and rethink my offer," Huffman said. "I will pay your old salary, plus ten percent, and I'll get you an appointment with the U.S. Marshal's office to increase your authority. On top of that, I promise you that you will find me a fair and reasonable employer."

"No thanks," Morgan said.

"Sorry to hear that. My intent is to run the whiskey and the gambling and the prostitution out of my construction camp and to get this railroad focused on laying tracks. From what I hear of you, I thought you might be the man to help me do it," Huffman said.

Huffman left for a moment, but came back. He handed Morgan the boxes of cartridges for the pistol.

"Think on my offer and send me a telegraph if you should change your mind," he said. "If this territory is going to ever amount to anything, it's going to need good men to help it along."

Morgan watched him leave at the same brisk pace he had arrived with, as if he were a man that always found some reason to hurry him. When he was gone, Morgan shifted his attention to the new saloon closest to the tracks for a moment, but saddled the zebra dun and rode away without stopping at the establishment. He crossed the Arkansas by ferry and followed the old road up the Grand River to within sight of the stockade and barracks at Fort Gibson where he struck the Fort Smith Road.

He was halfway to the settlement at Webbers Falls when he dismounted under a shade tree to give both himself and the horse a break from their travel. He ate his lunch while he watched the stretch of road south of him where it cut through a swath of tall grass prairie between the low timbered ridges rising up to either side of it.

Before he finished eating, a lone rider became visible working up the road toward him at a trot. And as the rider came closer, he recognized the distinct way the man rode slumped in the saddle, and then he recognized the man. He waved his hand once and waited.

Dixie Rayburn waved back at him, but he was slower to recognize Morgan sitting in the shade and was within a stone's throw of the tree before he lowered the short shotgun he was carrying, rested it on his thigh, and laid it across his saddle forks.

"Long time, no see," Dixie said.

Morgan expected his former policeman to be happier to see him. Dixie only looked tired, and Morgan noticed his bandaged hand.

"I've seen a fair piece of country since we last met," Morgan said.

"I haven't gone fifteen miles from Ironhead either way since you left, but I feel the same way," Dixie said as he stepped down from his horse. "I'd shake your hand, but this bandage makes that kind of awkward."

The two men took a seat on the ground in the shade, and both of them stared at the road to the south instead of looking at each other.

"Had any trouble?" Dixie asked.

"Some. You?" Morgan asked as he took a closer look at Dixie's hand.

"A bit," Dixie replied.

"What happened to your Rebel cap?" Morgan pointed at the narrow-brimmed Stetson on Dixie's head. "Thought I would never see you without it."

"Lost it."

Again, there was silence between them. Morgan offered him a slice of canned peaches, but Dixie shook his head and sipped from his canteen.

"To tell you the truth, Morgan, everything's gone to Hell in a handbasket."

"Railroad trouble or police trouble?"

"Both. Reckon I bungled the job. Hell, I wasn't ready for it, and you and I both know that."

"You bungled it? I don't recall things exactly going smoothly when I was wearing the same badge you've got pinned on your vest."

"You don't know the half of it."

Dixie relayed a short rundown of what had transpired in Ironhead and Canadian since Morgan had left. Morgan's only response to the news was an occasional movement of his head or a simple question to get the finer details. He didn't tell Dixie that the Katy's new superintendent had offered him Dixie's job.

"Is that why you're packing that sawed-off Roper?" Morgan gestured at the shotgun lying across Dixie's lap.

Dixie held up his bandaged hand. "Not real handy with a rifle or a pistol with this."

"Best thing you can do is to let that heal," Morgan said. "You've put the word out, and there's a good chance that Duvall and this Hilltopper you told me about will be caught soon."

"You know that isn't true. Half the outlaws in the world are running free in the territory."

"Duvall won't head for the brush. He's a town man, and you'll catch him down with a telegraph faster than you will chasing him on horseback."

"That's why I went after the Hilltopper."

"That, and maybe for what he did to your hand."

"He killed Saul and I let him get away with it. Had the drop on him and let him do this to me."

"Sometimes they get away. Sad fact of the peacekeeping trade."

"The only fact I know is that I wasn't cut out for this kind of work."

"Give it time and let that hand heal up, and things will look better," Morgan said. "This territory needs good men like you."

Dixie stuck a stem of grass in one corner of his mouth and shook his head. "You're right, it needs good men, but good men don't have to wear a badge to lend a hand."

"There's some that don't call it that anymore."

"What do they call it?"

"Eufaula. Indian name."

"I prefer Ironhead."

"Me, too, but it won't matter when me and the rest of them starve out. Nobody will ever remember the place was even there."

Morgan kicked the dun up a trot to keep pace with Dixie. "I'm not so sure the town will starve out. Not if there's more people like you willing to try to make a go of it."

"Ain't that the Traveler's horse you're riding?" Dixie asked.

"That it is."

And they didn't say anything else to each other for the last six miles into Webbers Falls.

Chapter Forty-Four

The road Morgan and Dixie followed led them past several farms and cabins, and men and women tending their cotton patches and cornfields in the fertile soil of the Arkansas River bottoms. A little farther on they rode into Webbers Falls, a Cherokee town and a steamship landing downstream of a rock ledge that spanned the wide river and created a low set of falls.

The town itself was little more than a few houses and cabins, a livery and some warehouses, and two general stores lining a stretch of dusty dirt road that led down to a boat dock and a shallow ford above the falls. Morgan remembered from earlier visits that one of the storekeepers would sell you a drink or two if he knew you and wasn't afraid you would report him to the Cherokee courts or the law at Fort Smith. He also remembered another thing about the storekeeper.

When they dismounted and left their horses at the hitching rail in front of the store, Morgan carried Dixie's shotgun up onto the porch with them.

"Fellow that owns this place has an eye for guns," Morgan said to Dixie before they went inside. "He'll buy or trade for one if he can get it at a fair price, although you've mangled this one pretty good when you sawed off the barrel."

"I gave it to you."

"I've no need for it, and it's best you put a few dollars in your pocket before you turn gentleman farmer on me," Morgan said.

The storekeeper was an old, white-haired Cherokee man with a stately bearing and wearing a white dress shirt with the celluloid collar attached and a cravat around it. The instant he recognized Morgan he waved the two of them over to him where he stood behind his counter.

"Hello, Clyde," the storekeeper said. "Where's your badge? Last I recall you were a deputy marshal for Judge Story's court, but I heard you had quit him and taken a job with the railroad."

"You heard right, but that was a while ago," Morgan said. "As it is, I'm currently unemployed and in need of a drink. Thought you might be the man that could fix that."

"Give you a job or a sip of whiskey?" the storekeeper asked.

"Whiskey," Dixie said. "A sip or two of that and we'll forget about needing jobs."

Morgan jerked a thumb in Dixie's direction. "This galoot with me is Ben Rayburn. He worked as a policeman for the Katy until recently."

"You the one that put out the word about some fugitives that might be coming through here?" the storekeeper asked. "A big man and another one? Two Cherokee deputies from down at Tahlequah rode through here this morning looking for them. They said some railroad lawman over in the Choctaw Nation was asking for help."

"That's me," Dixie said. "Any strangers through here the last two days?"

"You're the first one."

"Well how about a little sipping liquor to introduce ourselves to each other properly. And I don't mind saying I could use a drink after what I've been through lately."

The storekeeper looked around the room as if to make sure they were the only ones present, and then he produced a glass bottle of unlabeled, clear whiskey and three glasses. Morgan laid the sawed-off Roper shotgun on the bar while the storekeeper poured them all a drink. The Cherokee man tried to act like the gun didn't interest him, but Morgan saw him cut his eyes at it twice.

They sipped the moonshine in silence and looked out the front door at the dirt road as if it held great interest.

"Tarnation!" Dixie said. "A few more sips of this stuff and I might not remember my name."

"Make it myself," the storekeeper said. "Smooth going down, but it packs a punch when it hits bottom."

Morgan had to agree with the last part. Already, beads of sweat were popping out on his forehead, or maybe that was simply because it was a hot day and the open door and the two open windows in the store did little to cool the room. He shrugged out of his frock coat and laid it across the bar on top of the shotgun.

"Hot as Hades in here," he said.

The storekeeper nodded. "What have you got under that coat, Clyde? Are you here to drink or are you here to trade?"

Morgan slid his hand under the coat and took hold of the shotgun. He was about to show it to the storekeeper when the sound of a walking horse outside stopped him.

He could barely make out the head and one front leg of the horse through the open door, as whoever had ridden it tied it to the hitching rail beside their own. The horse's visible leg was wet up past the knee, as if it had been ridden across the shallow ford above the falls.

The sound of heavy footsteps reverberated on the porch, and shortly thereafter a big man filled the door frame, silhouetted by the sun at his back. Morgan had never seen the Hilltopper or heard of him until Dixie had told him of recent events on the railroad, but a man as big as the one in the doorway could be none other.

The Hilltopper already had his hand on the butt of his Colt's

Dragoon when he stepped in the store, a reasonable tactic for a hunted man until he had a chance to see the lay of the land. The sight of the three men staring back at him didn't give him reason to let go of his pistol. He could have run for it, but he didn't. Instead, he stopped and stared back at them with no hint of panic showing on him. He was either too mean or too fearless to take flight, or else he wasn't sure yet how bad of a bind he had put himself in by walking through the door.

Dixie was nearest to the door, and had put down his whiskey glass and his left hand was moving down towards the Confederate Navy holstered on his belt. That, and the look on his face assured Morgan beyond a doubt that he had guessed the man's identity.

"How's that hand, Reb?" the Hilltopper said.

The storekeeper was quick to see that trouble was at hand, and made as if to move out of the way.

"Stand where you are, Indian," the Hilltopper said. "And you, Reb, you keep inching for your pistol and I'm going to finish that ear trimming I promised you."

"Let me meet your new friend," Morgan said.

Dixie took a slow step backwards, and then another one, allowing the Hilltopper and Morgan to have a full view of each other. Morgan's left hand hung beside the Remington holstered on that hip, and the Hilltopper was quick to notice it.

"Who the hell are you?" the Hilltopper asked.

"Morgan Clyde, and I'm guessing you're the one they call the Hilltopper."

"Clyde, huh? I heard of you."

"And I've heard of you. Aren't we a pair?"

"Morgan," Dixie warned.

"Law dogs everywhere you go," the Hilltopper said. "Man can't even slip in and have himself a drink without stepping on them."

"Morgan, this is my trouble," Dixie said.

Morgan ignored him, never taking his eyes off the Hilltopper. "Would it do any good if my friend here said you were under arrest?"

"Not one damned bit," the Hilltopper said.

"There's another way we could do this."

"What's that?"

"You could run," Morgan said. "I promise I won't laugh."

Dixie shifted his feet and a floorboard creaked beneath his weight. Maybe that was why the Hilltopper pulled his pistol, or maybe he had picked his moment then and there.

Dixie stumbled backwards, groping clumsily for his own pistol, and making a poor job of it with his left hand. Meanwhile, Morgan remained where he was, to all appearances as calm as he had been when sipping his whiskey earlier. The Hilltopper's pistol was free of his holster and coming up towards Morgan, and still Morgan hadn't made a move to draw his Remington. But his other hand was under that frock coat of his, and the clack of the shotgun hammer being drawn back beneath that cloth was followed almost instantly by the boom of the twelve-gauge. He didn't even pick the gun up, but simply fired it where it lay pointed down the bar towards the door.

The buckshot Dixie had loaded the shot shell with took the Hilltopper in the chest and staggered him back two steps onto the porch. He glared at his riddled, bloody chest and then back at Morgan. He wobbled side to side, as if about to fall, but the Dragoon pistol clenched in his fist was working its way back up.

Morgan pulled the Roper shotgun out from under his coat, cocked the hammer once more, and put another round of buckshot from the hip into the Hilltopper's face. The giant fell backwards and hit the flat of his back on the ground with both of his big, booted feet resting on the top of the porch steps.

Morgan laid the shotgun on the bar top and drew his

Remington and walked out onto the porch to look down at him. Dixie wasn't far behind him.

"He was a big devil," Morgan said.

"Was," Dixie repeated. "He don't look so tall now."

Morgan holstered his pistol and went back in the store and took up his unfinished glass of whiskey. He lifted the glass as if in toast to the storekeeper, and then he tossed the rest of it down.

"Sorry about that," he said, and took up the shotgun and went out the door.

He held out the shotgun to Dixie.

"No, you keep it. I thought you were going to sell it to that storekeeper in there," Dixie said.

"I don't think he's in a dickering mood anymore."

"I told you I don't want it."

"It does have too long of a hammer throw. Takes some getting used to."

"That ain't the reason I gave it to you, and you know it." Dixie pointed at the Hilltopper's mangled body. "That's the reason. I've lost the stomach for this kind of work."

"It's an ugly business some days." Morgan shoved the shotgun inside the bedroll tied behind his saddle and swung up on the dun. "You want me to help you load him so you can take him back to Ironhead?"

"Don't reckon I do," Dixie said, still staring at the Hilltopper's ruined face.

"Well, what are you waiting for?"

Dixie reached down and jerked his gray wool cap out of the Hilltopper's belt. He gave it a quick examination, ran his finger through a buckshot hole through one side of it, then pitched the hat he wore on the porch and crammed the cap on his head with a satisfied twist back and forth.

"There now, that's better," he said, and then he mounted his own horse.

Morgan rode up to the porch where he could see into the open door. "How much for a burying?"

The storekeeper stepped into the doorway, but no farther. "You're leaving him on my steps?"

"The law has been served."

"Four dollars," the storekeeper said. "There's a man here that will normally do it for two, but that one's twice as big as he ought to be."

Morgan pitched him the coins, and then he and Dixie rode away.

"Morgan?" Dixie asked after a little time passed.

"Yeah?"

"You still have trouble sleeping?"

"Sometimes."

Dixie twisted in his saddle and looked back across the river at the store on the far bank behind them. "Maybe I ain't the only one who ought to quit the peacekeeping trade."

They headed southwest down the well-worn trail to North Fork and Ironhead beyond it.

Chapter Forty-Five

A coughing spell woke Red Molly up somewhere in the wee hours of the morning, and she went out into the darkness to keep from waking Ruby Ann and Hannah. She crossed the short distance to the back entrance to the Bullhorn, and stood there until the worst of her coughing was past, then she slipped inside the saloon.

Noodles was snoring from his cot at the far end of the bar, but it took her a moment to find the source of the other sleeper snoring all his own. She lit a lamp and kept the wick trimmed low, and held it high and cast the dim light about the tent. There, atop two tables pulled together, lay Pork Chop flat on his back and asleep with his mouth wide open and snorting like a bull on the fight. How two men could sleep so soundly with both of them making that kind of noise, she didn't know.

Another cough ripped out of her chest, and it was all she could do to muffle the sound with a hand clamped to her mouth. She put the lamp out and went to the front door, intending to take a walk about camp. She was halfway out it when she saw something moving across the street and well behind the store at the edge of the woods.

The only thing over that way was the tent Duvall had set up for Helvina Vanderwagen, but there was no lamplight showing through that tent, for it was still a good hour or more until daylight.

Whoever it was, was moving slow and being very cautious, as

if they didn't want to be seen. That would also explain their moving in the darkness. Any early riser about their business would simply walk down the street.

Molly stayed where she was, catching shadowy glimpses of the figure as it worked its way past Helvina's tent. She was almost certain it was a man, but she couldn't be sure. And then she couldn't see whoever it was anymore.

Somebody touched her from behind and startled her. It was Ruby Ann.

"You scared the living daylights out of me. What are you doing up this early?" Molly said, and then, knowing Ruby Ann wouldn't answer her, "I woke you up with my coughing, didn't I?"

Ruby nodded in the dim moonlight shining into the doorway.

"Somebody's slipping around over by Helvina's tent," Molly said.

Ruby eased past her and took a look of her own. She soon pointed in the direction of the hotel. Molly took another look, and as soon as she did she saw that same sneaking form disappear into the hotel.

"I got an idea who that is," Molly said. "I'd swear that was Duvall."

Ruby Ann shook her head, not as if she disagreed, but because of something else.

Molly went to the bar and found herself a bottle of whiskey without lighting a lamp again. She drank straight from the bottle, and when she noticed how her hand shook she took another drink.

"Go back to bed," she said to Ruby Ann.

Ruby Ann went out the back of the saloon, leaving Molly alone with her whiskey and the two snoring men.

Molly sipped the whiskey, waiting for her hands to quit shaking, wanting the bravery that the alcohol could provide her, and thinking about the man she had seen across the street. She was almost sure that lurker was Willis Duvall, for there was something about the way he walked. The posses had been unable to flush either him or the Hilltopper from the brush, but perhaps he had simply lain low nearby, and was slipping back to hide in the hotel while Helvina figured out a way to help him permanently escape.

Escape, the word caused the bile to rise up in her throat. He would be gone before long, off to wherever. The more she thought about it the more she was sure he would get away. Men like him rarely answered for what they had done, not his kind with the money to buy their way out of things and to purchase them a new story and start somewhere else. Time would wash away his crimes, and soon nobody would remember what had happened at a little backwater place like Ironhead.

But she wouldn't forget, not ever. And he wasn't going to get away with what he had done to her and Ruby Ann, and that poor Hannah. No, he wasn't.

She put down the whiskey and went out the back door at a fast walk. She slowed when she reached her tent, and slipped quietly inside it. The dim shape of her roommates on the bed and the sound of heavy, slow breathing convinced her that both of them were asleep, and she was careful not to make any noise when she opened her dresser drawer and felt amongst her things there for the pistol Tuck had given her.

She didn't find the pistol, and at that same moment she heard the gunshot from across the street at the hotel.

Chapter Forty-Six

The sound of the gunshot got others' attention besides Red Molly. She was only halfway across the street to the hotel when one of the deputy marshals from Fort Smith fell in beside her. She saw a brief glimmer of moonlight on the pistol he was holding, and then they were standing outside what would be the front entrance and lower balcony to the hotel facing the train tracks when it was finished.

"You stay here." The marshal cocked his pistol and took a long, quick step into the doorway.

She listened to the soft scuff of his boot soles as he passed farther into the room. He sounded as if he was almost to the back of the building when another gunshot racked off pine siding.

She ducked low and peered into the building from the bottom of the door opening and along the moonlit floor. In a moment, she heard someone curse softly, and thought it was the marshal.

"Bring me a lantern," he called to her in a voice not much louder.

By the time she had retrieved a lit lantern from the saloon, there were already several people standing outside the hotel. A couple of them followed her inside the building.

"Over here," the marshal said.

She shifted directions and moved the lantern towards the sound of his voice. The first thing that fell into the kerosene glow was the figure of a man slumped in a chair. When she was closer she saw that it was not Duvall sitting there, but Bill Tuck.

The marshal took the lantern from her and held it high so that the rest of the room was lit up. It was meant to be the kitchen at some point, and a back door from it overlooked Helvina's tent. Tuck sat facing that doorway, as if he had been watching that tent.

"Best you go on and don't look at this," the marshal said.

But Molly had already seen the bullet hole in Tuck's forehead, and the rifle on the floor at his feet that he must have been holding when he was killed.

"Got him right between the eyes," said someone behind her who was less concerned with the sensitivities of a whore.

Molly was still trying to get over the fact that it was Bill Tuck dead, and not Willis Duvall. And then the marshal's hold on the lantern shifted, and she saw Ruby Ann's body lying there with Tuck's nickel-plated pistol still clutched in her outflung, dead hand, and a pool of blood beside her head.

"Looks like she did for herself, as soon as she was through with him," one of the men pressing up behind Molly said.

"You men get back," the marshal said.

Those behind Molly scrambled back some, but not far.

"Wasn't she one of Tuck's doves at one time?" the marshal asked Molly.

"Yes," Molly answered after finding her voice.

"Well, whatever he did to her, he won't be doing it anymore."

"He wasn't the one. She thought he was somebody else."

"What's that?"

But Molly didn't answer him, for she was already leaving out the back of the building.

"Not a thing for a woman to see," one of the onlookers said. "Even for a tough one like Red Molly."

Molly didn't hear that, for she was already to Helvina's tent.

The gunshots must have woke the New York woman, for there was now a lamp lit inside the canvas, and Molly could hear her either rummaging around in there or getting dressed. She didn't ask for an invite, nor did she say anything when she pushed her way into the tent.

Helvina stood beside her bed tying a robe about her waist to cover her.

"Duvall. Where is he?" Molly asked.

"First, I'll tell you to get out of my tent, and never to come in here unannounced or without my permission," Helvina said. "And then secondly, I'll tell you that I haven't seen Willis since the night they chased him in the woods."

Molly took another look around the room, not believing her.

"What was that shooting about?" Helvina asked.

"Bill Tuck's dead, and so is Ruby Ann."

"Ruby Ann? Is she that mute girl that wanders around and is always staring at everyone?"

"She's wasn't a mute."

"Willis said she was a mute."

"Your Willis is a liar."

Molly went back outside and left Helvina staring after her. She crossed the street to the Bullhorn, and found Noodles and Pork Chop sitting up and somewhat alert.

"What happens, Signora?" Noodles mumbled and held up one hand to shelter his eyes from the lamplight she held over him.

"Wake up. I need you."

He rubbed his face and then blinked his eyes several times. "I say what happens? I think I hear shooting."

"I want you to go wake Hank Bickford. The blacksmith, you know him? He and his wife have set up one of those pointy topped army tents where the bathhouse used to be."

"I know him," Noodles said.

"Then go tell him I need him to build another coffin. Two coffins."

Pork Chop went to the door and stood there scratching at the seat of his pants with one hand while he flipped a suspender over his shoulder with the other.

Molly looked to him. "Pork Chop, would you ride over to North Fork and get Father Pickins?"

"I could do that. This have anything to do with that over yonder?" He was pointing out the door towards the hotel.

"Ruby Ann killed Bill Tuck, and then she killed herself."

"What did Bill ever do to her?"

"He didn't do anything to her."

"But she killed him, just like that?"

Molly poured herself another whiskey, but paused with the glass almost to her lips. "It was an accident."

And Molly couldn't quit thinking what a sad accident it was. Tuck waiting in the hotel hoping Duvall would show at Helvina's tent so he could get his revenge, and Ruby Ann approaching Tuck in the dark thinking she was going to kill a different man and killing herself when she realized the mistake she had made. How did things get so messed up?

And she began to cry, and for the first time in a long time she didn't try to stop herself.

Chapter Forty-Seven

Morgan and Dixie arrived in Ironhead in time to walk up the hill with the funeral procession. Everyone in Ironhead turned out, even some of the train men who brought up a supply train from Canadian that morning stopped their work and helped carry the coffins to the cemetery. For some of them remembered Ruby Ann before the bad thing that somebody did to her the past spring, and remembered what a pretty, young whore she had been and how she loved to talk more than anything. And others remembered Bill Tuck, most not with any sense of loss, but seeing such a hard man put below the ground was a novelty worth seeing.

Even Helvina Vanderwagen had showed up for the funeral, and it had shocked Molly when Pork Chop told her that Helvina had donated thirty dollars to help pay for the burying and the service. She wore a black dress with a black veil hanging down from the little hat that covered her face, and even the lace gloves on her hands were black. She stood alone behind the rest of them, and said nothing to any of them.

The coffins Hank Bickford had built were of simple yellow pine, and not so pretty or sanded so smoothly as Saul's box had been, for he hadn't been given the time to practice his skill as he would have liked. He stood with his wife, hugging her to him with one arm, and the other wrapped around his children, a boy and a girl. The girl wasn't much younger than Ruby Ann had been when Molly first met her in Sedalia.

Both coffins were lowered down into the graves side by side while the small crowd watched in silence. Molly had started to protest Ruby Ann resting for eternity beside a pimp like Bill Tuck, but in the end, they convinced her that the preacher could do a single graveside service if the graves were close together. And Molly consoled herself with the thought that Ruby Ann was past caring who she kept company with.

Preacher Pickins stood at the head of the graves and read from his Bible, and a few among the attendants nodded their heads at a verse or two he quoted. But Molly didn't hear much of it. She watched Dixie beside her, staring down at the ring of wild flowers she had put on Ruby Ann's coffin lid with his eyes sagging and so sad.

And then she looked across both of the graves to where Morgan stood with his black hat held by the brim in both hands before him, and the wind whipping his thick black hair and lifting his coattails. He hadn't said a word to her on their way to the cemetery, and never once did she catch him looking back at her.

When the service was finished, Preacher Pickins let her throw the first handful of earth into Ruby Ann's grave, and then everyone started back down the hill except for Hank Bickford and Pork Chop, who stayed behind to finish the burial.

Molly found herself walking beside Morgan, and she said nothing to him until they were halfway to her saloon.

"Are you staying?" she asked.

He looked beside them across several people to where Helvina walked back to her tent. "No."

"What did you say? I didn't quite make that out."

He looked back at her, and then at the crude beginnings of the settlement that they all still thought of as Ironhead. "Maybe, but I've got things to attend to first."

"What things?"

He didn't answer her for his attention had shifted to the man standing beside the trail through the woods, as if he were waiting for someone to pass. It was Deacon Fischer standing there, and she saw Morgan flip his coattail behind his pistol as they neared the man.

"Hello, Clyde," the Deacon whispered like a dying gasp.

Morgan stopped not a body length from him. "Are you looking for me, Deacon?"

The Deacon nodded his chin once, ever so slightly.

"There's been enough killing," Morgan said. "No more today."

The Deacon took hold of his coat lapels, held them open to show he carried no weapon, and then let them drop.

"I only want to talk to you," he croaked again.

"You and I have nothing to say that hasn't already been said," Morgan answered.

"Lots to be said. I came to ask your forgiveness."

That seemed to take Morgan aback, and he gave the Deacon a closer look, from the bandage on his throat to the bones showing on the backs of his thin hands.

"If you want to square things between us, you be gone when I come back," Morgan said. "I've heard you talk crazy before, and that's as far as I'll go with you."

The Deacon flinched a little when Morgan called him crazy, a quick flick of his eyelids and a tightening of his lips, but that was his only reaction.

"It took twenty stitches to sew up the cut you left in me," he said.

"That's going to leave a nasty scar," Morgan said.

The Deacon gave that subtle drop of his chin again.

"Scar like that is hard to forget," Morgan added.

"We've all got things best forgotten." The Deacon's voice was so quiet that Molly could barely hear those last words.

Morgan moved on, and flipped his coat back over his gun when he was well away from the Deacon. "Crazy bastard."

"When are you coming back?" Molly asked him as she matched his stride, but not looking at him when she said it.

"Why so many questions, Molly? You know me. I go where the work is."

"Just asking. No reason at all," she said with the anger plain in her voice. "It's not like I give a damn."

She heard him stop and could feel him watching her back as she went past him and ducked into the Bullhorn. She stopped and waited a few steps inside the tent, wondering if he would follow her, but he didn't.

She took a deep breath, straightened the slump from her shoulders, and spied Noodles behind the bar. "I want you to go ask Hank Bickford to come talk with me when he's finished with the graves."

"Something happen again, Signora?" he asked her.

Signora, be damned, but she was getting to like the sound of that. "Damn right something is going to happen. Hank is a good carpenter besides his blacksmith work, and I intend to hire him to make this place look a little finer."

"Finer? I don't know what this means?"

"Italians," she said with mock disgust.

"Sicilian," he corrected her.

"Well, does your Sicilian self know how to paint?"

"I can paint."

"Well, good. As soon as you get back I want a new sign put out there on the post by the front door."

"A new sign?"

"Yes, a new sign."

"I make you a good sign."

"You spell worse than I do. On second thought, you let me paint the sign."

"What is it going to say? This new sign?"

"Molly O'Flanagan's. That's all."

"Only your name?" Noodles asked.

"My name."

Pork Chop watched them both from his card table, and had heard it all. He quit shuffling his cards when she looked his way.

"Are you planning on staying here?" he said.

"They'll have to drag me off by my heels with a yoke of oxen, boyo, if they want me gone. I'm Red Molly, belle of the tracks, a full cunning woman and beholden to no man, and let anyone that says any different say it to my face."

"Molly O'Flanagan's," he repeated as he started to shuffle the cards again. "Got to admit it has a ring to it."

Chapter Forty-Eight

Morgan was on his way to find where Dixie had gone when Hank Bickford's young son ran him down.

"Miss Vanderwagen wants to see you," the boy said. "She told me to ask you nicely and to tell you to please come."

"She did, did she?"

"Yes, sir. Her tent's over there behind the hotel."

Morgan ruffled the boy's hair and gave him a coin for his trouble. He watched the boy run off and then headed for the hotel. He saw the tent where the boy had said it would be, setting some fifty yards behind the hotel at the edge of the woods. He straightened his coat and readjusted his hat and started towards it.

"It's Morgan," he said when he stood outside the closed door flaps.

"Come in," Helvina's voice answered him.

He pushed his way through the door flaps and saw her with her back to him at the far end of the room. She wore some kind of house robe, and when she turned to him he saw that the front of it wasn't closed and that she wore nothing underneath it.

"What are you doing, Helvina?"

She gave a slight, pouting frown. "That's the first thing you say to a woman obviously intent on seducing you? Really, Morgan?"

"You try this with me after everything you've done?"

She let the robe drop off her shoulders, standing before him nude and with one knee slightly cocked in an alluring pose, and her dimpled chin lifted. "Don't you find me beautiful anymore?"

"You proved a long time ago you didn't want me."

"I didn't want to be married to you anymore," she said as she stepped closer to him. "Not the same thing as not wanting you, not at all."

He couldn't help but look at her, and to remember things. She had always been a passionate woman.

"It will never work between us. Too much has happened that neither of us can forgive," he said.

She gave a soft chuckle, and she was close enough to him by then that he could smell her perfume. Close enough that he was almost touching her.

"What's a little fun between old lovers? Something to take our minds off our troubles? No expectations and no acting out our lies. No games, Morgan. I see you wanting me."

"Helvina . . ."

"I'm not trying to win you back," she said in a sultry whisper. "But don't you get lonely sometimes?"

She pressed her body against him, her face upturned to him and her eyes closed. "Make love to me Morgan. Make love to me like you used to. Just this once."

He felt her arms on his shoulders, then felt her slowly pulling him deeper into the room towards her bed. And he looked down at her, the slim waist and flat belly above her hips, the high, firm breasts with their nipples already hard and excited, and at the perfect face upturned to him with those pouting lips ready for him to kiss them.

So perfect she was, and yet so ugly. He had never really noticed that before as he did then. He pulled her hands from his neck and stepped back from her. "Like hell, I will."

"What? Don't you tease me," she said. "I know you're teasing me. Come lay down with me and let's do it like we used to. I remember all the things you like."

"Helvina, you're only doing this to prove to yourself and to me that you can, or because you're scared and want somebody to hang on to until the feeling passes," he said. "You did me that way once, but I'm not the fool for you I was then."

"You were the one that was a fool? Did you really just say that?"

"I thought you were something you aren't, and I'm sure you thought of me the same," he said. "But we both know each other now, and as you said, there's no room left for cruel games."

She picked up her robe and jerked it on. When she turned back to him her lower lip began to tremble and her hands were clenched in fists beside her. He knew her well enough to know how her temper worked. She had never been one to tolerate not getting her way. He also noticed that she hadn't tied her robe closed. Angry, yes, but still believing in the power of her looks and wielding them like a weapon.

"You stupid, arrogant, stubborn man," she said. "You haven't changed one bit."

He smiled at that and shook his head. "You broke my heart, you turned my son against me, and cut me a thousand other ways that you can't even imagine, but it's you I feel sorry for."

"Oh, you're always so melodramatic, and putting the blame on everybody but yourself," she said.

He turned and went to the door.

"You're actually leaving?"

He looked back at her one last time as he laid hand to one of the door flaps. "To put it frankly and in the local vernacular, woman, I can say quite confidently that I'd rather hump a mule."

And then he went out the door and let it fall closed behind him.

"Morgan Clyde!" she called after him.

But he kept on walking.

"I hate your sorry guts," she said, and he heard her throw something against the tent wall. "You never were enough man for me."

There was a new train coming down from the south, and he tracked the black smoke from the engine's stack closing in on the station. He made a stop to retrieve his traveling bag and to see to the keep of his horse, and then went to the depot house to catch that train.

Chapter Forty-Nine

Willis Duvall waited until long in the afternoon before he left his hiding spot in the creek bank. The Hilltopper had led him on a winding course through the woods to get there, and it had been too dark then to properly see. As it was, he had no clue where he was. And he was hungry, terribly hungry.

There had been no other sounds of anyone searching for him, and he hoped that they had given up the chase. The only problem was, he didn't know which direction he should go to keep from blundering upon them. The only thing he knew was that he was somewhere north of the Canadian River, and that meant he was within a few miles of Ironhead, a place he would as soon stay away from. He studied the sun through the treetops for a brief moment, but quickly gave that up as a waste of time.

Frontiersmen and backwoods sorts were supposed to have all kinds of ways of determining the four compass directions and navigating their way through wilderness, but he was a town man and such things were beyond his scope. Any choice he made was simply a wild guess, no matter how much time he took in the deciding of it, so one direction was as good as the other, and all he could hope was that he didn't end up back in Ironhead.

He took off walking with the sun behind him. His socks had provided him little protection from the sharp rocks and sticks and thorns, but now even they were in shreds and he was practically barefooted. And he walked tenderly and slowly because of it, stopping often to pick something from one foot or the other. What was done was done, but amongst the things he regretted, one that struck him the strongest right then was being so drunk when he left Canadian that he forgot his shoes.

He found a dead, broken limb lying on the ground, and used it for a walking stick. He tried to think of what he would do when he found his way back to somewhere civilized, and what he must say to the authorities when the time came. Who would believe the word of a colored woman over a man such as he? Given time, the whole affair would blow over.

And the directors on the board? With proper persuasion and the right kinds of offers some of them might consider how far he had built their railroad before they decided to replace him and pay him at least a portion of the shares they promised him on completion.

Such thoughts lifted his spirits, and he forgot about his hunger and his pained feet for at least a little while. Yes, his situation bordered on the dire, but he had come back from other predicaments. And he would do it again. There was no way Helvina could build her hotel without him. As soon as he was away, he would contact her. She was a difficult woman, but even she would have to listen to reason. With the return of the money she had taken from him, he would be well on his way to recouping his fortune.

His determined daydreaming was interrupted by a tangle of brambles that barred his passage. He was looking for a way around the thicket when he saw sunlight through the trees ahead of him, as if there was a clearing there. The promise of possibly escaping the confines of the dense woods excited him so, that he plunged through the briars and clinging limbs, unheeding of how they cut and scraped him and tore his clothes.

The patch of sunlight ahead was nothing but a small clearing consisting of no more than a few acres and full of tree stumps where some farmer had cleared back the forest. A patch of chest-high green cornstalks and a tiny log cabin lay on the far side of it. He stopped at the edge of the woods and watched the cabin for signs of life. He had watched it for a long time and seen no one when he heard what sounded like laughter somewhere not far from him. Women's laughter.

He stayed within the timber and moved towards the sound. If it was some local citizen that belonged to the cabin, perhaps they would be unaware of the manhunt for him and could be convinced to carry him to the nearest settlement. He would be cautious, and study them for a while to be sure of his approach.

Another creek crossed his way, but this time it was not a shallow trickle and spotted with dry stretches like the one that had hid him earlier. Instead, it was perhaps thirty yards wide and deep enough to swim in, exactly as the women were doing when he slipped up on the high bank above them and not far downstream.

Not women, but young girls. Five of them, all Indians, and the oldest of them somewhere in her teens. It was a hot day, and their clothes lay piled on a rocky shoal not far from where they frolicked in the shallows below it. He told himself he should move on. Go back to the cabin, and if there was no one there, then search it for food and a pair of shoes. Or maybe there was a horse close by.

But he didn't leave. Most of the Indian girls were submerged deep enough to have to tread water and so young to be of no interest to him, but the oldest one, perhaps tired of swimming, left her friends in the deeper pool and waded in waist-high water. He hid behind the trunk of the tree, and the old hunger came back to him. Her body was ripe with young womanhood, and the thought of that tight, young, naked flesh caused him to move when he lost sight of her as she moved nearer to the high creek bank.

He moved a few yards, found another tree to hide behind, and then leaned out over the bank so that he could see upstream to the place where she had disappeared to. He immediately found that he had misjudged the distance and that instead of being upstream from him, she was directly below him. She looked up and saw him at the same time he saw her, and she screamed.

He hadn't the time to properly run before all of them were screaming. And they were still screaming and calling to someone for help when he ran behind the cabin and through the corn patch.

Someone in a wagon was rattling across the clearing towards the cabin when he entered the woods once more. It wasn't long before he could hear whoever was in that wagon calling to the girls, and the girls calling back to them.

He moved as fast as he could, tortured with every step. Nothing he could think of would lift his spirits or distract him from the pain in his feet. The damned board. It was all their fault. Couldn't they see that he was a man destined for great things? So what if he liked the ladies? Every man had his vices, and who had he ever hurt that mattered? Not some whore. Not some colored woman. The people that would judge him wouldn't stoop to say hello to them if they passed them on the street.

The woods before him abruptly ended, and this time he found himself facing a far larger clearing. Part of it appeared to be natural prairie that had been expanded over time with the axe and fire. Several cabins and framed homes dotted it, and he could see tended fields and livestock grazing in fenced-in pastures. And maybe a half-mile away was some kind of town or settlement, and beyond that he could see a line of trees that looked like they marked a river or creek bank.

North Fork Town, he remembered his workers and surveyors

talking of it. That had to be what he was looking at, for supposedly that was the only other settlement besides Ironhead between the two forks of the Canadian River. And if he was right, then there was also supposed to be a road from there that led to Webbers Falls and then on to Fort Smith. Or maybe a boat could be had to take him downriver until he could board a steamship.

He waited until it was dark, then he walked to the settlement. Twice, dogs barked at him, but neither time did their owners come out of their homes to see what had made them noisy. The only light burning in the handful of buildings came from what looked like some kind of tavern or roadside inn, and he crawled through that split oak rails of a corral and hid in the darkness of a large and leaning hay barn while he watched the lamplight burning in the window of that building down the street. The barn roof above him was in disrepair, same as its leaning walls, and in places the shakes were gone or blown off in some storm, and he could see patches of stars and the moon through those holes.

He had no way of knowing who was in that tavern, or whatever it was. All of the other buildings lining both sides of the one-wagon street that ran through them seemed to be places of business, or once had been. If there was a businessman in there, then perhaps he had a chance. A businessman would listen to a good deal when he heard it. Maybe mention his account in the Chicago bank that didn't exist, and maybe suggest a generous reward for the man that would help him.

The search parties out looking for him had surely come through there, but he had little choice but to take the chance. Even if he was recognized, money would buy most men's silence. Or the promise of money.

He smoothed his hair back as best he could, and tucked his tattered and filthy shirt back in his waistband. There was no helping his feet, but he did remove what was left of his socks. A barefoot man wouldn't be so out of place among the native heathens one usually found in the Nations. And he was already working up the story he would tell to explain his condition and appearance.

He left the barn and walked until he stood in front of the place he had been watching. A long porch with a swaybacked roof over it fronted the building, and he took one last look at the lamplight burning behind one of the front windows before he stepped up on the porch and knocked on the door.

"Who's out there?" a gruff voice from within said.

"I was thrown from my horse crossing the river," Duvall said.

"I said who's out there?"

"I hate to bother you at this time of night, but I need help."

He saw a face peering at him out of the lit window, and then he heard a dog growling from within. "I mean you no harm. I was thrown from my horse."

The door was jerked open and inward, and he found himself bathed in a swath of light. A man stood in that doorway brandishing a shotgun and aiming it at him. Two hounds burst out of the door in a scramble of toenails on the porch boards. They growled and circled him.

"He's down here," the man with the shotgun cried. "I got him."

Duvall stumbled backwards off the porch and fell at the foot of the steps leading up to it. One of the dogs bit him on the arm as he was getting to his feet.

"You stay where you are." The man with the shotgun was still silhouetted in his doorway. "You move and I'll shoot."

Duvall was debating whether the man really would or not when he heard others coming. He heard the trotting hoofbeats of their horses, and soon saw the glow of the lanterns some of them carried.

They surrounded him, six of them, and all men in big hats and carrying rifles. Their spurs and their bridle bits rattled every time their nervous horses stomped and blew out their nostrils and shook their heads.

"Go fetch the father," one of the men said to a comrade.

The one that gave the order rode his horse into the barking dogs, scattered them, and then scolded them until they retreated. Then he rode up against Duvall and held the light close so that he could see the man he was looking down at.

"Who are you?" his voice had a strange accent and inflection.

"I was thrown from my horse. I was crossing the river and . . ."

"I asked your name."

The lantern also let Duvall see his captors more clearly, and he saw that the one close to him was an Indian. And then he saw the badge the man wore.

"Who are you to be accosting me like this? I simply knocked on that man's door to ask him for help."

"Me? I'm Sergeant Harjo, and these men with me ride for the Creek Lighthorse."

"I assure you the charges against me are unfounded, despite what you may have heard."

"And what charges are those?"

Several of the Indian policemen with him laughed.

"I am Willis Duvall, superintendent of the MK&T Railroad."

"Well, thank you for that information, Superintendent. But I already knew that. You see, I was in your camp several times when you were still in Ironhead. Was there when you paid my tribe for running your railroad across our land, and I was there when those bushwhackers almost put an end to your railroad."

"Then you know me for the man I am," Duvall said, gathering himself and feeling a little better about the situation. Take command at the first opportunity, that's the way you did it.

Bluff until you had the feel of things.

"I know that there's people combing half the territory looking for you and the Hilltopper, and I know what they say you and him did back there."

"I tell you those are lies. Accusations made by my enemies. You either let me go, or see me to Fort Smith and turn me over to the court there. You Indians have no jurisdiction over a white man."

"We don't care so much what you did back in your camp, Mr. Willis Duvall. What we care is what you did to our girls at the Blackburn farm."

"What girls?"

"You're a poor liar, especially for a white man."

The rider that the sergeant had sent away came back followed by another Indian man wearing overalls and a floppy hat and driving a wagon with a young girl seated beside him. Again, the sergeant held the lantern so that Duvall's face was revealed.

"That's him," the girl said.

"Are you sure?" the sergeant asked.

"I'm positive."

Two of the Lighthorsemen dismounted and grabbed Duvall. They shackled his wrists behind him, and their attentions were not gentle.

"What is this about?" Duvall said.

"You know what this is about," the sergeant said. "The girl here told us how she caught you watching her and her cousins bathing in the creek."

"That's a lie."

"Put him up in the back of the wagon."

Rough hands drug him to the rear of the wagon, and then they picked him up bodily and threw him on the tailgate. One of the Indians climbed into the wagon bed and sat on the sideboard with a rifle pointed at his head.

"Leave the girl here," the sergeant said. "She doesn't need to see this."

Duvall heard none of that, for he was too busy watching the rifle pointed at him.

The girl climbed down from the wagon seat and went inside the building with the man with the shotgun and the mean dogs. The remaining Indians, except for the one guarding Duvall, rode off a ways and clustered their horses together. Duvall could hear them talking in their native language, and it sounded like an argument.

"Let's go," the sergeant said when they came back.

The wagon took off with a lunge and a bounce of its hind wheels through a rut. Duvall fell over on his side without his hands to catch him. He righted himself and looked to the man in the back of the wagon with him.

"Are you taking me to Fort Smith or to Ironhead?"

The sergeant was riding alongside the wagon bed and it was him that answered. "We're taking you to a suitable tree."

"What?"

"Tribal law says that a rapist gets a lashing. Whipped like the dog he is."

"You have no right . . ."

The sergeant went on. "Of course, a repeat offender gets the death penalty, and you, sir, from what we hear, appear to be a repeat offender."

"I did nothing to those girls. I merely came upon them by accident, and they mistook my intentions."

"We looked at the tracks you left. That isn't the story they tell."

The wagon rattled along until they reached a point where the road to Ironhead once more entered the timber. They stopped the wagon under an immense, tall oak with fat limbs that reached almost horizontally out over the road. The one in the wagon with Duvall set aside his rifle and caught the end of a rope one of them threw to him. It was a common manila lariat of the kind cowboys used to rope steers, with a simple eye tied in it. Two more men climbed into the wagon bed and pulled Duvall to his feet.

"I'm a white man. You have no right . . ."

The Indian with the rope slipped the loop over his head and drew it tight on his neck. One of the men still on his horse threw the rope over the limb above the wagon, and then he rode over to the tree trunk and tied the end of it to a lower limb.

"I'm the superintendent of the MK&T Railroad. I am a white man," Duvall said. "You will stop this now."

"He says he's a white man. The law says we have to hand white men over to their courts," the sergeant said.

"Hard to tell in the dark," one of the others answered. "But he looks like an Indian to me. Osage maybe."

"Kaw, I'm thinking," said another.

"You got anything you'd like to say to him?" the sergeant asked the farmer Indian driving the wagon.

"No."

"Then drive ahead."

Duvall was already on his tiptoes when the man driving the wagon chucked to his team of horses and they lunged against their harnesses. The wagon bed slid away, and there was nothing but air beneath Duvall and the choking bite of the rope.

One by one, the Lighthorsemen put out their lanterns. Duvall's legs had quit kicking by the time they followed the wagon back towards North Fork Town.

Chapter Fifty

William Pinkerton unlocked the main door to the agency's headquarters at 80 Washington Street, Chicago, Illinois, barely after daylight. His staff had yet to arrive, and the gas lamps were yet to be lit.

He entered his personal office in the dark, set his keys, his walking cane, and his satchel down on his desk, and lit the two gas lamps on the wall. The darkness was slowly replaced by the soft white light put off by the lamps, and it was then that Mr. William Pinkerton saw the man reclined in a chair opposite his desk with one leg crossed casually over the other knee.

He was a tall man, dressed quite nattily in a gray and black checkered coat, vest and cravat, and a black bowler hat. A smoking cigar was stuck in one corner of his mouth.

"I hope you don't mind me waiting for you," the man said.

"What do you want?"

The man seated there held a pistol, a large pistol, and he gestured with it towards the desk. "Have a seat, Mr. Pinkerton. William, I presume, or is it the other brother, Robert?"

"William," the young man said, adjusting his suit coat and taking a seat at his desk. His lower point of view put him more on level with the pistol bore aimed at his chest. "And, who, sir, might you be?"

"Morgan Clyde."

"Who?"

"Quit pretending that you don't know my name. You paid the

Indian Territory a visit looking for me not so long ago."

"What do you want?"

"How about we wait for your brother to show up? I don't intend to repeat myself."

"My brother is in Pennsylvania on business and will not be back for some time."

"Well, then, you will have to relay my message."

"And what is your message?"

"Don't bandy words with me, and don't think I haven't noticed that belly gun you've got hidden behind your coat lapel," Morgan said as he cocked his own revolver.

"I never argue with a man who's holding a gun on me." Pinkerton placed both hands on his desktop where they were in plain sight. "Have you come to kill me, Mr. Clyde?"

"Some years ago, after the war, my former wife, Miss Helvina Vanderwagen, or some of her family, hired your agency to see to it that I quit seeking her and our son."

"I am not at liberty to discuss the terms we come to with our clients."

Morgan straightened a little in the chair and jerked the cigar out of his mouth and held it in the air between them. "I'm not talking about terms. I'm talking about three of your detectives jumping me."

"They were only instructed to frighten you, yet you killed one of them and severely wounded the other two." Some of the calmness had left Pinkerton's voice.

"I'm not a man who frightens easily, Mr. Pinkerton."

"No, I suppose not."

Morgan shoved the cigar back in his mouth and clenched it between his jaw teeth until it gave him a half grin. "Some of your detectives came after me again not a month ago. Said they were doing so at your orders."

"And what may I ask became of them? May I surmise they

are no longer in my employ?"

"You surmise what you want to."

"You're here and they're not."

"That's a fact." Morgan drew on the cigar until the end of it burned bright, then he exhaled a string of smoke rings that floated lazily above them in the dim light.

"You left out the part where you beat one of my detectives at Ironhead Station on the MK&T line, and how you threw another out of a moving train," Pinkerton said.

"If you hire civil men, I will treat them civilly."

"We are both aware of the hostility between my father's firm and yourself. What do you intend by this meeting?"

"Your father and I once had an understanding when he was running things." Morgan ground the cigar out in an ashtray on the edge of the desk, and squinted through the smoke at his captive. "I had the same kind of talk with him that I'm having with you right now, and we came to an agreement."

"I'm aware that my father was willing to forgive you due to some extenuating circumstances brought about by our detectives' first encounter with you at the behest of the Vanderwagen family."

"They broke my jaw with a pair of brass knuckles, and three of my fingers with the butt of a pistol."

"As I said, extenuating and complicating circumstances. An unfortunate event on both sides."

"I wasn't that mad when I came in here, but I'm getting that way," Morgan said. "Gets worse every time you open your mouth."

"I merely am answering your questions. And for that matter, do you seriously expect me to believe you would shoot me right here in my own office with a number of my detectives about to arrive here at any moment, and the Chicago Police Department on especially good terms with my agency? You would never get away with it."

"I don't expect to get away with it."

Those words and the way Morgan said them changed the look on William Pinkerton once again. Morgan watched him swallow, and saw him glance at his walking cane once, and then down behind the desk at one of his desk drawers. He would be willing to bet that the cane had a knife or a rapier inside it, and that there was a pistol in that drawer to go with the one he carried in a shoulder holster under his coat. Morgan disliked the man, but he had to admit he was no coward.

"A friend of mine once told me that the worst part of the kind of profession you and I find ourselves in is that none of our business is ever finished," Morgan said. "You see, you make more enemies than friends, and for every enemy you tend to, you make two or three more to replace him."

"There is some truth in that, yet I fail to see where you are leading me."

"I want this business between your agency and myself finished. No more detectives on my trail, no more rough stuff. I leave you be, and you do the same for me. Finished."

"And what if I do not agree?"

"Then I'll come back here and finish our conversation."

"Your confidence borders on arrogance."

"You sit behind that desk of yours with all your detectives and hired muscle at your command, and you tell yourself what a powerful thing your detective agency is. But ask yourself, did all that power prevent me from waiting for you this morning? Who's going to stop me from putting a bullet in your brainpan? Nasty things, bullets. Make a mess of that fine suit of yours."

Morgan rose from his chair, and as badly as the Pinkerton boss tried not to, he flinched a little at the sudden movement.

Morgan leaned closer to him. "You can send more men after me, but you better hope they get me. Because the next time I come back, you will like it much less than this little visit of ours."

William Pinkerton's lower jaw was trembling, whether out of fear or anger, it didn't matter to Morgan. He reached inside the man's coat and removed the Colt Police from the shoulder holster, then he reached across him and took a snub-nosed Smith & Wesson Number 2 from the desk drawer.

"I'll leave your guns at the front door," he said as he went out of the office. "Wouldn't want you to hurt yourself with them."

William Pinkerton listened to the sound of Morgan's footfalls going down the hallway, and when he thought it was safe he got up and went to the front door and opened it onto the street. He looked right and left, but there was no sign of Clyde or where he had gone.

One of his detectives, a woman who specialized in keeping their criminal files updated and modern, came walking down the sidewalk.

"Who was that I saw leaving?" she asked.

"That was none other than Morgan Clyde."

"Do you mean to tell me that was really Clyde? All this time hunting him, and he shows up right here in your office?"

He gave her a cold look, and she was quick to notice it.

"I'll go right now and send a wire to the police, and then I'll put the word out to our detectives in the city," she said.

He put an arm across the doorway to block her. "No need of that."

"What? You have said more than once that Morgan Clyde is an embarrassment that the agency can't afford or tolerate."

"Perhaps, but Mr. Clyde and I had a most interesting meeting just now, and we have come to terms."

"Terms?"

"Yes, terms. We won't bother him anymore and he won't kill me."

"The gall of the man."

"Yes, quite a bit of gall to him, but I now see what my father must have seen in him." He moved his arm and offered the door to her. "What say we get to work? I'm sure you have all kinds of files to work on, and I'm quite sure I can find other projects more profitable and less troublesome to the company than Mr. Clyde."

"We could catch him before he ever gets out of the city."

William Pinkerton took one last look down the street and then shrugged. "You are probably right, but why take a chance?"

HISTORICAL NOTES

1. It may cross readers' minds that the violence of the Indian Territory has been greatly exaggerated for the sake of fiction; however, the *Indian Progress,* a short-lived newspaper in Muskogee, I.T., reported in 1875 that there had been fifteen murders by gun or knife between the years 1873 and 1874 around Caddo Station, one of the stops on the Katy line.

2. The Roper cylinder shotgun—This shotgun, first produced in 1867, was offered in both 16-gauge and 12-gauge configurations. While it wasn't the first revolving shotgun or the first breechloader, it was the first to incorporate threaded, removable chokes to configure the spread and patterning of shot fired through it, and one of the earliest shotguns to incorporate center fire, reloadable cartridges. Those cartridge cases were steel instead of brass or paper, which came into use later with other shotguns. The gun was also unique in the fact that its fixed rotary magazine was encased in a can-shaped receiver, unlike the external rotating cylinder on early percussion Colt revolving shotguns that mimicked the design of that company's percussion revolvers and rifles.

Sylvester Howard Roper was a machinist and an inventor of sewing machines and steam carriages prior to his work on the shotgun design. He worked for the Springfield Armory during the Civil War and perhaps that experience with firearms led him to invent and produce the first removable choke tubes that could be threaded into a shotgun's barrel, the same choke setup used in the Roper cylinder shotgun. He worked with Christopher Spencer to design the shotgun and received a patent for it, the same Christopher Spencer who also designed the Spencer repeating rifle, a firearm whose fame in the Old West is perhaps only secondary to Winchester's lever guns and Colt's revolvers. Roper and Spencer also collaborated on the first pump action shotgun patent, granted in 1882.

Roper himself receives greater acclaim for his inventions in the early American automobile and motorcycle industry. His Roper steam velocipede of 1867 is touted by many as the very first motorcycle. He was killed in a crash while racing one of his velocipedes around a bicycle track in Cambridge, Massachusetts, in 1896. Prior to the crash, he was clocked at a whopping forty miles per hour. He was almost seventy-three years old when he felt this last need for speed. Shotguns and motorcycles, Roper was perhaps the first American outlaw biker.

3. Webbers Falls—Walter Webber, an influential man among the Old Settler Cherokees, founded Webbers Falls in 1818. There he built a trading post, a salt works, and made other money transporting goods and people across the river. Soon other Cherokee, many of them planters and slaveholders, settled along the riverbanks. The settlement lay on a trail that ran west from Fort Smith, Arkansas, and during the days of '49, many a gold hungry emigrant crossed the river at the falls on their way to California to strike it rich. Through the decades, the settlement saw its share of excitement: slave revolts, fur traders, wild Indians come to trade from the plains to the west, and soldier explorers sent to learn the far reaches of the Great American Desert. "Rich Joe" Vann, the wealthy Cherokee plantation owner and steamship magnate, lived there before his famed death

from a boiler explosion while racing his steamboat, the *Lucy Walker,* against another vessel on the Ohio River. Stand Watie, the only Indian brigadier general of the Civil War and famed for his raids leading the Cherokee Mounted Rifles, also made his home there.

4. Salt plain—the salt plain that Morgan crosses in the novel exists near current-day Jet, Oklahoma. The salt is the leftover remains of an ancient inland sea. The first recorded white men to visit the area were members of the Sibley expedition in 1811. They named the area the Grand Saline.

5. Alabaster Caverns—The cave in which Morgan must find his way out of is actually the Alabaster Caverns, the world's largest natural gypsum cave, and located a few miles south of the town of Freedom in northwestern Oklahoma. The main passage is approximately three-quarters of a mile long, with several other side branches. Legend has it that in the 1920's a group of schoolboys on a field trip stumbled across a hidden chamber beneath a sinkhole skylight in the cave system. There they found a human skeleton, an old, dry-rotted saddle, and a kerosene can. With that legend in mind, and the fact the Francisco Vázquez de Coronado's expedition in search of the Seven Cities of Gold in 1540–41 passed through the country not too far way, I decided to have Morgan find a Spanish conquistador's skeleton and the horse bones.

6. Texas fire starter—The torch Morgan uses while trying to find his way out of Alabaster Caverns might seem a hastily improvised item created solely for the benefit of fiction, but Charles Goodnight, the famous Texas Ranger and trailblazing cattleman, told in his biography of how early day Texans charred cotton cloth lightly in a fire, dampened it with water, and then

coated it with gunpowder. The cloth, thus prepared, was run through a short length of hollow switch cane. A bit of it could be pulled out at a time, put to flame with a spark from a flint and steel, and used thusly as a lighter wick. You could then start your campfire with it, or light your pipe or cigarette. Once done, you simply pinched out the wick's flame and drew it back inside the cane. Call it an early day Zippo lighter, if you will.

7. In this novel, Red Molly O'Flanagan finally reveals her story of where she came from, fleeing Ireland during what has become known as the Great Famine, or the Great Potato Famine. While her story is purely fictional, the things she suffered were based on real events other poor Irish immigrants between 1847 and 1851 experienced coming to North America. It has been estimated that of the 100,000 Irish that sailed to British North America in 1847, an estimated one out of five died from disease and malnutrition, including over 5,000 at Grosse Isle in the quarantine camp. They died from typhus, dysentery, malnutrition, and other ailments incurred during the often-poor ship conditions while making the trans-Atlantic crossing.

8. MK&T Railroad—The Katy, as it was called, never received rights to any Indian Territory land other than its 200-feet right of way for the tracks it laid. Originally, there was talk of a land grant of some three million acres within the territory, but arguments within Congress and the courts over the legality of such a grant and its conflict with earlier Indian treaties and tribal sovereignty ended the land grab. However, on December 25, 1872, the Katy did cross the Red River and reach Denison, Texas, being the first railroad to cross Indian Territory and connect Missouri and Kansas to the Lone Star State.

9. I originally named Erastus Tuck, aka the Arkansas Traveler, after a famous song and fiddle tune written somewhere around 1840. At the time, I had no more motive than liking the name, and the lyrics telling of an Arkansas backwoodsmen encountering a city slicker fit with the Traveler's hillbilly character. Beyond that, I had only a vague concept of what the Traveler's experiences in the Civil War would be. I merely knew that I needed to place him at Gettysburg whereby he and Morgan Clyde could first come into conflict. I was in for quite a shock when it came time to research Arkansas Civil War regiments and to find one that fit the plot of the second novel as I began to create more background for the Traveler's character. Only one Arkansas Confederate regiment fit the bill on all counts, and that was Company A of the Third Arkansas Infantry, the only Arkansas regiment to serve the entire war in the east and to see most of the major battles. At the time, I was thinking what a great stroke of luck it was for me to find an Arkansas regiment that fit the plot and background for the Traveler's character that I had begun in the first novel. But the oddest surprise came when I noticed that all the companies within the Third had nicknames, as was a pretty common practice for other regiments on both sides of the war, Confederate and Union. And what was the nickname for Company A? They were known as none other than the Arkansas Travelers, as if I had planned it all out beforehand. Sometimes the truth is truly stranger than fiction.

ABOUT THE AUTHOR

Some folks are just born to tell tall tales. **Brett Cogburn** was reared in Texas and the mountains of southeastern Oklahoma. He had the fortune for many years to make his living from the back of a horse, where cowboys still step on frisky broncs on cold mornings, and drag calves to the branding fire on the end of a rope from their saddle horn. Growing up around ranches, livestock auctions, and backwoods hunting camps filled his head with stories, and he never forgot a one. In his own words, "My grandfather taught me to ride a bucking horse, my mother gave me a love of reading, and my father taught me how to shoot straight. Cowboys are just as wild as they ever were, and I've been fortunate enough to know more than a few."

Somewhere during his knockabout years cowboying, training horses, and working in the oil field, he managed to earn a BA in English and a minor in history. Brett lives with his family on a small ranch in Oklahoma. The West is still teaching him how to write.

[illegible]

[illegible]

Attn: Publisher

10 [illegible] St., Suite [illegible]

[illegible]

The employees of Five Star Publishing hope you have enjoyed this book.

Our Five Star novels explore little-known chapters from America's history, stories told from unique perspectives that will entertain a broad range of readers.

Other Five Star books are available at your local library, bookstore, all major book distributors, and directly from Five Star/Gale.

Connect with Five Star Publishing

Visit us on Facebook:
https://www.facebook.com/FiveStarCengage

Email:
FiveStar@cengage.com

For information about titles and placing orders:
(800) 223-1244
gale.orders@cengage.com

To share your comments, write to us:
Five Star Publishing
Attn: Publisher
10 Water St., Suite 310
Waterville, ME 04901